One More Dance

Wayne Forster

Newstream Publishing

Published by Newstream Publishing
41 Hartford Drive, Lower Sackville, NS, Canada, B4C 3S1
www.newstreampublishing.com

This story is a work of fiction. All the characters, organizations, or events portrayed in this novel are either the product of the author's imagination or are used fictitiously.

Printed in the United States of America
Cover design: Sari Naworynski
Interior design: Jetlaunch

ISBN: 978-0-9689528-1-8

To my mother.
I regret that I did not finish this while she was still with us.
I miss her very much.

Acknowledgements

Writing is a solitary endeavour. Publishing a book is not. It requires the help and support of many people. This book was no exception.

My thanks to Gwen Davies who taught me a lot about writing fiction and provided an excellent critique of the initial manuscript. You were a constant source of invaluable feedback and encouragement. Thank you to Marianne Ward. Your editing challenged me to re-think and revise key sections of the book, and helped me strengthen my characters. The result was a much better piece of work. Thanks to Sari Naworynski for your patience in working with me to come up with the cover design. Thanks also to James White for your help with the historical research, and to Jon Tattrie and Corinne Hewitt for your assistance in navigating the publishing process.

And most importantly, thank you to my wife Helen. It might be cliché-ish for an author to acknowledge their spouse or partner when they write a book, but without your patience, support, and love, *One More Dance* would never have happened. You gave me the freedom to put aside the demands of everyday living to focus my time and energy on this project. I love you more each day.

Chapter 1

Saturday night. The best dance night of the week. Better bands. Bigger crowds. More sailors.

Josie pulled hard to loosen her apron string, lifted the apron over her head, rolled it up in a ball, and tossed it in the bin. She yanked out the bobby pins holding the bandette in her hair, folded the bandette in two, and stuffed it in the pocket of her uniform.

"I'm heading out, Mr. Gorman. See you Monday."

"Ok Josie. Have a good weekend."

She flashed her boss a mischievous smile as she headed for the door. "I always do."

Saturday night. Dance night. She'd ask Becky to go with her. They'd go to the Strand. Josie preferred it to the Masonic Hall. The Masonic Hall was closer, just three minutes walk from Miss Bennett's boarding house where she and her sister roomed with four other girls. But the Strand had better music—and they never checked for liquor.

Becky had worked the early shift, so Josie figured she'd been home since four, had her supper, and was probably up in her room. Josie had worked until nine. Hopefully, Becky hadn't gone to bed early. Josie really wanted to go dancing.

It was less than a five-minute walk from Gorman's Restaurant on Hollis Street to the boarding house. Like every other Saturday night, dozens of people were already out on the street, heading for dances, going to the movies, or just strolling the downtown.

Like the young sailor and his giggling girl walking arm in arm. *They're in love*, thought Josie. *At least until his ship sets sail.*

Josie crossed the street to the harbour side and headed north up Hollis. She always walked as if she was in a race, especially when she was going to a dance. Not very lady-like according to Miss Bennett, but her "nature" as her mother always said. Before long, she had arrived at the house. She scampered up the steps, took her key out of her uniform pocket, unlocked the door, dashed into the foyer, and bolted up the stairs. She hadn't seen Miss Bennett coming down and almost ran her over.

"No running in the house, young lady," shouted Miss Bennett. "How many times have I told you that?"

Probably a hundred times, thought Josie. And a hundred times not to draw so much water for her bath, and a hundred times not to spend so much time on the phone, and a hundred times to turn the radio down, and a hundred times this, and a hundred times that. "Sorry, Miss Bennett. It's just that I'm going to the Strand and I don't want to get there too late."

"Another dance?" said Miss Bennett. "That's all you young girls think of these days, going to dances, and parties, and..."

The sound of her landlady's voice tailed off as Josie hurried down the hall to Becky's room. She could see that Becky was still up, from the light shining out from under her door, so she went right in without knocking. Becky was in her slip, brushing her hair in front of the mirror. "Josie!" screeched her sister, crossing her arms to cover her breasts. "How about knocking?"

"Why, because you'd have a *man* in here?"

"I could be getting undressed and somebody could be walking by the door."

Poor Becky. Josie knew she could only tease her younger sister to a point. She was shy and easily embarrassed. If she tormented her too much, Becky would get upset. And the last thing she wanted to do right now was upset her. She needed a companion for the dance. "Ok, I'm sorry," said Josie. "Next time I'll knock."

"Ya, sure," said Becky.

"Anyway," said Josie, "wanna go to the dance at the Stand?"

"Oh, I don't think so. I'm tired. I worked some extra shifts this week. I think I'll just stay home and do some ironing before I go to bed."

Josie grinned devilishly. "There's gonna be sailors there."

"Is that all you ever think about, Josie—sailors?"

"C'mon, Becky. You know I don't like to go alone. I'll help you with your ironing tomorrow."

"Sure you will."

"I will, I promise. Pleeeze Becky. I really want to go dancing."

Becky sighed. "Oh, alright. Give me fifteen minutes to get dressed."

"I'll be back in ten. Make sure you're ready."

Josie went to her room and picked up a few pieces of clothing she had strewn on her bed. She found a half-empty pint of lemon gin in her dresser and stuffed it in her purse. She took a quick trip to the bathroom to check her lipstick before returning to Becky's room. This time she knocked before entering. "Are you ready?" she asked.

"I can't go," moaned Becky.

"What? What do you mean you can't go?"

"I can't go. Look." Becky turned sideways and stuck out her leg. There was a long run in her stocking on her left calf. "I can't go looking like this!"

"Don't you have another pair?"

"No. My other two pairs are on the rack."

"Well, just go get one. I'm sure they're almost dry. Even if they're a little wet, so what?"

Becky slumped down on her bed. "Why do these things always happen to me? I always have the worst luck. Nothing ever goes right."

"It doesn't look that bad. Besides, nobody's going to ask you to dance anyway."

"Oh, shut up."

Josie went over to Becky's clothes rack, removed one of the pair of nylons that were hanging there, and gave them to Becky. "Here, they're dry enough. Put them on."

"But..."

"Put them on!"

Becky did as she was told.

"And take off that dress. I'm not going anywhere with you in that ugly dress. Wear that blue polka dot one Mom gave you."

"You're telling me what to wear now?"

The sisters headed out the door for a night of fun, Becky in her polka dot dress.

Chapter 2

It was a beautiful late June evening, warm and calm, without a hint of wind. The harbour was like glass, save for the rolling wake from a patrol boat heading out. The sun had already gone down, but it wasn't yet completely dark, with the horizon aglow in orange and yellow, spreading across a cloudless sky. Peaceful, almost.

Josie and Becky turned onto Salter, walking arm in arm as they always did, and headed up to Barrington. As they climbed the hill, they could hear the music coming from the Masonic Hall at the corner. At the top of Salter they turned right onto Barrington, passing directly in front of the main doors to the Hall. Several people were going in, including a group of four exuberant young sailors. One of the sailors noticed them approaching, broke off from his buddies, and jumped in front of them, blocking their path. He stared directly at Josie, ignoring Becky completely. "Hey, sweet cheeks, why don't you join us at the dance?"

Josie could smell the liquor on his breath. "Sorry, we'd love to," she said with a smile, "but we're going to the Strand."

"What's the Strand?"

"It's another dance hall just a few minutes from here."

"Is it better than this place?"

"*We* think so. The music's better and there's usually a bigger crowd."

"Well, why don't I get my buddies and we'll join you."

"Suit yourself."

The young sailor turned and ran into the hall. Josie and Becky resumed walking. Once they were clear of the hall, Becky began walking faster, pulling on Josie's arm.

"What are you doing?" complained Josie.

"What am *I* doing?" Becky shot back. "What are *you* doing, inviting all those boys to join us?"

"Are they coming?"

Becky looked back over her shoulder. "No, I don't see them yet."

"Then don't worry about it."

Within a few minutes, they were at the Strand. The sailors hadn't followed. Josie assumed they had found something more interesting at the Masonic. In any event, although she had not let on to Becky, she was actually relieved. If they'd accompanied her and Becky to the Strand, they'd have expected a few dances. She didn't want to feel obligated. She wanted to be free to decide for herself who she was going to dance with. No strings attached.

Even though it was only a little past nine thirty, there was already a big crowd on the dance floor. From a quick scan of the room, Josie could see there were more guys than girls, as usual, and almost all the guys were sailors in uniform. Some would be local boys with their regular girls, but most would be fresh off the ship. *This should be a good night for dancing*, thought Josie, smiling to herself.

Although Josie and Becky always walked arm in arm in the street, once they got to a dance Josie liked to strike out on her own. Not totally abandon her sister—no, she wouldn't do that; she'd still keep an eye out for her—but not stick so close together. Josie found it more likely that a sailor would ask her to dance if her little sister wasn't tagging along behind her. That wasn't always easy because Becky usually tailed her like a puppy to its new master. But Josie had developed a few tricks to get rid of her. "See if you can find us a table in the corner," she said to Becky. "I'm just going to take a walk around the floor. I'll join you in a minute."

Josie knew there probably wouldn't be any available tables, but it would buy her enough time to make one pass around the room. A group of Canadian sailors were standing by the canteen, so she headed in that direction. As she walked by the group, one of them made eye contact, stepped out from the others, and approached her. "Excuse me, Miss. Would you like to dance?"

Without responding, Josie grabbed his hand and pulled him on to the dance floor. The band was part way through a slow number.

"I hope they play something livelier," said Josie to the young man. "Do you know how to jitterbug?"

"Uh, well…"

Before he had time to respond, the slow song was over, and the band had started to play something more up-tempo. The band leader came to the microphone. "And now for all you gals and guys who like to swing, here's that big Glenn Miller hit, 'Chattanooga Choo Choo'!"

"That's the one!" yelled Josie, as she yanked her startled dance partner toward her and spun him around like a top. It was soon evident that the young sailor was completely out of his element, as his arms and legs flailed about in all directions without any resemblance to the jitterbug or any other dance known to mankind.

"Just follow my lead," said Josie, as she swivelled her hips and swayed back and forth, alternately pulling him towards her and pushing him back. But it was no use. He was completely over-whelmed. Panic set in his eyes as beads of sweat began to form on his forehead. He looked like a caged animal desperately trying to find a way to escape. At just that moment, Becky appeared alongside them, shouting to Josie over the blare of the music. "I found us a table."

"For Pete's sake, not now Becky. I'm dancing."

"But I got someone to save it for us and I don't think they'll hold it for very long."

Josie was annoyed at the sudden intrusion, but for the young sailor, Becky was an angel of mercy. He saw his opening and went for it. "No, you go ahead," he said to Josie. "I have to use the bathroom, anyway." He slowly backed away at first, then bolted for safety. Josie shrugged her shoulders, then followed Becky off the dance floor to their table. "He couldn't dance for beans," she mumbled to her sister.

The rest of the evening went much better. Josie had several dances, some two-steps, some jitterbugs, some with Canadian sailors, some with American sailors, even one with a Norwegian who kept asking her to come back to Norway with him as his bride when the war was over. Becky had danced as well. Not as often as Josie, but enough to keep her happy. Josie liked to see her sister having a good time.

As the night wore on, though, the dance floor grew increasingly crowded as more sailors piled in. That caused two problems. First, there was less room to dance, especially for swing numbers. Second, there was more competition for female dance partners. That was great for Josie and the other local girls, but it was starting to cause some pushing and shoving between the sailors, who had to start lining up for the next available girl.

The noise level in the hall had also risen, partly because of the larger crowd but mostly because everyone was getting a little drunk. You couldn't buy alcohol at the dance, so you'd have to sneak it in. Girls would have a flask of rum or whisky in their purse or a sailor might have a small one tucked into a sock. You weren't allowed to openly drink alcohol in the building, so you'd get a half cup of pop at the canteen, then add alcohol from your flask when you thought no one was looking. Everyone did it, and everyone knew everyone did it, but you kept up the charade. The Strand was pretty good about it; they didn't give you a hard time, as long as you weren't too open about it. But some dance halls were pretty strict, especially if there were officers present. They'd have someone walking around looking for alcohol, and if you were caught, the booze was confiscated and you were shown the door. Josie even heard about sailors being reported to their commanders.

As the crowd swelled and the noise rose and the alcohol flowed, Becky began to get a little edgy. "Maybe we should go now," she said to her sister. "It's getting late."

But Josie wasn't ready to leave. "Just a few more dances."

Josie scanned the floor and spied a sailor she had danced with earlier. He was standing alone sipping a drink. She remembered that he was a very good dancer, particularly with the fast numbers. Besides, he hadn't tried to pick her up like a lot of the guys did, especially as it got later in the evening. Josie figured he probably had a girlfriend or a wife back home, although that didn't stop a lot of them. She headed over. "How about one more dance before my sister and I have to go?" she said to him, extending her hand.

"Sure," he answered, with a broad smile.

The band was still going strong, but their music was getting lost in the hubbub of the crowd. Josie and her partner were doing their best to follow the beat and stay in rhythm but were constantly being jostled by other couples. At one point, Josie winced in pain as someone stepped on her heel. She was not enjoying this.

Suddenly, Josie heard a disturbance not far from them. Men were shouting and women were screaming. Josie and her partner stopped dancing and strained to see what was going on. All at once, a massive wave of humanity moved towards them, creating a circular clearing and revealing the source of the commotion. A fight had broken out between two sailors.

Josie pushed her way through the crowd to get a front row view of the action. One of the combatants was the lovesick Norwegian she had danced with earlier. The other was an American. They were going at it hot and heavy, with fists flying in all directions, some landing but most missing wildly. Cheering sections had emerged for each contender, with the Norwegian clearly the more popular. Through it all, the band kept playing and the rest of the room kept dancing, either unaware of, or uninterested in, the fracas.

As the fight continued, the American appeared to be gaining the upper hand, landing several short jabs to the face of his much larger but more inebriated opponent. Likely sensing the tide was turning against him, the Norwegian charged headlong at the American, wrapped his muscular arms around him in a bearhug, and drove him backwards into the spectators, almost directly at the spot Josie was standing. As this mass of manhood barrelled towards the onlookers, everyone tried to jump out of the way. But Josie froze. Before she could react, someone slammed into her, driving her straight back. She felt herself falling, unable to control her body, feeling helpless, terrified!

Abruptly, she came to a complete stop. Someone had caught her before she had crashed to the floor. Two arms encircled her from behind, pulled her away from the crowd, then lifted her to her feet. She righted herself and turned to face her rescuer.

"Are you all right, Miss?" asked a tall, fair-haired young man.

The accent was British. He was in civvies. Josie was drawn immediately to his eyes. They were the bluest she had ever seen. Like the sky on a clear autumn day. And caring. Genuinely caring. Inviting, even. Josie couldn't stop staring at them. She felt a strange sensation flow through her body. Unfamiliar, but warm. Pleasing, but unsettling. She could feel her heart beating in her chest.

"Miss?"

Josie felt disoriented. "What?"

"Are you all right?" repeated the man. "You almost took a nasty spill."

"Oh, uh, yes, yes... I'm fine," said Josie, slowly coming out of her fog.

"Would you like to sit down?"

"Yes. Thank you."

The man helped her to a nearby chair. He stood over her, as if shielding her from danger. She looked up at him. Into those eyes. She felt that warm sensation again.

"Those two numbskulls," said the man. "You could have been badly hurt."

"I'm okay now."

"Are you here alone? Is there someone I should fetch?"

"I'm here with my…" Becky! Josie had forgotten all about her. She hadn't seen her since she'd left her at the table, and she now worried that she may have gotten hurt in all the pushing and shoving. "I have to find my sister," she muttered.

"Let me help you," said the man.

Josie nodded, and with her new-found friend close behind, she headed to the table where she had left Becky. Her sister wasn't there. Panic washed over her. "Oh my God, I've lost Becky! I've lost my sister!"

"Relax, you haven't lost her. She's probably gone looking for you. You stay here in case she returns, and I'll go find her. What does she look like?"

"Well, she's seventeen, she's about my height but skinnier, much skinnier. And not much of a figure, if you know what I mean." Josie moved an open hand up and down in front of herself to illustrate her point. "Her hair is lighter than mine, not as long, and curly. She's sort of cute, I guess."

"What is she wearing?"

"A blue polka dot dress."

"Might she have gone outside?"

"Not without me. I'm sure of that."

"I'll find her, then. She has to be in the hall somewhere."

"She's kinda shy. I'm not sure she'll come back with you even if you find her."

"Leave that to me."

The tall stranger made his way across the dance floor as Josie leaned back in the chair to wait. She felt more at ease now. For some reason she was confident the Brit with the blue eyes would bring Becky back safe and sound. He had a reassuring way about him.

By now, the earlier ruckus on the dance floor had subsided. A few people were still milling about where the fight had taken place, but most had resumed dancing. No one seemed the worse for wear. Josie spotted two Navy MPs speaking to the Norwegian against the wall in the corner. The Norwegian seemed quite jovial, smiling broadly and playfully putting his arm around one of the MPs. They were handling it very calmly, talking him down before escorting him off the premises.

It wasn't long before Becky and the Brit appeared. Josie stood to greet them. The Brit walked slowly over to Josie and stood directly in front of her. She looked up at him. He smiled. "I told you I'd find her."

She stared into his eyes, unable to pull away, as if something was holding her there, something hypnotic, mesmerizing. It beckoned her, drawing her in, inviting her to enter the unknown. She succumbed, unable, unwilling to resist. She plunged deeper, abandoning her reality. The pulsing rhythms of the music and thumping drone of the crowd faded into the background, replaced by the sound of her own beating heart. No one else seemed to exist. Just him, and those eyes. An eternity passed. Time seemed to stand still.

Becky snapped her out of her trance. "Can we go home now? Before there's another fight?"

"What? Oh, yes, I guess we should go. It's getting late." Josie turned to the young Brit. "Thank you so much for everything you've done for us tonight. You've been like a knight in shining armour."

"Absolutely my pleasure," he responded. "Do you need a cab?"

"No, our boarding house is just a short walk from here," said Josie. "We'll be fine."

They gazed at each other in awkward silence.

"Good night, then," said Josie.

"Good night," said the Brit.

Josie turned to Becky, offered her arm, and the two of them headed for the exit.

"Wait!" shouted the Brit. Josie and Becky stopped in their tracks and turned to face him. He looked directly at Josie. "I never got your name."

"Josie."

"I'm Peter." The tall Brit with the captivating eyes now had a name. "Why don't you let me walk both of you home." There was a hint of pleading in his voice.

Josie hesitated. Becky glanced at her to see what she was going to say. Josie never allowed a guy to walk her home when she and Becky were out at a dance together, which was practically every dance. When they were together, it was just the two of them. No guys. But this was different. "Okay," she said.

The three of them left the Strand and headed for the boarding house with Peter in the middle, Josie on his left arm, and Becky on his right. The conversation on the way back, though, was entirely between Josie and Peter. They talked about how warm the weather was that night, how big the crowd was at the dance, and how good the music had been. They laughed about the fight between the Norwegian and the American, and how everyone had picked sides. And Josie said how lucky she was that Peter had been there to catch her. Before long, they were at the boarding house, standing on the sidewalk in front of the entrance. Peter glanced at Josie and smiled, then looked down at his feet, his hands in his pockets. Josie motioned to Becky to go inside, but Becky wasn't taking the hint.

"Becky?" whispered Josie.

Finally it dawned on the younger sister. "Oh, uh, well, uh, I'm, I'm going to bed," she stammered. "It was nice meeting you, Peter."

Peter smiled. "Nice meeting you as well."

Becky scampered up the steps and entered the house.

"Thank you for rescuing me tonight," said Josie.

"Thank you for falling into my arms," replied Peter. Josie felt her face flush ever so slightly.

"I hate when they fight at dances," she said.

"Well, actually, I'm glad there was a fight tonight. Otherwise, I might never have met you."

They stared at each other intently for several seconds. Josie broke the impasse. "I can tell from your accent you're English, but you're not wearing a uniform. Are you a sailor?"

"Yes, I am. Oh, and by the way, you're the one with the accent, not me."

Josie didn't get the joke. "Why no uniform?"

"Well, to be honest, I was out earlier this evening selling American cigarettes and I didn't think it would look good if the local authorities spotted a member of His Majesty's Navy selling contraband cigs. Didn't want to draw attention to myself."

"How'd you do?"

"Sold my last carton to a policeman for two bucks."

They both roared with laughter. As their laughter subsided, Peter changed the subject. "What are you doing tomorrow?"

Tomorrow was Sunday and Josie and Becky always went to mass at St. Mary's on Sunday mornings. But not this Sunday. "Nothing," she replied.

"Would you like to spend the day with me? I have shore leave until five."

Josie's pulse quickened with anticipation. "What would we do?"

"Well, perhaps we could go to a park somewhere. Somewhere quiet, somewhere where we could be alone. We could bring something to eat, perhaps have a little picnic. I have some chores to do on the ship first thing in the morning but I could stop in for you around eleven."

Josie recalled stories she'd heard about local girls going off with sailors to remote places and coming back with "bad reputations." And sometimes more than that. She didn't want to be one of those girls. But she'd be careful. She decided to chance it. "Sounds like fun."

"Then it's a date."

"A date."

They stared at each other for several seconds, smiling.

"I was thinking," said Peter, "I never got to dance with you."

"What do you mean?" said Josie.

"At the Strand. With all the ruckus, I never got to dance with you."

"Well, you never asked me."

Peter hesitated. "Okay, I'm asking you now."

"What?"

"Will you dance with me?"

"Here?"

"Sure."

"On the sidewalk?"

"Why not?"

Josie laughed. "You're crazy!"

Peter took Josie by the hand, pulled her gently towards him, and began waltzing with her while humming a tune.

"You're shaking," he said.

"It's chilly," she replied.

They both laughed.

They danced for a minute or so, Peter continuing to hum his tune, but neither saying a word. Peter then halted the dance and pulled Josie even closer to him, so close she could feel his breath on her face. "May I kiss you?" he said.

Josie nodded. Peter placed his forefinger under Josie's chin, gently lifted her head, gazed into her dark eyes, turned his head ever so slightly, leaned in, and kissed her softly on the lips, lingering for a while before slowly pulling back.

Josie sighed a deep sigh. "I better go in," she said.

"I'll wait until you're safely inside."

Josie turned and walked slowly up the steps, unlocked the door, opened it, and turned back to see Peter still standing on the sidewalk below.

"Tomorrow," he said.

"Tomorrow," she said, smiling.

Chapter 3

Josie was awakened by the sound of someone tapping lightly on her door. She lifted her head and squinted at the clock on her night table. It was five minutes to eight. "Who is it?" she mumbled, still groggy with sleep.

"It's me."

Becky.

"Come on in." Josie yawned, rolled over onto her back, and stretched her arms to bring herself back to life. The door opened and her sister entered the room.

"Are you still in bed?" shrieked Becky. "We're going to be late for breakfast. You know Miss Bennett doesn't like it when we're late."

Breakfast on the weekends was always at eight o'clock sharp. Sunday was the only day of the week that Miss Bennett served bacon and eggs. If you were more than ten minutes late, you missed out. You might manage to scrounge up a strip of cold, leftover bacon, but that was about it. "I'm not here to serve stragglers," she'd always grumble. So, you'd have to fix your own breakfast, maybe some porridge but usually just toast and tea.

This particular morning, Josie was in no hurry. "You go ahead. I'll be down in a few minutes."

"Well, don't be too long," said Becky. "We also have to get ready for mass."

"I'm not going to mass today."

"What?" snapped Becky.

"I'm not going to mass today."

"What do you mean you're not going to mass? You have to go to mass. We always go to Sunday mass."

"I don't have to do anything."

Becky rolled her eyes. "Don't be so stubborn. It's just that we go every week."

"Well, not this week."

"What's so different about this week?"

"I have a date".

"A date? With who?"

"Peter."

"Peter? The guy from last night?"

"Yeees, the guy from last night."

"On Sunday morning?"

"Well, he has to get back to his ship for five, so he's picking me up here at eleven and we're going out for the day. Maybe go to a park for a picnic."

Becky clearly didn't like this change in the normal routine. "So, who's going to take me to mass? We always go together."

"Go with Claire. She always goes to Sunday mass."

"I don't like her," whined Becky. "She gossips too much."

"You don't have to like her, just go to mass with her."

Josie didn't feel like discussing the matter any further. "I'm going on a date with Peter and I'm not going to mass. You can go with someone else if you want. You better go down for breakfast or you'll be late."

Becky shook her head and left.

Josie got out of bed, threw her housecoat on over her night-gown, grabbed a towel, face cloth, and a bar of soap, and headed for the bathroom at the end of the hall. When she was finished washing, she went back to her room, selected her best "picnicking" clothes, dressed, brushed her hair, and proceeded downstairs to see what was left of the morning meal. By the time she entered the dining room, it was almost ten minutes to nine. Becky wasn't there. Josie assumed she was back in her room getting ready for mass. Two of the other girls were still at the table, chatting and sipping on their tea. Miss Bennett was clearing the dishes.

"I'm not cooking any more bacon and eggs," said Miss Bennett, without looking up at Josie. "You know breakfast is at eight."

"I'm sorry. I overslept."

"I don't know how you girls can sleep so much," said Miss Bennett. "You're wasting your life away in bed. I've been up since five thirty, did some laundry, and prepared breakfast. I did half a day's work before you even got up."

Josie felt like saying, "Good for you!" but knew it was best not to say anything. She stood quietly, expecting another scolding. But Miss Bennett was apparently finished with her reprimand.

"Anyway, go in the kitchen and make yourself some toast and tea. You need to eat something."

Josie headed for the kitchen while Miss Bennett continued to clear the table. Just when Josie thought she was in the clear, Miss Bennett called out to her again. "And there may be a piece of coffee cake left over from last night's dinner. It's on the cake stand."

Josie smiled to herself. Maybe the old witch had a heart after all.

Once Josie had finished eating, she cleared her own dishes, went back upstairs, brushed her teeth, put on some lipstick, and made her bed. Peter wasn't arriving until eleven, but she decided to go down to the parlour early and wait for him there. Maybe listen to the radio to kill some time. As she reached the bottom of the stairs, Becky was heading out the front door, with Claire.

"Say a prayer for me," Josie called out to her sister.

Becky looked back. "Are you sure you don't want to go to mass with us?"

"I can't. I'm waiting for Peter."

"We might be back before he gets here."

"I can't chance it. If he arrives and I'm not here, he may think I've stood him up, and he'll leave."

"Why don't you just tell Miss Bennett you're expecting a visitor."

"Are you kidding?"

"Then, just put a note on the door."

"Go!" ordered Josie, motioning Becky away with her hand.

Josie went into the parlour, sat down on one of the large wingback chairs, and turned on the radio that was on the table next to the chair. Miss Bennett always kept the radio on the same station, which played mostly "old-fashioned" music, as Josie called it (Miss Bennett called it "classical"), as well as news programs like "Carry On, Canada" which was usually about the war or something the government in Ottawa was doing. She wasn't pleased when the girls changed the station, so they'd wait until she was out running errands or had gone to bed for the night. At night, though, they'd have to keep the volume down, which took all the fun out of listening to the jazz tunes. And they had to turn it off by ten. This particular morning, Josie knew Miss Bennett was still in the house, so she left the dial where it was. But after several minutes of announcements about government rationing, and reports from the front in Europe, and music by someone named "Bock," she turned it off.

As time dragged, her thoughts turned to the day that lay ahead. Where would they go, what would they do? Would they go on a picnic, like he had suggested? If that was the plan, hopefully he'd bring the food, because Miss Bennett wouldn't likely give her any. And what would he be wearing? Would he be in his civvies again or his uniform? She hoped he'd be in uniform. Would he like her dress? Should she change into another one? No, she might not have time. This one was fine. He'd like it. What would they talk about? Would they talk about last night's dance, or their favourite movies, or favourite songs? Or would he talk about the war? She hoped not. She didn't like talking about the war. But most importantly, would he kiss her the way he had kissed her last night?

She found herself checking the clock on the mantle every few minutes. At five to eleven, she got up from her chair and went to the window to see if Peter was coming up the street. No sign of him yet, so she sat back down. By eleven o'clock, he still had not arrived. *No need to worry*, she thought, *he was probably delayed.* Maybe his morning chores on the ship took longer than expected. She tried to recall if he had said he'd pick her up *at* eleven or *around* eleven.

At about a quarter past eleven, Josie heard the front door open. Her heart jumped. For a split second she thought it might be Peter but quickly realized he wouldn't just walk into the house. It was probably Becky and Claire returning from mass.

Becky poked her head into the parlour. "Is he here?" she whispered, straining her neck to survey the room.

"Not yet," said Josie.

"Maybe he's not coming," said Becky.

Josie didn't want to consider what she knew Becky was thinking, that Peter had stood her up. That he was just another sailor trying to see how far he could get with the local girls before shipping out. She needed to convince herself that Peter was different. That he wasn't like all the others. That the kiss last night had meant something.

"He'll be here," said Josie, trying to sound unconcerned. "He probably got delayed with his ship chores. Anyway, he said he'd be here *around* eleven, so he's not actually late."

Becky seemed unconvinced. "Well, anyway, I'm going up to change. I'll see you later."

By eleven thirty, Peter had still not arrived. Josie felt her hopes fading. In her mind, she knew there could be a hundred reasons why he was late. But in her heart, she felt only pain. The pain of longing for something that now seemed out of reach. The pain of embarrassment when Becky and the other girls would find out what had happened. The pain of anger that she had allowed herself to fall for someone she had just met, a total stranger.

At eleven forty-five, Josie got up from her chair and went to the window in one last desperate hope that she'd see her blue-eyed Brit running frantically up the street. Nothing. Dejected but resigned, she went upstairs to her room. She closed the door behind her and sat down on the side of her bed, staring straight ahead. A jumble of thoughts raced through her mind. It was silly of her to think that this sailor would be any different than the thousands of other sailors who had passed through Halifax during this war. Of course he was looking to get lucky last night, and when all he got was a kiss, he moved on. But what a kiss. Josie had been kissed before, but never like that. Never had a kiss made her shiver. Then, maybe he was just a great kisser. Maybe that was his specialty. Maybe that was the way he kissed every girl. Maybe she was just another girl to him. Another potential conquest. But then, why did he make a date for Sunday? Why did he suggest they go on a picnic? He could have just brushed her off. Why did he get her hopes up? Maybe because he *did* really like her. Maybe last night *did* mean something to him. Maybe he had every intention of keeping the date. Maybe something happened to him. Maybe something terrible.

Josie caught herself. Her thoughts were running out of control. She had to come to her senses. He wasn't coming, that was it. Last night was like any other Saturday night. She had gone to a dance and met some sailors, like she had done so many times since arriving in Halifax. Nothing different had happened. Time to move on. Get back to normal.

She glanced at her clock. Five past noon. Dinner was at twelve thirty, so she still had time to change out of her dress and make it down on time. Sunday was the only day of the week that Miss Bennett served dinner at midday. Every other day of the week the girls were on their own for dinner, or lunch, as most of the girls called it. During the week, Josie and Becky would usually eat lunch at Gorman's or skip it altogether. Maybe just grab a coffee on their break.

Josie got up from her bed and went to her closet to pick a change of clothes. Just then she heard the muffled sound of the doorbell downstairs. Could it be? Her heart raced as she opened her door and peered out, straining to listen. Then she heard it. His voice. The British accent. Unmistakable. It was him. It was Peter.

A chill went through her. She stepped quietly into the hall and positioned herself so that she could see over the rail and down into the foyer without being detected. There he was, absolutely dashing in full uniform, speaking with Miss Bennett. As Josie looked on, Miss Bennett started up the stairs. Josie dashed back into her room, quietly closed the door, sat on her bed, and waited. Within a few seconds she received the anticipated knock. She opened the door to find a stern looking Miss Bennett facing her.

"There's an English sailor downstairs who says he has a date with you," said Miss Bennett. "Is he correct?"

"Yes. His name is Peter," replied Josie.

"A date? On Sunday?"

"We're going on a picnic."

"A picnic," said Miss Bennett, her voice rising mockingly. "So that's what they're calling it these days."

Josie smiled a forced smile but didn't reply.

"Does this mean you won't be joining us for dinner?" said Miss Bennett.

"Sorry," Josie replied.

She was anxious to go downstairs to meet Peter, but Miss Bennett wasn't finished with her yet. "I wish you had given me some advance notice that you would not be joining us for dinner. I would not have prepared as much food, and I would not have set a place for you."

Again, Josie remained mum, fighting the voice in her head. The silent treatment seemed to work.

"Be on your way, then," grumbled Miss Bennett, as she turned to go back down the stairs. She had taken no more than a few steps when she wheeled around and stared Josie straight in the eye. "Just be careful. You know what these sailors are looking for."

"I can take care of myself."

"I hope so, for your sake," said Miss Bennett, as she left the room.

Josie rolled her eyes. The blue-eyed Englishman was not the first sailor she had ever gone out with. She knew how to protect herself if she needed to. Anyway, this seemed different. This seemed real. It was that kiss.

She grabbed her compact off her dresser, checked her lipstick and hair, fluffed up her dress, threw her purse over her arm, took a deep breath, and headed down to meet Peter. He was at the bottom of the stairs, slowly pacing back and forth. As she came into his view, he looked up, meeting her eyes. Josie felt her knees weaken. His eyes were even bluer than they had been last night, contrasting against the brilliant white of his uniform. His smile was as warm as she had remembered. In the light of day, he was even more handsome, more dashing.

He rushed to greet her as she reached the bottom step. "Please forgive me," he said. "I am so, so sorry I'm late. You wouldn't believe what happened on the ship this morning. Everything went wrong. It took forever to get things straightened out. And I had no way of getting in touch with you because I didn't have your phone number. I thought for sure you'd be gone by the time I arrived. And I wouldn't have blamed you."

Josie was so excited to see him that she barely heard his apology. But she didn't want to appear to be too lovestruck. A girl had to maintain her composure, make sure the guy didn't take anything for granted, make him work a little. She peered at him with a sly grin on her face. "Is this the way you treat all the girls?"

"No, no, honestly," said Peter.

"Because you don't get a second chance with me. I don't get stood up a second time."

Peter stood speechless, like a child that had just been scolded. Josie smiled mischievously. Realizing then that he had just been toyed with, Peter broke into laughter, shaking his head.

"Are you still taking me on a picnic?" asked Josie.

"Of course."

Josie offered him her arm. "Then let's get going. You've already lost over an hour of our date."

Peter suggested they go to a park known as "The Dingle." One of his chums on the ship had told him it was a good place to take a girl on a picnic. Josie wasn't sure if that meant it was a good place for the *girl* or a good place for the *guy*. In any event, she had heard of The Dingle but had never been there. It was on the Northwest Arm, an inlet at the far west end of the city. The trolleys didn't run out that far, so they'd have to take a cab.

Peter had brought along the "provisions," as he called them, purloined from his ship's kitchen, which he was carrying in a small duffle bag. The only thing missing, he said, was something to wash down the food. Since the liquor stores were closed on Sundays, Peter had the cab driver stop at a bootlegger, where he bought two quarts of beer.

The sun was just peeping through the clouds as they arrived at the park. The air had been a little chilly in the morning but had warmed up nicely as the day wore on. A light breeze blew off the Arm. It looked like it was going to be a perfect afternoon for a picnic.

The park was teeming with people—sailors and their girls stretched out on the grass, small clusters of sailors without dates walking along the paths, families eating at tables, old men playing checkers, kids throwing stones into the ocean. Although there was a small sand beach, the water was still too cold for swimming. But a young couple had taken off their shoes and stockings, had waded in up to their knees, and were splashing each other playfully.

Peter took Josie by the hand as he led her along one of the paths. She tingled at his touch. His hand was strong but smooth. And comforting. Josie felt safe. At ease. And excited.

Peter said he wanted to find a spot that had some privacy but was still open to the warmth of the sun. After several minutes, they found the ideal location—a clearing on the top of a hill to the rear of the park, away from the paths. The clearing was protected at the back and on both sides by thick forest. To the front stood a smattering of alders and small bushes but an open sight line to the water, and the boat houses and stately homes on the other side of the Arm. From their vantage point, they had an almost panoramic, if partially obstructed, view of the park below, but enough tree cover to be practically unseen.

Peter helped Josie up the sharp incline to the clearing. He selected a relatively flat area, opened his duffle bag, took out a bed sheet, and spread it out on the grass. Next, he took all of the utensils out of his bag, one by one, and positioned them in a neat, orderly fashion on the sheet, creating two perfect place settings—two knives, two forks, two small plates, and two cups. He then took out all the food and laid it neatly on the sheet. He had brought slices of ham and turkey, some potato salad, two apples, two scones, butter (which was rationed on shore but plentiful on board), even salt and pepper. Finally, he took out the two quarts of beer. Satisfied that the preparations were complete, he turned to Josie and smiled. "Ladies first."

Josie returned the smile and sat down on the sheet, in front of one of the settings. Peter sat down directly across from her.

"Pretty fancy," said Josie.

"I tried to bring the good china, but the head steward wouldn't let me," joked Peter.

He distributed the food between them and invited Josie to begin eating. He grabbed one of the quarts of beer, took a pen knife out of his pocket, and popped the cap off the bottle. He then passed a cup to Josie and took one for himself. "Are you alright with beer?" he asked.

"Sure," said Josie.

"What do Halifax girls usually drink?"

"A lot of the girls like lemon gin." Josie definitely didn't want to tell Peter the other name the locals had for lemon gin, the one referring to a certain item of ladies clothing!

Peter filled both cups to the brim. "Cheers," he said, raising his cup.

Josie reciprocated, lightly tapping Peter's cup. They both took healthy swigs, then started into the food. As they ate, they looked up at each other and smiled from time to time, but neither spoke. Josie wondered if she should kick off the conversation first or wait for him. Was he shy? He didn't seem shy. But she had to get the ball rolling. She opened her mouth to speak. But at the same time, Peter did the same.

"Oh, I'm sorry," he said. "Were you going to say something?"

"No, you go ahead," said Josie.

"I was just going to ask you to tell me a little about yourself. I don't even know your last name."

"Bourdeau. Josephine Bourdeau."

"It sounds French."

"It is."

"I didn't really pick up a French accent. Do you speak French?"

"Yes, a little. I understand all of it. My father is French, but my mother is English, so we grew up speaking mostly English."

Her mother and father. She missed them. She wondered if they missed her. She hadn't seen them in over two years, when she went home for her sister Agatha's wedding. She wrote to them, of course, from time to time, but that wasn't the same. Besides, it was Agatha who would write back because neither of them could read or write. So, Josie was never quite sure she was getting her parents words or Agatha's.

"Have you lived in Halifax all your life?" asked Peter.

"Oh no, I just moved here when the war started. To find a job."

"You must have been quite young."

"Are you trying to find out how old I am?"

"No! No! I, I…"

"Because a gentleman doesn't ask a lady her age."

"No, I just…"

Josie decided to let him off the hook. "I was almost 20 when I came to Halifax. I'm 22 now."

Peter looked relieved. "So, where is home?" he continued.

"Just a little fishing village on the coast, about a six-hour bus drive from Halifax."

"What's the name of it?"

"Oh, you've never heard of it."

"Tell me anyway."

"Perch Cove."

"Never heard of it."

"Told you."

They both laughed.

Now it was Josie's turn to interrogate her new friend. "And you, sir, do you have a last name?"

"Churchill. I'm Winston's son."

"Really?" shrieked Josie, falling for the prank.

"No," laughed Peter. "I'm just teasing you. My last name is actually Harris."

Josie slapped Peter playfully on the arm. They both had a good laugh at her expense and continued their conversation while finishing off their food and beer. Peter told Josie he was from Lancashire in northern England and had joined the merchant marine in '35 when he was only fifteen. When the war broke out in '39 he enlisted in the regular Navy. He also talked a little about his parents and his two brothers and three sisters back in England, and they shared stories about childhood adventures and even old school sweethearts. Josie talked about her family, her job at Gorman's, and what it was like to live at Miss Bennett's. Neither one discussed the war. It was a subject most people didn't want to talk about.

The war. *When will it end?* thought Josie. It had been going on for almost three years. Everybody was saying that now that the Americans were in, the tide would start to turn in favour of the Allies. But nobody knew for sure. Sometimes it seemed like it would never end. Sometimes it seemed that the news about battles lost and ships sunk and fathers and sons and brothers never coming home would go on forever.

With their tongues growing tired and all the food and beer gone, Peter began cleaning up, stuffing the utensils and empty beer bottles back into his duffle bag. He then sidled over to Josie so that they were directly facing each other, almost touching. Staring intently into her eyes, he reached up and brushed the back of his index finger down her cheek. "You're very beautiful, you know."

Josie felt a fluttering sensation in her chest as her face flushed ever so slightly. Her body heaved as her breathing quickened. She tried to look away to ease the powerful emotions building inside her—but she couldn't. His eyes were like magnets drawing the two of them closer and closer together. She couldn't resist. She didn't want to resist. She remembered their kiss from last night and craved the excitement of it once more.

She didn't have to wait long. Peter tilted his head slightly and leaned in. This time she met him half way. Their lips touched, softly at first, then more firmly, more passionately. He put his arms around her and pulled her towards him. She put her arms around him and held tight. She could feel her breasts melding into his chest, the space between their bodies quickly vanishing.

They slumped slowly to the ground together, lips never parting. Their kisses became more feverish, more lustful, as they explored their senses with abandon. Peter skillfully unfastened one of the buttons on the front of her dress, slowly slid in his hand, and softly caressed her firm and full flesh. Josie felt her nipples swell as Peter's warm hand brushed across them. She was losing control, gladly, as an intoxicating wave of pleasure flushed through her.

The next several minutes were a haze – a trance-like melange of enchantment, delirium, and delight. A sense of euphoria swept over Josie, unlike anything she had ever experienced before, a feeling so intense and powerful it both excited and startled her.

She could feel the blood coursing through her veins, her body alive, her senses tingling. Uncertainty clouded her mind. Should she accept him? Should she succumb to her desires? Should she...?

Chapter 4

Josie buttoned her dress as Peter folded the bed sheet and jammed it into his duffle.

"My watch starts at five o'clock," said Peter. "We should start to make our way back."

Josie nodded. He took her arm and guided her as they descended the steep bank to the path below. Once on level ground again, they headed towards the entrance to the park, walking slowly, their arms around each other's waists. Neither one said a word.

When they arrived at the entrance, Peter went to the canteen to ask one of the workers to call a taxi. Josie waited at a picnic table nearby. Shortly after, Peter returned and sat down next to Josie. "The bloke at the canteen said the taxi should be here in ten to fifteen minutes."

Josie just smiled.

Peter gazed at her. He reached out and stroked her hair, running the strands between his fingers. "My ship sails before dawn tomorrow."

This was the moment Josie had feared, the moment when the sailor thanks the girl for the "good time" they've had, that it's been fun, that he'll always cherish their time together, that he will never forget her. That's the way it was in wartime. You grabbed your bits of bliss when you could. Nothing was permanent. You lived for today because there may not be a tomorrow. Josie knew she wouldn't be the first girl to hear the line. It happened all the time.

But she didn't want it to happen to her.

"I'll write to you often," said Peter. "And I'm sure I'll be back in Halifax before long."

Josie so very much wanted to believe him. Maybe right now, at this moment, he actually did mean it. But three days from now, a week from now, a month from now, would she be just another pretty girl he had met in another port in another part of the world? "Peter, it's okay. You don't have to say that."

"What? No, I promise. I *will* write."

Josie looked down, averting her eyes. Peter lifted her chin and stared into her eyes.

"Josie, listen to me carefully. From the first time I saw you, I've thought of nothing else. You have been on my mind every minute, every second. I've never felt this way before. Ever. You are the most amazing woman I have ever met. Now, do you believe me when I say I will write to you?"

Josie's eyes grew misty. She believed him. She trusted him. Completely. Unabashedly. "Yes. Yes, I believe you."

"Then kiss me."

Their lips met once again, more passionately than before, hungrier, yielding to the fervour pulsating through their veins. They pressed furiously against each other, unwilling, unable to stop. Josie could feel herself letting go again, surrendering to her cravings, oblivious to her surroundings, unaware of time.

They were interrupted by a bellowing voice from behind the canteen counter. "Hey Romeo, your cab's here."

Peter and Josie broke off their embrace and laughed like schoolchildren. She grabbed him by the hand, yanked him up from the picnic table, and pulled him across the parking lot to the waiting cab, laughing as they went. Once in the cab, they snuggled close and continued where they had left off, savouring every minute together.

By the time they arrived back at the boarding house, it was almost four thirty. Peter would have to hurry not to be late for his watch. He asked the driver to wait for him for a few minutes and then take him to his ship. Peter and Josie got out of the cab and stood on the sidewalk in front of the house, facing each other. He held her hands in his. "I guess this is it."

Conflicting emotions swept over Josie. She felt both sad and happy. Sad because he was leaving but happy because she now had someone to miss. Happy to be sad, in a strange way.

The whole thing was crazy. She had known him less than a day. They were strangers, really. But he didn't feel like a stranger. He felt like someone she had known her entire life. Someone she was meant to be with.

"Don't forget to write," she said.

"I'm going to need your postal address. Jot it down on a piece of paper so I won't forget it."

"I'll get some writing paper from Miss Bennett."

"Hurry!"

Josie scurried up the steps and into the house. She went to the end of the hall and knocked on Miss Bennett's office door. No answer. "Miss Bennett?" she called out. Still no reply. She searched the rest of the main floor but Miss Bennett was nowhere to be found. She ran up the stairs to see if any of the girls had seen the old lady, stopping at Becky's door first. "Becky, are you there?"

"Yeah."

"Are you decent?"

"Come on in."

Josie entered the room. "Do you know where Miss Bennett is?"

"She went out about two hours ago. I think she was going to the bank and then to the grocery store. I don't think she's back yet."

"Oh, that's just great," sighed Josie. "Do you have any writing paper?" she asked her sister.

"No, but Miss Bennett should have some."

"Becky, why do you think I'm looking for her?"

"Sorry, I didn't know. You'll have to wait until she gets back."

"I can't!"

Josie raced back down the stairs and went to Miss Bennett's office door. The girls were forbidden to go into her office unless she was there, and even then, most of the time she wouldn't actually let them into the room. She'd greet them at the door instead. The girls used to joke that she must be a German spy hiding top secret documents. In any event, no one dared face her wrath by entering uninvited.

But this was different. This was an emergency. Josie decided to chance it. Yet despite the urgency of the situation, she still felt uneasy as she slowly turned the door knob, pushed the door back slightly, and peeked into the room. Confirming that Miss Bennett was indeed not there, she stepped in and quietly closed the door behind her.

The room was like no other in the house. Windowless, dark, dreary even, with the only light coming from a small lamp on the desk. There was a fireplace at the far end, unlit, framed by two ornate chairs and a heavy wooden coffee table on a dark burgundy floral rug. In one corner stood a tall mahogany chest, in another a bookcase. The walls were covered in a dark, pattern-less paper with gaudily framed oil paintings barely breaking the bleakness. Porcelain ornaments were strategically placed throughout, on the mantle, on the tall chest, on the bookcase. It had a feel of formality about it; severity; gloom. A lot like Miss Bennett herself.

Josie made her way to the desk. She spotted a fountain pen and ink well on the right but no paper. She opened the top righthand desk drawer. No paper there either. But something else caught her eye. A framed photograph. It seemed to be staring up at her. Curious, she took the picture out of the drawer and held it under the lamp for a closer look. It was a head and shoulders portrait of a blond-haired strikingly handsome young man, no more than a teenager, in full military uniform.

A bolt of light suddenly pierced the dark room. Startled, Josie looked up to see a silhouette standing in the doorway. A voice shrieked out from the shadow. "What are you doing in my office?"

It was Miss Bennett.

"You know you are forbidden to be in this room when I am not here," she shouted angrily. "Explain this intrusion, young lady!"

"I, I..." Josie stammered.

Miss Bennett spotted the picture Josie was holding. "What are you doing with that?"

"I was just looking at it."

Miss Bennett rushed at Josie and snatched the photograph from her hand. "Give me that," she yelled. "Where did you find this?"

"It was in your top drawer."

"What were you doing in my drawer?"

"I was looking for some writing paper."

"Writing paper?"

"Yes, I need to write down our postal address and give it to Peter so he can write to me."

"Peter?"

"Yes, the English sailor you met earlier."

The veins bulged in Miss Bennett's neck. "And that gives you the right to trespass in my office? To violate my privacy?"

"Well, I..."

"Get out! Get out of my office! Right now!"

"But..."

"Get out!"

Josie felt her blood beginning to boil. She wanted to say something nasty to her landlady but held her tongue. Instead, she glared angrily at her before storming out of the room and running full speed through the foyer and onto the street where Peter was pacing back and forth.

"What took you so long?" said Peter. "I thought you had forgotten about me. Did you get a piece of paper from your landlady?"

"No. That old battle axe wouldn't give me any."

"Why not?"

"Because she's an old battle axe, that's why."

Peter didn't wait for an explanation. "Wait here," he said to Josie. He went to the cab, opened the front passenger side door, stuck his head inside, said something to the driver, and came back with a small scrap of paper and a pencil. He handed both items to Josie. "Here, write down your postal address."

Josie obliged, using Peter's back as a writing surface, and handed the paper and pencil back to him. He folded the paper and stuffed it in his jacket pocket.

"I have to go," he said, smiling at Josie and caressing her hair.

"Wait!" shouted Josie. "I almost forgot." She turned and ran back into the house, returning shortly after. She handed Peter a small photograph. A photograph of herself. "This is so you won't forget what I look like."

"I won't forget," said Peter, as he slid the photo into his pocket. "Now I really have to go."

Simultaneously, the two lovers lunged at each other and hungrily devoured each other's lips, clinging to every second of pleasure, refusing to let go, yearning for time to stand still so the moment could last forever. But it couldn't. Peter pulled himself free, opened the back door of the car, and got in. As the vehicle pulled away from the curb, he rolled down the window and waved. Within seconds, the car turned left onto Bishop and disappeared out of sight.

Josie lingered on the sidewalk for awhile, staring down the street, not wanting to go back into the house just yet. Once inside, her life would return to normal, to what it had been less than twenty-four hours ago. Before those blue eyes, before the kiss, before the Dingle.

A voice from behind snapped her back to reality. "What are you doing standing out here alone?"

It was Claire, the busy-body, returning from her walk.

"Oh, nothing, just enjoying the sunshine," said Josie.

"Are you coming in for dinner? We're having roast beef tonight." Claire then proceeded to tell Josie exactly how she liked her roast beef to be cooked, and how her mother always cooked it, and what style of potato was best with roast beef, and what vegetables you should serve, and every other excruciating detail about roast beef dinners that you'd ever want to know. Or not know. Josie nodded occasionally, only half listening, as they went back in the house together.

Indeed, life had returned to normal.

Chapter 5

Monday was always the worst morning of the week. Back to work. Back to the grind. And the weather this particular Monday morning didn't help. After a warm and sunny weekend, it was cool, foggy, and damp.

Josie and Becky were both working the morning shift, which began at seven, so they were up early, had breakfast together, and were out the door by six forty-five. Neither one had said much to the other at the breakfast table, but as they walked down Hollis, Becky couldn't hold back her curiosity. "So, how was your date yesterday?"

"Good," replied Josie, matter-of-factly.

"Where did you go?"

"To the Dingle."

"Isn't that a make-out place?"

"It's *not* a make-out place, it's a park. We had a picnic."

"But did you make out?"

Josie glanced over at Becky and smiled. "That's between Peter and me. It's none of your business."

"So, you *did* make out."

"None of your business, I said."

"Sorry. Don't be so touchy."

The two sisters walked in silence for a bit until Becky piped up again. "Do you think you'll ever see him again?"

"Of course," said Josie. "He'll probably be back in Halifax before too long. And he's going to write to me often." As she heard herself speak the words, they sounded more confident than she felt.

The sisters crossed the street to Gorman's.

Gorman's. Josie liked working there. The girls all got along well together. Of course, she wished she made more money. Not that Mr. Gorman was cheap or anything. He paid as much as any other restaurant owner in Halifax. And the tips had certainly been better since the Americans had joined the war. But waitressing was waitressing. She could only make so much. And with what she was getting, it was hard sometimes to pay the rent and still have money left over to buy some nice clothes.

The crowd was light this morning. A few men in suits grabbing a bite to eat before heading to their office jobs, a couple of construction workers, the odd bedraggled sailor who had probably been up all night drinking and was trying to sober up with a cup of coffee. Josie had even recognized one of the girls from Ava's down the street, no doubt relaxing after "servicing" the troops the night before.

Even when they didn't have a lot of customers to wait on, there was always plenty for the girls to do on the Monday morning shift. Top up the salt and pepper shakers, load the napkin dispensers, fill the ketchup and mustard bottles, make coffee, put out the cream and sugar. Although the Saturday night crew was supposed to clean up after their shift, they often did no more than a lick and a prayer, leaving a lot to do on Monday morning— sweeping the floors again, wiping off the counters, tidying up the bathrooms, and on and on. So, by the time mid-morning had arrived, Josie was more than ready for a break. Usually the girls took their breaks in the storage room at the back, where they'd have a cup of coffee and a cigarette, if they smoked, which most of them did. Then they'd sit and gossip about other girls, or talk about boyfriends or husbands or kids, or trade stories about oddball customers.

But this morning Josie decided to take her break outside, across the street. She propped herself up on a short ledge on the side of one of the buildings, lit a cigarette, took a deep drag, tilted her head back, and exhaled. She squinted as the smoke burned her eyes, sweeping it away with the back of her hand. Josie didn't smoke very often, but every once in a while she found a cigarette helped her relax. This was one of those times.

The air had warmed a little from earlier in the morning, and the fog had lifted from over the land but still engulfed the harbour. In the distance, Josie could hear the faint sound of the foghorn, which always reminded her of home.

Home. She'd left shortly after the war started, moving to the big city to find a better job. Back home she'd cleaned houses and minded children, but she wanted more than that. And Halifax was the place to find it. Everyone was moving here. At least, all the young people. The war was a terrible thing, but it had created lots of jobs for young women. Jobs as waitresses, secretaries, store clerks, factory workers. Josie had even heard about girls getting jobs as welders at the shipyards.

And there was a lot more to do in Halifax. Dances almost every night of the week, movie theatres with all the top films from Hollywood, ice cream parlours where you could get a sundae or a float. And the shopping! Clothing stores, and shoe stores, and jewelry stores, where even if you couldn't afford to buy anything, you could always look in the windows and dream. There was none of that where Josie came from. One measly general store with two gas pumps out front. That was it. No, she missed her parents for sure, but she never regretted moving away. She was happy here. Free. Alive. Life was good. And she had met and fallen in love with a handsome English sailor. That never would have happened if she hadn't moved to the city.

Peter. She missed him already. She'd thought about him all evening. He was the last thing on her mind before she went to sleep and the first thing on her mind when she woke up. She'd thought about him all morning at work, especially whenever a sailor came into the restaurant. Where would his ship be by now?

Was he safe? When would he be back in Halifax? Was he missing her? When would he write?

The backfire from a passing truck interrupted her daydream. *Oh my God*, she thought to herself, *I've lost track of time. My break is probably over.*

She dropped her cigarette on the sidewalk, stubbed it out with her shoe, and raced across the street to the restaurant. As she entered, her eyes met Mr. Gorman's. He was standing behind the counter. Without saying a word, he pointed to the clock on the wall behind him. She was three minutes late. Mouthing a silent "sorry," she strapped on her apron, grabbed her order pad and pencil, and got back to work. The rest of the shift passed uneventfully. Traffic picked up quite a bit at lunchtime, with the businessmen and clerks and secretaries from nearby offices making their daily visits. Josie and Becky both got off at four, so they walked home together. By then, the fog had disappeared completely, and it had turned out to be a very pleasant day. When they arrived at the house, they went up to their rooms to change and clean up for dinner.

At dinner, Miss Bennett seemed to be in a particularly sour mood. She was never jovial at the best of times, but this evening she seemed even worse. Typically, she'd make comments (usually critical ones) about the prevailing topic of conversation among the girls at the table or complain about some aspect of the upkeep of the house, like the girls not picking up after themselves in the laundry room or taking food into the parlour after meals. But at least she'd speak. Tonight, she barely said a word. Once or twice Josie thought that Miss Bennett had glared directly at her, and she wondered if that had anything to do with their confrontation the day before. Or maybe it was just her imagination.

Josie never knew how to read Miss Bennett. She was always very strict, but at times she'd do something nice for you, like bring a bowl of soup up to your room when you were sick or give you an extra blanket on an especially cold night. Some girls thought she was *too* tough on them, like a school mistress or a drill sergeant.

They wanted more freedom, more flexibility, fewer rules. Those girls usually didn't stay long. But Josie knew there were a lot worse boarding houses in the city than Miss Bennett's. At least you got two good meals a day, a clean, safe place to live, and no rats. For that, Josie could put up with Miss Bennett's crankiness.

After dinner, Josie and Becky got together in Josie's room, as they often did, to gab and keep each other company. They'd talk about things that happened at work, or what they were going to do on the weekend, or news from home. Becky would often tell Josie about things that Claire, the gossip, had told her. Then Josie would tell Becky that she was gossiping just like Claire by repeating what Claire had said. Then Becky would say it wasn't the same, that only the person telling the story the first time was the gossip, not the repeater. It was all in good fun.

This time, Becky had something else on her mind. "Did you notice that Miss Bennett was really grouchy tonight? I mean, grouchier than usual."

"I think it was my fault," said Josie.

"Your fault?"

"Yesterday she caught me in her office looking for some writing paper."

"Josie, you know we're not allowed in her office when she's not here. I told you to wait for her to come back."

"I couldn't. I had to give Peter our mailing address before he went back to his ship."

"Geez. What did she say?"

"She blew her top. She yelled at me to get out."

"Wow. Sounds like she was really mad. You shouldn't have gone in."

"Maybe not, but I don't think that's the main reason she was so upset."

"What do you mean?"

"I found a framed picture in her desk drawer and I was looking at it when she came in. When she saw me with it, she ran at me and grabbed it out of my hand. That's when she *really* got mad. She didn't want me to see that photograph."

"A photograph of what?"

"A young man in a military uniform. Very handsome. But very young."

"Did you recognize him?"

"No, I've never seen him before. And I didn't dare ask her about him."

"Hmm, I wonder who he is?"

Josie began running all the possibilities through her mind. Was he Miss Bennett's father, when he was young? Was it a family member, like a brother away in the war? Was it a former lover? What a tantalizing notion, although Josie couldn't imagine Miss Bennett with a lover, former or otherwise. And it couldn't be a deceased husband because she went by "Miss" Bennett, not "Mrs." Bennett. It was a mystery, for sure.

"Did you ever hear her talk about any relatives, a brother or someone else?" Josie asked Becky. "Maybe something you heard from your sidekick Claire?"

"No, I never heard her mention anyone," said Becky.

"Miss Bennett never mentioned anyone or Claire never mentioned anyone?"

Becky glared at Josie. "Neither. And Claire's not my sidekick."

"I would love to find out who it is," mused Josie, more to herself than to Becky.

It would be their final word on the subject for the evening. Their conversation switched to the usual topics, until they ran out of things to say and hugged each other goodnight. Once Becky had left, Josie changed into her nightgown, brushed her hair, and went to bed. But sleep didn't come quickly, as it usually did. Her imagination raced with thoughts of Miss Bennett. Who was this mysterious woman? Where had she come from? What secrets did her past hold?

For the first time in two days, Peter never crossed her mind.

Chapter 6

It was an excruciatingly long next few weeks for Josie. She knew that it could take as many as three weeks for letters to arrive from servicemen overseas. From Peter, perhaps more, depending how long he was at sea and where he was sailing to. The mail was delivered every day of the week except Sunday. Miss Bennett would distribute any letters for the girls, sliding them under their door if they weren't in their room. Nothing had arrived for Josie in the first three weeks since Peter had set sail.

Uncharacteristically, Josie hadn't gone to any dances since the one at the Strand where she first met Peter. For three consecutive Saturday nights, when Becky had asked if they were going dancing, Josie had said she wanted to go to a movie instead. She'd always say she really wanted to see the film that was playing, that she'd heard so many good things about it. Becky had told her she liked to go to the movies too, but they couldn't meet any new boys at a movie. Josie said she wasn't interested in meeting new boys.

By the end of the fourth week, there was still no letter from Peter. Then, one day, as Josie entered the house on her return from work, Miss Bennett stopped her in the foyer. "A letter came for you today, Miss Bourdeau. I put it under your door."

Josie's heart jumped. She flew up the stairs in a flash and flung open her door. There it was, on the floor. A chill ran through her. She snatched it up quickly and sat down on the side of her bed. With her hands trembling, she tore open the envelope and began to read. Within seconds, the reality hit her. It was not from Peter.

It was from her sister Agatha, relaying news from home. In her excitement, she had neglected to look at the postmark. Her heart sank. She tossed the letter aside and threw herself on the bed.

By the Natal Day weekend in early August, it had been five weeks since she'd met Peter. Still no letter. Josie reminded herself to be patient. There could be dozens of reasons why she hadn't heard from him. Perhaps he was still at sea and hadn't had an opportunity to post his letter. Perhaps it was held up with the censors, who checked every piece of mail to make sure it didn't contain anything the Germans could use to their advantage. Perhaps it had gotten lost in transit. Perhaps Peter had lost her mailing address. Perhaps he was injured and couldn't write. Perhaps worse. The unthinkable. She didn't want to consider that possibility. No, she would just have to wait. His letter would come, eventually.

Six weeks in, nothing. Eight weeks, still nothing. Of late, she'd been in the habit of asking Miss Bennett almost daily if there was any mail for her, but she'd stopped doing that because Miss Bennett was getting annoyed with Josie's "pestering." A couple of times she had even checked the mailbox herself after she saw the mailman drop by. That was risky, of course, because Miss Bennett would have been furious if she had caught her. The mail had to be checked by her first, then distributed to the girls. But it didn't matter. Josie hadn't found anything anyway.

With each passing day, she was growing more despondent. If Peter had indeed written to her, she should have received the letter by now, despite any possible delays. Even if he had lost her mailing address, he could always send it general delivery and it would eventually get to her. No, there were now only two possibilities. Either he hadn't written to her at all, or he was dead. Josie felt guilty for wishing it was the latter.

As the weeks went on with no letter, Josie's demeanor began to change. She was quieter, less talkative, less outgoing. She hardly spoke at the dinner table most nights. And even during her usual late night chats with Becky, she didn't say much. Ironically, Becky was becoming the more talkative one.

Then there was the dancing. Josie hadn't been to any dances over the summer—not one. She had even stopped going to the movies. Becky had started going with some of the other girls at the boarding house, rather than stay home every Saturday night. She and Josie used to go everywhere together. Now, they hardly went anywhere. Josie was not herself. She had gone from a happy, fun-loving flirt to a sad, lonely stick-in-the-mud.

One night, in Josie's room, Becky tried to snap her out of it. "Josie, let's go to a dance this weekend."

"Oh Becky, you know I don't feel like going to dances right now."

"Why not? You used to love going to dances."

"That's when I wanted to meet guys. I have a guy now."

"But he hasn't written to you."

"He will."

"Are you sure?"

"Yes, I'm sure. Anyway, I don't want to talk about this. If you want to go to a dance, go with someone else."

"But we always used to go together."

"Well, things change."

"Then how about a movie? We haven't been to a movie together in weeks. We don't have to meet any guys there."

"Oh, I don't know, Becky."

"C'mon. I hear there's a Clark Cable movie on at the Capitol. You always like him. It's called *Blowing in the Wind*, I think."

"*Gone with the Wind*," Josie corrected her.

"Yes, that's it. *Gone with the Wind*. So, what do you say? You need a night out. It'll be fun."

"Well…"

"Please, Sis."

"Oh, alright, we'll go to the movies Saturday night."

Becky gave Josie a big hug. "Thanks, Sis."

Saturday night was cool and crisp. The day had been nice, but the temperature had dropped several degrees by evening. Late August, and it was already starting to feel fallish. According to the radio, *Gone with the Wind* was one of the most popular movies ever. It had sold out everywhere it had played. A blockbuster, they called it. And they were finally showing it in Halifax. So, Josie and Becky decided to go early to make sure they got a good seat. Even so, when they arrived at The Capitol, there were long lineups on both sides of the theatre, stretching north and south along Barrington. They were in for a long wait.

As they stood in line, Josie stretched her neck, looking up the queue. Something had caught her attention.

"What is it?" asked Becky.

"It's him!" Josie said excitedly.

"Who?"

"Peter."

"Peter? Your Peter?"

"Yes, my Peter."

"Are you sure?"

"Positive. It's him. Look."

Josie pulled Becky toward her so that her sister could see up ahead. "See that tall guy in the British Navy uniform with his back to us, standing next to that shorter guy? It's him. I can see the blond hair under his hat."

Becky wasn't as sure. "Oh, I don't know. It looks a bit like him from the back, but there's lots of British sailors with blond hair."

"It's him. He's back in Halifax like he said he would be. He's come back to see me."

Before Becky could stop her, Josie left her place in line and made a beeline for her Peter, ignoring the glares and grumbling of others in the line. She came right up behind him. She was now even more certain that it was him. "Peter?" she said.

He didn't turn around.

She touched him on the arm. "Peter?"

This time he turned around. But it wasn't him. It wasn't Peter. It was just another sailor. Someone she didn't recognize. She was crushed. And embarrassed. "I'm sorry," she said, disheartened. "I thought you were someone else."

"Hey, luv," said the unknown sailor, "I'll be anyone you want me to be." He then laughed and turned to his buddy to share the joke.

Josie went back to her place in the line and stood next to Becky. She stared straight ahead without saying anything. Becky tried to console her. "Well, it *did* look like him from behind."

Josie didn't say a word. In fact, she didn't say much for the rest of the evening. Usually, she'd make comments to Becky about the movie. Not this time. Nothing. Becky stayed mum as well, for the most part. The only time she really spoke to Josie was at the intermission, when she told her she was going for popcorn and asked her if she wanted anything. Josie gave her a blunt "No."

Josie's silence continued on their way home. Becky tried a couple of times to strike up a conversation by making comments about certain scenes in the movie, but Josie would either respond with a grunt or simply say nothing at all. And for the first time that Becky could remember, they didn't walk arm in arm. When they arrived at the boarding house and went upstairs, Becky followed Josie into her room, expecting their usual late night chat. But Josie was not in the mood. "Becky, not tonight. I'm tired and I just want to go to bed."

"Are you alright?"

"I'm fine."

"It's okay, Josie, there's lots of other guys out there. You'll find somebody else."

Josie felt her anger rising but said nothing. Becky kept talking. "You know, Claire said the same thing happened to her cousin. She met this sailor at a dance—well, he was an American, but it's still the same—and she fell head over heels for him. He said he'd write to her too, but he never did. Well, she was devastated.

She almost went into a depression. But she eventually got over it, and now she's married to a local guy and has three kids."

Becky barely paused to take a breath. "Claire says this happens all the time. Local girls fall for sailors and the sailors will tell the girls anything to get what they want. Then they leave and you never see them again. They do this everywhere they go, in every port, all over the place. And Clair says…"

Josie exploded. "I don't give a *fuck* what Claire says. I just want to go to bed. Now leave me alone!"

Becky looked stunned. She had never seen Josie this angry. And she had never heard her curse like that. She also looked hurt. Her big sister had never hollered at her like that before. Ever. She slowly backed out of the room and closed the door behind her.

Tears welled in Josie's eyes as she undressed, put on her nightgown, and got into bed. Emotions raged through her as her head throbbed—anger, embarrassment, betrayal, despair. Anger for being lied to. Embarrassment for being such a fool. Betrayal by the man she had given herself completely to, body and soul. Despair that she might never find love again.

She pulled the covers over her face and cried herself to sleep.

Chapter 7

Josie woke with a start. She glanced over at the clock on her night table. It was twenty-five to nine. She laid back on her bed and stared at the ceiling, thinking about the previous night, processing what had occurred. She had lost her temper. She had jumped down Becky's throat. She had said things she shouldn't have said.

Why had she acted like that? Because she was angry, that's why. At Becky? No, Becky had done nothing wrong. At herself. Angry at herself for falling in love with some sailor she had just met, who she didn't know from Adam. Angry at herself for believing his lies, for giving herself to him, for opening her heart and letting him in.

How did she let this happen? This had never happened to her before. She never swooned over guys, they swooned over her. She was Josie. Carefree, happy-go-lucky Josie. Love was for Hollywood movies or her married sisters back home. She just wanted to have a good time.

She hated to admit it, but blabber-mouth Claire was right. This *did* happen all the time. Sailors arrived in port, met local girls, told them whatever they needed to tell them to get what they wanted, then sailed off to the next port to pull the same trick on their next victim. Hey, there was a war on. What did you expect? Josie just never thought it would happen to her.

But she wasn't going to let it happen again. No, she would never let another sailor break her heart. She would never let another sailor lie to her, betray her, embarrass her. She was going to go back to being the old Josie, the fun-loving, devil-may-care Josie, the Josie that went to all the dances and flirted with all the boys.

But first she had to apologize to Becky.

Since it was Sunday morning, she was already much too late to join the girls for their weekly group breakfast. So, she took her time washing and getting dressed before heading downstairs to look for her sister. As she entered the dining room, she spotted Becky helping Miss Bennett clear away the breakfast dishes. Miss Bennett looked up, glared at Josie, and was about to say something when Josie cut her off.

"I know, I'm too late."

"Again," snapped Miss Bennett, before disappearing into the kitchen.

Josie knew that Becky had seen her come in but hadn't acknowledged her. She was wiping off the table as Josie sidled up to her. "Good morning."

"Good morning," said Becky, still not looking up.

Josie searched for what to say next. "Are you going to mass this morning?"

"Yes," said Becky.

"I think I'll go too."

"Suit yourself."

"Do you want to go together or are you going with Claire?"

"Are you sure you want to go with me?"

"Yes, I'm sure."

This time, Becky paused before speaking. "We can go together, if you want."

"Great. Let's meet in the parlour at twenty to ten."

"Okay."

Josie was about to go into the kitchen and ask Miss Bennett if she could have a cup of tea and some toast but then thought better of it. Besides, she wasn't all that hungry. She went back to her room to get ready for mass. When she went downstairs at twenty to ten, Becky was already waiting for her in the parlour. This time, Becky glanced up.

"Let's go," said Josie, smiling.

She turned and headed out the door, and Becky followed. When they got on the sidewalk, Josie offered Becky her arm. Becky held back for just a second, then hooked her arm around Josie's. They walked slowly and silently together for a couple of minutes until Josie finally broke the ice. "Becky, I'm sorry that I hollered at you last night. I shouldn't have done that."

Becky didn't respond.

Josie continued. "I wasn't mad at you, I was mad at myself. I was mad at myself for being so stupid to fall for that lying jerk. And I took it out on you. I shouldn't have. It wasn't your fault. You didn't say anything wrong. I'm sorry."

"I never heard you say that word before," said Becky.

"Well, when you're mad, you say things you shouldn't say."

"You'll have to go to confession."

Josie chuckled to herself. Here she was trying to apologize and her sister was worried about her confessing her sins. If she only knew.

They walked the rest of the way to the church without saying another word. At one point, Becky rested her head against Josie's shoulder. Josie knew *then* that all was forgiven. After mass, Josie suggested they walk up Spring Garden Road to the Public Gardens. It was a bright, sunny Sunday and the park was full. Josie couldn't help but notice all the sailors strolling along with a girl on their arm. She wanted to go up to the girls and say, "Don't believe them! They're all liars! They'll break your hearts!" But she didn't. She and Becky found a bench overlooking the pond and just sat and watched the ducks floating by.

As Josie let the sun warm her face, she tried to relax and clear her mind. But she couldn't. Her mind kept jumping back to last night, to her anger and embarrassment. "I still can't believe I fell for that guy," she blurted out.

"Well, he was kinda good looking," said Becky.

"He was a creep."

Josie pondered whether creep was the best word to describe him. Rascal, scoundrel, rat also came to mind. She decided creep was as good as any.

"You'll find somebody else," reassured Becky.

"I don't want to find somebody else. I'm going back to being the old Josie. Going to the dances, dancing with lots of guys, just having fun."

"Are you going to dance with sailors?"

"Yeah, I'll dance with sailors. There's nobody else to dance with. But I'm not going to fall for them. They can fall for me, but I'm not falling for them."

Enough of that, thought Josie. She changed the topic. They started talking about the weather. And work. And a dress Becky had seen in a shop window on Barrington.

After she and Becky had had enough of watching ducks, they got up from the bench and explored the rest of the park. They were getting hungry, so they left the park and headed down Spring Garden to find a place to eat. After they had eaten, they went back to the house to spend the rest of the day doing as little as possible.

Everything was now good between the sisters. No lasting harm had been done.

Chapter 8

True to her word, Josie started going back to the dances. The very next week. She and Becky had Saturday off from work, so on Friday night they went together to the Masonic Hall, just like in the old days. As expected, the place was packed with sailors, trolling for girls. But Josie felt upbeat. She felt free. She was going to enjoy herself.

It didn't take long before a sailor asked her to dance. He was an American. No more than eighteen or nineteen, Josie figured. And not that good-looking. But Josie didn't care. She just wanted to dance, to have fun. She said yes. Instantly, he grabbed her hand and pulled her onto the floor. He turned out to be a very good dancer, and twirled Josie round and round in perfect step with the music. When the song was over, he wanted to dance with her again. But she turned him down, laughing loudly. "Sorry, only one dance to a customer," she told him.

The night continued much the same, with sailors constantly getting her up on the floor. Yanks, Canucks, Brits, Norwegians— even some whose uniforms or accents she didn't recognize. For all she knew, she could be dancing with German spies. But she didn't care. She was having too much fun. And she was at her flirtatious best, with her coy smile, her sparkling eyes, and her long hair flying in all directions. She felt alive!

At one point, as she was gently letting down one overly amorous sea dog who wanted another spin around the floor, she heard a woman's voice from behind shout out her name. She turned to see who it was and immediately recognized one of her coworkers. "Doris!"

Doris was the head waitress at Gorman's. She had shown Josie the ropes when she had first started, and they had been friends ever since. Doris would trade shifts with her whenever Josie asked, if she could, and Josie would do the same for her. They'd also cover for each other when necessary.

"Let me introduce you to my friends," said Doris, still shouting over the noise.

Doris had a sailor on each arm and was enjoying the attention. All three appeared a little glassy-eyed. "This is Tom from Connecticut," she said, gesturing to the one on her right arm, "and this is Bill from North Carolina," nodding towards the one on her left.

"South Carolina," corrected the one named Bill.

"North, South, whatever. Anyway, Josie, why don't you join us. We have a table over against the wall somewhere."

Doris was married, but that didn't stop her from going to dances and hooking up with sailors. She had been married only six months when her husband shipped out overseas. That was in 1940 and she hadn't seen him since. She'd confided in Josie once about how lonely she was by herself. She didn't go out for about a year after he left but then figured he was probably chasing girls overseas, so why shouldn't she have some fun here. Besides, she hardly knew him before they got married and admitted she sometimes had a difficult time remembering his face.

Josie mulled over whether or not to join her friend. Tagging along with Doris would be fun, but she wasn't quite sure what kind of fun. Then she remembered what she had promised herself that morning in bed a few days ago. "Sure, why not."

Doris was delighted. She extricated herself from her two companions, hooked her arm in Josie's, and escorted her to their table as the Americans followed close behind. When they got to the table, Doris zipped open her purse and showed Josie the contents. There was a quart of rum inside, about three-quarters full.

"Go get some cups for the four of us, and some mix," she ordered her two sailor boys.

When they returned, Doris distributed the cups and poured out stiff drinks for each of them, glancing around to see if anyone was watching, although nobody seemed to be paying any attention whatsoever. She then passed around the mix, which because there was so little of it between the four of them, barely diluted the rum. She then lifted her cup, exhorted the others to do the same, and proposed a toast. "To our fighting men overseas."

"Here, here!" shouted one of the Americans, who Josie thought was Tom. Or maybe Bill. She couldn't remember.

Doris downed her drink without coming up for air, forcing the Americans to follow suit. Josie debated for a second, then, not wanting to be a killjoy, did the same. As the liquor slid down, she felt a burning in her chest. She had drunk rum before, a few times, but not this strong a drink, and not this much all at once. With the first round completed, Doris snatched everyone's cup and poured out a second round, trying to put equal amounts in each one, and again, pointlessly trying to hide what she was doing. The bottle now empty, she gave everyone back their cups, spilling a little from one of the American's.

"Hey!" he squawked, "that's valuable stuff."

"Sorry," said Doris.

Josie took her cup and looked at the rum. "But we don't have any more mix."

"Then we'll have to drink it straight," said Doris with a wide grin.

"To the American Navy!" roared Tom from Connecticut, raising his cup over his head.

"Here, here!" chimed in Doris. Bill from South Carolina raised his cup. Josie raised hers too. Almost in unison, the four drinking buddies brought their cups to their mouths and began to pour. Like before, Doris and the two Americans downed theirs without stopping. But Josie took a little more time to finish hers. This one burned too, but not as bad as the first. As the liquid slid down her throat, a warm sensation flowed through her body. The rum was beginning to work its magic. For no apparent reason, Josie started giggling. Then Doris started giggling. Before long, the four of them were laughing out loud, though no one had said or done anything remotely funny. Rum did that to you.

"Another drink," demanded Tom, pushing his cup towards Doris.

"That's all I have," said Doris. "The bottle's empty."

"What? No more rum? We need more rum. Find us a bootlegger."

"To the bootlegger's!" declared Doris, wrapping her arm around Josie's neck.

Like four musketeers, Doris and Josie and Tom and Bill stumbled towards the exit, laughing and playfully jostling each other as they went. All of a sudden, Josie stopped. "Becky!" she shouted. "I forgot about Becky."

"Who's Becky?" asked Tom.

"Becky, your sister?" said Doris to Josie.

"Yes."

"What about her?"

"Well, we came here together. I can't leave her here by herself."

"Bring her with us."

"Oh, I don't think she'll want to come. She doesn't drink."

"So what. Bring her along anyway. She can keep an eye on the rest of us."

"Oh, I don't know."

"Ah, c'mon Josie. We're havin' so much fun. Don't leave me now."

"Well, we'll have to find her."

"Okay, let's start looking."

Doris instructed the two Americans to wait by the exit while they searched for Becky. The hall was crowded, so Josie figured it might take some time to find her, but within a minute or two they spotted her dancing with a young man in civvies. Josie went right up to her, cutting in front of her dance partner. "You know Doris."

"Hi Doris," said Becky.

"Doris has invited both of us to, um, a party," said Josie. "So let's go."

"Wait, what?" said Becky. "What kind of a party?"

"Just a party. C'mon, there's other people waiting for us."

"But I'm not finished my dance."

"I'm going with Doris and I'm not leaving you here by yourself, so you have to come with me. Grab my hand."

Becky shrugged, apologized to the young man, and took Josie's hand. As they walked together towards the exit, Becky sniffed Josie's breath. "Have you been drinking?"

"A little," said Josie.

The two Americans were waiting at the exit. Doris handled the introductions. "Becky, this is Tom and Bill. Guys, this is Becky, Josie's sister."

"Hey, cutie," said Bill.

"*Baby* sister," warned Josie.

The group of now five revelers poured out of the Masonic Hall onto the sidewalk. Tom flagged down a taxi and they all crowded in, Becky and Josie in the front seat and Doris between the two Americans in the back.

"To the bootleggers!" shouted Tom.

"Which one?" asked the driver.

"Jimmy's on Queen," said Doris.

Becky leaned over and whispered to Josie sitting next to her. "I thought we were going to a party."

"We are," said Josie, "but we have to go to the bootlegger's first."

When they arrived at Jimmy's, Doris asked Tom to give her some money. He gave her two American one-dollar bills. She passed one to the driver. "Can you wait here for us? We'll only be a few minutes."

The driver nodded.

Doris turned to Josie and Becky. "You two wait here. We'll be right back. Is there anything special you want, Josie, or is rum okay?"

"Lemon gin. I'd like some lemon gin," said Josie.

Doris and the two Americans jumped out of the cab and disappeared around the back of the bootlegger's house. As soon as they were gone, Becky confronted her sister again. "Josie, I don't think this is such a good idea. We should go home."

"Don't be such a stick-in-the-mud," said Josie. "You don't have to drink if you don't want to, but we're going with Doris. You're the one who talked me into going to the dance, so now I'm going to have some fun."

About five minutes later, Doris and her two friends reappeared, with the Americans each carrying a brown paper bag with the goodies. They piled back into the rear seat.

"We got two quarts of rum and some beer for us and a quart of lemon gin for you, Josie," said a beaming Doris. "All courtesy of the U.S. Navy. Jimmy even had some mix."

Doris asked the driver to take them to a place where they could enjoy their booty without getting hassled by MPs or the city police. He took them to a small, vacant, heavily wooded lot next to a cemetery further uptown. It was perfect. There, they could drink themselves silly without being bothered and without bothering anyone, because, as Bill joked, nobody in the cemetery would say a word.

Since they didn't have any cups, they drank straight out of the bottle, and chased it with the mix. Josie had the bottle of lemon gin all to herself. She had offered some to the others, but they had all passed.

Josie tried to keep pace with her friends, swig for swig. Bill even came up with a little drinking game, about trying to name the song he was singing. But he wasn't much of a singer, and the booze didn't help, so the others soon lost interest.

Before long, Josie began to feel the effects of the alcohol. While the first couple of drinks at the dance had made her feel all warm inside, the lemon gin was starting to make her feel a little woozy. Her speech began to slur noticeably. At one point, she tried to do a little jig to amuse the Americans, but stumbled awkwardly to the ground, laughing. Righting herself, she squinted through the dim light. "Hey, where's my baby sister?"

She spotted Becky sitting on the ground by herself away from the rest of the group, and stumbled over to her.

"Aren't you joining the party?" said Josie, garbling her words.

Becky looked up. "Don't you think you've had enough, Sis?"

Josie didn't respond, instead taking another swig from her bottle of lemon gin.

"How long are we going to stay here, Josie?" said Becky.

"Why, don't you like this place?"

"I'm getting a little chilly."

"Then have a drink. It'll warm you up."

"You know I don't drink. Besides, you guys have pretty much finished everything."

Josie lifted her liquor bottle to her face and peered into it. "Mmm, you're right!" She then staggered over to the others and approached Doris, who was sitting on the ground, laughing with the two Americans.

"Doris, we're running out of booze."

Doris looked at her own bottle, which was also nearly empty. "I think you're right," she answered. She then stood up to make the announcement. "Everybody, we're taking this party to my place. There's more booze there. Call me a cab."

"You're a cab," bellowed Tom, laughing hilariously at his own corny joke.

The lot where they had been partying was on a side street but not far from a main thoroughfare where they would be able to hail a cab. It was now well past midnight, but cabs ran late in the city during the war, especially on the weekends. The trick would be finding one in that part of town.

By this time, Josie could barely stand up on her own. Becky helped her to her feet and put her arm around her waist to prevent her from falling. Josie still held the bottle of lemon gin in her hand, but it was now completely empty. Becky took it from her. She asked Josie if she was okay. Josie mumbled something incoherent.

The five of them trudged up the street with Doris leading the way, weaving back and forth as she walked. Becky was struggling to keep up with the others, as she literally had to drag Josie with her. This was no mean feat, given that Josie was twenty pounds heavier than Becky, and now almost a dead weight.

When they finally arrived at the corner, Becky suggested to Doris that she let her hail the cab, to which Doris raised no objection. Becky then sat Josie down on the curb and stepped out into the street. After about ten minutes, she spotted a cab approaching and flagged it down. They all piled in and Doris gave the driver her home address. But Becky clearly had other ideas. "Driver, before you go there, can you drop my sister and me off at sixty-nine Hollis?"

"What, you're not coming to my place?" slurred Doris.

"No, I really need to get Josie home. But thanks anyway."

Doris just shrugged.

When they arrived at the boarding house, Becky pulled Josie out of the cab and bid farewell to the others, who were oblivious to her gesture. As the car sped away, Josie mumbled something.

"What?" said Becky.

Josie mumbled again. Her head was slumped down and her eyes were closed.

"What did you say, Josie?"

Becky put her ear up to Josie's mouth. This time, she heard her.

"I think I'm gonna be sick."

"You think you're going to be sick? You can't be sick here, not on the sidewalk!"

"I'm gonna be sick," Josie repeated.

Becky took Josie around the side of the building, where a walkway led to the back. The area was dark, but there was enough light coming from the street that they could see to make their way. By this time, Josie's body was starting to heave uncontrollably. It was only a matter of seconds before everything would let loose. Becky positioned Josie with one hand against the wall, head down, far enough away that she hopefully wouldn't throw up on her own shoes.

Then it happened. Like an explosion. Shooting out from her like a cannon, splashing against the wall, splashing back on her shoes and her dress. Becky rubbed Josie's back in circular motions, trying to comfort her. "Let it out, Josie. Let it all out. Get rid of all that bad stuff."

Josie vomited again and again, moaning in agony, her body heaving, retching. Each time there was less coming out, as her stomach began to empty. But that only made the ordeal more painful, more tortuous, more miserable. At long last, there was a lull in her suffering. With her head still down, Josie wiped her mouth with the back of her arm.

"Are you feeling any better?" said Becky, still rubbing Josie's back.

"I think I'm going to die," moaned Josie.

"You're not going to die. We just need to get you to bed. You need to sleep this off."

"My head is spinning. I can't lift my head. I can't move."

"I'll help you. C'mon, you can do it."

Becky put her arm around Josie's back and under her arm to help hold her up. They walked back to the sidewalk, up the steps, and into the house. Josie kept her head down the entire time.

"Try not to make any noise," Becky whispered, as they made their way up the stairs. "We don't want to wake anyone up."

Although it took some time, they made it to Josie's room without incident. Becky sat Josie on the bed. Immediately, Josie plopped herself down, rolled over on her side, and tucked her knees up in the fetal position. She moaned. "I don't feel very good, Becky."

"I'm going to get a cold cloth to wipe your face. I'll be right back."

Becky went out into the hall and returned shortly after with a small, damp facecloth. She sat down on the side of the bed, pushed back Josie's hair, and gently patted Josie's face with the wet cloth. "Does that feel better?"

"Mmm," mumbled Josie.

Becky kept patting Josie's face with the cloth, turning it over periodically to the damper side. Josie didn't say a word or move a muscle. Then, all of a sudden, she sat up in the bed. "I'm gonna be sick again."

"You can't throw up here. Try to hold it," pleaded Becky. "We've got to get you to the bathroom."

Becky helped her sister to her feet and they stumbled towards the bathroom as fast as they could. But they didn't make it. Halfway down the hall, Josie let fly. Vomit spewed everywhere. On the floor, on the walls, everywhere.

"Oh my God!" wailed Becky.

Becky grabbed Josie around the waist and dragged her into the bathroom, closing the door behind her. Josie vomited again on the bathroom floor before Becky had a chance to plop her sister on her knees in front of the toilet. Josie vomited again, this time into the toilet. By now, there was nothing left in her stomach; she was just bringing up bile. Yellow, watery bile. She then went into the dry heaves, her body retching forward again and again and again, but nothing coming out. *I want to die*, she thought to herself.

Eventually, the heaving subsided. She struggled to breathe. She felt exhausted. She could feel Becky's hand on her back, rubbing back and forth. She tried to lift her head out of the toilet, but the room started spinning, so she put it back down.

She heard a scream. "What was that?" she mumbled to Becky.

Becky rose from her knees and looked out the bathroom door. "It's Shirley," said Becky.

"What happened?" mumbled Josie.

"She walked in your throw up in her bare feet," said Becky. "I think she woke everybody up. I see all the lights on."

"Oh God," moaned Josie.

Within seconds, Josie could hear Claire's voice behind her. "What's wrong with Josie?"

"She's sick. She's been throwing up," said Becky.

"Wow. Is it the flu?"

Becky didn't respond.

"Yeah, it's the flu, you birdbrain," mumbled Josie, barely audibly.

"What?" said Claire.

"Nothing," said Becky. "Help me get Josie back to her room before Miss Bennett shows up."

Just then, they heard the unmistakable bellow of their landlady coming from the hallway.

"Too late," said Claire.

It was indeed too late. A moment later Miss Bennett was at the bathroom door. "What is going on here?!" she barked.

"Josie's sick," said Becky.

"Sick?" Miss Bennett sniffed. "I smell alcohol. Has she been drinking?"

Becky didn't answer.

"Has she been drinking? You had better tell me the truth, young lady!"

Becky hesitated. "Yes, she has."

"Well, this is totally unacceptable! Totally unacceptable! I will not abide by this kind of behavior in this house. Now you get this mess cleaned up right now, Miss Becky, and get your sister to her room. I will deal with her in the morning."

With that, Miss Bennett stormed out.

"Okay Sis," said Becky, "we have to get you to bed. Can you stand up?"

"I'll try," said Josie.

With considerable effort, Josie managed to get to her feet, but she had to keep her head down because the room still felt like it was spinning. Becky wet a cloth and wiped the dried vomit from Josie's face and arms. She then took Josie back to her room, with

Claire's help. Josie's clothes reeked of vomit, so they undressed her, except for her bra and panties, and put on her night gown. Becky then laid Josie down in her bed and covered her with the bed sheets. "I'll take your dirty clothes with me and wash them tomorrow," said Becky to her sister, who managed only a grunt in reply.

The last thing Josie remembered was Becky kissing her on the forehead.

Chapter 9

The voice was faint, as if far away, then grew louder and louder. She sensed movement: gentle, rocking movement. A form appeared, as darkness turned slowly to light. Milky and cloudy at first, then gradually coming into focus. She squinted to make it out.

It was Becky, looking down at her. "Josie. Josie. It's time to get up."

Little by little, consciousness returned. She was in her bed, in her room. Becky was with her, trying to wake her up. She struggled to see her, as the piercing light from her window burned her eyes. Her head ached, as if someone was squeezing it in a vise. She felt queasy, her insides rolling like an ocean swell. Her mouth was dry.

"Josie, it's almost eleven o'clock. You have to try to get up."

Josie opened and closed her mouth several times, trying to generate some moisture. "Water," she mumbled, almost inaudibly.

"What?" said Becky.

"Water. Get me some water."

Becky left the room and returned shortly after with a glass of water. She helped Josie sit up in bed and brought the glass to Josie's lips. Josie took a small mouthful. "I have to lie down," said Josie. "I feel dizzy." Josie laid back down and closed her eyes.

"You have to try to get up, Josie. Try to put something in your stomach."

"I can't eat now."

"It'll make you feel better."

"Nothing'll make me feel better."

Becky left the room again and this time came back with a wet facecloth. She gently wiped Josie's face, folded the facecloth in two, and laid it across Josie's forehead. "C'mon, I'll help you get up."

"No, just leave me here. I'm just going to stay in bed for the day."

"You can't. You have to get up. Miss Bennett wants to speak with you."

"Miss Bennett? About what?"

"About last night."

"Last night?"

"Yeah, last night. Don't you remember?"

Josie strained to recall the events of the previous evening. Some were clearer, others a blur. "I remember going to the dance, and then meeting Doris, and then going to the bootlegger's with Doris and those two American sailors. And I remember drinking lemon gin at that place next to the cemetery. And I think I remember getting sick."

"You threw up in the hall upstairs and all over the floor in the bathroom."

"Oh my God. Did I? Did anyone see me?"

"Everyone was up."

"Miss Bennett too?"

"Miss Bennett too. I'm sure that's why she wants to speak with you. I think you're in trouble."

All the more reason to stay in bed, thought Josie. She certainly didn't enjoy Miss Bennett's lectures at the best of times. And with the way she was feeling right now, it was the last thing she wanted to do. But putting it off would only make things worse. It would only make Miss Bennett angrier. She might as well face the music and get it over with. Then she could go back to bed and sleep off this hangover. "Okay, I'll try to get up. Give me a hand."

With Becky's help, Josie rolled over and sat on the side of her bed. As she lifted her head, the room began to spin, so she dropped her head and stared at the floor with her arms resting on her knees. Becky wiped Josie's face again with the cloth.

"You have to try to stand up," said Becky.

"Just give me a few minutes."

Josie remained on the side of the bed for several minutes, raising her head slowly, little by little, feeling dizzy each time she did so, but holding herself still until the dizziness subsided and her sense of balance returned. Before long, she was sitting straight up. "I think I'll be okay now."

"Are you sure?"

"Yeah, I just need some time."

Eventually, Josie told her sister she felt ready to stand and walk a little. Becky then helped her make her way to the bathroom so she could freshen up. Once she was finished, Becky guided her back to her room and helped her get dressed. She then sat Josie down at her dressing table and brushed her hair. "How do you feel now?"

"Like I've just been run over by an army truck."

Becky chuckled. "At least you still have your sense of humour."

"I'll need it with Miss Bennett."

"Are you going to speak with her right now?"

"I might as well, if she's not busy."

"Are you worried?"

"Nah, she's been upset with me before. I'll just say I'm sorry and that it won't happen again."

"Well, I'm going back to my room. Let me know how you make out."

As Becky headed out the door, Josie called to her. "Sis?"

"What?"

"Thanks."

They smiled at each other the way sisters do.

Josie picked up her compact from her dressing table and stared at herself in its small mirror. "I *do* look like I've been run over by an army truck," she said aloud. She brushed some powder under her eyes and dabbed her forehead. She then took out a tube of lipstick and applied a fresh coat. Getting up from the dressing table, she walked across the room, picked up the glass of water that Becky had left on the night table, and took another sip. Her hand was shaking. She took a deep breath, then headed downstairs to face her fate. When she reached the bottom of the stairs, she stopped for a second, took another deep breath, then walked straight to Miss Bennett's office. She knocked lightly on the door.

"Come in."

Miss Bennett was seated at her desk, head down, writing something in a notebook. The room was in shadows, lit only by the lamp on the desk. Josie recalled the last time she had been in this room. It looked and felt exactly the same: dark and gloomy. She waited to see if Miss Bennett would acknowledge her presence, but the old woman kept writing in her notebook.

"Miss Bennett, Becky said you wanted to speak with me about something?"

Miss Bennett looked up. She put down her pen. "Yes. Yes, I do."

There was no side chair by the desk, so Josie wondered if Miss Bennett would invite her to the sitting area by the fireplace for their conversation. But she didn't. She just sat upright in her chair, staring at Josie. Josie moved closer, so that the light from the lamp now illuminated them both. She waited for Miss Bennett to say something, but her landlady just kept staring at her. After what seemed like an eternity, the old woman finally spoke.

"Last night, in the middle of the night in fact, I was awakened by a commotion coming from the girls' rooms upstairs. When I arrived on the scene, I discovered you, Miss Bourdeau, in the bathroom, bent over the toilet bowl, vomiting. With my keen sense of smell, I was quickly able to determine that alcohol was the cause of your *illness*. I was also able to determine, both from the sickening stench and with my very own eyes, that you had vomited all over the bathroom floor. After instructing your sister to clean up your mess, on my way back downstairs to my room, I discovered, to my absolute disgust and revulsion, that you had also vomited all over the floor and walls in the hall."

"I'm very sorry, Miss Bennett. I…"

"I'm not finished, Miss Bourdeau. As if the events of last night were not disturbing enough, this morning I was alerted by our neighbor, Mr. Simpson, that someone had vomited on the side of our building. He discovered it on his morning walk with his dog when he noticed rats and other vermin milling around the spot. Now, of course, Mr. Simpson assumed that the culprit was some drunken sailor passing by. But connecting this piece of information to the events of last evening, my suspicions immediately fell on you, Miss Bourdeau. When I confronted your sister with my hunch, she tried to protect you at first, but I eventually extracted the truth from her."

Josie lowered her head, embarrassed. "I don't remember that."

"I'm not surprised you don't remember it, given the condition you were in."

Josie realized she was in trouble. She would have to come up with her best *mea culpa*. "Miss Bennett, I am so very sorry. I am so ashamed of myself. It will never happen again, I promise."

"You are right. It will never happen again. At least, not in this house."

Josie was puzzled. "What do you mean?"

"Miss Bourdeau, I run a respectable establishment here. I provide a clean, safe place for young women to live, protected from bad influences that can lead them down the wrong path in life. I don't allow drinking on the premises and I certainly don't want drunkards living here."

Josie resented the inference. "I'm not a drunkard."

"Miss Bourdeau, your behaviour last evening was deplorable, despicable, disgraceful. You allowed yourself to become so intoxicated that you had no control over yourself or your actions. You disturbed the sleep of all the girls, you desecrated their home, and you set a terrible example. And you endangered my reputation."

"Your reputation?"

"If Mr. Simpson finds out that it was one of my own girls who vomited on the side of the building, what impression will that give him about my establishment? If word spreads that girls here are getting drunk and throwing up all over the place, what do you think will happen to my reputation? Do you think mothers and fathers will want their young daughters living here? No, Miss Bourdeau, your behaviour is inexcusable, and I won't take the chance that it might happen again."

Josie started to get a funny feeling in the pit of her stomach. "What are you saying?"

"I'm saying that I can no longer allow you to live here. You must move out."

"What?" screamed Josie. "You can't do that!"

"Oh, but I can, and I will. I alone decide who stays at my establishment and I no longer want you living here."

"But that's not fair!"

"Oh, I think it's perfectly fair. Your behaviour was totally unacceptable, and now you must pay the consequences of your actions, Miss Bourdeau."

"But kicking me out for this. I said I'm sorry. Please, Miss Bennett."

"The decision has been made. Nothing you can say will change it."

Josie's eyes welled with tears, as much from anger as sorrow. "But where will I go? Where will I stay?"

"I'll give you one week to find another place. You have to be out of this house with all your belongings by next Saturday."

"How am I going to find another place in one week? You know how hard it is to find a place to live in this city."

"You're a resourceful young lady. You'll find something."

Josie was in a daze. Her mind raced from thought to thought. The thought of having no place to stay. The thought of being out on the street without a home. And then she thought about her sister. "What about Becky?" she asked Miss Bennett.

"Miss Becky is free to stay here if she wishes. I have no problem with her. She has always behaved as a young lady should."

"But I have to look after her. She's my baby sister."

Miss Bennett glared at Josie through the corner of her eye. "With all due respect, Miss Bourdeau, from what I observed last evening, I would say she was the one looking after you."

Josie felt rage building inside her. How could Miss Bennett do this to her? How could she be so nasty, so vicious, so cruel? So she got drunk and threw up. It had only happened once. Why couldn't she just accept her apology? Why did she have to kick her out? It was because she had caught her in her office, that was it. She'd been hard on her ever since. As though she hated her. Well, Josie hated her too. This time, she wasn't going to hold back. She had nothing to lose. She was going to tell Miss Bennett exactly what she thought of her.

"You're just a mean old witch! You've never had any fun in your life and you don't want anyone else to have any fun. You don't have any friends because nobody can stand you. None of the girls here like you. They all hate you. But I hate you the most. And I'll be glad to be out of this prison!"

Miss Bennett's eyes widened, and her face flushed slightly, but she kept her composure. "One week," she said calmly.

Josie stormed out of the room, slamming the door behind her as hard as she could. She bolted up the stairs to her room, flung open the door, slammed it shut, and threw herself onto her bed. What was she going to do now? Where was she going to live? How was she going to watch over Becky? What if her mother found out?

Her head now throbbed worse than ever.

Chapter 10

Resourceful or not, finding a place to stay in one week would not be easy. With thousands of young women flooding into the city from the countryside to find work during the war, just like Josie and Becky had done, accommodations were scarce. Adding to the demand were the many wives of Canadian sailors from outside the province who wanted to be close to their husbands when they came into port on shore leave. And landlords were taking advantage of the situation, jacking up room rates beyond belief. Most of what limited supply was available, Josie couldn't afford. Or what she could afford wasn't fit for a dog to live in. Putting up with crotchety old Miss Bennett was starting to look good. Josie soon regretted her night of fun with Doris.

By Thursday, Josie still hadn't found a place, despite spending every night after work patrolling the streets of Halifax searching for vacancy signs or knocking on doors of known rooming houses. She had asked every girl at Gorman's if they knew of any available places and had even started querying customers. She had checked the want ads in the newspaper and found a few listings, but every time she called, either the price was too high or the room was already taken. She also checked bulletin boards in several stores. Nothing available. Nothing. Not a single suitable room in the whole city. At first, she had confined her search to the downtown area, so that she could be within walking distance of work, the shops, and the dance halls. But as the week wore on, she widened her search to include the North End and west all the way up to Connaught, resigning herself to having to ride the trolleys. But it didn't help. Still nothing.

With only two days to go before her deadline, things were looking bleak. Josie began to worry that she might end up on the street. Or worse still, have to move back home with her parents. Then, Thursday afternoon at the restaurant, she caught a break. While talking to a customer about her situation, the customer said something that gave Josie an idea.

"Are you Catholic?" he asked.

"Yes," said Josie.

"Too bad you weren't a refugee."

"What do you mean?"

"Well, if you were a refugee, you could stay at the Sisters of Service. But they only take young Catholic women who are refugees from a foreign country, usually escaping from the war."

"Where is it?"

"It's at the corner of Barrington and Tobin, only a five-minute walk from here."

The location would be perfect, thought Josie. She could stay there until she found something better. "What if I pretended to be a refugee?"

"That wouldn't work. The Sisters meet the refugees at the pier when their ships come in. They have to be processed through the government officials, and everything. Unless they're stowaways."

"Stowaways?"

"Well, I heard about one young woman who was a stowaway. She went to the local Catholic church and the priest there contacted the Sisters. So, they took her in."

"How do you know so much about this place?"

"My brother's the handyman there."

Josie felt a rush of excitement. This could be the solution to her problem. "Thank you," she said to the customer.

"For what?"

"Oh, nothing."

Nothing indeed. Josie thought of nothing else for the rest of her shift. She spent all afternoon mapping out her plan in her head. She'd go see Father Fitzgerald at St. Mary's, right after work. She liked him. He was a nice priest. Very kind. She'd tell him about her predicament and ask him for his help in getting her into the Sisters of Service. Even if she wasn't a refugee, surely he would understand her situation. It would only be for a short time, she'd assure him, until she could find another place.

As soon as her shift was over, she raced home to the boarding house, changed out of her uniform, and headed up to St. Mary's. Entering the side door of the church, she went down the hall to Father Fitzgerald's office. The door was open. Father Fitzgerald was seated behind his desk, head down, writing on a piece of paper. She tapped lightly on the door. He looked up. "Yes, Miss?"

"I'm so sorry to bother you, Father," said Josie, "but could I speak with you for a minute?"

"Of course, my child," he answered, waving her in.

There was a chair in front of the desk, but since he hadn't offered it to her, she decided to remain standing. She didn't want to seem too forward. "I don't know if you recognize me, Father, but I'm Josephine Bourdeau. Josie? I'm one of your parishioners."

"Yes, yes, I do recognize you. What can I do for you?"

"Well, Father, I have a problem."

Father Fitzgerald's demeanour turned serious. "What kind of problem, my child?"

Josie looked down at the floor. "Well, Father, I did something wrong, and I'm going to go to confession for it, I promise, but now it's gotten me in trouble."

She now had the priest's full attention. "What did you do?"

"This is very embarrassing."

"No need to be embarrassed around me."

"Well, I got drunk, and I threw up all over the floor at my boarding house, and the landlady is throwing me out, and I only have one more day to find another place, and I've looked everywhere around the city, and I can't find anything, at least nothing I can afford. And I have nowhere to go. I'm afraid I'm going to be out on the street, and I'm afraid what might happen to me if I end up homeless. I don't know what to do."

Josie knew she was rambling, but she was hoping to generate some sympathy from the priest. She had also stretched the truth a little, saying she had one more day to find a place, instead of two, but she was desperate.

The priest, for his part, seemed slightly relieved, as if he was anticipating something far worse. He responded in a soft tone. "Well, Miss Bourdeau, I sympathize with your situation. A lot of people are having problems finding accommodations in the city during the war. But I'm not sure how I can help. The parish doesn't own any boarding houses or accommodations of any kind."

Josie looked up at the priest. "What about the Sisters of Service?"

A puzzled look came over the priest's face. "The Sisters of Service? Well, ah, their residence is for newcomers to Canada, refugees from the war, immigrants fleeing their home country. It's not for local girls."

"But what if you spoke with them and told them about my situation? Coming from you, wouldn't that carry some weight?"

"I'm afraid I couldn't do that. That would not be appropriate. If I did that for you, I'd have to do it for everyone. I'm sure you can understand that."

"But I heard that the church sometimes refers women to the Sisters."

"Well, yes, occasionally. But, again, they would be refugees, not local girls."

"But it would only be for a short time. Just until I found something else. I've got nowhere to go."

The priest smiled sympathetically. "I'm sorry, my child, there's really nothing I can do."

Josie stared at him for several seconds without saying anything. She felt a pressure building in her chest. What was she going to do if she couldn't find a place to stay? She covered her eyes with her hands. She moaned and lamented about her life being ruined, about God hating her for her sins.

Father Fitzgerald jumped out of his chair and rushed over to her. He wrapped his arm around her shoulders. "My child, please, you mustn't say those things. God loves you very much."

"Then why won't he help me?"

The priest inhaled, then let out a deep sigh. "Let me call the Sisters right now. I can't promise anything, but I'll see what I can do. Please wait in the hall while I make the call."

"Oh, thank you. Thank you so much." She rose to her feet and went out into the hall. Father Fitzgerald closed his office door behind her. A few minutes later, the office door opened and Father Fitzgerald came out to give Josie the news. "Okay, they'll take you."

"Bless you, Father. Bless you."

"But it can only be for a short time. You have to keep looking for a place."

"Oh, I will. I promise."

With that, Josie thanked Father Fitzgerald again and left the building. As she stood on the sidewalk in front of the church, she took a deep breath. Maybe things were starting to turn her way after all.

Chapter 11

Josie placed the last piece of clothing in her suitcase and snapped the lid shut. The time had come. Becky had cried and cried when Josie had first given her the news. She had begged Miss Bennett to give Josie another chance, but to no avail. Josie wasn't surprised. She had killed any chance at a reconciliation with her outburst. Miss Bennett would never take her back after that.

Josie wouldn't be able to stay at the Sisters of Service for very long. As soon as she could find another place, she'd have to leave. For the time being, Becky would pick up any mail that arrived at the boarding house for her, which wasn't much, except for the occasional letter from Agatha. She wouldn't write to Agatha just yet; she'd wait until she had a more permanent address. Then she'd let her family know that she had moved.

She had asked Miss Bennett if she could come and visit Becky from time to time. Miss Bennett had hesitated at first but then agreed, provided Josie visited with her sister in the parlour. She wasn't allowed upstairs. Josie didn't think that was very fair, since all the girls could have family members up in their rooms, but she wasn't in much of a position to argue. She also wasn't allowed to stay past nine in the evening. That, plus the fact the upstairs was off limits, meant that she and Becky wouldn't be able to have their late-night chats before going to bed. She'd miss that. And she knew Becky would too.

Josie didn't have much to pack. All her clothes and her personal belongings fitted into her one suitcase. Becky had offered to walk with her to the Sisters of Service, which was about ten minutes from the boarding house, and take turns carrying the suitcase, which was a bit heavy with all the stuff in it, but Josie had said she preferred to go alone. She could have taken a cab, but she had to save her money for the new place. The cost of rooms had gone up quite a bit in the city since she had first moved into Miss Bennett's. Another aftereffect of the war. In any event, it was a nice day for a walk, and she was in no hurry.

The only thing left for her to do now was to say her goodbyes. The girls had just finished their Saturday morning breakfast, so most of them would be in their rooms. If not, she'd likely find them in the dining room or in the parlour. Becky accompanied her as she made her rounds. She managed to speak with everybody. All of them wished her good luck. Some said they'd miss her. Claire cried and gave her a great big hug.

Becky walked with Josie to the front door. The two sisters embraced, holding each other tight, not wanting to let go. But it was time.

"We'll see each other at work when we have the same shift," said Josie.

Tears began streaming down Becky's face. "I know."

"And I'll visit often, even if Miss Bennett doesn't want to see me."

"I know."

"And we can still go to mass together on Sundays. You'll be right on my way."

"I know, I know."

They hugged again, then Josie kissed Becky on the cheek. "I love you, baby sister."

"I love you too."

Josie turned to leave. Abruptly, she stopped, turned around, and looked down the hall. She had one more thing to do. "Is she in?" she asked Becky.

"Miss Bennett?"

"Yeah."

"I think she's in the kitchen."

Josie put down her suitcase and walked through the dining room into the kitchen. Miss Bennett was putting something in the refrigerator.

"I'm leaving now," called out Josie.

Miss Bennett closed the refrigerator door and looked up. She folded her hands in front of her. "Very well, then."

The two women stared at each other for several moments, seemingly waiting for the other to speak first. A range of emotions swept through Josie. Anger, frustration, sadness, regret, guilt. She didn't know if she should apologize to Miss Bennett or if she should wait for Miss Bennett to apologize to her, although she really didn't expect to receive one from the woman. And she didn't.

"I understand you'll be staying at the Sisters of Service," said Miss Bennett instead.

"Yes, for a short time, until I find something more permanent."

"How did you manage that? I thought they only took immigrants or refugees."

Josie smiled. "I used that resourcefulness you said I had."

Another awkward moment of silence followed.

"Are you all packed?" said Miss Bennett.

"Yes, my suitcase is in the hall."

"You have everything, then?"

"Yes. If I've forgotten anything, Becky can get it to me."

"Do you need a ride? I can call a taxi."

"No, thank you. I'm going to walk. It's not far."

"Well, then, goodbye."

"Goodbye."

Josie stood motionless. When it was obvious Miss Bennett wasn't going to say anything else, Josie turned to leave. Just as she reached the kitchen door, she looked back over her shoulder. "Miss Bennett?"

"Yes?"

Josie hesitated, struggling with what she wanted to say, what she *should* say. "I'm sorry."

Miss Bennett's stern expression softened ever so slightly. "Good luck, Miss Bourdeau. I hope you learn from this experience."

Josie turned and walked away. Becky was waiting for her at the front door. "Did you talk to her?"

"Yes."

"What did she say?"

"Nothing much. She just wished me luck. Anyway, I'm off. I'll stop by tomorrow morning and we'll go to mass."

"Okay. Are you sure you don't want me to go over with you?"

"No, I'm fine. It's just a short walk."

With that, Josie stepped out of the building and descended the few steps to the sidewalk. She turned and looked back at the place that had been her home for the past three years. Memories started flooding into her thoughts. Fond memories. All the late night chats with Becky. All the chatter and the teasing between the girls at mealtime. The practical jokes they'd sometimes play on each other.

And then there was Miss Bennett. Despite all her faults, and with everything that had happened between the two of them, Josie had to admit that the old lady hadn't treated her that badly. She'd always felt safe and secure at the Bennett Boarding House. She was going to miss the place. And oddly enough, she'd probably miss the old "battle axe" too.

It took her about twenty minutes to get to the Sisters of Service. She stopped once to rest and switch hands on the suitcase and another to have a cigarette at the park in front of the Nova Scotian. She didn't know if the nuns allowed smoking on their premises, so she decided she would have one before she got there. That would do her for the day.

When she arrived, she knocked on the door and was greeted with a warm smile by a short, chubby nun with round, puffy cheeks. When Josie introduced herself and said she had been sent by Father Fitzgerald, the nun bubbled with excitement. "Oh, we are so glad to have you, my dear. Won't you come in. I'm Sister Annette."

Josie could see right away that it was a busy spot. People were coming and going. A group of girls were in a room to the left of the entrance sitting around a table. They were knitting, and talking and laughing as they worked. A handyman was fixing a broken spindle on the stairs. It was definitely a lot nosier than Miss Bennett's. As she was taking everything in, she realized that the nun was speaking to her.

"We're quite full right now, but Father Fitzgerald mentioned you'd had a bit of misfortune recently and needed a place to stay until you found something else, so we're happy to accommodate. We normally have two girls to each room, but we've set up a cot for you in one of the larger rooms. I hope that's okay."

Josie told her it would be fine.

"The two girls you'll be rooming with are both from Poland. Now, they don't speak very much English, but they are very nice. I'm sure you'll like them."

Josie told her she was sure they would get along just great.

"Maybe you can teach them a little English."

Josie told her that she would try.

Sister Annette took Josie upstairs to her new accommodations. The room was plain, with white walls, but well lit by a large window framed with white lace curtains. The furnishings were sparse, consisting of two single beds and the cot set up for Josie, two chairs, one small dresser, and a free-standing clothes rack. There was no closet. Crucifixes hung over each bed and there was a picture of the Virgin Mary on one wall. Josie's cot looked sturdy, with a thin, stuffed mattress. A sheet and a blanket were laid out on top, folded, along with a towel, a facecloth, and a bar of soap.

"I hope you'll find this satisfactory, Josie," said Sister Annette. "I know it's probably not what you're used to, but I hope it will tide you over until you get back on your feet."

The nun's words echoed in Josie's head. "Until you get back on your feet." It sounded distressing. Josie wondered what Father Fitzgerald had told them about her situation.

"It's fine, "said Josie. "Thank you very much."

Sister Annette then took a few minutes to give Josie the names of the other nuns in residence, explain the rules of the household, the meal schedule, bathroom privileges, and other details to ensure everything functioned properly. "If you need anything, let us know. We're always around somewhere, either upstairs or downstairs. Otherwise, we'll see you at lunch in about forty minutes."

Josie thanked her again. The nun then made her exit.

Josie went to the window and gazed out onto the street below. She stood in the middle of the room and surveyed her surroundings. This was her home now. For how long, she wasn't sure. A week? Two weeks? Longer? Who knew? But one thing *was* clear. A new chapter in her life had just begun.

Chapter 12

"In nomine Patris, et Filii, et Spiritus Sancti, Amen."

The bishop bowed to the congregation, ending the mass. Josie made the sign of the cross, kissed the crucifix on her rosary, and stuffed the rosary in her coat pocket. As she and Becky slid out of the pew, she whispered to her sister. "Wait for me. I'm going to light a candle."

Josie went to the candle rack at the front of the church, dropped a dime in the donation box, lit a candle, knelt on the kneeler, and said her prayer. When she had finished, she blessed herself and went back to Becky who was waiting for her in the aisle.

Lighting a candle after midnight mass had become a bit of a Christmas tradition for Josie since she'd moved to Halifax. She'd ask God to take care of her parents and her brothers and sisters, and she'd ask him to try and end the war, although she doubted even God could do that.

Christmas. Already. A lot had happened over the past few months since she'd left Miss Bennett's. She hadn't stayed at the Sisters of Service for long, a little over two weeks. A room had become available above Gorman's, so she'd jumped at it. It would be perfect, she had thought. Right where she worked. As it had turned out, it wasn't quite so perfect. For one thing, board was not included, so she had to provide her own meals. She was permitted a hotplate in her room to cook for herself, or she could eat at the restaurant at a discount, but she had calculated that between the room rent and her food, it was costing her more to stay at Gorman's that it had at Miss Bennett's. And she wasn't eating nearly as well.

Her room was fine, perhaps not as nice as her old room, but better than the one at the Sisters of Service. However, the atmosphere was quite different. At Miss Bennett's, she'd been boarding with five other women, including Becky, all roughly her own age, all single, and generally all from similar backgrounds. At Gorman's, by contrast, there were five tenants: two women, including her, and three men. The other woman was an elderly lady who didn't come out of her room much. Rumour had it her husband had died unexpectedly and left her with a mound of debt, forcing her to sell her house to cover the obligations. Mr. Gorman had taken her in as a charity case, more or less, because he had been a good friend of her husband's.

The three men, meanwhile, included a Chinese man who worked in the laundry at one of the hotels in the city and didn't speak much English, a nice young man who was a travelling salesman and therefore usually on the road, and a middle-aged man who nobody seemed to know much about. Josie had heard a rumour that he worked for the government trying to find out if there were any German spies in the city. But that was just hearsay; although Josie did see him leave the building once in the middle of the night.

Basically, the tenants at Gorman's hardly knew each other. In fact, they rarely spoke, except to say hello or make small talk about the weather when they passed each other in the hall. By contrast, the girls at Miss Bennett's were like a family. They ate their meals as a group, they'd gather in the parlour to listen to the radio and chat, and they often went places together.

Josie was also starting to have mixed feelings about living where she worked. She had taken the room primarily because of its convenience, but she soon realized there were some disadvantages to being so close to her job. For one, she found it difficult to mentally separate her social life from her work life. The job was always on her mind because it was right there in front of her. For another, her proximity made it easier for Mr. Gorman to ask her to work late or to get her to help him with something in the restaurant. And then there was the noise. If she was in her room trying to take a nap on her day off or after her shift, and the restaurant was still open, she could hear the sounds of voices and the clanging of pots and pans coming from downstairs.

But it wasn't all bad. It was safe, relatively clean, and within her budget. It was a place to live. And she needed a place to live.

Of course, not living at Miss Bennett's meant she saw less of Becky. They still went to mass together (when Josie went, which wasn't every Sunday), and to the occasional dance together. And they saw each other at work when they were on the same shift. But it wasn't the same as living in the same house. At Miss Bennett's, Becky's room was right next to Josie's, and they'd have long talks practically every night before going to bed. They couldn't do that now. As a result, Becky had started spending more time with Claire. They'd go to mass together when Josie didn't go, they'd go shopping together, and they'd go to dances together when Josie was going with someone else. Even when Josie and Becky went to the dance together, Claire would often tag along.

Josie was glad to see Becky making friends. She had turned eighteen in October and it was time for her to come out from under Josie's coattails, so to speak. It also worked to Josie's advantage at times. When the three of them would go to a dance, Josie could leave Becky with Claire and not worry about her. She could then go off on her own. And if she wanted to go somewhere after the dance, Becky could go home with Claire. But there was a flipside. Josie worried she was losing that special relationship with her sister, that special bond only they had. Yes, they were still sisters, and they always would be, of course. But they were also friends. Best friends. Josie didn't want that to change.

In fairness to Becky, though, Josie had also started to broaden her own social circle since moving out of Miss Bennett's. She was now chumming around a lot more with Doris, her co-worker at

Gorman's and the "instigator," as Becky had called her, of that fateful night. Josie had to agree with Becky that Doris was more than a bit on the wild side, and you had to be careful where she took you, but she was also a lot of fun. And she really seemed to like Josie. She had said they were "best pals."

Being best pals with Doris, however, meant that Josie was drinking a lot more than usual. Doris always had a pint or a flask of rum with her whenever she went to a dance. She'd even sneak some into a movie. And if she ran out, she could always convince some guy to get some for her. But Josie noticed that Doris never seemed to get really drunk; like falling-down, pie-eyed drunk. And she never got sick. She knew how to hold her liquor.

Josie was getting better at holding her liquor too, thanks to her friend. Doris had shown her how to pace her drinks and spread them out over the evening. She had told her to use water as mix, not soda pop, because pop made you drunk faster. And she had advised her to stick to one type of liquor for the night. If you were going to drink rum, drink rum. If you were going to drink lemon gin, drink lemon gin. "It was mixing the lemon gin with the rum that night that made you sick," she had told Josie.

Chumming with Doris also meant meeting lots of guys, both sailors and local boys. Being married didn't stop Doris. She always needed to have a man on her arm. And she had no trouble getting them. She was attractive. Not "gorgeous" attractive but attractive enough to catch a fella's eye. She was like a magnet. Men were drawn to her.

Doris and Josie made a good pair. They'd arrive at the dances together, stroll around the floor, flash a few flirtatious smiles, and before long they had dance partners. They'd dance one or two numbers, slip outside for a nip of rum from Doris's flask, then head back in to find new partners. After the dance, they might go to a blind pig (one of the many illegal watering holes in the city) for a drink, maybe hook up with a couple of sailors and find a secluded place for some necking and petting, or maybe just drink and flirt. But they always stuck together. They never left each other alone. Strength in numbers.

Except for this one time. After a dance at the Strand, Doris and Josie went to a blind pig for a drink. Doris started talking with this American sailor. Soon after, they went outside. About ten minutes later, Doris came back in and went over to Josie. "I'm taking him back to my place. Are you okay by yourself?" Josie took a cab home by herself that night, which was fine. Doris could do what she wanted. She was a grown woman. Josie just liked hanging around with her. It was nice to have a close friend.

When you're someone's friend, though, you also have to take the bad with the good, as Josie found out one tragic day in mid October. The Germans had torpedoed and sunk the *Caribou* passenger ferry on its way from Nova Scotia to Newfoundland, killing over one hundred and thirty people. One of those killed was Doris's first cousin, who she was very close to. They had grown up together as kids. Doris had taken it pretty hard, so Josie had stayed up with her all evening trying to console her. It was a rough night.

But this night, Christmas Eve, Josie wouldn't be with her friend Doris. She'd be with her sister Becky, at midnight mass. And she'd spend all Christmas Day with her. Each Christmas, Miss Bennett would allow the girls to invite one family member to spend Christmas Day with them at the boarding house, including joining them for Christmas dinner. Some of the girls, of course, would be away for Christmas, spending the holiday with their families across the province or in other parts of the country. So, there wouldn't be a huge crowd. But it was a nice gesture, nonetheless. For the girls who didn't have any other plans, it at least made Christmas a little special. And it was perfect for Becky. Since she and Josie weren't going home to their parents' place for Christmas, she could invite Josie over and they could spend the whole day together. Josie was even allowed upstairs now, as Miss Bennett had loosened her earlier restriction about a month previously. And she could stay until ten o'clock, rather than nine. "But just this once," Miss Bennett had reminded Becky. Josie had smiled when Becky gave her the news. "Maybe the old lady has a heart after all," she had said to her sister.

Becky and Josie had a big day planned. Josie would come over after lunch and they'd open the presents they had bought for each other. At two o'clock they'd go to the Christmas concert at the Masonic Hall. After that, they'd come back to the boarding house and get ready for dinner. After dinner, they'd go see the Christmas lights at the Nova Scotian and listen to the carolers at Cornwallis Park. Once they'd had their fill of Christmas songs, they'd head back to Miss Bennett's, go up to Becky's room, and gossip until Josie had to leave.

Josie slept in Christmas morning. It had been past one thirty by the time she'd got back to her room after midnight mass. Since the restaurant was closed on Christmas Day, she had to have her meals in her room. She'd basically skipped breakfast because it was so late, instead fixing herself a cup of tea, then warming up some soup on the hotplate for lunch. After wrapping Becky's present, she picked out a dress suitable for the occasion, and a pair of shoes to wear indoors, then got dressed, brushed her hair, and put on some lipstick. She then put on her coat and boots, and headed for Miss Bennett's with her shoes and Becky's present under her arm.

The day was cold and crisp but clear. Snow had fallen over-night, making for the perfect Christmas scene. Josie always loved a new snowfall. It made everything look so clean, as if hiding all the world's imperfections. When she arrived at the boarding house, she rang the bell and was greeted almost immediately by Becky who had seen her coming up the street through the dining room window. They gave each other a big hug, then Becky took Josie's coat and hung it up in the hall closet. Josie removed her boots and put on her shoes. They then raced up to Becky's room.

"What did you get me?" squealed Becky, barely giving Josie a chance to catch her breath.

"What did you get *me*?" said Josie.

"I wanna open mine first," pleaded Becky.

The two girls sat on Becky's bed, their legs folded under them, and Josie handed Becky her present. Becky tore off the wrapping paper and flipped open the box. It was a red and white floral-patterned head scarf. Becky took the scarf out of the box and stretched it out it front of her. "Oh, it's beautiful! I love it."

Becky folded the scarf into a triangle, put it over her head, and tied it under her chin. "How do I look?" she said, turning her head to one side and lifting her nose in the air.

"Fabulous, dah-ling," replied Josie, doing her best Tallulah Bankhead impression.

The two sisters laughed like giddy schoolgirls.

"Later, I'll show you how to tie it up in your hair," said Josie. "It's all the style now."

Becky placed the scarf back in the box. She went to her dresser, opened the top drawer, and took out a small, gift-wrapped box. "I hope you like it," she said, handing it to Josie.

Josie slowly unwrapped the box and opened it. Inside was a brooch with six turquoise stones in the shape of flower petals mounted on twelve sterling silver leaves. In the centre were three blue stones.

"Oh my God," gasped Josie. "How much did you pay for this?"

"It was on sale," said Becky.

"How could you afford this?"

"I've been saving up for it for awhile."

"Becky, this is too much."

"Don't you like it?"

"I love it! But you shouldn't have spent this much."

"It's not as much as you think. And anyway, it's none of your business how much I spent on it. It's a gift, and I wanted to get it for you. I thought of you as soon as I saw it."

Josie looked at Becky and smiled. Her eyes filled with tears. "It's beautiful. Thanks so much, Sis. Now I feel I didn't give you enough."

"You gave me enough. I love my scarf."

The two sisters sat admiring Josie's new brooch for a few moments, then Josie pinned it on her dress. They went to the bathroom so she could check it out in the mirror. It was beautiful, for sure. After they got back to Becky's room, Josie removed the brooch, placed it back in the gift box, and put it in the top drawer of Becky's dresser for safe keeping. By then, it was time to head to the Masonic Hall for the Christmas concert.

The concert lasted about two hours. There was a big crowd in attendance, mostly families with children. A lot of children. Children with their mothers, but without their fathers, who were off fighting the Germans. There were all the normal Christmas songs, and a few patriotic war songs, and a skit about baby Jesus in the manger with Mary and Joseph and the Three Wise Men. They even had a real lamb on stage. A Protestant minister closed with a prayer, asking God to "keep all our boys in uniform safe." It was a sombre ending to what had been a welcomed distraction from the reality of wartime.

Back at the boarding house, Josie and Becky freshened up, then went down to the parlour to wait for dinner. Becky had told Josie that Miss Bennett wanted everyone seated at the table and ready for grace at precisely five o'clock. Miss Bennett had decorated the table with a beautiful Christmas-themed table cloth, an elaborate centrepiece, and a lit candle at each end. She had brought out her best china and silverware, and her crystal drinking glasses. Josie was terrified of touching anything for fear of breaking it.

There were eight people seated around the table: four of the girls from the boarding house, including Becky; three invited guests, including Josie; and Miss Bennett. Eleanor hadn't invited anyone, but Shirley had brought along her sister Mildred, who lived alone over in Dartmouth and worked as a doctor's receptionist. Marie had invited her brother Thomas, who was a civilian clerk with the Navy. It was quite different having a man at the table, but he was very nice and he fitted right in with the girls. Even Miss Bennett liked him.

As usual for Christmas dinner, and only for Christmas dinner, Miss Bennett had hired outside help, a husband and wife team, the Morrisons, to cook and serve the meal. That freed her to sit with the girls (and one guy, in this case) and oversee the proceedings—at the head of the table, of course. The meal was splendid, truly a Christmas feast. The main fare was turkey, with the tastiest stuffing Josie had ever eaten (even better than her mother's), and all the fixings—mashed potatoes, carrots, turnips served in ice-cream-scoop shapes, cranberry sauce, tea biscuits, and even butter for the biscuits, which was rationed and hard to come by. For dessert, there was warm apple pie topped with a slice of cheese. To drink, you had your choice of milk, tea, or coffee. And to top it all off, Miss Bennett gave each person one Christmas chocolate.

Everyone filled themselves to the brim and seemed to be having a good time, chatting and laughing throughout dinner. Josie even thought she saw Miss Bennett smile once. After the meal, Miss Bennett invited the group into the parlour to listen to some Christmas music on the radio. Everyone sang along, in the spirit of the season. When the music ended and the news came on, Miss Bennett turned off the radio. She said Christmas was not the time to hear about war. Eleanor then suggested that everyone should relate a story about their most memorable Christmas. Thomas volunteered to go first. As he entertained the gathering with embarrassing stories about his sister Marie as a child, Becky leaned over to Josie, who was sitting next to her, and whispered in her ear. "I have to talk to you about something."

"Right now?" said Josie.

"No, when we go back up to my room."

Josie didn't think too much of it at the moment, but as she sat half listening to Thomas, she recalled how Becky hadn't talked much at dinner. Becky wasn't overly chatty to begin with, but she had been particularly quiet, even for her. Josie glanced over at her sister. She seemed uneasy. Something was definitely on her mind.

The Christmas diners remained together in the parlour until almost nine o'clock when it was time for the outside guests to depart, except for Josie. Miss Bennett had called a taxi for Thomas and Mildred, and it had arrived. They thanked Miss Bennett for her hospitality and said goodnight to everyone. Once they had left, Miss Bennett wished the remaining girls a "Merry Christmas," and turned to leave. But not before addressing Becky. "Remember, no later than ten o'clock."

Becky and Josie headed up the stairs. When Josie entered Becky's room, she threw herself on the bed. "I think I gained ten pounds tonight."

Becky didn't respond. Instead, she kept pacing back and forth from one side of the small room to the other. Josie knew there was something eating at her sister. "Is there something wrong?" she asked.

Becky stopped pacing and sat on the side of her bed, next to Josie. "I have to talk to you about something."

"Okay, what is it?"

"I've been going out with this guy for the past few months. His name is Albert."

"You never told me about this."

"No, I wasn't sure if it was serious."

"Is it serious now?"

"Maybe."

"Is he a sailor?"

"Well, he's in the Navy but he has a shore job."

"So, he's a slacker."

"A what?"

"A slacker."

"What's a slacker?"

"Someone who doesn't want to fight overseas."

"It's not that he doesn't want to fight overseas. He went to basic training, and when he wrote the aptitude test, they said he was so smart they wanted him to work in the office in Halifax."

"So, he's a smart slacker."

"He's not a slacker!"

"Okay, he's not a slacker. So, what's he like?"

"He's really nice. He was the guy I was dancing with that night when you dragged me away so you could go with Doris. You remember him."

Josie didn't remember him. "Okay."

"Actually, you probably *know* him. He's originally from down home. He moved up here with his parents when he was thirteen. Albert Blanchard. They used to call him Bertie when he was a kid. He'd be a couple of years older than you, but you would have seen him in school."

Josie wracked her brains to try to remember who Becky was talking about. Then it dawned on her. "Bertie? Goofy Bertie with the big ears?"

"He's not goofy anymore. And his ears aren't all that big."

"Well, they must have shrunk. Or his head got bigger."

Josie could see she was getting Becky upset. "Okay, so you're going out with Bertie."

"Albert," Becky corrected.

"Albert, right. So, if he's a nice guy, good. I'm happy for you. I'm glad that you have a boyfriend."

Becky didn't respond. Josie could tell there was something else. "Is that all you wanted to talk to me about?"

"Well, that's the first part," said Becky.

"What's the second part?"

"Well, he's starting to pressure me."

"Pressure you for what?"

"To do it."

"To do what?"

"You know. *It.*"

Becky raised her eyebrows and stared right at Josie. She was giving her all the signals. She was talking about "it," putting out, going all the way. Josie's eyes widened. "Wow. So, did you say no?"

"Of course I said no! What do you think I am? I told him I was saving myself for marriage. That I wanted to be a virgin for my husband."

"What did he say to that?"

Becky took a deep breath, then exhaled. "He suggested we get married."

Josie erupted. "What! Married? You don't wanna get married now! You're too young!"

"I'm eighteen. Beatrice was only seventeen when she got married."

"And do you want to be like Beatrice?"

"What's wrong with Beatrice?"

"Well, she married the first man that ever paid any attention to her. She never went out with any other guys. Now, she's got four kids and her husband is at sea halfway around the world. She's basically living with Mom and Dad. She never goes anywhere. She's never been to a dance. Or a party. Nothing. Is that what you want?"

"It doesn't mean I'd have four kids. And we wouldn't be living with Mom and Dad. We'd get a place up here."

"Becky, Becky," pleaded Josie. "You don't want to get married during wartime. Your husband gets sent overseas, he gets killed, you're a widow, maybe with a baby, or expecting. Then what? Your life is over."

"They're not going to send him overseas."

"They might. With all the boys being killed, they might need him."

"But if I don't marry him, I'm afraid I'll lose him. He says not being able to do it with me is driving him crazy."

Josie smirked. "They all say that."

"But what if he means it?"

Josie thought for a second. "You know, there's other ways to keep him without marrying him."

"How?"

"Well, you don't have to go all the way to satisfy him."

"What do you mean?"

Josie realized Becky had no idea what she was referring to. She'd obviously never done what Josie was about to suggest. Josie had to make sure she explained it the right way. "Well, you could give him a hand job?"

"A what?"

"A hand job."

"What's a hand job?"

"Well, it's where you take the man's thing, you know, his thing, in your hand, and you rub it and stroke it up and down until, you know, he's done. Until he comes."

Josie demonstrated the technique, moving her hand up and down on the imaginary "thing." Becky's eyes widened wider than Josie had ever seen them. She looked mortified. "What? You must be joking! I'm not doing that!"

"Why not?"

"I'd have to touch it."

"It's not going to bite you."

"Isn't that a sin?"

"It's less of a sin than going all the way and having a baby when you're not married, or getting married and regretting it all your life."

"Oh, I don't know Josie. It seems dirty."

"Get him to wash it before you do it."

Becky scowled at her sister. "That's not what I meant."

The two of them sat silently. Josie could see that her sister was processing this startling new information. She wondered if Becky would ask her how she knew about these "hand jobs." Whether she was speaking from personal experience. She was relieved when she didn't.

Before long, it was time for Josie to leave. Neither sister brought up the topic again. Josie retrieved her Christmas gift from Becky's dresser, thanked her again for it, and made her way downstairs with her sister accompanying her. She put on her coat and boots, slipped on her gloves, gave Becky a big hug, and waved goodbye. As she walked alone down Hollis to Gorman's, a light snow began to fall, covering the ground like a fluffy blanket. She stopped and looked up, letting the flakes land gently on her face. The light of the moon shone through the flurries. Her sister had a boyfriend. She was growing up. She wasn't a little kid anymore. It made her feel happy. And sad.

Chapter 13

"I now pronounce you man and wife."

Albert looked up at the priest. The priest nodded. Taking full advantage of this divine permission, Albert wrapped his arms around his new bride and planted a huge one on her lips, much to the delight of the congregation gathered in the church. Becky turned beet red. Apparently feeling that Albert was lingering in the moment too long, the priest cleared his throat, signalling to the amorous groom that it was time to release his bride so that the ceremony could continue. Once the ceremony had ended, the newly married couple proceeded down the aisle and out the church to receive congratulations from family and friends, and the traditional shower of thrown rice.

Josie had no idea if Becky had taken her suggestion about how to keep from losing Albert without losing her virginity. Becky hadn't told her and Josie hadn't asked. All Josie knew was that Becky had managed to convince Albert to wait until June before they got married. She had always wanted to be a June bride.

Josie thought that everything had gone very well. She had been the maid of honour and Albert's youngest brother, Raymond, the best man. Becky looked lovely in her wedding dress, a long sleeved, full-length gown given to her by her mother-in-law. Albert's mother had hoped that a daughter of her own would wear her wedding dress some day but since she had had only boys, she had asked Becky if she would wear it, and Becky had graciously accepted. The dress was quite elaborate, with overlays of lace on the shoulders and sleeves, though Josie thought it looked slightly yellowed. But no one seemed to notice. At least no one said anything.

Uncle Ted, who owned the only car in the village, drove the bride and groom from the church to Josie's parents' house, beeping his horn continually as he went. Women waved from their front steps, men lined the road with their hands in their pockets, and children raced behind the car with their bicycles, trying to keep up. A wedding was a big thing in a small place.

At the house, Josie helped Becky change from her wedding gown to her wedding day clothes, a two-piece light brown outfit. Albert remained in his suit. Throughout the afternoon, Becky and Albert played host to dozens of visitors who came to offer the couple best wishes for a long and happily married life—blessed with lots of children, of course. Becky's mother and her sisters Beatrice and Rose served sweets and tea to the guests. Her father took the men out to the fish shed behind the house for a nip of rum.

At six o'clock, the immediate family sat down for the wedding dinner. The house was full. Josie's father had to borrow tables and chairs from some of the neighbours to accommodate everyone. Two tables had been set up for the adults in the living room and one table for the children in the kitchen. At one adult table were the bride and groom; the maid of honour and the best man; the parents of the bride, Charles and Sarah; and the mother of the groom, Edith. At the other adult table were the bride's oldest sister Rose and her husband Joseph; her sister Beatrice; her sister Agatha and her husband Lawrence; her sister Margaret; her brother Harry; and her sister-in-law Greta, her brother George's wife. The crowd would have been even larger had it not been wartime, as several of the men were either overseas or stationed somewhere in Canada and not able to make it to the wedding. Albert's two older brothers were somewhere in Europe; Beatrice's husband Cecil was at sea; Margaret's husband Leonard was in Debert; and brother George was training gunnery crews in England. Harry had almost missed the wedding, as well, but just happened to be on shore leave in Halifax for a few days and was able to make it home.

Becky's father gave the toast to the bride and groom. As per tradition, he welcomed Albert into the family. Harry also said a few words and threatened to give Albert a "thrashing" if he didn't take proper care of his baby sister. It was all in good fun. Albert thanked everyone for coming and asked them to pray for those family members who were not able to attend. He said he wished his father had lived long enough to see this day. "He would have loved you," he said to Becky.

After the meal, the women cleaned up and the men went out for a smoke. All the while, the children ran free, hooting and hollering and having a great time. Weddings were one of those few occasions when the adults let the kids do whatever they wanted. Total freedom.

Once the dishes had all been washed, dried, and put away, and the men were back indoors, Beatrice brought out two cribbage boards and two decks of cards. "Who wants a game a crib?" she shouted.

Before long, there were two crib games underway, one at each of the adult tables. Those not playing just mingled about, chatting, or enjoying a smoke, or sipping on a cup of tea. Becky and Albert were sitting next to each other on chairs they had put against the wall, holding hands, whispering to each other, kissing from time to time. Josie smiled as she watched them.

As the crib games wound down, Harry pulled out the old phonograph from the alcove, put on a waltz number, and waved over Albert and Becky. "Come on. Bride and groom. First dance," he said.

Lawrence and Raymond pushed the tables to one side to create a dancing area. Becky seemed reluctant, but Albert pulled her up off her chair and into the middle of the room. The couple danced alone together for a minute or two, while the others looked on, smiling and clapping. Albert then urged everyone to join them. Agatha and Lawrence were first up, followed by Becky's parents. Albert's brother Raymond then went up to Josie and asked her to dance. Josie frowned. "Do you know how to waltz?" she asked him.

"Of course," he replied. "You'll see."

As the waltz ended, Raymond called over to Harry. "Do you have anything livelier?"

Harry flipped through his parents' stack of records and pulled one out. It wasn't Glenn Miller or Benny Goodman, but it was the liveliest one they had. He put it on. Raymond grabbed Josie's hand and twirled her around. Margaret and Greta jumped up and began dancing together. Harry yanked Albert's mother onto the floor, much to her delight, despite her mild protest. Everyone was having a great time.

As the night wore on, the children grew tired and restless and wanted to go home. It was time for the festivities to end. Albert and Becky were spending their wedding night at Beatrice's with the house to themselves. Beatrice and her three kids were staying with Greta and her son, who was thrilled because he got a chance to play with his cousins. Beatrice didn't mind either because she really didn't like being the only adult in the house when her husband was away. Harry was sleeping on the couch at Rose's. Agatha, Lawrence, and their two children were going back to their place. Uncle Ted was coming over to drive Margaret and her two girls home. They lived about ten miles away in another village. Everyone else lived within walking distance. That left Josie, Raymond, and Albert's mother, Ethel, spending the night at Josie's parents. Josie had her old bedroom, which she had shared with most of her sisters at some point in her life. Albert's mother stayed in George and Harry's old room. Raymond slept on the couch downstairs.

The next morning, Josie woke to the aroma of homemade bread baking in the oven. It brought back memories of when she was a little girl, getting up in the morning to go to school. The same smell. It made her feel warm inside. And safe. She got out of bed, put on her housecoat, brushed her hair, and went downstairs. Her mother was in the kitchen preparing another batch of bread. No one else seemed to be around.

"Good morning," said Josie.

Her mother looked up. "Good morning, dear," she replied, then returned her attention to her bread. "Did you sleep well?"

"Yes, I did. It was nice sleeping in my old bed."

"Well, you can sleep there any time you like, you know."

Josie smiled but didn't take the bait. "Where is everyone?"

"Your father and Raymond went down to the shore to get some salt cod. Albert's mother hasn't come down yet, so I assume she's still sleeping."

"I don't imagine you've heard from Becky yet."

"Last night I told them to come over for breakfast when they got up, but you know newlyweds. They're going to have to get up soon, though, if they're going to be ready for mass."

"But they went to mass yesterday."

"That doesn't count. Yesterday was a wedding mass. Today is Sunday mass."

It counts for me, Josie said to herself as she went to the cupboard and opened one of the doors. "Do you have any coffee, Mom?"

"No, but you can boil some water and make some tea."

Josie put two scoops of tea in the teapot. She then filled the kettle with water and placed it on the stove. When the water boiled, she poured it in the teapot. She let it steeped for a few minutes, then poured herself a cup. "Do you want a cup?" she asked her mother.

"I don't have time for tea right now," her mother replied.

Josie brought a chair over from the table and sat next to her mother, watching her work. She was tearing off clumps of dough with her hand, forming them into round balls, and placing three balls side by side in each of the pre-greased pans. As Josie sat sipping on her tea, she noticed that her mother was starting to show her age. She had been a beautiful woman, and still was, but the years, and the strain of bearing and raising eight children, had taken its toll. Wrinkles lined her face, dark circles puffed her eyes, and streaks of grey ran through her hair. And now, with the war, she no doubt worried constantly about her two sons in the services and her two youngest daughters in the big city, far away from home.

Her mother broke Josie's train of thought. "It was a lovely wedding, wasn't it?"

"Yes, it was," replied Josie.

"And Rebecca looked beautiful, didn't she?"

"Yes, she did."

"And happy. I think she's happy."

"I think so too."

"My baby girl. Married."

Josie didn't respond. She knew what was coming next. Her mother didn't disappoint.

"That leaves only one left."

"Harry?"

"You, Josie. I was referring to my daughters. I don't worry about Harry getting married. He's a man. He can provide for himself. I worry about my daughters. I want them to find a good husband who'll take care of them."

"I can take care of myself."

"But wouldn't you like to be married, and have children, and have a good husband to share your life with?"

"Some day. But I'm not ready yet."

"Not ready yet? How much longer are you going to wait? You'll be twenty-three in December. All your sisters were married by the time they were your age."

"Well, I guess I'm not like all my sisters."

"Perhaps you just haven't found the right man yet."

Josie thought she had found the right man once, but he had lied to her, deceived her. She wasn't going to let that happen again. "Perhaps."

Josie's mother wiped her brow with her apron. She was finished filling all the pans. "There. We'll just let that rise for a few hours and we'll have some fresh bread for supper tonight."

She walked over to the stove, picked up the kettle, brought it back to the sink, poured some water in the basin, and washed her hands. She then wiped them dry with a tea towel. "Raymond's a nice young man," she said.

"Albert's brother?"

"He looked very dashing in his suit yesterday. You and he made a handsome couple at the wedding ceremony."

Josie knew where her mother was going with this, and she didn't like it. "Mother, he's just a boy."

"No he's not."

"He's about Becky's age."

"Oh, I don't think so. He just looks young. I'd say he's about your age. He's right after Albert, and Albert is twenty-four."

"I'm telling you, he's no more than eighteen or nineteen."

"Oh, he's more than that. I'll ask his mother."

"No you won't!"

"Why not? Then you'll know."

"I don't need to know. I don't care how old he is, I'm not interested."

"He likes *you*. I could tell when he was dancing with you last night."

"Well, I don't like him."

"How can you say that? You don't even know him."

Josie was getting a little annoyed. She didn't need a matchmaker. "Mom, I'm not getting married. I'm not looking for a husband. So, stop it."

Josie's mother wasn't giving up just yet. "I'm not saying you have to marry him, but you could go out on a date with him. Rebecca told me you don't have a boyfriend right now."

Becky has to stop telling Mom about my love life, Josie thought to herself. "Mom, please. I don't want to talk about it anymore. Talk about something else."

"Very well. Sorry."

Neither one spoke for a few moments, then Josie's mother said, "Oh, I have something for you."

"For me?"

"It's in the cupboard above the sink. Can you get it? My hands are full of flour."

Josie placed a chair in front of the sink, stepped up on it, and opened the cupboard. The only thing in there was an old shoebox. She took it out and showed it to her mother. "Is this it?"

"Yes, that's it."

Josie stepped down from the chair and placed the box on the table. She then pulled the chair over to the table, sat down, and opened the box. Inside was a collection of items from her childhood: her first communion certificate; a small crucifix; a scapular of the Virgin Mary; a gold star she had won in a spelling bee in Grade 3; a photo of her with her arm around King, their family dog; a ring she had received as a gift from an aunt in the Boston States; and a small music box.

"What's all this, Mom? Were you house cleaning?"

"They're from when you were a little girl. I just thought you'd want them."

As Josie held each item in her hand, memories flooded in. Happy memories, like the feel of King licking her face; the tinkling of the music box; how proud her father had been when she won the spelling contest. But unhappy memories too. Like being forced to go to confession; or the jealousy of her older sisters when she received the ring from her aunt; or how heartbroken she was when King died. But these were things of the past, not the future. And they meant more to her mother than they did to her.

"Mom, this is very thoughtful but why don't you keep them. They're safer here with you. Somebody might steal them if I take them to Halifax."

"I thought you might want to show them to your own little girl someday."

"Well, when I have a little girl … *if* I have a little girl, I'll take them. For now, they're better here with you."

"Are you sure?"

"Yes, I'm sure."

"Very well."

Just then, they heard footsteps on the stairs. It was Albert's mother on her way down.

"Good morning, Ethel," said Josie's mother.

"Good morning, Sarah," she replied. "Good morning, Josie."

"Good morning, Mrs. Blanchard." Josie prayed Albert's mother hadn't overheard their conversation about Raymond. She didn't seem to be upset, so it looked like they were in the clear.

"I have some fresh bread, Ethel, and some molasses, and Josie just made the tea, if you'd like some breakfast," said Josie's mother.

Albert's mother smiled. "That would be nice."

"Josie and I will join you."

Josie's mother brought the bread and molasses over to the kitchen table. Josie fetched the tea cups, plates, spoons, and a knife for the molasses. She also brought over some cream for the tea. She then poured a cup of tea for her mother and one for Albert's mother. The two older women chatted while they ate, while Josie sat silently. They talked mostly about the wedding but also about their children and grandchildren. At one point, Albert's mother mused about how long it would be before Albert and Becky began a family.

Give them a break," Josie mumbled under her breath.

Once they were finished eating, Josie cleared the dishes off the table and put them in the wash basin. With the two older women now alone at the table, Josie's mother couldn't resist.

"By the way, Ethel, how old is Raymond?"

Josie glared over at her mother.

"Nineteen," said Albert's mother. "He turned nineteen in March."

Josie's mother looked sheepish. "Oh, I thought he was older than that."

Vindicated, Josie stood behind Albert's mother out of the woman's view and mouthed silently to her mother, "I told you."

Before long, Josie's father and Raymond returned with the salt cod. Soon after, Albert showed up at the door, without Becky.

"Where's your bride?" Raymond asked his brother.

"She's getting dressed for mass."

"Is she knocked up yet?" said Raymond, roaring with laughter, much to the displeasure of his mother who slapped him on the back of the head. Now Josie knew she *really* didn't like him.

Josie and her mother set the table for the second time that morning and the men all had breakfast. After they had finished eating and the table had been cleared away again, Josie went upstairs to get washed and dressed. Her mother had dictated that everyone was going to mass, no exceptions. Once she was ready, Josie went downstairs to join the others. Everyone was there except her mother, who was still in her room getting dressed.

"Mom's still not ready?" asked Josie.

"Has to look good for the Lord," her father joked.

Just then, Becky came in the front door. She was wearing a knee-length, short-sleeved summer dress with a pink floral pattern on a white background, and a dark pink belt. On her head she wore a pink hat with artificial white flowers. Around her neck was a beaded necklace. Her wedding ring glistened from the morning sun streaming through a window. *She looks beautiful,* thought Josie. *All grown up.*

As Becky entered, everyone stopped and stared. No one said a word. Raymond had been warned by his mother to keep his mouth shut when Becky arrived. Albert went over to her and held out his arm. She accepted it. She stood there, as if on display, blushing. For a few seconds, no one knew what to do. Then Becky's father started clapping and the rest joined in. By now, Josie's mother had come down the stairs and went over and hugged her daughter. One by one, everyone followed suit—Josie's father, Albert's mother, Raymond, and finally, Josie.

Josie thought Becky looked embarrassed, like she had done something wrong. The cat who swallowed the canary. Maybe that's what brides looked like the morning after their wedding night. But she also looked happy. Giddy, even. And she beamed when she looked at Albert, as if he were a god. Josie wondered if that was the look of true love.

The hugs for Becky completed, Josie's mother herded everyone out the door. They walked the twenty minutes to the church as a group, talking and laughing as they went. At the church they met the rest of the immediate family, all except Margaret and her girls who belonged to a different parish. As Albert and Becky entered, people smiled and waved at them, or came up and offered their best wishes. *This was life in a small community*, thought Josie. Everyone knew everyone else. It had its advantages and disadvantages. At times like this, it felt comforting. Everyone shared in your happiness. You were part of something bigger than yourself. You weren't alone. But sometimes you wanted to be alone. To live your life the way you wanted to, without everyone knowing your business. Without feeling like you were in a goldfish bowl with everyone staring at you. Free.

After mass, all the family members returned to their respective homes, then reconvened at Josie's parents' place after lunch where the adults played cards all afternoon and the children amused themselves outside. With Albert, Becky, Josie, and Harry returning to Halifax in the morning, everyone wanted to take full advantage of their time together.

At five thirty, the family sat down for a dinner of salt cod and boiled potatoes, with pork scraps and onions. It had always been Josie's father's favourite meal. There was plenty of home-made bread, and even butter for the bread, which Uncle Ted had dropped off the night before. For dessert, they had Beatrice's special apple cobbler.

After dinner, as usual, the women cleaned up and the men went out to the fish shed to smoke and drink rum. Josie managed to escape from the ladies at one point and join the men in the shed. Her father frowned disapprovingly as she bummed a cigarette from Lawrence and lit it up. When she asked for a drink of rum, he threatened to thrash anyone who gave her one. But when no one was looking, he slipped her a little nip.

The party broke up earlier this night than the night before. The children had school in the morning and the Halifax gang had a long train ride back to the city. Tears flowed as the older sisters hugged the younger sisters before heading home. They weren't sure when they'd see each other again.

The next morning, Uncle Ted showed up around nine-forty-five to drive the crew to the station in time for the eleven fifteen train. Josie's mother had been up early, preparing breakfast and a basket of food for the travellers to take with them. Josie's father had also been up early, fetching water from the well and lighting the stove to boil the water for tea. Josie had packed her small carrying case the night before, so once she had washed and dressed, brushed her hair, and put on some lipstick, she was ready to go. Becky and Albert had slept in the boys' old room upstairs, Albert's mother had bunked with Josie in the girls' old room, and Harry and Raymond had slept downstairs, Harry on the couch and Raymond in a makeshift bed on the floor. So, everyone was on the premises.

The goodbyes were emotional. Becky sobbed in her mother's arms as the two hugged. Her mother tried to hold it together but broke down when she said goodbye to Harry, her youngest son. "Becky now has Albert to look after her," she said, "and Josie says she can look after herself. But who is going to look after my baby boy, in the middle of the ocean in the middle of a war?"

For Josie, the toughest part was saying goodbye to her father. She loved her mother with all her heart, but her father had always been her rock, her lighthouse in the storm. She missed him so much. As they embraced, a solitary tear formed in the corner of his eye. Josie smiled, wiped the tear away with her finger, and kissed him on the cheek.

The drive to the train station took about forty minutes. Harry sat in the front seat with Uncle Ted, and Josie sat in the back with Becky and Albert. Uncle Ted talked Harry's head off the whole way, telling him about his fish buying business, filling him in on all the local news, and discussing the war. Albert and Becky mostly just cuddled and kissed, and Josie peered out the window at the passing scenery.

When they arrived at the station, Harry offered Uncle Ted some money for the gas, which he refused to accept. "We're family," he said. When Harry persisted, Uncle Ted took the money and gave it to Becky. "Save this for your first child."

On the train, they found a compartment with bench seats facing each other. Becky and Albert sat together on one side, with Josie and Harry on the other. It was a relatively quiet trip, each person seemingly alone with their thoughts. Before long, Becky and Albert were asleep in each other's arms, no doubt exhausted from their emotional and hectic weekend. At one point, Harry got up from his seat and wandered around the train, looking for fellow servicemen to commiserate with or young ladies to flirt with. With Becky and Albert asleep, and Harry gone, Josie found herself mesmerized by the constant, monotonous click-clacking of the train wheels on the track. She soon dozed off.

A few hours into the trip, they switched trains for the final leg into Halifax. That woke everyone up and got them talking. They talked about the wedding, about Becky and Albert's plans for the future, and about their respective parents. Josie asked Harry and Becky if they thought their mother was starting to look old. Both said they hadn't noticed. Shortly after, Becky got up to go to the bathroom. That left Josie alone with the two men.

"So, our baby sister is married, Josie," said Harry. "That leaves just you."

Josie admonished her brother with her eyes. "Not you too?"

"I know a fellow who would be perfect for you," continued Harry.

"Is he a sailor?" asked Josie.

"Yeah."

"Then I'm not interested."

"Why? What's wrong with sailors? I'm a sailor."

Josie was tempted to give Harry a long list of things that were wrong with sailors. Like they didn't write when they promised they would write. Like they only wanted one thing. Like they had a girl in every port. But she saw no point in upsetting him. "There's nothing wrong with sailors, I just wouldn't want to marry one. At least, not until after the war is over. You never know what's going to happen."

Harry lowered his head. He looked sombre. The comment had hit him hard. Josie wished she hadn't said anything.

"I have a friend you might like," said Albert. "He's not a sailor. He works with me in the office. He's a little quiet, but he's very nice."

When Josie didn't reply, Albert continued his pitch.

"We could double date, Becky and me, and you and my friend. We could go to the movies together, or to restaurants, or just play cards at our place. And if you and he were to ever get married, you and Becky could help each other with the children, and we could go on family picnics, and…"

Josie had had enough. "Why is everyone trying to get me married off? I told Mom and I'm telling you guys, I don't want to get married. So drop it!"

Albert leaned back in his seat, sufficiently chastised. Harry stared out the window. Neither one raised the topic again. When Becky returned from the bathroom, she noticed that her three travelling companions were ignoring each other. "Is anything wrong?" she asked.

Albert sat up and smiled at his bride. "No, sweetie, we're all just tired."

By the time they arrived in Halifax, it was just past seven thirty. It had been a long and tiring day. They retrieved their bags and disembarked, making their way through the station, into the lobby of the Nova Scotian, and outside to hail a cab. Albert and

Becky were going to their new flat on Brenton Street, between Morris and Clyde, and Harry was going back to his ship, which was set to sail in the morning. Josie had said she'd walk home since Gorman's was just on the next block, but Albert had convinced her to share their cab. He'd pay the fare, he said.

Just before Josie got in the cab, she pulled Harry aside. "I'm sorry about earlier."

"It's okay. I still love you."

They hugged each other hard.

When the cab stopped in front of Gorman's, Josie kissed Becky on the cheek. "I'll see you at work tomorrow." She then turned to Albert. "Take care of my little sister. Or you'll have me to answer to."

Albert smiled.

Finally, she turned to Harry. "Take care of yourself."

"I will," he replied. "And you take care of yourself."

Josie grabbed her bag and got out of the cab. As it sped away, she waved. She continued to wave until the cab was out of sight.

By this time of the night on Mondays, the restaurant was closed, so Josie went around to the back stairs. Everything seemed peaceful as she entered the building and walked down the hall to her room. There was the faint sound of a radio coming from one of the rooms and a light under the door of the Chinese man. Otherwise, all was quiet. Josie unlocked her door, stepped inside, and closed the door behind her. She stood in the middle of the small room, surveying the sight before her. It was a far cry from the warmth, comfort, and cheerfulness of her parents' home. *Her* home, too, where she had grown up. For the first time she could remember, she felt truly alone.

Josie unpacked her bag, grabbed a towel and a bar of soap, and went to the bathroom to take a bath. As she soaked in the tub, the events and conversations of the past few days echoed through her mind. Her little sister was married. Things would change. She'd see even less of her now. There'd be no more late-night chats. Becky would be with Albert, in their marital bed, attending to his "needs." There'd be no more going to dances together. Now that Becky was married, she didn't need to meet boys. There'd be no more just chumming around because she and Albert would now be chumming around with other married couples. And once Becky started having babies, it would be even worse. Becky would give up her job at Gorman's to look after her kids. Then Josie would *never* see her. Unless she was married herself. Unless she found a husband. Then it would be like Albert had said on the train. Then she and Becky would be close again. Like before.

It was almost dark by the time Josie finished her bath. She'd been soaking for quite a while. When she got back to her room, she didn't bother turning on the light. She changed into her nightgown in the semi-darkness, closed the curtains, and got into bed. It was a warm night, so she left herself uncovered. As she stared at the ceiling, she wondered what the future held in store for her. Would she get married? *Should* she get married? Maybe her mother and Harry and Albert were right. Get married, have children, and let your husband look after you, like all her sisters had done. That was the easy way. The practical way. Then she wouldn't have to worry about having a job or paying the bills or being safe. Maybe that was best. Maybe that was every woman's destiny. Maybe it was *her* destiny.

Or was it her destiny to live life to the fullest? To go to dances and parties, and drink when she wanted, and flirt with who she wanted to flirt with. Not beholden to any one man. Unfettered. Uncaged. Free.

And alone.

Chapter 14

"What'll you have, Hon?"

"How about a night with you?"

"Not on the menu, lover."

"In that case, I guess I'll have to settle for the T-bone special. Can you put an extra scoop of mashed on that?"

"Sure. And to drink?"

"I don't suppose you can get me a beer?"

"Sorry, I can't."

"C'mon, you must have a secret stash out back. You could sneak me some in a paper cup."

"I could, but do you see that guy in the suit sitting at that table over there? He could be a liquor inspector. Then we'd all be in trouble."

"Then, just a Coke."

Josie winked at the young sailor, stuffed her pad and pencil in her apron pocket, and went to place his order with the cook. Doris was behind the counter pouring coffee for a customer. As Josie passed by, Doris motioned to her. "I have to talk to you later about something."

"Okay. When?"

"Meet me out front after our shift."

Josie feigned fear. "Am I in trouble?"

"No, but maybe I am."

Josie shot a puzzled look at her friend as Doris tore a sheet from her pad, clipped it on the order wire, and nonchalantly returned to the floor to serve another customer. *What kind of trouble could she be in?* Josie wondered. Was it work related? Had she upset a customer who then complained to Mr. Gorman? Had she said something to Mr. Gorman that she shouldn't have? Or worse. Had she stolen something from the kitchen? It couldn't be that. Doris wasn't a thief.

Maybe it was something personal. Maybe her landlord was upset with all her late night partying. Maybe she had been caught selling liquor or contraband cigarettes. Or the unthinkable. Had she gotten herself "in trouble" with a sailor? That wouldn't have surprised Josie, with all the men she'd seen her with.

Josie could think of nothing but Doris all afternoon. Could her friend lose her job? Could she be evicted from her flat? Could she go to jail? Josie didn't even want to imagine what would happen to her if she had contracted VD, or, God forbid, was expecting. Her stomach felt like it was tied in knots. Now that Becky was married, Doris had become her best pal, her bosom buddy, her comrade-in-arms. She couldn't wait for the shift to be over.

At twenty past four, Evelyn and Louise arrived for the evening shift. Josie was just finishing up with a customer and Doris was cleaning around the wait station. At precisely four thirty, Josie went to the back room, took off her apron, threw it in the hamper, and returned to the dining area. Doris was still at the wait station. "C'mon, the shift's over, let's go," Josie said impatiently to Doris.

"Just a minute. I'm almost done," said Doris, calmly.

Josie couldn't wait. "Let Evelyn finish that."

"What's the big rush, girl?" said Doris, without looking up from her work.

"You were going to tell me something. About you being in trouble."

Doris paused. "Oh that. Patience, patience."

Doris wiped the counter, folded the dish cloth, and placed it at the back of the sink. She took off her apron, disappeared into the back room, and emerged seconds later. "Ready to go."

The two women walked out of the restaurant with Josie in the lead. They were barely out the door when Josie turned to Doris.

"Well?"

"Let's go to the park. I'll tell you there."

The five-minute walk to Cornwallis Park seemed like an eternity to Josie. She had to know what disaster had befallen her friend. The suspense was killing her. As she repeatedly ran through all the possibilities in her mind, she resolved to be supportive, no matter what Doris had done. She'd stick with her through thick and thin. If Doris was in trouble with Mr. Gorman, she'd put in a good word for her, try to convince Mr. Gorman to give her another chance. If she was expecting, she'd help her in any way she could. Help her look after the baby, even babysit if she needed it. Anything to help poor Doris.

When they arrived at the park, Doris plopped herself down on a park bench. Josie sat next to her. Doris reached into the pocket of her uniform, took out a pack of cigarettes and offered one to Josie. Josie waived her off, not wanting to delay the news another minute. Doris took a cigarette from the pack, lit it, took a deep drag, tilted her head straight back and slowly blew the smoke into the sky.

Josie had had enough. "Are you going to tell me or not?"

Doris leaned back in the bench and crossed her arms, with her cigarette dangling daintily between her fingers. She looked at Josie, pausing. At last she spoke. "I got a letter from my husband. He's coming home."

"On leave?"

"For good."

Josie was baffled. She was expecting disastrous news, like Doris was going to get fired, or she was going to be evicted, or she was going to have some American sailor's baby. This sounded like good news. She was both relieved and peeved. "You had me worried sick. I thought something terrible had happened to you. This is great."

"Not really."

"Why not?"

"He got injured. One of our own tanks ran over both his legs. Now he's crippled. That's why the army is sending him home. He's been declared unfit for duty. They're sending him home in a wheelchair. And I'm going to be expected to take care of him."

"But he's your husband. You're his wife. You're supposed to take care of him."

"He was only my husband for six months before he enlisted. I didn't know he was going to enlist. He didn't discuss it with me. He just went ahead and signed up."

"But everybody was signing up at that time. The war had started by then. You must have known he might enlist."

"The war hadn't started when we got married. Maybe *he* signed on for the war, but that's not what *I* signed on for when I got married. To look after a cripple for the rest of my life? If I had known that was going to happen, I wouldn't have married him in the first place. I'd have stayed single."

Josie didn't know what to say. The whole situation was confusing. Part of her wanted to admonish her friend for not wanting to stand by her husband during his time of need, especially since he had been injured serving his country. That was her duty. But part of her understood exactly how she felt; how the war had given her a raw deal. A young woman in her prime. She decided she should try and console her.

"Well, maybe it won't be that bad. He'll probably get a pension from the army."

"No, it will be bad, pension or no pension. I'm going to be completely tied down looking after him. My life, as I've known it for the past three years, is over. No more partying, no more dancing, no more sailors. It's over. Everything. You're going to have to find yourself a new drinking buddy."

The two friends sat silently for several moments. Josie stared straight ahead while Doris puffed slowly on her cigarette. Then Josie asked Doris when her husband would be getting home.

Doris groaned. "In three weeks. He's in England right now at a hospital getting some kind of treatment. Once he's finished with the treatments, they're sending him home. You know what that means."

"What?"

"Only three more weeks of freedom."

Josie felt sorry for her friend. She imagined how she'd feel if the same thing happened to her. If you were married to a serviceman you always lived with the possibility that they might not come back. But you never thought they'd come back a cripple. It was a horrible thing to even think about, but her brother Harry had once told her he'd rather be killed in action than be crippled for life. Especially if he was married. It would be better for both the husband and the wife, he said.

No, Doris mustn't think that way. At least her husband was still alive. Life was better than death. Doris would have to deal with it. And, as her friend, Josie would have to be supportive. An idea popped into her head. She turned to Doris. "How about we have one last fling?"

"One last fling?"

"Yeah, one last fling before your husband arrives. We'll go to a dance, meet a couple of sailors, get some liquor, have a good time."

"You mean, my last night of fun before my life is over?"

"Your life isn't over."

"It may as well be."

"So, what do you say?"

"I don't know."

"C'mon. For old times sake."

Doris looked at her friend. A smile crept onto her face. "Sure, whatever you want."

"Great. We'll go this Saturday night. There's quite a few ships in port, so they'll be lots to choose from at the dance."

"On one condition."

"What's that?"

"That you let me have the good looking one this time."

Josie laughed.

Doris got up from the bench, dropped her cigarette on the walkway, and crushed it out with her shoe. She hooked her arm under Josie's and the two friends walked out of the park to the corner of South and Hollis where they parted ways, Doris heading west up South to her flat and Josie north along Hollis back to her apartment at Gorman's. As they separated, Doris turned back and called out, "You're a good friend, Josephine Bourdeau."

Josie smiled. She hoped she was.

Chapter 15

The Strand was packed Saturday night, overflowing with sailors, as Josie had predicted. With guys far outnumbering gals, it didn't take long for Josie and Doris to be invited up on the dance floor.

Since this was Doris's "last fling," they had decided to be particularly fussy about which two sailors they would choose to escort them on their night of partying. Number one, they had to be handsome. Really handsome. Clark Gable handsome. And if only one of them was handsome, Josie had agreed to let Doris have the handsome one. It was only fair. This was her night. Number two, they had to be fun-loving. A little wild. No shy guys. No stick-in-the-muds. This was a night Josie wanted Doris to remember for the rest of her life. And number three, they had to have some money and be willing to spend it. After all, the guys would be paying for the booze.

With their guidelines established, the two predators ventured out in search of their prey. Drawing upon every weapon in their feminine arsenal, they were at their flirtatious best, surveying the field, moving from dance partner to dance partner, never lingering too long, assessing as many candidates as possible. Near the end of the dance, they made their choice. Two Canadian sailors. One was fair-haired, average height, and Hollywood handsome, with a playful, mischievous smile. That one was for Doris. The other was taller, darker-haired, and okay looking, who laughed at every word out of his buddy's mouth, whether it was funny or not. That one was for Josie.

Josie and Doris had danced with the two young men much earlier in the evening, although they hadn't exchanged names. At that time, the boys told them they had a few dollars they wanted to spend before shipping out and had asked the girls if they wanted to leave the Strand and go get some liquor. The girls were tempted but wanted to check out what else was available. In the end, they decided to find out if the earlier offer was still on the table.

They spotted their targets circling around the perimeter of the dance floor, so they positioned themselves where the two sailors would "accidently" bump into them. The tactic worked like a charm. With Josie in the lead, they moved directly into the sailors' path and feigned fright when the twosomes almost collided. The handsome one (the one for Doris) recognized them right away.

"Are you girls still here?"

"Yeah, but we're thinking of leaving," said Josie. "There's nothing much happening."

Doris smiled coyly at the handsome one. He took the bait.

"Why don't you join us?" he said. "We'll find a place to have some drinks. Start our own party. Our treat."

Josie looked at Doris, as if debating whether or not to accept the offer. Doris played along perfectly, shrugging her shoulders as if to say "Okay." She turned to the handsome one, offering him her arm. "Let's go, then."

The handsome one flashed his playful, mischievous smile, and took Doris's arm. The okay-looking one laughed loudly for no apparent reason and offered his arm to Josie, which she also accepted. The two couples then headed for the exit. Once on Argyle, the handsome one hailed a passing cab and the four of them piled in, all in the back seat.

"Take us to the nearest bar, my good man," said the handsome one to the cabbie.

"There's no bars in Halifax," said the cabbie. "No legal ones."

"Then take us to an illegal one."

"The Cavern on Dresden Row, driver," said Doris.

"You girls have done this before," said the handsome one.

"Once or twice," said Josie, winking at Doris.

"By the way, my name is Donnie," said the handsome one, "and this is my buddy Roy."

"I'm Josie, and this is my friend Doris."

"Great," said the handsome one named Donnie. "Now we all know each other."

Meanwhile, the okay-looking one named Roy had managed to put one arm around Josie's shoulders with his hand dangling precariously close to her breast. She was keeping a close eye on it.

"So, where are you boys from?" asked Josie.

"Windsor, Ontario," replied Donnie.

"That's a long way from the ocean," said Josie. "Why the Navy?"

"Because we figured we'd rather die in a ship on the ocean than in a foxhole in the ground," said Donnie.

Roy laughed as if he'd just heard the funniest joke ever told.

"What about you girls? Local, I assume?" said Donnie.

"Yep, good ol' Halifax girls," said Josie.

The cab pulled up in front of a nondescript three-storey house on Dresden. Donnie paid the driver and the four new-found friends exited the cab.

"Around the back, downstairs," said Doris.

"They call this place the Cavern?" said Donnie.

"It's not an official name," said Josie. "It's just what the locals call it."

Doris led the entourage through a dark alley along the side of the house and down a flight of stairs at the back of the building. A dim overhead light illuminated a wooden door whose plainness was broken only by a small peephole. She tapped loudly on the door twice. A few moments later, the door opened and a heavy-set man waved them in, closing the door behind them. As they entered, it was clear to see why they called it "the Cavern." Its low ceiling, its huge pillars holding up exposed wood beams, and its sparse lighting all gave the sense that you were underground. But the place was packed. Mostly sailors, but local civilians as well. More men but quite a few women too. And noisy. Very noisy. And smoke so thick it burned your eyes.

"You girls find us a table and Roy and I will get the drinks," said Donnie. "What are you girls going to have?"

Josie wanted to say, "lemon gin," but the memory of a previous lemon gin night with Doris popped into her head. "Rum and Coke for me."

"Same for me," said Doris.

All the tables were taken, but Josie managed to find two unoccupied chairs near one of the pillars. At least she and Doris would have a place to sit. The boys would have to stand. A few minutes later, Josie spotted Donnie and Roy, with drinks in hand, scanning the room, looking for them. Josie hollered over, but they obviously couldn't hear her above the clamor. She waved her arms back and forth to catch their attention, but that didn't work either. "Save my seat," she said to Doris. She then proceeded to retrieve the two sailors and escort them back to the spot by the pillar.

"We couldn't find a table," said Josie, as Donnie and Roy handed the drinks to the girls. "Only these two chairs. Sorry, but you boys will have to stand."

Donnie had another idea. "Or we could sit on the chairs and you could sit on our laps."

Roy seemed to like that suggestion. Grinning widely, he placed his drink on the floor, lifted Josie from her seat, plopped himself down on the chair, and pulled Josie onto his lap, wrapping his arm around her waist. "Like this?" he said.

Taking the cue from his buddy, Donnie sat down on the second chair and beckoned Doris over. Shrugging, Doris planted herself on his lap.

"There," said Donnie. "All nice and cozy."

The four new friends yakked and laughed and flirted while they drank their rum and Cokes. When they had finished their drinks, the boys went and got another round. And then another. As the alcohol worked its wizardry, the yakking grew louder, the laughing more boisterous, and the flirting more suggestive. Necks were nibbled and cheeks caressed. Hands wandered and were playfully slapped. After a fourth round of drinks, Donnie broke some news that threatened to put a damper on the evening's merriment.

"We're running out of money," he said. "The drinks here aren't cheap."

"Let's go to a bootlegger then," suggested Josie.

"I don't think we have enough for a bootlegger either," said Donnie.

Josie was miffed. "I thought you guys were going to treat us to a good time. You said you were going to buy all the liquor. We're not finished drinking yet. We're not even half-drunk."

Donnie was apologetic. "I'm really sorry. I didn't realize the drinks would be so expensive. They're not that expensive back home."

"Welcome to the warfront, junior," quipped Doris.

The four of them sat silently, racking their brains for a solution to their problem. No one wanted the party to end. Ironically, it was Roy who saved the day. "I know where we can get some booze. And we won't have to pay anything for it."

The others perked up. Doris was skeptical. "Free booze?"

"Yep," said Roy, clearly pleased with himself.

"Where?" asked Donnie.

"The junior officers' mess at Stad."

Josie was amazed at the Navy's apparent generosity. "They give it to you for nothing?"

"Well, not exactly," said Roy.

Doris clued in. "You mean you're going to steal it."

"Borrow it without giving it back," said Roy, with a huge grin.

Donnie jumped into the conversation. "That's crazy. You're not going to be able to get into the officers' mess."

"*Junior* officers' mess," corrected Roy.

"Junior, senior. You're still not going to be able to get in. Everything's going to be locked up solid. There'll be guards, MPs."

"I can get in," said Roy confidently.

Donnie was doubtful. "Yeah, how?"

"I can get in, trust me."

Donnie, Doris, and Josie all looked at each other, pondering Roy's solution to continuing the night's revelry.

"Let's do it!" shouted Josie.

Donnie and Doris hooted their approval, raising their arms in the air as if charging into battle. With the rum having dispensed of any collective common sense, the four musketeers marched out of the Cavern and onto Dresden Row to find a taxi to take them to the scene of the impending crime. Finding nothing on Dresden, the would-be gangsters stumbled down to Spring Garden where, after singing war songs for about ten minutes, they found a cabbie willing to get them off the street.

As they rode to Stadacona, a surge of excitement coursed through Josie's body. She was embarking on a caper, an escapade, an adventure fraught with danger. She was going to do something bad, something wild. And it scared her a little. But she loved it. It made her feel alive.

Within ten minutes, they had arrived at Stad. Roy told the cabbie to drop them off one block north of the base, so as not to draw suspicion. Donnie had just enough money left to pay the driver, so he settled up and the gang of four disembarked. As they stood in the near darkness on the street, Donnie put his arm on Roy's shoulder. "So, what's the plan?"

"Follow me," said Roy.

The three co-conspirators obeyed their leader and followed Roy down a short lane between two houses. At the end of the path was a gravel road running perpendicular to the path. On the other side of the gravel road was a chain-link fence, about eight feet high, topped with barbed wire. The fence ran parallel to the road in both directions for as far as they could see in the darkness. A few feet on the other side of the fence they could see a windowless, red-brick building, about forty feet high.

"We're supposed to get inside there?" said Josie.

Unperturbed, Roy headed left down the gravel road. The others followed. Seconds later, a large utility truck came into view, parked right up against the fence. Roy stopped beside the truck and waved the others over. "They've been parking this truck against the fence for the past few nights because the fence is broken, and they haven't fixed it yet," he said. "All we have to do is move the truck and we can get inside."

Donnie reached up and tried to open the truck door. "And how are we going to move the truck, wise guy? The door's locked."

Roy flashed his huge grin. He knelt down on the ground next to the truck's left front tire, reached in under the fender, pulled something out, and held it up for his friends to see. "Spare key," he said, beaming.

"He's smarter than he looks," Doris whispered to Josie.

"If we start the truck, it might wake up the neighbours," said Donnie.

"We're not going to start the truck," said Roy. "We're just going to put it in neutral and push the truck out of the way. Do you know how to drive, Josie?"

Josie had never driven anything in her life, but thanks to all the "liquid courage" she had consumed, she felt she could do anything. "A little," she said.

"Good. You get in the truck and put it in neutral. The rest of us will push. When we've pushed it far enough, I'll bang on the side of the truck and you'll put on the brakes."

Josie nodded in agreement. Roy unlocked the driver's side door, swung it back, and helped Josie up into the driver's seat. He then watched as Josie moved the shifter back and forth, grinding the gears.

Roy cringed. "The clutch!" Engage the clutch! The pedal on the left. I thought you said you could drive."

"I said a little," said Josie defensively.

Josie engaged the clutch and moved the gear shift back and forth trying to find neutral. "Is that it?" she asked.

Roy reached over her, grabbed the shifter, and maneuvered it until he found neutral. "That's neutral there. Hold it right there." He then jumped down from the cab and went to the back of the truck to direct the push. Roy and Donnie braced their shoulders against the back of the truck while Doris placed her two hands on the bumper.

"Okay," said Roy, "on three. One, two, three, push!"

The two men strained as hard as they could and Doris did her best to assist the effort, but the truck didn't budge.

"Okay, again," said Roy. "One, two, three, push!"

Again, the truck didn't budge.

"It should move," said Donnie. "It's on level ground. Are you sure it's in neutral?"

"It's in neutral," said Roy. "I think I know what's wrong."

Roy went back to the cab, opened the door, and climbed up beside Josie. He reached over her and pulled on the emergency brake, releasing it. He then returned to the back of the truck.

"The emergency brake was on," he said to the others. The three of them took their positions and tried again. This time, the truck moved slightly.

"Okay," said Roy. "We'll get it rocking back and forth and then give it a big push."

After a couple of tries, the truck started rocking nicely. By now, Roy and Donnie were doing all the work as Doris had packed it in. At the right moment, the two men gave it all they had and the truck began moving forward on its own. Once it had travelled far enough to expose the broken section of the fence, Roy banged on the side of the truck and Josie brought the vehicle to a full stop. Roy then went to the cab and opened the driver side door. He reached over Josie and put the truck back in first gear, then removed the key. Josie climbed down from the cab and joined her friends standing by the opening in the fence.

"After we get the booze," said Roy, "we'll come back through here and put the truck back where it was. Let's go."

The group slipped through the broken fence into the compound. Josie's heart beat faster as the thrill of what they were doing rushed through her.

"Which way?" asked Donnie.

"This way," said Roy, as he turned to the right, staying close to the red-brick building. They had walked about thirty feet when the forty-foot-high windowless building turned into a two-storey building with a full row of windows. There were no lights on inside. Another sixty feet further, they reached the far end of the building. As they turned the corner, they could see a large parking lot which was mostly empty, apart from two jeeps.

"See that building on the other side of the parking lot?" said Roy to the others. "That's where we're going. The junior officers' mess is in there."

"Great," said Josie. "Let's go. I'm getting thirsty."

"Just wait," said Roy. "I don't think we should walk straight across. It's wide open. Someone might see us."

"It's pitch black here," said Doris. "No one's gonna see us."

"Yeah, why is it so dark here?" asked Josie. "Shouldn't everything be all lit up."

"They keep the lights out at night to make it harder for the German bombers to see their targets if they ever attack the base," said Roy.

Josie was becoming impressed with how much Roy knew about so many things. She had underestimated him.

"Anyway," Roy continued, "to be safe, I think we should go around the parking lot to the right and come in the backside of the building. We'll follow the fence. The trees there will give us some cover. There's a smaller building near the water reservoir in the far corner of the compound. We can stay behind it, then scoot across the lawn to the mess."

"Sounds easy," said Doris somewhat sarcastically.

With Roy in the lead, the four accomplices made their way along the fence, behind the small building near the reservoir, and across the lawn to the building where Roy had assured them their treasure could be found.

"Around the back," said Roy.

With the others in tow, Roy made his way to the back of the structure. Suddenly, he stopped, looked right, then left, then right again. "There's supposed to be a door back here."

Everyone strained their eyes in the darkness to find a door, but there didn't seem to be one anywhere. Josie broke off from the rest of the group and began exploring farther down the side of the building. Within seconds, she had found the door. "Over here," she called to the others, trying to keep her voice down. When her friends arrived, she pointed to her discovery. "There it is." In the corner of an alcove, a Navy pick-up truck was parked with its back end against a door, leaving only half of the door visible. In the darkness it could be easily missed.

"Another truck?" lamented Donnie.

Roy went to the back of the truck to assess the situation. "I think there's enough room to get behind there. Doris, you're the smallest one here. See if you can slide in behind there."

Doris looked at Roy as if he had three heads. "Me?"

"C'mon, Doris," said Josie. "You can do it. One last fling, remember?"

Doris shrugged, then agreed to give it a try. Without much effort but a lot of complaining, she managed to slide behind the truck and reach the door. She turned the knob and pushed. It didn't open. "It's locked," she said.

"It's not locked," said Roy. "It's just stuck. The fella told me it's never locked. The canteen manager leaves it unlocked so some of his buddies can come in after hours and have a drink."

"The fella?" said Josie.

"Yeah, the fella I met at the Cavern while we were waiting for our drinks. He's the guy that told me all about this."

"Why is the pick-up truck parked against the door?" asked Donnie.

"I don't know," said Roy.

Roy knew a lot, thought Josie, *but he didn't know everything.*

"Try it again," Roy said to Doris. "Push hard."

Doris tried the door again, pushing a little harder, but obviously not hard enough. The door still didn't open.

"Let me see if I can get in there," said Donnie.

Doris slid out from behind the truck and Donnie slid in. After considerable effort, and more than a few scrapes to his arms from the rough brick on the side of the building, Donnie managed to reach the door. He turned the knob and pushed hard, but nothing happened.

"Try lifting the knob a little first, then pushing," suggested Roy.

Donnie following his buddy's instructions, turning the knob and lifting it up as far as he could, then pushing hard. It popped open.

"We're in!" shouted Josie.

"Shh! Keep your voice down," whispered Donnie.

Donnie opened the door wider and stepped in. The others climbed into the back of the pick-up and Donnie helped them over the tailgate and into the building. Once everyone was inside, Donnie closed the door behind them. The room they entered appeared to be a small foyer leading to another room. It was in total darkness, except for a faint light shining from underneath a facing door. Roy opened the door and the group entered a much larger room filled with tables and chairs. A long bar counter ran almost the full length of the right side of the room. The only light in the room was coming from behind the counter.

"This must be the mess bar," said Roy.

Donnie went behind the counter. On the back wall of the bar, metal rolling shutters covered the large assortment of liquor bottles. Donnie tried to lift the shutters, but they were locked. Looking around, he spotted a door at the back of the bar at the far end and opened it. He called out to the others. "Over here, everybody."

Josie, Doris, and Roy came running over, and crammed into the doorway of the storage room. Donnie smiled, extending his arm towards their prize. "I don't know why they'd lock up the bottles in the bar and leave the storage room unlocked, but there it is."

"Wahoo!" shouted Josie.

"I told you I could get us free liquor," beamed Roy.

"How much are we going to take?" asked Doris.

"We'll grab two bottles each," said Donnie.

Roy had other ideas. "I say we take two *cases*. You carry one and I'll carry the other," he said to Donnie.

"Are you crazy?" said Donnie. "We're going to drag two cases of liquor out of here and into a cab? Then what are we going to do with them?"

"We'll divide 'em up somewhere," said Roy, with a shrug.

While the two sailors were arguing about how much liquor they should steal, Josie had taken two bottles of rum out of one of the cases, found four paper cups in a cupboard in the bar, and had poured roughly equal amounts of rum in each cup. She then distributed the cups to each of her chums.

"Bottom's up!" she bellowed, and downed her drink without stopping. The rum burned as it went down straight, without any mix, but it also made her feel warm inside. She liked the feeling.

"Are we drinking here?" asked Doris.

"I am," declared Josie. "I was starting to sober up."

Doris decided to join her friend and took a swig of her drink. Then another. The two sailors, realizing that the girls weren't going anywhere for awhile, and knowing that they couldn't abandon them there, gave in. Everyone was going to stay and drink their ill-gotten gains.

Before long, the four merrymakers had reached their earlier level of drunkenness—and beyond. The rum flowed, the laughter roared, and the speech slurred. Soon, all four were plopped on the floor in the bar, oblivious to time and place. As the alcohol gradually removed all constraints, the men got friskier and the women more submissive. Doris and Donnie were going at it heavy, devouring each other's lips and tongues. Roy had Josie's blouse open, foundling her breasts while clumsily trying to undo her bra. Josie repelled his advances slightly at first but was now in such a fog that she was largely oblivious to what he was doing.

All of a sudden, the lights in the room came on. Startled, Roy jumped up, shaking Josie out of her stupor.

"Uh-oh," mumbled Roy.

Josie dragged herself to her feet, blouse wide open. Propping herself on the counter, she squinted into the now brightly lit room. There, standing by the entranceway, were two monstrous, fully-uniformed, billy-club wielding military police.

"I think we're in trouble," she whispered to her friends.

It was the understatement of her life.

Chapter 16

"Halt! Don't move!"

Josie and Roy froze in their tracks as the two burly MPs moved swiftly towards them. By now, Doris and Donnie had recognized that something was going on and had scrambled to their feet. The four accomplices were a sorry sight, lined up behind the bar, awaiting their fate.

"What are you people doing here?" shouted one of the MPs. "This is a restricted area!"

No one answered, but it didn't matter because the MP wasn't waiting for answers. He kept firing questions. "How did you get in here?"

"The door was unlocked," replied Doris, calmly.

"Try again, Miss."

"It was," insisted Josie.

The MP wasn't buying it. "Get out from behind the bar, the four of you. Right now!"

Roy and Donnie obeyed, exiting the bar into the outer room and snapping to attention in front of the MPs. Doris joined them, taking her good, sweet time. Instead of standing at attention, like the two sailors, she crossed her arms and smirked at the MPs. Josie, suddenly realizing she was half dressed, frantically began fastening her bra and buttoning her blouse. But not fast enough to suit the surly MP.

"Now, sister!"

Josie jumped, scooted out from behind the counter, and positioning herself next to Doris. The four of them presented quite a sight. Drunk. Dishevelled. Caught in the act. Their audacious adventure aborted. The MP who had been doing all the talking surveyed the collection of culprits before him. He stared suggestively at Josie who was still buttoning her blouse, before turning to the sailors.

"Wrong place to take your whores, boys."

"We're not whores," snapped Josie.

While MP number one was carrying out his interrogation, MP number two had gone behind the bar. He emerged shortly after, holding one half-empty bottle of rum and two completely empty ones.

"They got these from the storage room, Hank," he said to his colleague. "Looks like they were having a party."

The MP now identified as Hank smiled at Josie and her friends. "That's Navy property, folks," he smirked. "Now we can add theft to the break-and-enter charges."

"How do you know they're not ours?" sneered Doris.

"Because it says, 'Property of the Canadian Navy' on the bottles," said MP number two, clearly gloating.

Doris had no comeback. But Josie, emboldened by the rum, wasn't backing down that easy. "And these boys are in the Canadian Navy, so it's just as much their rum as it is anyone else's."

"It's for the officers," said MP Hank, raising his voice in anger.

But Josie wasn't backing down. "Why is everything always for the officers? What about the enlisted men? They deserve some rum once in awhile. They're fighting for our country too, you know."

MP Hank was clearly losing his patience with this brash "whore." "Look, lady. You broke in here illegally, you drank liquor that didn't belong to you, and you're going to pay the consequences. So clam up."

"We didn't break in, I told you. The door was unlocked."

"Tell it to the judge, sweetheart."

MP Hank then turned his attention back to the two sailors. "What ship are you on, boys?"

"We're both on the *Restigouche*," said Donnie, having difficulty remaining at attention in his inebriated state.

"We're going to escort you back to your ship, gentlemen. You realize we're going to have to report this to your commanding officer. He'll decide your punishment."

"What about us?" asked Doris. "Are we free to go?"

"You two girls are not going anywhere. We're turning you over to the Halifax police. You'll probably be charged, and go to jail."

"What?" screeched Josie. "Go to jail? For what? For havin' a few drinks of the Navy's rum?"

MP Hank was infuriated. "For break-and-enter into Navy premises. For theft of Navy property. For being drunk and disorderly. And if you don't watch your tongue, young lady, I'll tell the city cops to add resisting arrest!"

Josie pouted. "Well, that's just not fair."

Fair or not, her protests fell on deaf ears. MP Hank went behind the bar, found a phone, and called the city police. Josie couldn't hear the conversation, but he was on the line for several minutes. When he returned, he summoned the group. "Okay, everybody have a seat. When the city cops get here, you two ladies will go with them and you two boys will come with us. So, relax. I don't know how long it's going to be. Maybe you can take the time to sober up a little."

Josie opened her mouth to say something, but Doris touched her on the arm. Josie glanced at her friend, who was shaking her head from side to side. She took the hint. It was best to keep her mouth shut. They were already in enough trouble as it was.

For the next several minutes, no one said a word. Roy appeared to be falling asleep. Donnie was staring at the ceiling. Doris was playing with her hair and occasionally smiling flirtatiously at MP number two, who appeared to like the attention. MP Hank was standing erect, chest out, legs shoulder width apart, billy club at the ready, guarding his charges. Josie was sitting quietly. As she sat, she started to sense the effects of all the alcohol she had consumed. She felt groggy and a little queasy. She also needed to pee.

"I have to go to the bathroom," she announced.

"Officer MacKinnon," said MP Hank, "escort the detainee to the bathroom."

MP number two, who now had a last name, gestured to Josie to come with him. Josie got up from her chair and followed him out the main door of the room into a hallway. He pointed to a door on the left. Josie opened the door, entered the room, and flicked on the light. It was a small bathroom with a toilet, a urinal, and a sink. There was a circular mirror above the sink.

Josie closed the door behind her and turned the lock. As she sat on the toilet, she felt the room starting to spin ever so slightly. The queasiness in her stomach returned. Her tongue felt thick and chalky. She started to gag. She finished peeing and went to the sink. Staring into the mirror, the sight startled her. She looked terrible. Her lipstick was completely wiped away, her hair was a mess, and her face a pale shade of green. Her mother would not have been proud.

The gagging was getting worse. She felt like she was going to be sick. She stuck her head in the sink. Her body heaved as she tried to throw up, but nothing came out. Again she strained to rid her body of the poison inside, convulsing and jerking forward, but again, nothing. She moaned and writhed and prayed for some relief from her agony.

There was a knock on the door. "Miss, are you alright? Miss?"

It was Officer MacKinnon, who had obviously heard Josie's moans. Josie didn't have the strength to respond. Officer MacKinnon tried the door, but it was locked. "Miss, unlock the door," he said.

Josie reached over and unlocked the door without lifting her head out of the sink. Officer MacKinnon entered.

"Are you alright?" he asked.

"I feel sick," said Josie.

"Too much liquor, obviously. Here, have a seat on the toilet. Keep your head down."

Officer MacKinnon put his arm around Josie's waist and helped her to the toilet. He then grabbed a hand towel and wet it. Kneeling down in front of her, he gently wiped her face, then folded the towel and placed it on the back of her neck. He began stroking her back to comfort her. After thirty seconds or so, he took the towel from her neck, wetted it once more, and wiped her face again.

"Feeling any better?" he asked.

"A little," replied Josie.

Officer MacKinnon continued for several minutes to comfort Josie as best he could, rubbing her back and wiping her face with the wet towel from time to time. He then told her he'd have to take her back inside, that his partner would be wondering where they were. He wetted the towel again, folded it, and gave it to Josie. "Hold this on your forehead," he said. He helped Josie to her feet and slowly escorted her back to the room with the others.

When they entered the main room, MP Hank barked at his fellow officer. "What took you so long?"

"She was sick," said Officer MacKinnon.

MP Hank showed no sympathy for Josie's condition. "Maybe she should have considered that before she stole the Navy's rum. Anyway, the city police can deal with her."

Officer MacKinnon helped Josie to a chair and Doris came over to try to assist her friend. Josie kept the wet towel pressed against her forehead.

The phone behind the bar rang. MP Hank walked over and answered it. He returned shortly after.

"The city police have arrived," he told them. "Officer MacKinnon, please let them in and bring them here."

Officer MacKinnon left the room and reappeared a short time later with two city police officers. They approached MP Hank and shook hands. "These are the two civilians I reported," said MP Hank, pointing to Josie and Doris. "As I told your Captain, they broke into these premises with these two servicemen, stole property belonging to the Navy, and are obviously drunk in a public place. We're turning them over to your authority. We'll take the two servicemen back to their ship where they'll be turned over to their commanding officer for appropriate disciplinary action."

One of the city officers approached Doris, motioned to her to stand, grabbed her arm, and led her out of the room. The other approached Josie, who still had her head down.

"She's feeling a little sick," said Doris.

"As long as she doesn't throw up in our car," said the officer, as he took Josie's arm, lifted her to her feet, and led her to the exit. As they were leaving, Doris called back to the two sailors. She smiled.

"It was fun while it lasted, boys. Maybe we'll do it again sometime."

Donnie raised his eyebrows and shrugged. Roy just grinned.

The two officers escorted Josie and Doris out of the building and into their police cruiser parked out front. They put the girls in the back seat. Josie kept her head down and continued to hold the towel to her forehead, although it was starting to dry out. At least she was feeling a bit better. The nausea was subsiding.

As they drove to the police station, Josie noticed that it was getting light outside.

"What time is it?" she asked the officers.

"Twenty minutes to six," replied the one sitting in the passenger seat.

Josie couldn't believe it. They had been up all night. She had completely lost track of the time.

"So, what happens now, boys?" asked Doris.

Again, the officer in the passenger seat did the talking. "We're taking you to the station. You'll be booked, charged, and placed in the women's cell. Then you'll appear before a magistrate—a judge—to answer to the charges. After that, it depends on the judge."

"So, how long will that take?"

"Booking you won't take too long, but today is Sunday, and the court doesn't sit on Sundays. So, you'll have to spend the night in jail, then appear in court Monday morning, or afternoon, depending on how many cases there are."

Doris didn't like the sound of that. "But I have to work Monday. Couldn't we just pay a fine or something?"

"The judge decides on the fines, not the police. Besides, you're going to be charged with break and enter, and theft. Those are serious charges. You could go to jail for quite a while."

The reality of the situation hit Josie for the first time. If she and Doris had to spend any length of time in jail, they would probably lose their jobs. And if they lost their jobs, how were they going to pay their rent? Maybe it was a good thing, after all, that Doris's husband would be home in a few weeks. At least he could pay her bills with his Navy pension. But that wouldn't help Josie. She started to regret suggesting they have "one last fling." Josie had done it for Doris's benefit. Now, they were both about to pay a hefty price for her thoughtfulness.

By the time they arrived at the station, Josie was feeling a little better, a little more alert. Her stomach had settled down, although she still felt a bit light-headed. As she and Doris exited the car, she turned to her friend. "I think we're in trouble."

"They're just trying to scare us," said Doris. "Don't worry, we'll be fine."

Josie wasn't so sure. "I hope you're right," she said. "I hope you're right."

Chapter 17

The police station occupied the entire basement level of the City Hall building and had all the feel of a subterranean hell-hole. Dark, dingy, and poorly ventilated, its walls were coated in grime from the building's coal bins situated directly underneath. With its small, stuffy, and less than sanitary holding cells, it was not the place for a proper young lady.

The officers escorted Josie and Doris from the car, down a flight of concrete steps, and into the basement entrance of the station. They continued down a narrow hallway, through a door to an open foyer, and into a small room where they were processed, photographed, and fingerprinted. The officers then took them into a slightly larger room containing a long table surrounded by chairs, where they were asked to have a seat. One of the officers then left the room while the other stood by the door.

As Josie sat there, the effects of her night of heavy drinking began to set in. While the queasiness she'd experienced earlier had subsided, she now had a splitting headache, the shivers, and an extremely dry mouth—all the classic signs of a massive hangover.

"I need a drink of water," she said to the officer by the door.

"You'll have to wait," he said.

"But I'm thirsty."

"You'll have to wait until Detective Clark gets here. I'm not allowed to leave you unattended."

Josie moaned but decided not to argue. She'd wait.

About ten minutes later, a slim, tall, moderately handsome man in a brown suit and dark green tie came into the room holding a file folder. He sat down at the head of the table and opened his folder.

"Can I have my drink of water now?" Josie said to the officer by the door. The officer glanced over at the man in the brown suit, who nodded approval. The officer then left the room.

"I'm Detective Clark," said the man in the brown suit. "So, which one of you is Josephine Bourdeau?"

"Me," said Josie.

He turned to address Doris. "So, then you must be Doris Hebb."

"Yes sir," Doris replied, sounding uncharacteristically deferential.

The detective looked at a sheet of paper in his folder. "Break and enter into the junior officers' mess at Stadacona. Theft of Navy property. Drunk in a public place. These are serious charges."

He looked up at the two women, obviously waiting for some response. Josie and Doris looked at each other. At that moment, the door opened and the officer entered with a glass of water, placing it on the table in front of Josie. With her hand slightly shaking, Josie picked up the glass and downed the water without stopping.

The detective was still waiting for an explanation. "Well?"

Doris took the lead. "We met these two sailors at a dance," she began, "and they said they knew where we could get some free liquor. So, we just followed them."

"And then you helped them break into the mess," said the detective.

Doris found herself stuck for words. "Well, uh…"

Feeling slightly refreshed from the water, Josie piped in. "We didn't break in. The door was unlocked."

"Unlocked," said the detective sarcastically.

"Yeah."

The detective wasn't buying it. "You expect me to believe that the Canadian Navy, in the middle of a war, would leave its buildings unlocked overnight?"

"Well, it's true," said Josie.

The detective glared at her. "I don't believe you and neither will the judge. And anyway, how did you get into the compound in the first place? The MPs said that your sailor friends didn't register at the front gate."

Josie and Doris looked at each other again. "We came in through a hole in the fence," said Doris, looking down at her feet. "At the rear of the compound."

"A hole in the fence?" repeated the detective. "So, you *did* break in after all. Into the compound."

Neither Josie nor Doris had a comeback. But the detective wasn't done. "And then you stole the liquor."

"We *drank* the liquor," said Doris.

"You drank liquor that didn't belong to you," said the detective. "That's stealing."

Josie jumped in. She still thought she had a good counter argument. "The sailors said the liquor was just as much theirs as it was the officers' because they are all part of the Canadian Navy. So, you can't steal something that's already yours."

The detective laughed. "Oh, that's a good one. I'm sure the Navy brass would look at it the same way. That's why they keep their booze under lock and key. To share it with the enlisted men."

"The storage room wasn't locked," mumbled Doris.

"What was that?" asked the detective.

"Nothing," muttered Doris.

"Okay," continued the detective, "we've talked about the break and enter, and the theft of Navy property. The other charge is being drunk in a public place. Are you going to dispute that, too?"

Josie and Doris couldn't deny that one.

"I didn't think so," said the detective, "given that I can smell the booze all over both of you. So, we are charging you with these three offenses. The police court doesn't sit on Sundays, so you'll appear before the judge tomorrow morning, Monday. At that time, you'll enter a plea—guilty or not guilty. If you plead guilty, the judge will outline your punishment. If you plead not guilty, he'll schedule you for trial. In the meantime, you'll be held here in our women's holding cell until your court appearance."

A rush of fear flowed through Josie's body. What had started as a lark was now turning into a nightmare. She was sobering up very quickly.

"Do you have any questions?" asked the detective.

"What about bail?" said Doris.

"If you plead not guilty and the case goes to trial, you'll be able to apply for bail at that time. For now, you're held here without bail until your court appearance tomorrow."

Josie dreaded asking what was on her mind at the moment, but she had to know. "If we plead guilty, will we go to jail?"

The detective eyed Josie solemnly. "If you plead guilty or if you are found guilty at trial, you could be sentenced for up to two years in the city prison, or for more than two years at a federal penitentiary. It's all up to the judge."

Josie gasped. Her heart started pumping rapidly. She struggled to breathe. Prison? Penitentiary? Was it possible or was the detective just trying to scare them? She couldn't go to prison. She would lose her job. Becky would disown her. It would kill her mother.

"Do you have any other questions?" said the detective.

"Should we get a lawyer?" asked Doris.

"If it goes to trial, I suggest you get a lawyer. Anything else?"

Josie sat stunned, tears swelling in her eyes. Doris hung her head.

"If not, constable, you can take Miss Bourdeau and Mrs. Hebb to the holding cell."

The detective closed his folder and left the room without saying another word. The officer, who had been standing by the door during the entire interrogation, motioned to Josie and Doris to go with him. He ushered them back to the central foyer, through a door, down a couple of steps, and into a small holding cell. The cell consisted of wooden benches running along the two sides and a sink in one corner with a paper cup dispenser above it. There was no mirror. An under-sized window at the very top of the back wall, protected by iron bars, was the only link to the outside world. The room was dimly lit, with one overhead bulb and only a smidgen of outside light passing through the window. There were no other prisoners in the cell.

"You'll be given something to eat at mealtimes," said the officer, "but nothing in between, so don't ask. You'll also be allowed to use the facilities at mealtimes if you need to. The ladies' bathroom is across the hall from the cell. An officer will escort you, then return you to the cell."

"What if there's a medical emergency or something?" asked Doris.

"If there's an emergency, just holler and someone will come. The dispatch office is just down the hall and they'll definitely hear you from there. But make sure it's an emergency. We're not going to come running for every little thing."

"I have to pee," said Josie.

"Me too," said Doris.

"Okay," said the officer, "I'll take you now. But only one at a time."

The officer ushered Josie out of the cell first, closed the bars behind him, and locked them with a large key, leaving Doris alone. He escorted Josie to the ladies' bathroom, waited outside the door until she was done, then took her back to the cell. He then motioned to Doris to come out of the cell, closed the bars behind him, locked them again, and left with Doris. With Josie now alone in the cell, the reality of the situation hit her. She and Doris were in deep trouble. When the officer returned Doris to the cell, as soon as he was out of earshot, Josie pulled Doris towards her.

"What are we going to do?" she said, panic in her voice.

"What can we do?" said Doris. "We'll just have to wait till tomorrow and see what happens."

Josie sighed. "Maybe we should call someone."

"Who?"

"I don't know. Maybe I should call Becky."

"What can she do?"

"Maybe her husband Albert can get us out. He works for the Navy."

"Josie, you heard the detective. We're here until we appear before the judge. We can't get bail. Besides, do you really want Becky to know you're in jail?"

Josie realized Doris had a point. Becky would probably lose her mind if she told her where she was. She'd tell Albert, who would tell his mother, for sure. Then the whole world would know. No, she couldn't call Becky.

Something else occurred to her. "We have to work tomorrow."

"Not if we're in here," said Doris.

"We'll have to call Mr. Gorman."

"We'll have to wait until the morning. Today's Sunday."

"What are we going to tell him?"

"I don't know. We'll tell him that we're sick."

"Both of us?"

"What else are we going to tell him?"

Josie had no answer for that one.

The two cellmates sat silently on the hard wooden benches. Josie began imagining what it would be like to be in prison. Dingy cells, lousy meals, and the same drab clothes every day. No dances, no movies, no fun whatsoever. And would she be safe? She'd heard stories about guards beating prisoners, and prisoners beating their fellow inmates. Hopefully, the stories weren't true. Then she began thinking about what her life would be like when she got out. She'd definitely lose her job at Gorman's, no doubt about that. Mr. Gorman would have to hire someone to replace her while she was in prison, and wouldn't hire her back when she got out now that she'd be a convict. Would she be able to find another job if she had a criminal record? Not a good job with a good employer, that was for sure. She'd end up cleaning toilets or some other dirty job. That's all she'd be able to find. And she'd lose her apartment, too. Mr. Gorman would rent it out to someone else. Would she be able to find a decent place to live or would she end up on the street? What kind of life would that be?

And what about her family? What about the shame she would bring to them? Could her mother survive knowing her daughter was in prison? What would her father say? He would be so disappointed in her. What would Harry say, and Beatrice, and the others? Would Becky shun her forever?

The rest of the day passed excruciatingly slow for Josie. With nothing to do to keep herself occupied, except for the all-too-brief meal breaks, her mood grew increasingly melancholic. The fact that she wasn't able to take a bath and change her clothes only made things worse. By suppertime, she had been in the same dress and undergarments for almost twenty-four hours. Just after seven, however, help arrived when two female soldiers from the Salvation Army appeared at their cell, accompanied by a uniformed policeman. They had brought soap, facecloths and towels, a hairbrush, and a small compact. They also offered to take the girls' dresses and undergarments, have them washed, and return them in the morning, and had brought along two sets of cotton pajamas and two housecoats for the girls to change into. Doris asked if they could bring some lipstick when they came back the next day. By the time they had each taken a turn in the bathroom cleaning up and changing into their nightwear, it was almost eight thirty. They were still locked in a dirty, stuffy cell, but at least they felt a little refreshed. The Salvation Army visit had provided a welcomed respite.

At about ten o'clock, an officer came to their cell with two sleeping bags. "These are your beds for the night, ladies. It's the best we have."

By now, Josie was exhausted. The stress of her arrest, coupled with a doozy of a hangover, had sapped all her energy. Despite the uncomfortable surroundings, she had to get some sleep. She stretched out a sleeping bag on the concrete floor, zipped it open, and crawled inside. Doris did the same.

Under ordinary circumstances, Josie would have had a difficult time falling asleep in such a setting—rock-hard concrete floor, unventilated room, phones ringing in the dispatch office just down the hall. But these were no ordinary circumstances. She had had a rough day. Maybe the roughest day of her life. So, despite the discomfort and the noise and the stagnant air, Josie went out like a light.

Chapter 18

Josie woke to the sound of loud voices. As she gradually shook off the cobwebs of sleep, she could make out the silhouettes of human figures standing outside the cell. When her eyes finally focused, they revealed a shapely young woman with knee-high white boots and too much makeup shouting at two uniformed police officers who were trying their best to get her in the cell. Josie unzipped her sleeping bag partway and sat up. She heard a familiar voice from behind.

"You're awake," said Doris.

Josie looked back. Doris was slouched on the bench.

"What time is it?" Josie asked.

"About two o'clock, I'd say."

"Did you sleep?"

"How could I sleep? The phone's been ringing all night. There's people coming and going. It's a regular circus in here. I don't know how you slept, but you were snoring pretty good."

"I was just beat."

Josie opened her sleeping bag the rest of the way and went to sit next to Doris. The young lady in the white boots was still shouting at the officers, something about knowing the mayor and the chief of police.

"One of Ava's girls, I imagine," smirked Doris.

"I think I recognize her," said Josie. "She comes into the restaurant once in a while."

Josie and Doris watched as the two policemen slid open the bars and nudged their new prisoner into the cell. All the while, she continued to berate them, more to their amusement than their annoyance. Even as they locked the bars and walked away, she kept up her verbal assault, occasionally throwing in some colorful language. As they disappeared down the hall, she gave up the attack and turned towards her new cellmates. When she saw Josie and Doris, her demeanour switched one hundred and eighty degrees.

"Hey girls," she shrieked in delight. "You're waitresses at Gorman's, right?"

"I knew I'd seen you at the restaurant. I'm Josie."

"Gladys."

"This is my friend Doris."

Doris waved half-heartedly in Gladys's direction.

"What are you girls doin' in here?" said Gladys, her expression changing from excitement to puzzlement. "You're not trying to give me competition, are you?"

"It's a long story," said Doris.

"We've been charged with break and enter, and theft," said Josie.

Gladys's eyes bulged. "Whoa! Hardened criminals."

"It's not what it seems," said Josie. "We were with these two sailors, and they told us they could get some free liquor, so they took us to Stadacona, and the door was unlocked, so we went in, and we found the liquor, so we drank it, and then the MPs came, and they called the cops, and now we're here."

Josie had explained the entire night's events in about fifteen seconds. And without even stopping to take a breath.

Gladys smiled coyly. "What a coincidence. I was with two sailors tonight as well."

Josie proceeded to give Gladys a more detailed account of their escapade and the predicament they were now in. She told her how the detective had said they could spend time in the city prison, or even federal penitentiary, and how they had to appear before the judge later that day.

"Who's the judge?" asked Gladys.

"I don't know," said Josie.

"Maybe I know him. I know a lot of the judges. I've been in court a few times before," she said with a wink. "I could put in a good word for you."

"Could you?"

"Sure. Us girls gotta stick together. I'll ask the coppers which judge is hearing your case."

Josie's spirits lifted. Doris just chuckled.

Josie asked her new-found friend what they should expect with the upcoming court appearance, given that Gladys had been in court before. Doris, meanwhile, had closed her eyes and was slumped against the wall. After Gladys had explained the inner workings of police court, ad nauseum, Josie started to get drowsy as well, and laid back down in her sleeping bag. Sleep, however, would prove elusive for the rest of the night, at least for more than a few minutes at a time. The wee hours of the morning were a busy time at the police station. Between the constant ringing of the phone in the dispatch office, the drunks being thrown in the men's lockup, and the police sirens wailing outside, the conditions were far from ideal for a visit to dreamland. A fight even broke out between two drunk men just outside the women's cell. It was quite a night.

By the time dawn arrived, Josie and Doris were anxious to get their court appearance over with, whatever the outcome. Surely the city prison or the penitentiary couldn't be worse than this. Around seven, a woman from the Salvation Army arrived with their clothes washed and ironed. She even had some lipstick, as Doris had requested. Shortly after, they received permission to call Mr. Gorman. They decided it would be best if they each called at different times. It would look suspicious if one of them called to say that they were both sick.

The calls were made without incident. Mr. Gorman seemed to buy their stories. But as soon as Josie had hung up the phone, a thought occurred to her. "I hope he doesn't come up to check on me in my room."

Around eight, after they had taken their turns changing and freshening up in the bathroom, an officer brought them a breakfast of scones with jam and tea. Just before nine, a different officer came to their cell, unlocked the gate, and slid it open.

"Josephine Bourdeau and Doris Hebb, come with me."

Josie's heart skipped a beat. This was it. She would soon know her fate. She was about to find out where she would be spending the next few years of her life. Would it be Dorchester Penitentiary or the city prison? She couldn't believe this was happening to her. How had she gotten herself in such a mess?

Josie and Doris looked at each other, then went over to the officer.

"What about me, sugar?" said Gladys.

The officer glanced at her sideways. "Not just yet, sweetheart."

The officer motioned for Josie and Doris to come out of the cell. He then slid the gate closed and locked it. "Follow me, ladies."

Josie and Doris followed the officer to the far end of the building into a small vestibule. He gestured to a door on his left. "Through here." Josie opened the door and walked in, followed by Doris and the officer. They were in a high-ceilinged, well-lit room with large four-pane windows on each side of the far wall. In the centre of the far wall was a heavy wooden desk on a raised platform. Behind the desk was a dark, throne-like chair with a high back. Directly in front of the raised desk sat a uniformed police officer at a long table, with his back to the desk. The table was strewn with papers and books, and he was writing in one of the books. In front of the officer, taking up most of the room, were rows of long tables, with chairs facing the front. Only a few of the chairs were occupied. Against the left wall ran two long wooden benches occupied by three people, all men. Josie realized they were in the courtroom.

The officer pointed to the benches on the left. "Have a seat there, ladies. You'll listen for your names to be called, then you'll stand and wait for further instructions. There's three cases before yours."

Josie and Doris sat down on the bench next to the three men. Two of them looked rather scruffy, while the third was dressed in a suit and tie. One of the scruffy men, sitting immediately to Josie's left, seemed to be having a difficult time staying awake. The other scruffy one was just staring straight ahead. The one in the suit and tie, who was at the far end of the bench, peered over at Josie and flashed her a broad smile. Josie smiled back, nervously.

The officer who had brought Josie and Doris to the courtroom was now standing at the front of the room in the right-hand corner, next to a small desk. Without warning, he bellowed to the assembled crowd.

"All rise. Judge Malcolm Williams presiding."

A stocky, balding, middle-aged man with a ruddy complexion and warm, welcoming eyes entered the room from a door in the left front corner. He climbed a short flight of steps and sat down in the throne-like chair behind the raised desk. Josie thought he looked a little like Santa Claus. Perhaps it was a good omen. Once the judge was comfortably in his chair, the officer instructed everyone to be seated. The judge then asked for the first case to be called.

"Everett Stevens," called out the officer. "Approach the bench."

Everyone in the courtroom looked over at the benches where Josie and the others were sitting. No one stood.

"Everett Stevens," called out the officer, this time louder.

Still, no one on the bench moved. Doris leaned over to Josie. "It must be him," she said, pointing to the scruffy one sitting next to Josie, who was snoring loudly. Josie reached over and shook the man's arm, waking him from his stupor. "Are you Everett Stevens?" she asked him.

"Yeah, who wants to know?" he replied groggily.

"The judge," said Josie. "I think you're up."

The scruffy one named Everett Stevens slowly rose to his feet and faced the judge.

"Approach the bench, sir," said the officer.

The man sauntered up to the front of the room, feet dragging, and stood facing the judge. The officer came over and stood next to him. "Your Honour, Mr. Stevens is charged with public intoxication. He was picked up by a patrolman the night before last on Barrington Street at about seven in the evening. He was harassing law-abiding citizens who were out for a leisurely walk. The arresting officer, Constable Clark, deemed that he was intoxicated and brought him to the station. Here is the Constable's full report, your honour."

The officer reached up and handed a folder to the judge. The judge opened the folder and scanned the report. "I see that you're a repeat offender, Mr. Stevens. What seems to be the problem? Not able to handle your liquor?"

"Well, judge," began the accused, "it all began a few years ago when my wife left me. I was heartbroken. I had been good to that women. I gave her everything she ever asked for. And she ran away with another man. My best friend, can you believe it? So, I started drinking. It was the only way to deal with the pain."

The officer standing next to him rolled his eyes. The judge leaned towards the accused and smiled. "I sympathize with your plight, Mr. Stevens, but that's no excuse for public drunkenness, and especially bothering people in the street. You're going to have to find a more legal way to deal with your heartache."

The judge leaned back in his chair and addressed the accused. "I'm fining you seven dollars plus costs of two dollars and fifty cents, Mr. Stevens. And I don't want to see you in my court again. Understood?"

The accused nodded sheepishly.

"Next case," said the judge.

The next person up was the other scruffy one, also for public intoxication. This time the fine was only three dollars plus costs since it was his first offense. Third up was the smiling guy in the suit and tie. He was being charged with smuggling liquor into the province from Maine by boat. He pled not guilty, claiming that while he indeed owned the boat, he was not the captain of the vessel and was not aware that his captain was smuggling liquor in from the States. The judge scheduled his trial for a later date. Once the smuggling case had been dealt with, Josie assumed they were next. She was right. Shortly after, she saw the officer turn to face the audience. "Josephine Bourdeau and Doris Hebb," he blared. "Approach the bench."

Josie's and Doris's eyes met as they both rose and walked slowly to the front of the courtroom, positioning themselves directly in front of the judge. As they approached, Detective Clark, who had interrogated them the previous morning, came to the front and stood next to Josie. As Josie's eyes met the judge's, her knees went weak and she began to shake. She had never been so afraid in all her life.

"Ladies, ladies, ladies. What are you doing in my courtroom?" said the judge.

The detective didn't wait for Josie and Doris to respond. "Your honour, these two ladies have been charged with break and enter, theft, and public drunkenness. They were apprehended by members of the military police after secretly and illegally entering the grounds of Stadacona Naval Base in the company of two ordinary seaman of the Canadian Navy, breaking into the junior officers' mess, and stealing and consuming large quantities of the Navy's liquor supply. The military police then contacted our department, and two of our officers went to Stadacona and arrested the perpetrators, bringing them to the station. The one on my immediate left is Miss Bourdeau and the other is Mrs. Hebb."

"How do they know each other?" the judge asked the detective.

"They work together as waitresses at Gorman's."

The detective then handed the judge a folder. The judge opened it, picked up a sheet of paper, read from the sheet for several seconds, then placed it back in the folder. He looked up at Josie and Doris. "These are serious charges, ladies. Do you care to explain what happened?"

Josie tried to speak, but no words came out. She completely froze. Her mouth went bone dry. Doris jumped in. "Your honour, we were at a dance and we met these two sailors. They wanted to have a few drinks, so we went to the Cavern."

"The Cavern?" said the judge, with a puzzled look.

"It's an illegal bar on Dresden Row," interjected the detective.

The judge frowned. "I see. So there's an illegal bar operating with the full knowledge of the police department. Interesting. Continue, Mrs. Hebb."

"Well, the sailors ran out of money to buy drinks. Then one of them said he knew where we could get some free liquor. So we went with them. We didn't know where we were going at first, until one of them asked the cab driver to drop us off behind the Stad. Well, this sailor knew exactly where to go. He took us to this hole in the fence that was blocked by a truck, so we followed him into the compound. Then he took us to this building and we got in a back door that was unlocked, just like he said it would be. That took us into the officer's mess. So we went behind the bar, and..."

Suddenly, Josie yelled out. "It was all my fault!"

A murmur went through the courtroom. The judge's eyes widened. Even the court officer perked up. Everyone seemed to be waiting on bated breath for Josie's next words.

"I beg your pardon?" said the judge.

"It was all my fault," repeated Josie.

"Do tell, Miss Bourdeau."

"Well, your honour, uh, your worship, um, your majesty..."

The judge smiled. "Your honour is fine."

"You see, your honour, Doris's husband is coming home in a few weeks from overseas. He's in the army, and he was wounded in action, and he's probably going to be crippled for life. He's been declared unfit for duty and they're sending him home for good. So, Doris is going to have to take care of him all the time, and she won't be able to go out to dances and have fun anymore. So I thought…"

Doris nudged Josie with her elbow and whispered to her. "I don't think this is helping, Josie."

"Let her finish," said the judge, who had apparently overheard the whisper.

Josie picked up where she had left off. "So I thought, what if I treat her to one last fling, one more night of dancing, getting a couple of drinks, and just having a good time? She didn't want to do it at first, your honour, because she didn't think it would be right, since her husband was wounded. But I talked her into it. I told her that her husband would want her to enjoy herself."

Doris lowered her head and stifled a laugh. The judge glanced over at Doris. Josie continued her story. "So we went to the dance at the Strand, where we met these two sailors, and they offered to buy us a drink. So we went to the Cavern. And again, your honour, Doris didn't want to go. But I told her that I was going anyway and I didn't want to go alone. You see, I just wanted her to have a good time, your honour."

"Obviously," said the judge, appearing quite amused with the story to that point. "Then what happened?"

"Well, the rest was pretty much like Doris said, your honour. We went to the Cavern, had a couple of drinks, and then the boys told us they didn't have any more money. We weren't too happy with that, of course. But then one of them said he knew where we could get some free liquor. I didn't want the night to end so soon, for Doris's sake, so we went with them. And then, like Doris said, they took us to Stad and we got in through a hole in the fence. And Doris was telling the truth, your honour. The door into the officer's mess wasn't locked. The sailor told us the guy in charge of the bar leaves it unlocked so that the enlisted men can go in and have a drink after hours. So, if the door isn't locked, it's not really break and enter. Right?"

The detective interrupted. "Your honour, the report from the MPs stated that the storage room where they keep the liquor is always locked, so they would have had to break in to that room to get the liquor."

"That's not true," interjected Doris, calmly. "The door to the storage room wasn't locked. I swear."

The judge appeared to be pondering Doris's claim. "Anything else, Miss Bourdeau?"

"No, that's about it, your honour. Like I said, it's my fault this all happened. Don't take it out on Doris. Send me to jail if you have to, but spare her, please. She has to take care of her crippled husband. He needs her home with him."

The judge mumbled something inaudible and leaned back in his chair. He folded his arms across his chest and looked up at the ceiling. Everyone in the courtroom strained their necks to hear his next words. Josie felt a heaviness in her chest, as if a huge weight was pressing down on her. Doris stood stoically. After what seemed like an eternity, the judge spoke.

"Ladies, I have no desire to send either one of you to jail. You obviously made some poor decisions during this escapade, which is one of the unfortunate effects of alcohol. But I rather think the major culprits here are the two sailors, who hatched the whole plan and led its execution. Your mistake was tagging along. My guess is that the sailors will receive no more than a slap on the wrist from their commanding officer, or perhaps a few days in the brig. It would seem unfair, then, for you two ladies to spend time in the city prison while your two accomplices get off relatively scot-free. Besides, prison is no place for two hard-working, upstanding young ladies such as yourselves, which I assume you to be, notwithstanding this brush with the law."

The judge then leaned forward and stared directly at Josie and Doris.

"So, I'm dismissing the charges of break and enter, and theft. However, I feel I need to send some type of message to discourage you from ever returning to this court. Therefore, I'm convicting both of you of the charge of public drunkenness and fining you each twelve dollars plus three dollars in costs. You will pay the bailiff. Ladies, have a good day. Next case."

Josie exhaled. Her eyes welled with tears of joy. She wasn't going to jail. Doris gave her a big hug. "I told you everything would be okay," she said.

Detective Clark escorted them to the bailiff's desk at the rear of the courtroom. As they approached the bailiff, Josie turned to Doris. "We don't have any money on us."

"Maybe they'll take an IOU," said Doris.

When they explained their predicament to the bailiff, he was unsympathetic. They would have to pay the fine or they would be placed back in the lock-up until they could arrange for payment. And the court didn't accept IOUs. (The bailiff had thought that suggestion hilarious.) When Doris asked if a policeman could drive them to her house to get the money, the bailiff became annoyed. "We're not a taxi service, ma'am," he said. They would have to call someone to bring the money to pay the fines. Josie didn't know how much money Doris kept at her place, but for Josie, fifteen dollars was a lot. It was more than half a month's rent. She had a few dollars in a small jewelry box back in her room, but she really lived payday to payday. After Mr. Gorman deducted her rent and meals from her paycheque, she didn't have much left. Just enough to go to a dance once or twice a week, or maybe a movie, or maybe buy a pair of nylons or a tube of lipstick. If she had to borrow fifteen bucks from someone to pay her fine, it was going to take her quite a while to pay it back.

"Who are we going to call?" Doris asked her friend. "I can't think of anyone I know who would have that kind of money lying around."

"What about Mr. Gorman?" said Josie. "He would have the money to lend us. Then he could just take so much out of our pay each week until everything was paid back."

"Are you crazy?!" screeched Doris. "We just told him we're sick and can't come to work, and now we're going to ask him for thirty dollars to get us out of jail because we've just been convicted of public drunkenness?"

Josie felt stupid. "I'm sorry, I don't know what I was thinking."

Doris sighed. "It's okay. Forgive me. I shouldn't have yelled at you."

The two women stood silently in front of the bailiff's desk. Then an idea popped into Josie's head. "I could call Becky."

"Would she have that kind of money?"

"Well, her husband Albert might. He's got a good job with the Navy."

"Then call her."

"She's working today. I'll have to call the restaurant. What if Mr. Gorman answers?"

"Then act like you're sick. Cough or sneeze, or something."

"He's going to wonder where I'm calling from. He knows I don't have a phone in my room."

"I'll call then. I'll tell him I need to talk to Becky about her shift tomorrow."

Josie turned to the bailiff. "Can we make a phone call? It's to call someone to come and pay our fines."

"We'll have to get someone to escort you," said the bailiff. He turned to Detective Clark who had been standing next to Josie and Doris all this time.

"Detective, can you go with them?"

"Yeah, I suppose," said the detective. "Come with me, ladies."

Josie and Doris followed the detective to his office. On the way they met Gladys being escorted down the hall by an officer.

"How'd you gals make out?" said Gladys.

"They dropped the break and enter and theft charges," said Doris. "We just have to pay a fine for public drunkenness."

"Peachy!" said Gladys. "You girls got off easy. Who was the judge?"

"Judge Williams," said Josie.

"Hallelujah!" screeched Gladys. "I get ol' Saint Nick. Today is my lucky day."

When they arrived at the detective's office, the detective gestured to the phone on his desk. "Make your call, ladies."

Doris lifted the receiver and dialed the number of the restaurant. She held the earpiece so that Josie could listen along with her. It rang twice, then someone answered. Sure enough, it was Mr. Gorman.

"Gorman's restaurant. May I help you?"

"Mr. Gorman, it's Doris," she said in a nasal voice.

"Doris! How are you feeling?" said Mr. Gorman.

"Well, not that good. I think I'm down with the flu." She coughed for effect.

"You don't sound very good."

"Can I speak to Becky, Mr. Gorman?"

"Becky? She's waiting on a table right now. Can I get her to call you back?"

"Um, well, I'm really tired. You know, because of my flu. So, I'm going to be taking a nap soon and I don't want to be woken up by her call. I'd like to speak with her right now if I could. It's about her shifts this week."

"Well, okay. Hang on. I'll tell her as soon as she's finished with this customer."

They waited for about two minutes, then Becky answered. "Hello?"

"Hi Becky, it's Doris."

"Hi Doris. How are you feeling?"

"Never mind that. Is Mr. Gorman standing near you?"

"No, he went back into the kitchen."

"Is there anyone else near you that could overhear our conversation?"

"No, I don't think so."

"Good. Now, I don't want you to say a word, I just want you to listen."

"What's going on, Doris?"

"I told you not to say a word. Just listen."

"Okay."

"Now, I'm going to put Josie on the phone and she has something important to tell you."

"Josie? Is she with you?"

"Becky, just listen!"

"Sorry."

"Now, I'm going to give the phone to Josie. I want you to pretend you're talking to me about your shifts this week. Can you do that?"

The other end of the line went silent.

"Becky?"

"I thought you just wanted me to listen."

"Just say yes."

"Yes."

"Okay, here's Josie."

Doris handed the phone to her friend.

"Becky, it's Josie. I just want you to listen carefully and say yes or no when I ask you a question. Okay?"

"Okay."

"Doris and I got ourselves into a little bit of trouble with the law. I'll explain everything later. But right now, we're at the police station and we need thirty dollars to pay our fines to be released. Otherwise, they'll put us in jail. Do you understand?"

Becky didn't respond right away. Josie hoped she hadn't fainted. "Are you still there, Becky?"

"Yes," came the reply at last.

"Do you understand what I'm saying?"

"Yes."

"I was wondering if you could call Albert and ask him to lend us the money to pay the fines. He'd have to bring it here to the station. We'd pay him back, of course. It'd be a loan. Do you think he'd do that?"

Again, there was no immediate response from Becky.

"Becky?"

"Josie…I mean…Doris…I don't know."

"Could you at least ask him? Yes or no?"

"Yeees."

"Okay, good. You tell Albert not to worry, we'll pay him back. We'll wait for him here at the station. And like I said, I'll explain everything to you when I see you. Okay?"

"Yes."

"Oh, and don't say anything about this to Mr. Gorman. We both told him we were sick today. If he asks you about the call, tell him Doris wanted to know if you could work a double shift tomorrow if we were still out sick. Okay?"

"Yes."

"Thanks so much for this, Sis. I love you."

"Yes."

Josie hung up the phone and turned to the detective. "Okay, someone is coming to bring the money for our fines. Can we just wait here till he comes?"

"I'm sorry," said the detective, "you'll have to wait in the lock-up."

"Why can't we just wait here?" asked Doris.

"Ma'am, this is my private office. I've got confidential calls to make on cases. Besides, standard procedure requires us to hold you in the lock up until your fines are paid. Then you'll be released."

"Can we wait out in the lobby?" asked Josie.

"Can't do that either, ma'am. You have to go in the lock-up."

"Are you afraid we'll make a break for it?" said Doris, sarcastically.

Detective Clark was clearly straining to maintain his patience. "You'd be surprised how many people try to skip out without paying their fines. Once they leave here, it's hard to track them down. There's so many transients in this town since the war started, they could be long gone before we come looking for them. So, we had to put this procedure in place. Nothing personal. We treat everyone the same."

Josie and Doris resigned themselves to the fact that they'd have to go back into the lock-up, at least for a little while longer. The detective escorted them back to the cell and locked the bars behind them. They were the only ones in the cell. "What's the name of the person who's going to come and pay your fines?" asked the detective.

"Albert Blanchard," replied Josie.

"We'll let you know as soon as he arrives."

The two women sat down next to each other on one of the wooden benches to wait for Albert. Josie hoped they wouldn't have to wait too long. The cell gave her the creeps. Hopefully, Becky had been able to reach Albert and, hopefully, he had agreed to pay the fines. She just had to keep her fingers crossed. Josie wondered how Becky was going to react when she told her the whole story, and whether Becky would tell their mother and father in her next letter to Agatha. If Agatha found out, the whole world would know.

"Well, friend," said Doris, "you promised me a night I'd never forget. You certainly kept your promise. It was a heckuva night." They both laughed. It was the first time Josie had laughed all day.

At about twelve thirty, Albert appeared at their cell door with an officer. Josie jumped up when she saw him.

"Miss Bourdeau, Mrs. Hebb," said the officer, unlocking the bars, "this gentleman has paid your fines. You are free to go."

Josie could tell right away that Albert was not happy. He glared sternly at her. "Albert, thank you so much for this," she said. "I promise we'll pay you back as soon as we can."

"I'm only doing this because Becky begged me to," he replied sharply. "It's against my better judgement."

Josie decided it would be best not to say another word. There was no sense stirring the pot. She and Doris followed Albert out of the station and into a waiting cab. Josie asked the driver to drop her off just up Morris Street from Gorman's. She'd have to sneak in up the back stairs so Mr. Gorman wouldn't see her enter the building. Doris asked to be dropped off at her place. As they left the police station parking lot, Albert went on a rant about how he had been "terribly inconvenienced" by the whole situation. About how he had left work before his lunch break to go to the bank to get the money, then taken a cab to the station, then all the "rigmarole" involved in paying the fines. He complained that he had missed his entire lunch break and insisted that Josie and Doris would repay not only the amount of their fines but the cost of the taxi fares as well. Josie and Doris just kept quiet. Eventually, he ran out of steam.

Josie sat in the cab, staring out the window and feeling enormously relieved. She wasn't going to prison. She wasn't going to lose her job. She wasn't going to end up on the street. Thanks to the kind judge who looked like Santa Claus. But then a depressing thought struck her. With Doris's husband soon returning from the war and Becky now married, who would she chum around with? Who would she go to dances with, or to the movies, or just window shopping? She really had no other friends.

She suddenly felt very alone.

Chapter 19

Josie managed to get to her room through the back entrance without being spotted. She got undressed, put on her nightgown, and hopped into bed, just in case Mr. Gorman sent someone to check on how she was feeling. Once in bed, she fell asleep almost immediately, exhausted from her ordeal.

As she slept, she dreamt she was back in the lock-up at the police station. Only this time, Doris wasn't with her. Instead, the cell was filled with a bizarre collection of odd-looking characters, some she recognized, some she didn't. The prostitute she had met in the cell, Gladys, was there, but her lips were three times their normal size, and there was bright red lipstick smeared all over her face. A huge woman, with mounds of flesh spewing out from her clothes, sat on the bench against the wall, eating a chocolate pie with her hands, chocolate smeared all over her face, the bench sagging under her enormous bulk. A bent-over, crippled, bedraggled old hag appeared to be mopping the floor, but she had neither a mop nor a pail. She looked up at Josie. "Don't just stand there," she said. "Fetch that other mop over there and give me a hand." But there was no other mop to be seen. Josie's sister Beatrice was also there, holding an infant in each arm, her belly bulging with another, with four small children whom Josie did not recognize, pulling at her dress, crying "Mommy, Mommy, Mommy" over and over. Josie tried to speak with her, but she didn't seem to notice that Josie was there. She just stared straight ahead, with empty, hollow eyes. But the eeriest creature in the room sat in an enormous wingback chair in the far corner, impeccably dressed, snow-white hair perfectly coiffed, but with grotesque, festering boils on her nose and forehead. She glared intently and menacingly at Josie, her piercing eyes boring into Josie's very soul. Josie knew instantly who she was. Miss Bennett.

As the dream moved from one strange scene to another, Josie found herself in the police court again, standing in front of the judge. But it was a different judge this time. He looked more like the devil than Santa Claus, with greased-back black hair, elf-like pointy ears, and a sinister sneer. He demanded to know what Josie was doing in his courtroom. When she tried to answer, he cut her off, roaring in a booming voice, "Guilty as charged! Send her to prison for twenty years!" Three faceless police officers dragged her out of the courtroom, as shackles suddenly clamped onto her feet. A priest appeared at her side, praying in Latin, making the sign of the cross on her forehead. The next thing she knew she was in a dark, dank cell, alone, dressed in striped prison clothes. But the clothes were torn and full of holes, and she felt cold. A rat scurried across the floor. Terrified, she jumped up on the bed. But the bed turned into a slab of concrete, with no mattress, and a large wooden block where the pillow had been. As she sat in horror, she could hear tapping on the bars in a small window above her. Faint at first, then louder and louder. She looked up. She saw nothing. But someone was calling her name. "Jo-sie, Jo-sie, Jo-sie." The tapping and the voice grew louder and louder, as she gradually emerged from her subconscious state. The dream was ending. She was waking up. Someone was knocking on her door. Groggy and still half asleep, she sat up on the side of her bed. "Who is it?" she mumbled.

"It's Becky," came the voice.

Josie dragged herself to her feet and opened the door. Becky stomped in. Without any formalities, her younger sister got straight to the point. "Okay, you have some explaining to do."

Josie sat down on the side of her bed and invited Becky to sit down next to her. She then proceeded to tell Becky everything that had happened, from the time Doris broke the news about her husband coming home to the moment they were released from the police station. She confessed everything—about breaking into Stad, about getting arrested, about appearing before the judge. Everything. Every sordid detail.

When Josie was finished, Becky started into her lecture. "You have to stop chumming around with Doris," she said, waving her finger like she was scolding a child. "Every time you're with Doris, you get into trouble. She's a bad influence on you."

"It wasn't Doris's fault," said Josie. "The whole night was my idea. I wanted to treat her to one last fling before her husband returned from overseas."

"Well, I hope it's your last fling too."

"What do you mean?"

"Josie, don't you think it's time for you to settle down, meet a nice guy like I did, instead of chasing sailors and getting drunk and ending up in jail? Next time, you might not be so lucky to find a kind hearted judge. Next time they might throw the book at you and send you to prison. How would you feel then?"

"Wow. Look who's so mature. My little sister has turned into my mother."

"Well, aren't I right?"

Josie didn't answer.

"You know, it wouldn't hurt you to start looking for a nice guy to marry," Becky continued. "You're not getting any younger."

"So you think I'm an old maid?"

"I didn't say that."

"Well, that's what it sounds like."

"I'm just saying you need to start looking to settle down."

"You don't go looking for love, Becky. It finds you."

"I'm not talking about love. I'm talking about getting married."

Josie was taken aback. She was surprised at what she had just heard. "So, do you love Albert?"

Becky hesitated for just a split second. "I'm very fond of him. He's a very nice man. He's good to me, we get along very well, I feel very safe and secure when I'm with him."

"You didn't answer my question. Do you love him?"

"I'm sure I will in time."

"In time?"

"Mom says you don't 'fall' in love. That only happens in the movies. Love develops and grows over time. She told me she didn't really love Dad when they first got married. She hardly knew him. But they grew to love each other very much."

"When did she tell you that?"

"When I told her that Albert had asked me to marry him. I told her I didn't know if I loved him. She said it didn't matter. Love would come later."

"Well, it matters to me. I want to be sure I love someone *before* I marry them. What would happen if I married someone and then *didn't* fall in love with them? I'd be miserable for the rest of my life. Stuck in a loveless marriage with five or six kids. No, I want to marry for love. I want to be swept off my feet."

"You were swept off your feet once, remember? That English sailor with the blue eyes. How did that turn out?"

It was as if Becky had taken a knife and stabbed her in the chest. She hadn't thought about Peter for some time. Now, a flood of conflicting emotions raced through her—anger, longing, hurt, tenderness, regret, hope, despair. She was overwhelmed. And speechless.

Seemingly oblivious to the effect of her comment, Becky continued her lecture. "Anyway, what you need is to meet some nice guys. Local guys, not sailors who are here today and gone tomorrow. The war will be over one day and all those sailors will be going back home, probably to a girlfriend or maybe even a wife. The local guys will still be here."

Josie didn't respond. She was still thinking about Peter.

"So, what do you think? Josie? Josie?"

Josie snapped out of her trance. "What?"

"What do you think?"

"About what?"

"About what I said."

"What did you say?"

"About meeting local guys instead of chasing sailors. God, Josie. Haven't you been listening to me?"

Josie thought about what Becky had said. Although she hated to admit it, her sister was probably right. There wasn't much of a future dating sailors. It would only end in disappointment—and pain. A sense of resignation came over her. Maybe she should start going out with local guys. Boring local guys. Guys like Albert. Guys who couldn't get into the Navy because they had fallen arches, or asthma, or some kind of deformity. Then their kids would be born with the same deformity. A club foot, or six fingers, or....

She snapped herself out of her daydream. "Maybe you're right, Becky. Maybe I should meet some local guys. But I don't know any local guys. All you ever see in this town is sailors. And most of the local guys are sailors too. At least, the best looking ones."

"What about Albert?"

Josie was about to say something nasty but caught herself.

"Well, except Albert, of course."

"You know," said Becky, "Albert has a friend that works in the same office as him. He could invite his friend over to our place for dinner Saturday night, and I could invite you, as my sister."

"I *am* your sister."

"You know what I mean. Anyway, not an official date, just a chance to meet each other. If you like him, great. You guys can take it from there. If you don't, no harm done. We just eat dinner. What do you think?"

Josie sighed. She wasn't going to be able to back out of this one. "What's his name?"

"Hector."

"Hector what?"

"Hector MacIsaac."

Hector MacIsaac. It doesn't sound like the name of a dashing man, she thought. "Oh, I don't know, Becky."

"C'mon, at least give it a try."

Josie rolled her eyes. She imagined an evening with Albert and his friend Hector, and Becky's so-so cooking. A far cry from the exhilarating, adventurous, dangerous evening she had just spent with Doris. But maybe a welcome change. Maybe it really was time for her to settle down a little. Stay out of trouble. And maybe she'd like Hector. Maybe he was very nice. And maybe, just maybe, he would be so handsome and debonair that he would sweep her off her feet.

But she doubted it.

"Alright, I'll come to your place for dinner Saturday night."

Becky screeched with delight. "Wonderful. I'll ask Albert to speak with Hector, then I'll let you know."

"Do you think Albert's going to want his friend to meet me after what happened?"

"You let me handle Albert."

Josie was beginning to realize that Becky already could handle Albert. *Otherwise,* she thought, *I'd still be in jail.*

Chapter 20

Becky served ham and scalloped potatoes for dinner, with mashed turnips and carrots, then bread pudding for dessert. Josie felt the ham was a little overcooked—not juicy like their mother's—but edible. Not bad for a new bride. Albert evidently liked it, taking a second helping. Josie wondered if perhaps his mother wasn't much of a cook.

Hector seemed nervous throughout the meal, picking at his food and constantly sipping on his tea, so much so that Becky had to refill his cup three times. On the third refill, Becky joked that it was a good thing Albert worked for the Navy and had extra tea coupons.

At Becky's suggestion, Josie had come early so she would be there when Hector arrived. Becky thought it would make the event seem less contrived, that Hector would think Josie was always at Becky's for dinner and not just there to meet him.

It was clear to Josie, though, that Hector knew exactly what was going on. He knew why Josie was there and he knew why he was there. She could tell by the way he kept staring at her. No doubt Albert had clued him in, notwithstanding Becky's attempts to make their meeting look like a coincidence. But Josie wondered how much Albert had actually told him. Had he tried to scare Hector off by telling him about Josie's drinking and partying, and her brush with the law? If he did, it apparently hadn't worked. He'd shown up anyway. Maybe he liked bad girls.

Despite his nervousness, though, Hector did attempt a few subtle "advances" toward Josie. At one point he commented that he liked her hair. Josie tried to find something complimentary to say about him in return, but there was nothing that really appealed to her, except maybe his tie. *When a man says he likes your hair,* she thought, *you don't say "I like your tie."* So she simply replied with a "thank you."

It was not so much that she found him bad-looking. It was just that he was rather plain. No distinguishing, alluring characteristics. Nothing that would catch a woman's eye. He wore a neatly trimmed pencil mustache that, at one point in the evening, he said was his Clark Gable look. But he was no Clark Gable. Not even close. The only thing about his appearance that stood out were his ears. They were unusually small—like there had been a mix up at birth and God had given him the ears of a mouse instead of the ears of a man.

Actually, he reminded her a lot of Albert. Roughly the same height, the same slender build, the same bland features. Except Albert had larger ears. But other than that, they could have passed for brothers.

Josie managed to get through the entire evening without making any negative comments about either Albert's or Hector's appearance. But that was mostly because she said very little at all. At Becky's constant urging, Hector talked a lot about himself. He talked about how he had enlisted in the Navy in 1940 but had failed his medical because they discovered he had an irregular heartbeat. So they gave him a desk job. That's where he had met Albert. Then he talked a lot about the job—how "tricky" it was, how he had to get every detail right or he could get in serious trouble with the Navy brass. Josie couldn't figure out exactly what he did, although it apparently had a lot to do with typing letters.

Hector also talked a lot about his family. He was from the Truro area. Both his parents were still living. His father managed a hardware store. He had four siblings; one older brother in the

Navy, one older sister who was married, and two younger sisters who were single and still living at home.

Albert and Hector also talked about the progress of the war, and how the tide seemed to be finally turning against the Germans. They talked about the Russian front and the Italian campaign, about the situations in Japan and Africa, about this battle and that battle, about this victory and that victory. Josie couldn't really follow everything they were saying and had never heard of many of the places they mentioned, but it sounded like things were going well for the Allies, and that the war might soon come to an end. One could only hope.

Albert and Hector also had a spirited discussion about rumours that a German spy had infiltrated their office. They wondered if it was true, and speculated on who it could be, what he was looking for, and what would happen to him if he were caught. Josie perked right up when she heard the word "spy." It sounded exciting. Maybe Albert's and Hector's jobs were more interesting than she had first thought. In fact, maybe one of *them* was the spy. When she jokingly suggested that possibility during the conversation, no one considered it the least bit funny. Especially Albert.

With the hour getting late, Hector said goodnight and headed home on foot. At Becky's insistence, Josie had agreed to stay over for the night. They'd sleep together like they used to do when they were kids, and talk girl talk until they fell asleep. Albert would sleep on the couch for one night. Josie could tell by Albert's reaction that Becky had not run her plan by him first.

All in all, though, it hadn't been an entirely unpleasant evening for Josie. The meal was fine, Hector seemed nice enough, and Albert hadn't been too nasty to her. And she always enjoyed spending time with her younger sister. Hector appeared to have enjoyed himself as well. As he was leaving, he thanked Albert and Becky repeatedly for inviting him and complimented Becky on an "excellent" meal. He told Josie how much he had enjoyed meeting her and said he hoped he would see her again soon. Josie just smiled.

As it would turn out, it wouldn't be too long before Hector's wish would come true. On the Wednesday following Saturday night's dinner, Becky informed Josie that she and Albert were going out for a drive in the country on the weekend, and they invited Josie to join them. Apparently, Albert's boss was going to be in Ottawa on Navy business for a few days and had offered Albert his car, with a full tank of gas, no less—which was quite a generous offer because gas was rationed and sometimes hard to come by.

Josie was reluctant at first. She loved doing things with Becky, but she wondered how Albert would feel about spending the whole day together. But she didn't want to say no to her sister, and since she didn't have anything else planned, she accepted the invitation.

What Josie didn't know at the time was that Becky was playing matchmaker again. She had told Albert to invite Hector as well. So, when Becky and Albert rolled up to Gorman's Saturday morning in a baby blue Buick to pick her up, Josie was more than a little surprised to see Hector sitting in the back seat, with a huge grin on his face. For a split second, she thought about backing out. But she was stuck. Becky's devious scheme had succeeded. She slid in the back next to her beaming admirer.

Albert had decided they would go to the Annapolis Valley. One of his co-workers had told him about the spectacular views from a look-off at Cape Blomidon, with a picnic area nearby, and about the abundance of roadside markets where you could buy local fruits and vegetables. None of them had even been to the Valley before, so everyone was anxious to see what it was like.

It was a beautiful summer day; sunny, warmer than Halifax, with only a slight westerly breeze. Once they were out of the city, they passed through mostly heavily wooded countryside, dotted by the occasional small farm or lumber yard. As they travelled, they talked mostly about the scenery, Hector often commenting on the types of trees they were seeing. The only other significant topic of conversation was marriage. It was a rather one-sided conversation, though, with Becky doing almost all the talking. She talked about how she loved being married, and all the advantages of married life over the single life. Josie knew what she was getting at but didn't take the bait. She even changed the subject once by asking Hector about a certain tree they passed on the side of the road.

About an hour or so into the trip, they arrived at the small town of Windsor. Past Windsor, the landscape changed dramatically, with stunning vistas of rolling hills, large swaths of cultivated farmland, and numerous orchards. About twenty minutes out of Windsor, as they came over a crest in the road, there in the far distance was a magnificent cliff of red soil, jutting out into a huge body of bright blue water.

"That must be Cape Blomidon," said Albert excitedly. "We're almost there."

It took them another forty-five minutes to reach their destination They passed through the small towns of Wolfville, Port Williams, and Canning, before Albert spotted the sign for "Blomidon Look-off." A few yards further, he pulled off the road into a small gravel parking lot. Although the lot was quite full, he managed to find a spot, and parked the Buick. As they exited the car and made their way to the lookoff railing, the view opened up before them—a breathtaking panorama of miles and miles of checkerboard farmland, framed by luscious maples and oaks, and bordered in the distance by the waters of the bay. They were so high up that Josie wondered if they could see Halifax.

As they all leaned against a wooden barrier, taking in the scene before them, Hector reached over and held Josie's hand. Instinctively, she pulled it away. He didn't try it again. After about fifteen minutes at the look-off, they got back in the car and drove farther up the road to a picnic area, where the road ended. Becky had packed a picnic basket, but Albert suggested doing a little exploring before they ate, so they left the food in the car and headed out. A short time later, they found a path leading through the woods to a cliff overlooking a broad tidal mud flat that extended far out into the bay. They could see several people walking barefoot on the flat with their shoes in their hands.

"Let's do *that!*" said Josie.

Albert found a pathway of stone steps descending the cliff, and waved the group over. The grade was so steep and the footing so tricky that the men had to help the women down, Albert holding on to Becky and Hector to Josie. Once at the bottom, they took off their shoes and set out, carrying their shoes with them. The first part of the flat was relatively dry, but it became muddier the farther they went. The mud was cool and invigorating, as it oozed between Josie's toes and over her feet. She loved it.

As they trudged along, Albert held on to Becky, who seemed to be having difficulty with her footing. Josie, however, was having no such problem and was soon far ahead of the others, with Hector struggling to keep up with her. Before too long, Josie had opened up such a gap that when she turned around, she could barely see Becky and Albert. She kept going, and soon could see the waters of the bay not far ahead of her. She decided she was going to walk as far out as she could, right to the end of the flats where the bay began. A few hundred feet farther, however, she came to an inlet of water that had not been previously visible. On the other side of the inlet was more mud flat. The inlet was no more than ten feet wide, she figured, but ran for quite a distance to her right. Determined to get to the other side, and calculating that it would take a considerable amount of time to walk around the inlet at its far end, she decided to wade across. Although there was a slight ripple in the water, it didn't appear to be very deep and she assumed it wouldn't be difficult to navigate. So she lifted her dress slightly and gingerly treaded in. The first few steps were fine, and the water was warm, so she kept going. Then, all of a sudden, the ground disappeared beneath her and she plunged feet-first into the water, sinking completely in over her head. She thrashed her arms and legs in the murky water, trying desperately to grab something to hold on to but instead felt herself being pulled deeper. She fought frantically to reach the safety of the surface, flailing and thrashing wildly, but to no avail. Panic gripped her. She didn't know how to swim. She didn't know what to do to save herself. The more she struggled, the less it helped. She felt herself tiring, her arms and legs growing heavier and heavier, the water thick, like syrup, smothering her. She sensed herself falling, farther and farther down, into the darkness. She was confused, unable to think clearly. She seemed to be drifting aimlessly. A calmness came over her. A stillness. Then, nothingness.

The next thing she knew, she was lying in the mud, dripping wet, coughing violently, and spitting up brown liquid. Her eyes stung from the salt water and her chest ached. Someone was slapping her back. She looked up. It was Hector. "Are you alright?" he asked.

She sat up, remembering where she was and what had just happened. "I thought I was going to die," she managed to say between coughs.

"You almost did."

Gradually, the coughing and the spitting eased, and Josie began to regain consciousness of her surroundings. Hector took off his shirt and wiped the mud from Josie's eyes and face. After a few minutes, he helped her to her feet and they made their way back to the cliff. It was slow going. Josie was badly shaken and still a little woozy, so Hector held her arm and helped her along. As they neared the cliff, they could see Becky and Albert sitting on a large rock. Becky waved to them, unaware of Josie's brush with death. But as Josie and Hector drew closer, she rushed to them. "What happened to you? You're soaking wet. And your hair is full of mud."

"She fell into the water," said Hector.

"Oh my God, are you okay?"

"She's okay now," said Hector.

177

"Josie, you have to be more careful. You know you don't know how to swim."

"I'm okay," she assured her sister.

Becky tried to clean the mud from Josie's hair, but it was so thickly matted that the effort was pointless.

Josie then realized she didn't have her shoes with her. "Did you see my shoes, Hector?'

"No," he said. "You must have lost them in the water."

Hector took Josie by the arm and the four of them trekked slowly and carefully back up the stone steps to the picnic area. Becky tried to draw more details from Josie about what had happened, but Josie said very little, except to continually reassure Becky that she was fine. When Becky pressed Hector, he downplayed the incident as well, particularly his role. Albert suggested that under the circumstances, they could skip the picnic, head back to the city now, and eat their lunch in the car on the way back.

Josie insisted that wasn't necessary. "No, I don't want to spoil your picnic," she said. "I want you to enjoy the rest of your day as you had planned."

"Are you sure?" said Becky. "You had quite a scare."

"It was nothing. It's over with now," said Josie. "Besides, the sun is drying my clothes and my hair, and I'll clean myself up better when I get home."

Reassured by Josie, they found a picnic table and enjoyed their lunch. When they had finished eating, they packed up and headed out. On their way back, they did a little sightseeing and stopped at a couple of roadside markets. Despite the urging of both Becky and Hector, Josie stayed in the car while the others shopped. At Becky's request, they also stopped at a shoe store in Wolfville to buy an inexpensive pair of sandals for Josie to wear home, which Albert paid for. Josie offered to repay him on her next payday, but Becky would not hear of it.

By the time they got back to Halifax, it was almost five thirty. It had been a long and tiring day, and everyone just wanted to get home. The first stop was Gorman's, to drop off Josie. As Albert brought the car to a halt in front of the restaurant, Hector jumped out and went around to the other side to open the door for Josie. After she had thanked Becky and Albert, she got out of the car and stood on the sidewalk. Hector closed the car door. He walked over to Josie, who had been waiting for him.

"You saved my life," said Josie. "I don't know how to thank you."

"You don't have to. I'm just glad you're okay. I'd have been devastated if anything had happened to you."

Josie smiled, leaned over, and kissed him on the cheek. She turned and went around the side of the building and up the back steps to her room without looking back. As she plopped herself down on her bed, she thought about what had happened. It had been an almost disastrous day for her.

But a good day for Hector.

Chapter 21

Monday at work, Becky cornered Josie during their morning break. "So, things are going well between you and Hector, I see."

"What do you mean?" said Josie.

"I saw you kiss him when we dropped you off Saturday."

"It was just a peck on the cheek, Becky. I was thanking him for helping me when I fell in the water."

"So, do you like him?"

"He seems like a nice fellow."

"You know what I mean. Do you like him as a boyfriend?"

"Becky! I just met the man a week ago. Don't get carried away."

"You had just known that English sailor for one day and you were getting pretty carried away then."

Josie's mood turned somber. She looked down at the floor. "That was different."

Becky took another tack. "I know he likes *you*."

Josie's mind was wandering. "Who?"

"Hector. Who else did you think we were talking about?"

"What about him?"

"He likes you."

"How do you know that?"

"He told Albert. He thinks you're very pretty. Besides, it was written all over his face, the way he looks at you."

Josie had noticed as well. It was hard to miss. But she wasn't going to admit it to Becky and give her any more ammunition for her matchmaking. "I hadn't noticed."

"Then you must be blind."

"Becky, I don't mind going to dinner at your place or taking a drive in the country, but I don't know if I want a boyfriend right now."

"Josie, we talked about this before. You agreed you had to settle down a little. You said you wanted to meet some nice guys instead of sailors all the time. So, Hector's a nice guy. Give him a chance."

Josie's brain was telling her that Becky was right, but her heart was resisting.

Becky kept up the pressure. "I know he wants to ask you out on a real date."

"How do you know that?"

"He told Albert. And he asked Albert to ask me to find out if you would say yes."

"Is that what this is all about?"

"Maybe. C'mon, what will it hurt? Go out with him, see what happens. Maybe you'll have a good time. If you don't, we can look for someone else."

"We?"

"Yeah, we."

Josie was torn. She couldn't really see herself "with" Hector, but she also realized she couldn't keep going the way she was going. And Becky was making a strong case. What did she have to lose? Maybe Hector would surprise her. And if not, she'd move on.

"Alright, I'll go out with him. But no promises beyond that."

"Great. I'll tell Albert tonight. Then you wait to hear from Hector. I'm sure he won't wait too long."

Becky turned out to be absolutely right. The very next day, Hector showed up at the restaurant shortly after noon and sat down at a table. Josie was serving another customer but had noticed him when he walked in. Their eyes had met and he had smiled at her before taking his seat. Josie was a little annoyed that he was disturbing her while she was working, but she was stuck. She had told Becky she would go out with him. She was half hoping he had changed his mind and wasn't going to ask her. Obviously not. When she finished with her customer, she went over to Hector's table.

"Hi," he said, looking up at her.

"Hi," she answered.

"Uh, how are you?" he asked.

"Fine," she replied. She could tell he was nervous, but she wasn't going to make this easy for him. It was up to him to ask her out, not the other way around. But he appeared to be having difficulty getting the words out. After an awkward silence, she eased the pressure on him. "Are you ordering lunch?"

Hector fumbled with the menu. "Oh, yeah, right. Umm, let's see. Umm. I'll have the…uh…the chicken noodle soup and… uh…a toasted western."

Josie decided to play it all the way. "To drink?"

"Umm…just coffee."

"Be right up."

Josie walked away smiling to herself. She was enjoying this, making him squirm. If he wanted her to go out with him, he was going to have to at least get up the nerve to ask. A girl had a right to expect at least that. She walked over to the server's station, poured a cup of coffee, and brought it back to him.

"There you go," she said. "Your soup and sandwich should be ready soon."

"Oh, thank you very much."

Josie walked away again, without lingering. When his soup and sandwich were ready, she brought them over and placed them on the table in front of him. "Enjoy," she said, then turned away quickly, not giving him an opportunity to reply. While Hector ate his lunch, Josie served other customers but kept an eye on him. When he had finished his meal, she went over. "How was everything?" she asked.

"Very nice, thank you," he said.

"Did you save any room for dessert? We don't have any pies today, but we have some nice bread pudding."

"No, no, thank you. I try to eat light at lunch."

"Anything else, then?"

"No, no. Just the bill."

Josie flipped open her order pad, totalled up Hector's bill, tore the sheet off the pad, and placed it on the table. "Okay, Hector. You have a nice day." She turned and started to walk away. She had taken no more than a couple of steps when Hector called out to her.

"Josie?"

She stopped, smiled with her back to him, then nonchalantly turned to face him, pretending to look puzzled. "Yes, Hector? Something wrong with the bill?"

"No, no. It's not that. Can I speak with you for a second?"

"Well, I'm kind of busy."

"It'll just take a minute."

Josie walked over, stood next to him, and waited for him to say something. He was clearly trying to build up his courage.

"Uh, were you speaking with Becky?"

"I speak with Becky all the time."

"No, but I mean about us."

"Us?" *Now I'm just being mean*, she said to herself.

"Yes, about us going on a date together. A real date, I mean."

"Well, she did say that maybe you were going to ask me out."

"Oh, good. Then it's settled."

"What's settled?"

"About our date."

"But you didn't ask me."

"Well, I assumed…"

"Don't assume. You have to ask me yourself. Not through Becky, or Albert. They can't answer for me."

Hector swallowed hard, while Josie waited for the question. Finally, it came. "Josie, will you go out on a date with me?"

Josie looked up at the ceiling as if debating how to answer. After a few seconds, she decided she had made him suffer long enough. "Yes, Hector, I'll go out on a date with you."

Hector let out a huge sigh of relief. He thanked her, then outlined his plans for their date. They would go see a movie at the Capitol Theatre Saturday night. *Suspicion* was playing, starring Cary Grant and Joan Fontaine, and Cary Grant was Hector's favourite actor. They would get a milkshake or a malt at the Green Lantern after the movie. Hector would pick her up at her place, they'd walk up to the Capitol, then he'd walk her home after the date. Josie said that was fine with her. He thanked her again, then left the restaurant, beaming.

On Saturday night, Hector picked up Josie at about twenty past six. They walked the short distance to the Capitol on Barrington and arrived in plenty of time to get good seats, as the movie wasn't starting until seven. Hector bought a box of popcorn and a soda for them to share. After the movie, they went to the Green Lantern, as Hector had promised. Josie had a strawberry milkshake and Hector a fudge sundae. After they had finished their treats, Hector walked Josie home. When they arrived at the bottom of the back stairs at Gorman's, Josie thanked Hector and told him she had enjoyed the evening. When he leaned in to try to kiss her on the lips, she turned her head slightly and the kiss landed on her cheek. He then said goodnight, and left.

As it would turn out, the movie night at the Capitol would be the first of many dates Josie and Hector would have over the next several months. No doubt emboldened by his initial success, he asked Josie out again the very next week. She turned him down, making some feeble excuse, but he persisted and asked her out again. The second time, she relented. In the weeks that followed, he would continue to ask her out, and she would continue to offer weak resistance, then cave. After a month or so, she abandoned any pretense that she might rebuff him, and their dates became an automatic weekly occurrence. Becky didn't help matters, either. At every opportunity, she encouraged Hector in his pursuit, often arranging double dates with her and Albert and constantly lauding Hector's virtues. Under the double-barrelled onslaught, Josie was powerless to resist.

As the number of dates increased, Hector also became bolder in his romantic advances, especially, of course, when they were alone, which was usually in Josie's room. What started out as pecks on the cheek turned to soft kisses on the lips, then heavy necking. Eventually, Josie allowed Hector to fondle her breasts under her bra, but nothing below the waist. At one point, Hector caught Josie glancing at an obvious bulge in his pants during a heavy petting session, took her hand, and placed it on the bulging area. Josie pulled her hand away. That time. Before long, she wasn't pulling it away anymore, and she would keep rubbing (only on the outside, she was adamant about that) until he'd jump up and run to the bathroom.

So, by late autumn, for all intents and purposes, Josie and Hector were going steady. Josie didn't use the term and often admonished Hector when *he* tried to use it, but in reality, they were steadies, seeing each other every weekend and not dating anyone else.

One night, though, her loyalty to her now steady beau would be tested. And the test would come from an unexpected source. An old friend.

Chapter 22

Josie glanced at the clock behind the counter. She still had five minutes. Time to finish her coffee but not enough time for another cigarette. Out of the corner of her eye she caught a glimpse of someone approaching.

"This seat taken?" said a deep but pleasant male voice.

Josie looked to her left. Standing there was a tall, good-looking young man wearing an American Navy uniform. She smiled coyly. "Help yourself."

The young man sat down on the stool next to her and gestured to a waitress passing by behind the counter. "Coffee please. Black." He then turned to Josie. "You work here?"

"Yeah. On my break. The waitress uniform give it away?"

The young sailor chuckled. "You got me there. I was just trying to start a conversation."

"And that's the best you've got?" Her comeback seemed to deflate him a little. She felt a pang of sympathy. "I'm just teasing you," she laughed, poking him on the arm. He lowered his head and laughed with her. She then turned to face him. "I'm Josie."

"Tom," he replied. "I suppose you get sailors trying to talk to you all the time, a pretty girl like you."

"Enough. Especially American sailors."

"Really? Why especially American sailors?"

"You guys are bold."

"Bold? Is that a good thing or a bad thing?"

"Well, that depends on the guy. If he's too conceited, it's a bad thing, and a lot of you guys are conceited."

"Conceited? What do you mean?" Tom seemed more curious than offended.

"Well, you know, you Americans always have more money than the Canadian boys or the Brits, and you like to show it off."

"And that's bad," said Tom, more as a statement of agreement than as a question.

Josie flashed a mischievous smile. "Yeah, except if you want to buy us something nice."

"Something nice?"

"Yeah, like a pair of nylons or some lipstick."

"You're quite the girl," laughed Tom, shaking his head.

Josie laughed as well, then glanced up at the clock. Her break was over. It was time to get back to work. She turned to the handsome American. "Nice talking with you, Tom."

As she walked over to the counter to drop off her coffee cup, Doris snatched her by the arm. "You were flirting with that guy, weren't you?"

"No I wasn't! We were just talking."

"No, that was flirting. And you, with a steady boyfriend."

"We're not going steady. We just go out on dates once in a while."

"So, you're available then?"

"What do you mean?"

"If I said I was going to a party Saturday night, and I wanted someone to go with me, you'd be available?"

The question caught Josie by surprise. "What about your husband? I thought you weren't going to parties anymore. I thought you stayed home with him every night."

"I'm getting tired of staying home with him every night. I haven't been anywhere in months. I'm going crazy. I need to get out. Have some fun. What do you say? You and me."

"You remember the last time you and I went out together to have some fun. We almost ended up in Dorchester."

"This will be different. No illegal stuff. No break and entering. This is a legitimate party. Only Navy officers. On board a ship. It'll be a fancy affair."

"How did you find out about this?"

"One of the officers invited me. He was here at the restaurant a couple of days ago. Said I could invite one of my girlfriends if I wanted to."

"Officers? I've never been to a party with officers before."

"Well, here's your chance."

"Saturday night?"

"Yup."

"What will I tell Hector? We usually get together Saturday nights. I can't tell him I'm going to an officers' party."

"Tell him you have to visit a sick friend. It's not a lie. I am sick. Sick of staying home on Saturday night."

It was a very tempting offer. Josie had always wanted to go to a big fancy party. No doubt they'd have a top local band and lots to eat and drink. The best of everything, probably. "What'll I wear?" she asked her friend.

"The best dress you own."

The best dress she owned wouldn't be good enough. She'd have to go out and buy a new one. She hadn't bought any new clothes in a long time, so this would be a good excuse to add to her wardrobe.

She picked the dress up the following day after work. Saturday afternoon she called Hector and told him they couldn't get together that night as usual because she had to visit a sick friend. She felt a little guilty lying to him, but it wasn't like they were engaged. If she wanted to go to a party, she could go to a party. She wasn't tied down to anyone. She could make her own decisions, and she had decided to go to this party. And she had decided not to tell him.

Doris had arranged for a cab to drive them to the pier where the ship was moored. They were leaving from Doris's, so Josie walked over to her place. The cab showed up around a quarter to ten. When they arrived at the ship, two officers in full dress uniform were standing at the bottom of the gangway, greeting guests. Josie and Doris got out of the cab and walked over to the officers. "Lieutenant Simpson's guests," said Doris.

The officer smiled, nodded, and waved them through. Once they reached the deck, there were several regular sailors directing the guests to a formal dining room where the party was being held.

When they entered the room, Josie's mouth opened wide. She had never seen anything like it before. Even the dining room at the Nova Scotian wasn't as elaborate as this—high, decorated ceilings with rows of bright lights; imposing ribbed columns supporting huge beams on both sides of the room; heavy, ornately sculpted wood paneling; plush carpet covering the floor, except for a hardwood area at one end; round tables draped with white linen tablecloths; long side tables brimming with food of all manner and description; and sparkling glass, silver, and gold everywhere.

Groups of officers in their dress whites were standing by the bar with drinks in their hands, or just milling about, as the room filled with guests. Most of the new arrivals were women, young women, many of whom looked to be even younger than Josie and Doris. A few seemed to be just teenagers. As the women arrived, most of them were taking a seat at a table, so Josie and Doris followed suit. They selected an unoccupied table on the left side of the room and sat next to each other with their backs to the wall, so that they were facing the middle of the room. The tables had been positioned around the perimeter of the room, leaving a large, open, carpeted expanse in the middle. At the far end was a small, one-step-up stage. In front of the stage was a hardwood floor dance area. A four-piece band was on the stage playing light music.

As Josie and Doris watched the room fill up, it soon became apparent what the drill was. The girls would wait until they were approached by an officer, who would then bring them over to the bar for a drink. They would then either proceed to the centre of the room and socialize with other paired-off couples or sit down at a table and chat, alone or with others at the table. After a drink or two and a little small talk, the officer would ask the girl to dance. Josie quickly clued in on what type of party Doris had brought her to. It was a party for officers away from their wives or girlfriends for long stretches of time who were looking for a little female companionship, a couple of drinks, and a few dances—a momentary distraction from the realities and risks of life at sea during a war. So long as it didn't go any further than that, Josie was okay with it. She understood it. She'd stay and have a few dances. Enjoy herself. As she waited to be "selected," she leaned over to Doris. "Have you seen the officer who invited you here?"

"He's over by the bar talking to another officer, but I don't know if he's noticed me yet."

"Do you think he'll remember you?"

"Maybe not. He saw me in a waitress's uniform. I look a little different in this dress. Besides, I have a feeling I wasn't the only woman he invited to this party."

Just then, two younger officers came over to their table.

"Would you girls like a drink?" said one of them.

"We thought you'd never ask," said Doris. She and Josie got up and went over to the bar with the two young men. After they ordered their drinks, the officers escorted the girls to the middle of the room where they joined dozens of other couples standing and chatting. True to form, after several minutes of small talk, the two officers downed the remainder of their drinks, told Josie and Doris to do the same, and escorted the girls onto the dance floor.

The rest of the evening went pretty much the same, with different officers buying them drinks, dancing a few dances, then moving on to other girls. As the time grew late, the crowd began thinning out. Josie noticed some of the officers were leaving with girls. She began to feel a little uneasy. After finishing a couple of dances with one of the officers, she excused herself and sat down at a table, telling the officer she needed to take a break and catch her breath. As she sat trying to decide if she should stay or leave, with or without Doris, she spotted a heavy-set older officer approaching. He had several stripes on his uniform and was covered in medals. He came up to her. "I've been waiting to dance with you all night," he said, extending his hand.

Josie noticed the white circle around his finger where a ring had been. She hesitated. The officer grabbed her hand. He hauled her up to the dance floor and gestured to the band. They began playing a waltz. As soon as the music started, he pulled Josie toward him, pressing her body tight against his. She resisted slightly but that only made him pull her closer. There was no point fighting him—he was too strong. She acquiesced and prayed for the song to be over soon. When the music finally stopped, she thanked him for the dance and moved to leave, but he had a firm grip on her hand and wasn't letting go.

"We're not finished yet," he said. He gestured again to the band and they began playing another waltz. As he did the first time, he pulled Josie close to him and pressed himself against her. As they danced, he thrust his right leg between hers, holding her buttocks so she could not push away. At the same time, he held her hand against his neck and pressed his cheek against hers. There was nothing she could do. After the second song ended, Josie again thanked him and again tried to pull away. "One more," he said. The third dance was just like the other two, this bulk of a man overpowering her, grinding himself against her. After the third dance, he finally released her. But he wasn't quite done with her yet. "Now we go to my cabin, my dear," he said with no emotion in his voice. "You're the one I've chosen."

Josie gasped. A sense of fear, coupled with disgust, swept over her. She stared at this ghastly old man with all his stripes and medals. There was no way she was going anywhere with him, especially not to his cabin. She could feel herself slightly trembling. "I'm sorry, I don't want to go to your cabin."

"I beg your pardon?"

"I'm not going to your cabin with you. I'm not that type of girl."

"You're not that type of girl? What type of girl are you?"

"Well, I…"

He cut her off in mid sentence. "I'll tell you what type of girl you are," he continued, in a low but forceful voice. "You're the type of girl who comes here, drinks our liquor, eats our food, struts around in your pretty dress and arouses our desires, then leaves us hanging?"

"I, I…"

"What type of party did you think this was, young lady? Didn't you know what you were getting into? Why do you think you were invited here? I'll tell you why. To provide these lonely men with some release, some pleasure from this miserable war. Where's your sense of patriotism?"

Josie turned to leave. He grabbed her arm. "I can make it worth your while. What do you want? Name it."

"I want you to let go of my arm. You're hurting me."

He held tight.

"If you don't let go of my arm right now, I'll scream at the top of my lungs."

The officer stared at Josie menacingly, then released her arm. She stared right back at him, defiantly, then walked away. She scanned the room for Doris and spotted her laughing and carrying on with an officer. When Josie approached her, she could tell her friend was feeling no pain. "Doris, I want to leave right now. Let's go."

Doris squinted at Josie and frowned. "I don't want to leave now. I'm just starting to have fun."

"Doris, I'm leaving. Are you coming?"

Doris was only half listening. The other half was laughing and flirting with the officer. "What?"

"I'm leaving. Are you coming with me?"

"You go ahead. I'll be fine. I'll catch up with you later."

Josie was reluctant to head home without her friend, but she knew there was little chance she could convince Doris to leave with her. As Doris had said, she was just getting started. But Josie was determined to leave. Doris would have to fend for herself, like she had done many times in the past. Josie got her coat and left, retracing her steps along the deck to the gangway. This time there were no sailors on the deck and no officers at the bottom of the gangway. In fact, there was no one in sight. She dashed down the gangway and onto the pier. Walking hurriedly, she made her way down the pier and onto Lower Water Street. With no cabs in sight, she scampered home on foot, arriving without incident, save for almost tripping over a bum on the sidewalk and enduring the hoots and lewd comments of the occasional drunken sailor still roaming the streets.

As she readied herself for bed, she came to a realization. She would have to stop chumming around with Doris. As much as she liked her, and had fun being with her, every time she went out with Doris, she got into some type of trouble. The first time had led to being evicted from Miss Bennett's. The second time had almost landed her in jail. And tonight? Who knows what could have happened to her? So far, she'd been lucky. But next time? There couldn't be a next time.

The next day, she called Hector and invited him to come over to her place that evening. They did what they usually did. And in the weeks and months that followed, through the Christmas season and into the cold winter, they would get together almost every Saturday night. Back to the old routine.

Routine. That was the word that best described her relationship with Hector by the spring of 1944. They had settled into a routine—going out together every Saturday night, usually to a movie or a restaurant or to Becky's for dinner; going back to Josie's room afterwards, her allowing Hector to go only as far as she dictated. She could live with that. No reason to change. It gave her something to do each weekend. And she didn't mind being with Hector. He was nice enough. Yes, she was comfortable with the routine.

Little did she know, however, that her next date with Hector would be anything but routine.

Chapter 23

It was a Sunday afternoon in April. April 16th to be exact. Becky and Albert had invited Josie and Hector over for dinner, for one o'clock. Which was unusual because it was a Sunday afternoon rather than a Saturday eve•ning. But not so unusual that Josie suspected anything was up. During the meal, however, Josie noticed that Hector seemed oddly nervous, and Becky particularly excited. She was soon to find out why. After they were finished eating, Becky asked everyone to bring their tea into the parlour and made a point of insisting that Josie sit on the chesterfield. Hector sat down next to her. Small beads of sweat began to appear on his forehead as he squirmed in his seat. Becky sat in an armchair directly facing them, leaning forward on the edge of the chair, smiling broadly. Albert sat in another armchair next to Becky, with a solemn look on his face. Josie sensed something was about to happen. "What's going on?" she asked.

Hector looked over at Becky. She nodded enthusiastically. He then got up from the chesterfield, knelt down on one knee in front of Josie, and took her left hand. A heaviness suddenly gripped Josie's chest. She looked over at Becky, frowning. Becky was grinning like a schoolgirl, bouncing in her chair. Josie turned to face Hector. "What are you doing?" she asked, her voice trembling.

Hector swallowed hard and looked up into Josie's eyes. He stared at her for several seconds, as a trickle of sweat ran down the side of his face. Breathing heavily, he began to speak. "Josephine

194

Bourdeau…" He stopped. His mouth was wide open, but nothing was coming out. He took another deep breath. "Josephine Bourdeau, will you marry me?"

Josie gasped. A sharp pain stabbed her in the back. Her chest felt like it was going to explode. Her body shook. Her throat tightened. She felt herself getting light-headed. She began panting rapidly. She couldn't breathe. She pulled her hand from Hector's grasp and jumped up from the sofa. "I need some air! I need some air!"

She raced out of the room, down the steps, through the front door, and outside onto the veranda. She leaned over the rail, sucking in oxygen as fast as she could. It wasn't coming fast enough. Her head seemed like it was spinning. She felt like she was going to faint. Within seconds, Becky was at her side. "Are you okay?"

Josie looked over sideways at her sister, then looked back, still hanging over the rail. She didn't respond.

"Hector's inside waiting for your answer," Becky said. "Are you coming back in?"

"No," said Josie, without looking up.

"Do you need more time?"

"I don't need more time. I'm not going back in, now or later."

"The man asked you to marry him, Josie. You owe him an answer."

Just then, Albert arrived on the scene. "Is she coming back in?' he said to Becky. "Hector's wondering what's going on."

"She'll be in in a minute. Go get her coat. It's chilly out here."

"I told you this was a bad idea," said Albert.

"Oh, shut up!" barked Becky at her husband. Albert said nothing. He went back inside.

Josie finally stood up. She turned to Becky, scowling. "You knew about this?"

Becky sighed sheepishly. "Well, yes, he told me he was thinking about it."

"And you encouraged him, I suppose?"

Wayne Forster

"Well, why not? He's a nice man, and he'll make a good husband."

"I don't *want* a husband!"

"Why not? You've been going together for months. I thought you liked him."

"Just because I might like a fellow doesn't mean I want to marry him."

"Josie, I don't understand you. You wanted to find a nice guy and settle down. Now you've found a nice guy and he's giving you a chance to settle down. Take it."

"Settling down doesn't necessarily mean getting married."

"What? What are you talking about? That's gibberish."

Josie didn't reply.

At that moment, Albert arrived with Josie's coat and gave it to Becky. He seemed about to say something, but Becky glared menacingly at him. He went back inside without saying a word. Becky put the coat over Josie's shoulders.

"Look," Becky went on, "I'm going back inside. Get your head on straight, come back in, and tell that man you'll marry him. He thinks the world of you and you're never going to find anyone better."

The words echoed in Josie's ears as Becky went back into the house. "You're never going to find anyone better." All at once, she could hear a multitude of voices in her head. "*You're never going to find anyone better. Hector is the best you'll ever find. You're not getting any younger. You'll end up an old maid. Marry him! Marry him! Marry him!*"

Josie leapt off the veranda onto the sidewalk and ran down the street as fast as she could, past startled couples out for a Sunday stroll, past children on bicycles, past barking dogs. She ran all the way down Morris to Gorman's, and up the back stairs. She didn't stop running until she was safely in her room with the door closed behind her. As she bent over trying to catch her breathe, panic gripped her. Becky and Hector would come looking for her. She couldn't stay in her room. That's the first place they'd

196

look. She had to get out of there right now. But where would she go? Where could she hide? She had to get away. Far away. So far away that they'd never find her.

She reached under her bed, pulled out her suitcase, and flung it down on the bed. She opened the top drawer of her dresser and rummaged around until she found what she was looking for, a small key. She unlocked her suitcase. Reaching inside a torn area of the lining, she pulled out a quantity of bills and counted them. Not enough. She needed more money. But where could she get it? There might be some money in the restaurant downstairs, although Mr. Gorman would have emptied out the till last night. Besides, it was Sunday and the restaurant was closed, so she'd have to break in. Not a good idea. She could ask one of the other tenants in the building for a loan. Not likely to get one—she didn't know them well enough. Doris! She'd ask Doris. She'd tell her that her mother was very sick and she needed bus fare to get home. That would work.

She stuffed the bills into her purse, then hurriedly packed, jamming in as many clothes, toiletries, and personal belongings as the suitcase would hold. Suitcase in hand, she locked her door behind her and scurried down the back steps to the street. Walking almost at a run, she headed up Morris to Doris's place. By the time she arrived, she was all out of breath. Gasping for air, she rang the doorbell. Seconds later, Doris came to the door.

"Josie. What are you doing here?"

"I need to borrow some money."

"Some money? For what?"

"My...my mother is very sick, and I...I need to go home, and I don't have enough money for...for bus fare."

Doris looked puzzled. "Well, what about Becky? Or Albert? Couldn't they give you bus fare?"

"They...they went down yesterday. I forgot to ask them."

"Why didn't you go with them?"

"I had to work."

"But you didn't work yesterday."

"Doris, are you my friend or not?"

"Yes, of course I'm your friend."

"Well, I need some money. Are you going to lend me some?"

"Okay, okay. Relax. How much do you need?"

"Uh, twenty dollars."

"Twenty dollars? For bus fare?"

"Okay, then, uh…ten dollars."

"Okay, I'll see what I have. Do you want to come in?"

"No, I'll just wait here."

Doris disappeared, then reappeared a few minutes later. She handed Josie five two-dollar bills.

"Thanks," said Josie, taking the money from Doris's hand. Doris looked at her friend. "Are you alright?"

"Yes, I'm fine. I'm just upset about my mother."

"Well, I hope she gets better."

"Thanks. I'll pay you back."

Doris just smiled and nodded. Josie turned and headed back down the street as Doris stood in the doorway, watching her friend depart.

Josie headed back down Morris toward Hollis. Where would she go? She had to get as far away as possible. What was the best way? She had to decide quickly. The train! She'd take the train. She headed to the train station, lugging her suitcase with her.

As was typical for a Sunday, the train station was packed, with long lineups at the wickets. Josie nervously scanned the crowd to see if there was anyone who might know her. Satisfied that she hadn't been discovered, she entered one of the queues. After several anxious minutes in line, it was finally her turn.

"Next," called the attendant.

Josie moved slowly to the wicket. She peered nervously at the board on the back wall. Sydney. Yarmouth. Moncton. Boston. Montreal. Toronto.

"Where to, Miss?" asked the attendant, without lifting his head.

Josie couldn't make up her mind. "Uh…"

The attendant looked up, leaned slightly forward, smiled broadly, and with just a hint of impatience said, "Miss? Where are we travelling to today?"

A sense of fear washed over her. Maybe this was a bad idea. Maybe she should just go back, tell Hector she'd marry him, have six kids, and live miserably-ever-after, like the rest of her sisters.

"When is the next train leaving the station?" she asked.

"The Ocean Limited leaves in fifteen minutes, at three thirty."

"Where is it going?"

"Montreal."

Josie took a deep breath. Last chance to back out.

"I'll take a one-way ticket to Montreal."

Chapter 24

The train didn't arrive in Montreal until seven o'clock the following evening, a twenty-seven-and-a-half-hour trip. The long trip had given Josie a lot of time to think; too much time, as she debated back and forth in her mind if she'd overreacted. It was the shock of it. Totally unexpected. She'd never thought for a minute about marrying Hector, or anyone else for that matter. Thinking about it gave her the shakes. When the train finally pulled into Windsor Station, her first thought was to find something to do to take her mind off Hector's proposal.

Before that, though, she had to find a phone and call Becky. By now, her sister would be worried sick wondering where she was. No doubt she would have checked her room at Gorman's. Maybe she would have noticed the suitcase was gone. She probably would have talked to Doris. Doris would have told her she came looking for money to visit their sick mother. Becky would know that was a lie. Hopefully, Becky wouldn't have called their parents. They'd be beside themselves with worry. She had to call Becky right away.

She found a pay phone inside the train station. She checked her purse to see if she had enough change to make the call, but she had no idea how much a call from Montreal to Halifax would cost. She could call collect, but what if Albert answered and refused to accept the charges? She decided to take her chances. She placed a coin in the slot and dialed zero. The operator came on the line.

"Yes," said Josie, "I'd like to place a collect call to Halifax."

"The number?" said the operator.

Josie gave the operator Becky's number.

"Your name?"

"Josephine Bourdeau."

After a couple of seconds, Josie could hear the phone ringing on the other end of the line. It rang three times.

"Hello?"

It was Becky.

"I have a collect call from Josephine Bourdeau," said the operator. "Do you accept the charges?"

"Yes," said Becky.

"Go ahead," said the operator.

"Hi Becky," said Josie.

"Josie? Is that you?" said Becky.

"Yes, it's me."

"Where in the world are you? We've been looking everywhere for you. I've been worried sick."

"I...uh...took a little trip."

"Are you down home?"

"No, no. You didn't call home, did you?"

"No I didn't. I talked to Doris and she said you had gone to her place to borrow some money for bus fare down home because Mom was sick. Then Doris said that you said Albert and I had gone down the day before. I told her that wasn't true. Then I thought maybe you had gone down on your own. I was going to call down home, but Albert said I shouldn't because if you weren't there it would only worry Mom and Dad."

"He was right. It's a good thing you didn't call."

"So, where are you Josie?"

"I'm...uh...I'm in Montreal."

"Montreal?! Montreal?! What are you doing in Montreal?"

"I...uh...I just had to get away for a while."

"Oh my God, Josie! Are you crazy? Get away from what?"

"From everything! From Hector, from you trying to marry me off, from everything."

"Oh my God, Josie, you're so irresponsible. If you didn't want to marry the man, you should have just said no. You didn't have to run off to Montreal. And blaming me? I didn't tell Hector to propose to you. He told Albert he was going to propose. That's how I found out. I didn't think you'd react this way. You've been going out with him for months. I thought you'd be happy. All I wanted was for you to be happy."

Josie could hear a trembling in Becky's voice. It sounded like she was starting to cry.

"Becky, are you alright?"

Becky didn't answer.

"Becky, are you still there?"

"Yes."

"Are you alright?"

"Yes, I'm fine."

Neither sister said anything for a few moments.

"You're right," said Josie, "I should have just told him I didn't want to get married. I guess I panicked. Everyone must think I'm terrible."

"You're not terrible. You just do some crazy things sometimes."

Josie sighed a deep sigh. "I guess I should go," she said. "This call is going to cost you a fortune."

"Don't worry about that," said Becky. "I'm just relieved you're safe. Where are you staying?"

"I don't know yet. I'll find a hotel somewhere."

"Josie, be careful. You don't know your way around Montreal."

"Don't worry about me. I'll be fine."

"How long are you going to stay there?"

"I don't know."

"Why don't you come home right away? You'll talk to Hector and straighten the whole thing out."

"I don't want to talk to Hector. There's nothing to straighten out."

"Josie, you owe the man an explanation."

"Becky, this is why I ran away! Everybody's always telling me what I should do."

"Okay, okay. I'm sorry. I just want you home."

"I'll be home when I'm ready. I just need some time away right now. Okay?"

"Okay."

"I love you, Sis."

"I love you too."

Josie hung up the phone. A tear slid down her cheek. She took a hankie out of her purse and wiped her eyes.

She took a deep breath. She was now ready to go out and have some fun. Maybe go to a dance. But first she had to find a place to stay. Something not too expensive but not too seedy, either. After about an hour's search, she settled on a hotel not far from the train station. It was a little more than she had wanted to spend, but all the cheaper hotels looked run down. This one wasn't the Waldorf Astoria, by any means, but at least it was clean.

After checking in, she went up to her room and unpacked. She took a hot bath, changed into some clean clothes, freshened her lipstick, brushed her hair, and headed down to the lobby to ask the front desk clerk if he knew of any dance halls in the area. He told her about a place down by the port where they had dances every night. A "lively" spot, he had called it.

It was about a quarter to ten when she arrived at the dance. A good crowd had already gathered but quite a different crowd than those at the dances in Halifax. There, the crowds consisted mostly of sailors and young girls, and more sailors than girls. Here, most of the people appeared to be civilians, except for a few soldiers in their khakis. And a lot more girls than guys. So many girls, in fact, that a lot of them were dancing together, something you didn't see very often in Halifax. And the crowd here seemed to be a bit older. There were lots of young people, to be sure, but also older couples, presumably married, and a few older men by themselves. In Halifax, it was all young people.

Josie checked her coat and entered the hall discreetly to get the lay of the land. Most of the tables were occupied, primarily by the older couples. Groups of young girls were standing about, waiting for guys to approach them. It would be stiff competition tonight. The guys could have their pick.

She also noticed that the canteen near the entrance was serving liquor, and people were openly drinking at their tables. Even on the dance floor. The liquor laws were definitely more lenient here than in Halifax. At least you could openly order a drink at a dance without having to sneak it in. The people here were obviously more open-minded, not like the stuffed shirts back in Halifax. Josie never believed those rules made much sense, anyway. Everyone knew people brought liquor to the dances, even the police. It was a joke. But tonight, that didn't matter to Josie. She wasn't there to drink. She was there to dance.

At the dances in Halifax, Josie would stroll leisurely around the perimeter of the dance floor trying to catch a sailor's eye with a flirtatious smile. It would always work. That was going to be more difficult here, given the makeup of the crowd, but she decided she had to give it a try. However, after two circles of the hall with no offers, she needed another approach. Normally, she didn't consider it appropriate for a girl to ask a guy to dance, but she had a feeling that she might have to make an exception in this case. Besides, nobody here knew her. What was the harm?

After scanning the room, she spotted a guy who she thought might be a good target. He looked older, with hair longer than most of the other men, but he was a fantastic dancer, jiving and jitterbugging like no one she had seen before, not even in the movies. Josie knew he would be a lot of fun to dance with. She followed him closely, waiting for a chance to approach him. It took some time, as girl after girl would grab him for a dance, often pushing other girls out of the way. Finally, he took a break, retreating to the bar. Josie jumped at the opportunity. She sidled up to him as he stood at the counter, paying for his drink. "You're quite the dancer," she said to him.

The man turned to her and leaned slightly forward, straining to hear her over the music. "Pardon?" he said in French.

Josie raised her voice a little. "I said, you're quite the dancer. I was watching you on the floor."

The man eyeballed Josie as he slowly took a sip of his drink. "You're English?"

"Yes," replied Josie.

"Where are you from?"

"Halifax."

"I've never been to Halifax. I hear it's a lively place."

"Not as lively as this place."

The man stared at Josie intently. He had a mysterious way about him. "So, you like the way I dance."

"Yeah, especially the way you jitterbug. You're very good."

"Do you jitterbug?"

"If I can find the right partner."

The man grinned. "Do you want to dance with me?"

"I thought you'd never ask."

He downed the rest of his drink, put the empty cup on the bar, grabbed Josie's hand, and hauled her onto the dance floor. Cutting into the middle of a swing number, he pulled Josie in and out, twirled her around, fast-stepped, pirouetted, boogie-woogied, flipped her over his hip, and even made some moves she'd never seen before. He was the best dancer she had ever danced with. No one in Halifax danced like this. Not even close. She loved it. She was in her glory. Free, wild, uninhibited. Letting everything out. Like she was born to do exactly this.

They danced two or three more jitterbugs, a couple of jives, and a waltz here and there. Josie kept up with his every step. He was clearly impressed. After one particularly bouncy jive, he grabbed her by the arm. "Let's get a drink," he said. He pulled her over to the bar and summoned the server. "Rhum noir, monsieur. Une double."

He turned to Josie. "And for the mademoiselle?"

"Nothing for me, thanks."

"What? The girls in Halifax don't drink?"

"Oh, we drink. It's just that I don't feel like drinking tonight."

"Oh, come on. One drink. What will that hurt? Don't make me drink alone."

Josie sensed her resolve weakening. He was probably right. One drink wouldn't hurt. Just to be sociable. "Okay. Lemon gin and 7-up."

"Lemon gin?" He turned to the server. "Avez-vous du lemon gin?"

The server nodded and went to get their drinks. When they arrived, Josie's new friend paid for the drinks and passed Josie her lemon gin. "Let's find a table," he said. "We'll talk."

The man led her over to an empty table.

"So, what's your name, English girl from Halifax?"

"Josie."

"Hmm, Josie. I like the name. I'm Victor. So, what do you do in Halifax?"

"I'm a waitress."

"A waitress! Hmm. Josie the waitress from Halifax."

Josie wasn't sure if he was making fun of her. "And what do *you* do, Victor from Montreal?"

"I'm an artiste."

"An artiste?"

"A painter. I paint mostly portraits of people. Oil on canvas."

Josie was fascinated. "Wow! I've never met a painter before."

"No? No painters in Halifax?"

"None that I would know. Except maybe house painters."

Victor burst out laughing. Josie hadn't meant it to be funny.

"Would you like to see my paintings?"

"Yeah, sure."

"Okay, let's go."

"Right now?"

"Bien sur. Why not?"

"Well, I…"

"Are you with somebody?"

"No, but…"

"Okay then. We'll finish our drinks and then we'll go. My studio is only three blocks from here."

"Well, okay," said Josie, somewhat hesitantly.

When they were finished their drinks, Victor stood up. "Bon. Are you ready?" he said.

They stopped at the coat check to get their coats. Victor motioned to Josie to lead the way and they left the hall and out into the cool evening air. Josie wondered if she was doing the right thing, leaving with a man she had just met. In a strange city. Late at night. On the other hand, it was kind of exciting. An artist. In Montreal.

His studio was in a warehouse district, on the third floor of an old brick building that had seen better days. Mortar was crumbling in several spots, many of the grime-caked windows were cracked, and the wood trim on the front door was splintered and rotting. It reminded Josie of some of the buildings on the waterfront in Halifax.

Victor pushed open the stuck, unlocked front door with his shoulder and ushered Josie into a dimly lit hallway. "This way," he said. He proceeded down the hallway a short distance and turned onto a steel staircase. Josie delayed for a split second, debating whether she should keep going, then followed him up the staircase. They walked up two flights, then through a doorway into another dimly lit hall. They passed two doors and stopped at the third. Victor pulled out a key and unlocked the door. Flinging the door open, he swept his hand as if making a grand announcement. "Voilà. My studio."

The first thing that struck Josie was the mess. Paintings were scattered everywhere—leaning against the walls, stacked against chairs and wooden crates, propped up on easels. A large, paint soaked, light grey cloth covered part of the floor, with sheets of sketches on white paper strewn about. Against the left wall ran a long, heavy wooden table with thick legs. The top of the table was littered with cans and containers of paint brushes, jars of paint and other liquids, blank canvases, and an assortment of items that Josie assumed were the tools of the artist's trade. Paint was splattered everywhere—on the walls, on the floor, on the table, everywhere. The only somewhat tidy spot was the far left corner of the room, where a small wooden stool faced a beautifully ornate backless couch.

The second thing that struck Josie were the paintings themselves. She remembered he had said he painted mostly portraits of people, but these were all of women, almost all young women. Attractive young women. Some were head and shoulders only but most were of the entire body. And in all of the full body portraits, the women were either nude or partially nude. As she studied his work, she felt both anxious and captivated. They were indeed beautiful paintings.

Josie also realized that the studio doubled as the artist's home. There was a bed against the right wall, mussed and unmade, and a kitchen-like area in the back right corner with a fridge, stove, sink, small cupboard, and a small table with two chairs. The only thing dividing the living area from the studio was a rather ratty curtain hanging from a rod that was attached to the steel girders of the ceiling. The curtain had been drawn out about eight to ten feet.

Victor watched as Josie surveyed the surroundings. "Well, what do you think of my studio?"

Josie chose her words carefully. "Wow, it's quite the place."

Victor smiled. "That could mean two different things."

"No, I mean…"

"It's okay. I know it's a mess. But what do you think of my paintings?"

"They're all of women," said Josie.

"I specialize in portraits of women."

"They're all naked."

"I try to capture the beauty, the allure of the female form. The face, the neck, the shoulders, the breasts, the hips, the buttocks.

I want to show the softness, the smoothness, the perfection of women. Clothes get in the way."

He walked over and picked up a painting propped up against a chair and placed it on an easel. It was a full nude of a young, dark-haired woman. He motioned Josie over. "What do you think of this one?"

Josie recognized the backless couch the woman was spread out on. She stared at the painting. "She's beautiful," she said, almost inaudibly.

"Like you," said Victor.

Josie blushed slightly. She felt both flattered and uneasy.

Victor went over to the heavy wooden table, reached under and pulled out a bottle of dark rum from a shelf, and placed it on the table. "Would you like a drink?" he asked Josie. "I only have dark rum. No lemon gin."

"No, no thank you."

"Voyons, it will help you relax."

"I'm relaxed."

"You seem a little tense. Is it because of my paintings? You don't like seeing women in the nude?"

"Well, it's just that I'm not used to seeing things like that."

"You've never seen paintings like this in Halifax?"

"No, never."

"But you like them."

Josie had to be honest. "Yes, I do."

Victor smiled a faint smile, but said nothing, while Josie wandered around the studio examining some of the other paintings. He took an empty glass from the top of his table, blew into it, poured some rum, and downed it in one gulp. He called over to Josie. "Well, if you don't want any rum, how about some coffee?"

Josie was relieved. At least he wasn't going to ply her with liquor. "Coffee sounds great. Cream, no sugar."

"I don't have any cream. Or milk."

"Okay, then just black."

Victor went behind the curtain to his small kitchen. A few minutes later he came back with a cup of coffee and handed it to her. She took a sip. It was strong but hot. It warmed her inside. Meanwhile, Victor poured himself another drink. He watched intently as Josie continued to study his work. "You are wondering about something," he said. "I can see it in your face."

Josie was impressed that he could read her like that. *It must be the artist in him*, she thought. "Well, now that you mention it, I was wondering, did all of these women pose for you?"

"Of course. All my paintings are from live models. I don't work from photographs or from my imagination. These are real women."

"So, all of these women took their clothes off in front of you?"

"Of course."

Josie took another drink of her coffee. "Did you know all of these women before they posed for you?"

"Some I did. Some I had just met. Like you."

Victor poured himself another drink. He walked slowly over to Josie and stood inches from her, his eyes fixed on hers.

"Would you like me to paint you?"

Josie was startled by the question but not surprised. The thought had already crossed her mind that he might ask her. It both titillated and unsettled her. Part of her was disgusted at the idea, but part of her wanted to be like the other women in the paintings. Alluring, seductive, yet so naturally beautiful. Her breathing quickened. "Oh, I could never do that," she said, stumbling over her words.

"Pourquois pas? Why not?"

"I could never take my clothes off in front of a stranger."

"There's nothing to be afraid of. The nudity is not sexual. I'm an artiste. It's just my work. It's what I do."

"Well, it's not what I do," countered Josie.

"Are you ashamed of your body? You shouldn't be. C'est beau. It's beautiful. It's completely natural. It's what God gave you."

Josie found it strange that God was being brought into the conversation. "I'm not ashamed of my body. I just don't want to show it to everybody."

"You're not showing it to everybody, you're just showing it to me. So that I can paint you."

"But other people will see the painting."

"No one will know who you are. They'll just see a mysteriously beautiful woman, confident and strong, powerful and proud. I'll paint you as I see you."

Beautiful, confident, strong, powerful, proud. It sounded so right. Then why did it feel so wrong? Josie was confused. She couldn't think straight. She began to feel a little light-headed, like the room was floating. She wondered if it was the strain of the situation, her mind torn between two conflicting urges, two incompatible impulses.

Victor went to the other side of the room and came back with a long, dark burgundy robe. He offered it to Josie. "You can go behind the curtain, take off your clothes, put on the robe, and come back here."

"I can't." she said, meekly.

"Why not?" he said.

"I feel like I would be committing a sin."

"You are listening too much to your priest. I don't think God would be upset. But it is up to you. I want to paint you because I know I can create a beautiful piece of art, but I don't force anyone to do anything they don't want to do. Ask yourself, does it feel right to you?"

Josie stared at him for a few seconds. She then took the robe, went behind the ratty curtain, took off every piece of clothing, donned the robe, and came back to him. He took her by the hand and slowly led her over to the backless couch in the corner. "Now, take off the robe and lie on the couch, facing me, your legs together."

She pushed the robe back off her shoulders and let it fall to the floor. She sat on the side of the couch, then reclined, facing him with legs together, as he had instructed. Although the couch was warm, she shivered, her breathing laboured and uneven.

He walked over to one of his easels and removed the painting that was on it. He grabbed a blank canvas and placed it on the easel. He then went back to his table, prepared his paint palette, selected his brushes, sat down on the stool facing Josie, and began to paint.

Josie had no idea how long it took to complete the portrait. He had insisted that during the entire sitting she look directly at him, not anywhere else. As a result, she had no sense of time. It was like there was no other reality, just his eyes. Her only break from his hypnotic gaze was when he got up to change brushes or replenish his paint. But those were just brief moments of relief, too brief to enable her to return to the real world.

Without warning, he put his brush down on his palette, placed the palette on the floor, and turned the easel to face Josie. "What do you think?"

Josie couldn't believe what she was seeing. It was her, for sure, an excellent likeness. But it was more than that. It was raw and refined at the same time, majestic yet simple. It was like he had captured not only her body but her very soul. It both pleased and frightened her. "It's amazing," she mouthed, knowing that the word did not remotely describe what she was feeling. As she stared at the painting, however, she began to feel self-conscious. "Can I put my clothes back on?"

"Not yet. We have to let the paint set a little to see if I need to do any touch-ups."

"Well, can I put the robe on for now?"

He retrieved the robe from the hook where he had hung it and passed it to Josie. She put it on, tying the sash in the front.

"I'll warm up the coffee while we wait," he said.

A short while later, he called out from behind the curtain. "Coffee's ready. We'll sit at the table in here."

Josie joined him on the other side of the curtain. He was standing by the sink with his back to her. She sat down at the small table. He came over carrying two cups. He placed one on the table in front of her and sat down with the other in his hand. Feeling a bit out of sorts from the sitting, Josie welcomed the coffee.

"How are you feeling?" said Victor.

"I feel a little tired," said Josie.

"It's probably from the sitting. Everyone feels tired afterwards. It's very exhausting, posing for a portrait. Why don't you lie down on the bed for a minute while I check the painting?"

Josie wondered if that was a good idea, lying in a stranger's bed, but it had already been a long day and she was so tired she had to rest, if just to close her eyes for a few minutes. As she lay, though, her mind drifted into a state of semi-consciousness, half asleep, half awake. At times, she was vaguely aware of her surroundings. At other times, she felt like she was in a dream, with random, disjoined images flashing before her. Strange images. Images of her naked portrait staring back at her, with her breasts twice their normal size. People she did not recognize gawking at the portrait, some laughing, some angry. Then she saw her mother, staring at her portrait, crying. She tried to explain to her that it was art, but her mother did not seem to be aware that Josie was even there. The image then switched to a church and a man kneeling in front of the altar, praying, his back to her. She approached him from behind and tapped him on the shoulder. He turned slowly. It was Hector. He looked at her sadly, his cheerless, glum expression piercing her soul. But just as quickly as he had appeared, his faced dissolved. Another face appeared, blurred at first, but gradually growing clearer. It was Victor, trying to wake her up. "Josie," he said, "no touch-ups needed. C'est fini. We're all done. You can get dressed now."

Victor went back to the studio side of the room. Josie sat up, shaking off the effects of her brief nap. She retrieved her clothes and got dressed. She then joined Victor to have another look at her portrait. It was even more beautiful now—softer, richer.

"Are you happy with it?" said Victor.

"Very much," said Josie. "Are *you* happy with it?"

"Ah oui. It is beautiful. But I had a beautiful subject."

Josie blushed again slightly. She couldn't tell if Victor was flirting with her or just being the artist. A short time ago he was a complete stranger, but now she felt a connection to him, like he had known her for a long time. Intimately. Being naked in front of a man had that effect.

"What time is it?" said Josie.

"I do not know," said Victor. "I do not have a clock. But it must be at least two or three in the morning."

"It's late. I should be getting back to my hotel."

"I don't know if there are any taxis running this time of the night."

"Then I'll have to walk."

"Where is your hotel?"

Josie wasn't exactly sure what street her hotel was on but gave Victor the name. He knew where it was.

"That's a bit of a walk," he said. "You could stay here for the rest of the night and get a taxi in the morning."

Josie wondered if Victor had something else in mind besides just painting her. He had been a perfect gentleman so far, but she couldn't take the chance.

"Thank you, but I think I better get back to my hotel."

"Then I'll walk you back."

"Oh, you don't have to do that."

"Mais oui. I insist. A young woman should not be walking the streets by herself at this time of night."

Josie protested mildly but when Victor insisted once again, she thanked him and accepted his offer. On the way, they talked at length, Josie about her family and her background, Victor about his work. She told him about Hector's proposal and how she came to be in Montreal. She appreciated that he had just listened and hadn't judged her. By the time they reached the hotel, Josie felt they had become almost friends.

But now it was time for them to go their separate ways. "It was nice meeting you, Victor," said Josie.

"It was nice meeting you, Josie."

"If you're ever in Halifax, look me up at Gorman's Restaurant on Hollis."

"You never know. I might just do that."

Josie reached in and gave Victor a kiss on the cheek. "Good luck with your art," she said.

"Good luck with your life," he answered. "Bonne chance."

Josie turned and entered the hotel. As she walked through the lobby towards the stairs, she reflected on the evening. She had done something off-beat, maybe a little crazy. Something she couldn't tell Becky about, or any of her friends or family for that matter. She had posed nude for a painting!

She was glad she had come to Montreal. Maybe she'd stay a little longer.

Chapter 25

Josie slept in until almost ten o'clock. It had been after three before she'd gone to bed following her "adventure." Once she'd washed and dressed, she went down to the front desk to reserve another night's stay.

After a late breakfast at a restaurant near the hotel, she headed out for the day. She did some sightseeing, visiting Dorchester Square, the Clock Tower, Mont Royal, and her favourite spot, Notre Dame Basilica. The Basilica was so beautiful, it sent shivers through her body. She also had enough money to do a little shopping, buying a necklace for Becky and a pair of nylons for herself.

Around six, she decided to head back to the hotel. As she walked, she reflected on the previous couple of days. She had needed this. To get away. To get away from Hector, from Becky, from everything. Sure, she'd have to face the music on her return, but she had no regrets about what she had done. It was the right thing for her. At the right time.

This would be her last night in Montreal, she had decided. She'd head home tomorrow. Not that she wouldn't have liked to stay longer if she had more money. She liked this city. It had a different feel to it. You didn't feel the war here, as much. Not like Halifax, where reminders of the war were everywhere. Ships filling the harbour and sailors filling the streets. Not many sailors in Montreal. Which was a good thing, given her bad experience with sailors. At least a certain sailor.

What would she do on her last night here? Go to another dance? Maybe meet another artiste like Victor? No, she'd already done that. Or maybe meet someone else interesting, like an actor. No, there probably weren't too many actors in Montreal. Maybe she'd just find a bar that played good music, have a drink or two, and see what happened.

After dropping off her parcels in her room, she went out for supper at a nearby restaurant. She took her time eating, to kill time, as it was too early to go to a bar and she didn't feel like sitting in her room doing nothing. After she left the restaurant, she took a leisurely walk around the neighbourhood before returning to her room to change, freshen up, and head out on the town.

The front desk clerk told her about a jazz bar within walking distance. It was in the lobby of one of the bigger hotels in the downtown area. She arrived just before ten, found a table, and ordered a drink. A quartet was playing a cool jazz number, but the crowd was sparse and there was only one couple up on the small dance floor.

Josie sipped slowly on her drink and felt the familiar burn. She wouldn't drink too much tonight, just enough to get a bit tipsy. She leaned back in her chair. For the first time since leaving Halifax, she felt truly at peace. For the first time since Hector's *stupid* proposal. Why did he have to go and ruin everything? Everything was just fine the way it was. They were doing okay. Having a little fun. Then he had to propose. The idiot!

Anyway, she didn't want to think about Hector right now. She just wanted to enjoy her drink and relax. Clear her head. Take in the surroundings. Savour the moment. Be free. That's what it was all about. Freedom. Freedom to do what she wanted, not what someone else wanted her to do. Not what Hector wanted her to do or what Becky wanted her to do or what her family wanted her to do. What *she* wanted to do. And right now, she wanted to enjoy her drink. She stretched out in her chair and threw back her hair. She smiled a self-satisfied smile. Life was good. At this spot, at this moment, she didn't have a worry in the world.

As the time wore on, a few more people trickled into the bar. Her eyes surveyed the crowd. One of her favourite pastimes was people-watching—trying to figure out who they were and what they did, whether they were married or single, what type of person they were. On this night there were a few couples, but Josie noticed the majority of the patrons were men, mostly in business suits, three or four sitting together at the same table.

As she continued to scan the room, she inadvertently made eye contact with a man sitting alone. He smiled at her. She smiled back, but quickly looked away. A few seconds later, she looked over at him. He was still looking at her. He smiled again. She looked away, smiling. He was a well-built, ruggedly good-looking man in a suit and tie, a businessman she guessed. And he looked older, probably in his late thirties. She continued to look away from him, not wanting to appear too interested, but she could see through the corner of her eye that he was coming over to her table, drink in hand.

"What's a pretty girl like you doing in a place like this?" he said.

Josie looked up. She surmised he was English. Not a hint of a French-Canadian accent. "Is that the best line you've got?" she said.

He chuckled. "Mind if I join you?" he said.

Josie motioned for him to have a seat.

"I'm John," he said.

"Josie," she replied.

"Are you from around here?"

"I'm from Halifax."

"Oh, Halifax. I've been to Halifax on business."

"What type of business are you in?"

"Military equipment. I'm based out of Toronto but we have a factory here in Montreal."

"Your company must be making a lot of money these days."

"We're doing okay."

Josie tried to see if he was wearing a wedding ring, but his left hand was below the table. "Does you wife mind it when you travel away from home?" she said.

"I'm not married," he replied. "See, no ring." He lifted his left hand quickly then put it back down below the table. "What about you? Is there a man in your life?"

"No."

"Do you work?"

"I'm a waitress."

"You must be very busy as well with all the ships in port."

"Yes, Halifax is a hopping place these days. Lots of sailors."

"I can imagine." He took a sip of his drink. "What brings you to Montreal?"

Josie hesitated. She didn't want to tell him the real reason. "I…I'm visiting an elderly aunt. She's not well."

"You're not with her tonight?"

"Um…her son is with her tonight. He's giving me a break."

He smiled. Josie wasn't sure if he was buying her story. It didn't sound believable in her own head.

"I see that your glass is almost empty," he said, changing the subject. "Can I get you another?"

Josie remembered her pledge not to drink too much this night, but she hadn't really felt the first one, so decided a second wouldn't hurt. Besides, he seemed nice enough. "Okay," she said.

"What are you drinking?"

"Rum and Coke."

The businessman downed his own drink, then waved over a waiter and ordered drinks for both of them. When the drinks arrived he offered a toast. "To Montreal."

They clinked their glasses together.

As they drank, they continued to chat—mostly small talk about Montreal, Halifax, Toronto, the music. Josie didn't talk about Hector, or her family, or anything too personal. And he didn't talk about his business. Said it was "top secret." As the night wore on they continued to talk, had another drink, and danced a few dances. While walking back to their table after one such dance, he made a suggestion. "Listen, my company has a suite upstairs. There's a party there tonight. Rather than pay for these over-priced drinks here, why don't we go up to the suite and join the party? The drinks are free."

Josie was enjoying the company of her new acquaintance. She was having a good time and didn't want it to end. Not just yet. Going to a party sounded like fun. "Okay. Let me get my purse."

He placed his hand on the small of her back and gently led her out of the bar and into the hotel lobby. They took the elevator to the suite on the top floor. He unlocked the door and swung it open. "After you," he said.

Josie entered. It was a spacious, classy-looking room with a large bed, a long dressing table, an armoire, and two arm chairs around a small table. She spotted a bar in the corner. But there was no one else in the room. "I thought you said there was a party going on here," she said.

He closed the door behind him. He took off his suit jacket and threw it on one of the armchairs. "I guess everybody must be gone," he said.

Josie began to feel a little uneasy. She was alone in a hotel room with a stranger.

"Anyway," he said, "we can still have a drink. Right?"

"Just one," said Josie. "Then I'll have to go."

"What's your rush?" he said.

He went to the bar, poured two drinks of rum, handed one to Josie, and took the other in his right hand. Raising his glass, he offered his second toast of the evening. "To us."

Josie took a sip of her rum. It burned strong. "This is straight," she said.

"There was no mix," he replied.

He downed his drink in one gulp and put his glass on the dressing table. He then took Josie's glass out of her hand and placed it on the dressing table as well. Moving closer to her, he lifted her chin with his index finger. "You're very beautiful," he said.

He leaned in and tried to kiss her. She turned her head away. He then put his left arm around her, pulled her quickly towards him, and kissed her hard on the lips. She slowly pushed him away and broke his embrace.

"I should go," she said.

She turned to leave but he grabbed her hand. It was then that she saw it—the band of white flesh on his finger where a ring had been. He *was* married.

She yanked her hand out of his grasp. "You lied to me," she said to him.

"What?"

"You said you weren't married."

"I'm not."

"Yes, you are. I can see the white ring where you're wedding ring was."

He looked at his hand. He shrugged. "Okay, I'm married. So what?"

"I don't mess around with married men."

"Why should it matter to you? I'm the one who's married."

"It matters."

"Look, we're two people alone in Montreal. Nobody knows we're here. Let's just have some fun."

"I don't have fun with married men."

"You were having fun drinking the booze I bought you."

Josie stared angrily at him. "I think I better go."

Josie grabbed her purse and started for the door. He jumped in front of her, blocking her exit.

"Get out of my way!" she said.

As she tried to push past him he grabbed her by the arm.

"Let me go," she said through gritted teeth.

"You're not going anywhere, you little whore."

"Whore? Who are you calling a whore?"

"You accept my drinks, you flirt with me all night, you get me all aroused. And then you just want to leave me hanging? You're not leaving here until I get what I want."

For the first time, Josie felt afraid. "I'll scream!"

"Go ahead. Nobody will hear you on this floor. It's all suites."

"I'll scream anyway!"

"You scream and I'll beat the shit out of you."

He tightened his grip on her arm and pulled her towards the bed.

"Ow! You're hurting me!" she said.

"I'll do more than hurt you," he replied.

She tried desperately to pull away, but he was too strong. He threw her on the bed and quickly jumped on top of her before she could squirm free. She tried to scream but he put his large hand over her mouth. With his other hand he pulled off his tie and stuffed it into her mouth. She gagged. She tried to scream but no sound came out. With both of his hands now free, he held her down with one hand and pulled off her panties with the other. Struggling to keep her pinned to the mattress as she fought to escape, he managed to pull down his pants and boxers to his ankles, then kicked them onto the floor, leaving himself now naked from the waist down.

Panting heavily, he tried frantically to spread her legs and penetrate her with his now full erection. With every ounce of strength she had, she fought back, squirming and twisting and struggling to free herself. But he continued his assault, pushing down harder with his body while spreading her legs with his hands. She tried to push him off, but he was too strong. She punched him again and again on the back of his head, then pulled his hair, but it had no effect. He seemed immune to her feeble attacks and hell-bent on doing what he had intended to do. Her strength almost depleted and her legs now spread wide apart, he moved in to claim his prize. He lifted his lower body to position himself for the thrust. As he did so, his head lowered, so that his cheek pressed right up against Josie's face. She seized her last opportunity. With one free hand, she pulled the tie from her mouth. Opening her mouth wide, she clamped down on his cheek with her teeth and bit as hard as she could, almost instantly drawing blood. He screamed and jumped back, falling off the bed. Josie drew every bit of strength she still had and scrambled to her feet. But he righted himself quickly and stood facing her, only a few feet away, blood streaming from his face, naked from the waist down, his member now beginning to wilt. "You fuckin' little bitch! Look what you did to me!"

Josie knew she had to act quickly. In a few seconds, the shock would subside and he would regain his senses. Then he would beat her senseless—and rape her. Then maybe kill her.

She recalled something her brother Harry had once told her, about the weakest part of a man's body and how to exploit that weakness if she ever had to. Well, she had to. Now. She waited for the precise moment. She'd get one and only one chance to get it right. Her attacker provided the opening. He removed his hand from his cheek and looked down at the blood dripping through his fingers. She pounced. Quickly moving towards him, she kicked him as hard as she could in his scrotum. He keeled over, writhing in pain.

She grabbed her purse on the dresser and ran out the door. She couldn't wait for the elevator—she'd have to take the stairs. She raced down the hallway and located the stairwell at the far end. She bolted down the stairs two steps at a time, stumbling more than once. It was then that she realized she was barefoot. Her high-heels had come off in the attack. She obviously couldn't go back for them. She'd have to do without them.

She hadn't paid attention to which floor the suite was on, so she had no idea how many flights she had to go down. Although gasping for air, she couldn't stop to rest in case he was right behind her. But what if he took the elevator and beat her downstairs? What if he was waiting for her in the lobby?

She saw the sign—MAIN FLOOR. An arrow pointed to the left. She turned the corner and saw a door a short distance away.

She opened it slowly and peered out. She could see part of the lobby. There was no sign of him. She opened the door fully and stepped out. She looked around. Still no sign of him. She made a beeline for the front door and out onto the street.

She peered into the darkness to get her bearings. Her hotel was to the right. Or was it left? No, right. She was fairly sure. She glanced back at the hotel entrance to see if he was coming. No sign of him still. She scurried up the sidewalk, sometimes running, sometimes walking to catch her breath, frequently glancing back over her shoulder. *Where is that hotel?* she said to herself. *I think it's this way.* Her mind was clouded. She couldn't think straight. Was she lost? *No, it's around this corner. Yes, this way.*

She stubbed her toe on the curb and squealed from the pain. She stopped for a second to rub it but knew she couldn't linger. He might be right behind her. She hobbled along as fast as the pain would allow.

She was beginning to tire. She stopped and leaned up against a building to rest. She looked back, down the street. No one was following her. Catching her breath, she continued on. A minute or two later, she caught a glimpse of a taxi cab passing on a cross street just up ahead. *A cab! That's what I'll do. I'll get a cab to take me to my hotel.* She picked up her pace. Within seconds, she was at the intersection where the cab had passed. She looked up and down the street but saw nothing. It was gone. She slumped against a lamppost.

She had to keep moving. *Where is that hotel? I can't remember what street it was on. Oh my God, I'm lost!*

She kept walking. *It's got to be here somewhere. It didn't take me this long earlier.* She kept walking.

She sensed there was someone behind her. She could hear footsteps. Heavy footsteps. A man's footsteps. And they were quickening, picking up their pace. Could it be him? Could he have found her? She started walking faster, then faster and faster. Now she was running, stumbling, frantically trying to get way. Was it him? Had he found her? She had to know. Still racing forward, she looked back over her shoulder. Suddenly, she slammed into something solid. It stopped her dead in her tracks. It was a man! His arms were wrapped around her! She screamed.

"Oh, excusez-moi, mademoiselle. C'est ma faute. J'suis désolé."

Josie looked up. It wasn't him. It was a complete stranger, an older man. She regained her composure. "I'm sorry. It was my fault. I wasn't looking where I was going."

"No, it was my fault," insisted the man. "I came around the corner too fast."

As they were talking, another man walked by them and nodded, continuing up the street at a brisk pace. It was the man who had been behind Josie. Another stranger. Not her attacker. She felt both relieved and embarrassed.

The man Josie had run into glanced at her bare feet. "You're not wearing any shoes? Are you alright?"

She searched for a believable explanation. "No, I'm alright," she said, forcing a smile. "It's a funny story, really. I was at a dance, and…and somebody stole my shoes. I just need to get back to my hotel."

"What hotel are you staying at," said the man.

Josie hesitated. Should she tell him? Was she being too suspicious? She gave him the name of the hotel.

"It's just around the next corner," he said. "You're almost there."

Josie thanked the man and hurried to the corner. He was right. There it was. She was inside the hotel within seconds. Before crossing the lobby she took a moment to gather her composure, push back her hair, and straighten her dress. She remembered her attacker had torn off her panties. It didn't matter. No one would be able to tell.

She scurried through the lobby, making eye contact with the front desk clerk. He smiled, then frowned. Josie could only imagine what he was thinking.

She took the elevator to her room. Once inside, she locked the door behind her, sat on the side of the bed, and let out a huge sigh. As she sat there, though, a thought occurred to her. Had she told him where she was staying? Had she given him the name of her hotel? Maybe she had. Yes, she thought she did. No, she hadn't. She couldn't remember. They had talked about so many things. Panic gripped her. What if she did tell him? He'd come looking for her. He'd find her. He'd finish her off.

She couldn't stay there. She had to get out of the hotel as fast as possible. She couldn't take the chance. But where would she go? She couldn't go to another hotel. What if he tracked her down? Besides, she couldn't afford another hotel room. No, she had to get out of Montreal altogether. She had to get back to Halifax. She had to get to the train station. She could walk there, it was close enough. But what if he was outside waiting for her. She'd take a cab. She'd ask the desk clerk to get her a cab.

She hurried and put on a clean pair of panties and a pair of shoes. Her hands were shaking as she quickly brushed her hair and applied a fresh coat of lipstick. She packed her suitcase as fast as she could and headed down to the lobby.

"I have to leave right away," she said to the clerk. "Can you call me a taxi?"

"Is everything alright, Mademoiselle?" said the clerk.

"I just have to leave right away. It's an emergency."

"Very well, Mademoiselle."

The clerk called for a taxi. Josie settled her bill and waited in the lobby for the taxi to arrive. She was still shaking. Every second that passed was torture. Any moment she was terrified that he would walk through the door. The cab seemed to be taking forever. Finally, it arrived and took her to the train station.

The station was virtually empty. She went to the ticket counter. "I want a ticket on the next train to Halifax," she said.

"The next train to Halifax doesn't leave until seven-twenty in the morning," said the clerk.

"What time is it now?"

"It's ten after midnight."

"I'll wait."

Josie purchased her ticket and went to sit down on a bench for the long wait. As she sat there, her emotions welled up inside her. Her breathing quickened, her chest heaved, her lips quivered. She started sobbing, tears streaming down her face. She let it all out. Every fear, every rage, every shame. Every painful, agonizing memory of the past few hours.

She just wanted to go home.

Chapter 26

With a jerk, the train began to move. Ever so slowly at first, then faster and faster, until it was at full speed.

She was safe now.

Josie fell back in her seat and slumped against the window. She fought the heaviness in her eyes, but it was a losing battle. She was exhausted. Consciousness ebbed and flowed like breakers on a beach. Before long, she was out like a light.

When she woke, it took her a few seconds to remember where she was. So much had happened to her over the past few days that she was losing all sense of time and place. Squinting, she gazed out the window, as farmland whizzed by. Then it came to her. She was on a train heading home.

She stretched her arms high above her head, trying to shake the cobwebs. Her mouth was dry. She needed something to drink. After tidying her dress, brushing her hair, and touching up her lipstick, she left her berth and headed for the dining car. It was mealtime and the dining car was very busy. A clock on the wall told her it was a quarter to one. She had slept for almost four hours. After ordering a ham sandwich and a glass of milk, she found an empty table and sat down. As she ate, she scanned the room—young women like her, soldiers and sailors in uniform, businessmen in suits, mothers with their children, old men alone, old women alone. At one point, her heart skipped a beat. She had spotted a man who, from behind, looked like *him*. But when the man got up, it wasn't her attacker. It was just a man. An ordinary man.

She had to stop thinking about him, forget about him, forget she had even met him. Put the whole thing out of her mind. Erase the incident from her memory, like it had never happened. In a way, it felt like it *had* never happened. Like something unreal. A dream. Or more like a nightmare. Yes, she had to think ahead. She had to think about getting back to Halifax.

Why had she gone to Montreal in the first place? She should have stayed home. Then none of this would have happened. That man could have killed her. They would have found her in some alley with her throat slit. Or fished her bloated body out of the harbour. And all because a guy had proposed to her? A nice guy, at that. A guy probably too good for her. Why hadn't she just said no to him instead of running off like some frightened child? Why was she so impulsive? What was wrong with her?

What was she going to say to him? She couldn't face him. Not after what she had done to him. Becky had probably told him that she had gone to Montreal. There wasn't much more to say. Her actions said it all.

What was she going to say to Mr. Gorman? How was she going to explain her absence? She wondered if Becky had said anything to him. She probably did. He would have asked her why her sister hadn't shown up for work. He wouldn't be happy with the answer.

Josie finished her sandwich and milk, and went back to her berth. The day passed slowly. There wasn't much to do. She took a few short naps and walked around the train a few times but mostly just stared out the window at the scenery. Later, she went for supper, where she chatted for almost an hour with a nice elderly lady from Moncton who was returning home after attending her sister's funeral in Montreal. By seven thirty, Josie was back in her berth for the evening. After washing and changing, she went to bed about nine o'clock. She had a broken sleep, having napped throughout the day, and got up the next morning around six.

After breakfast, she went back to her berth to pack her things. Just after eight thirty, the train arrived in Halifax.

As Josie walked the ten minutes from the train station to Gorman's, she wondered if she should tell Becky about the incident. It would upset her, for sure. She'd also probably chastise her for going to Montreal in the first place; for putting herself in danger. Maybe she'd just keep it to herself.

After dropping off her suitcase in her room, she headed down to the restaurant to face the firing squad. As she entered, she scanned the room for Becky. It was just after nine and the place was still crowded from breakfast, so she didn't spot her sister right away. Then she saw her, back turned, wiping down one of the tables. She approached her from behind. "Becky?"

Becky turned. "Josie!" she screamed. "You're back!"

"I'm back."

Becky put her arms around Josie and squeezed her tight. "I'm so glad you're home. I was worried about you."

"I'm glad to be home."

Josie took a look around the restaurant. "Did you tell Mr. Gorman I was in Montreal?"

"Yes I did," said Becky."

"I suppose he wasn't too happy."

"No, he wasn't."

"What did he say?"

"Well, at first he was like the rest of us. He was worried about you, not knowing where you were. When you didn't show up for work Monday morning, I went up to your room to see if you were okay. I knocked, but there was no answer. I tried the door and it was locked. Then I got scared. I went and got Mr. Gorman to come and unlock your door. You weren't there, but your dresser drawers were open and most of your clothes were gone. I checked under the bed and your suitcase was gone as well. Then Tuesday morning, after you had called the night before, I told Mr. Gorman you were in Montreal. He got pretty mad."

Josie bowed her head. She felt both embarrassed and ashamed. "Where is he now?"

"He's gone to the bank. He should be back soon."

"I guess I'm going to have to apologize to him."

"I think that would be a good idea. And pray he gives you your job back."

Josie was puzzled. "What do you mean?"

"Well, he's already hired someone to replace you. He didn't know if or when you were coming back. He said he had a business to run."

Josie groaned. The last thing she needed right now was to lose her job. But before she had time to think about it much further, Mr. Gorman came in the door. He spotted her immediately. She went right up to him. "Hello Mr. Gorman," she said, timidly.

He smiled sardonically. "Well, the prodigal waitress has returned."

"I had to get away for a few days."

"So I heard. And you didn't bother to tell me?"

Josie searched for the right answer. "I had to leave in a hurry."

Mr. Gorman raised an eyebrow. He didn't seem impressed with Josie's explanation. He walked away and headed toward the kitchen. Josie followed him. "Mr. Gorman, Becky said you hired someone to replace me?"

Mr. Gorman kept walking. "I didn't know if you were coming back. I couldn't leave myself short."

"Well, can I come back to work now?"

Mr. Gorman stopped and turned to face Josie. "Come in to my office."

Josie followed him through the kitchen and into his office in the rear. He motioned for her to have a seat, closed the door, and sat down in his chair behind the desk. Looking her straight in the eye, he leaned forward, his hands clasped in front of him. "You're a good waitress, Josie. The customers like you. But I don't know if I can depend on you. You don't show up for work for four days and don't even take the time to leave me a note?"

Josie looked down. She had no defense.

"And that's not all," he continued. "I found out you lied to me."

Josie looked up, puzzled. "What do you mean?"

"One day last summer, when you said you were sick, you weren't sick at all. You were in jail, weren't you?"

Josie was stunned. He knew the truth. There was no point denying it. A feeling of impending doom swept over her. She lowered her head. She couldn't look him in the eye. "How did you find out?"

"When Becky told me you had disappeared and no one knew where you were, she was worried about you. So, I spoke to a friend of mine at the police station, a sergeant, about how we might try to find you, how we might track you down. When I mentioned your name, it rang a bell for him. He looked you up in the records. And, lo and behold, there you were, arrested for break and enter and theft, and eventually fined for public drunkenness. And when he mentioned that a Doris Hebb was also arrested and fined, it dawned on me. That was the day both you and Doris called in sick. I found that odd at the time that you'd both be sick on the same day, but I had no reason to doubt either of you. Now I know you were both lying."

Josie didn't know what to say. She felt both embarrassed and afraid—afraid she wasn't going to get her job back. "Mr. Gorman, I'm so sorry. I promise I won't do anything like that again."

"How can I be sure, Josie? You can't come to work because you're in jail, and you lie to me about it. Then you run off for four days without telling me. I can't take the chance that you won't go and do something crazy again. I have a business to run. Besides, I can't just let go the girl I just hired to bring you back. It wouldn't be fair to her."

"What if she doesn't work out? Can I come back then?"

Mr. Gorman slowly shook his head. "I'm sorry, Josie. I think it's better if you try to find another job."

Josie felt a lump forming in her throat. She swallowed hard. Her lower lip quivered. She bit down hard on it. She wasn't going to let him see her cry. Rising from the chair, she turned and headed for the door. Just as she was about to leave, she turned to Mr. Gorman. "What about Doris? Did you fire her, too? For lying to you?"

Mr. Gorman sighed heavily. "I can't fire Doris, she's my head waitress. She practically runs the place. But I gave her a stern warning."

"*A stern warning*", thought Josie. "*Doris gets a stern warning and I get fired.*

She felt the anger building inside her. She was mad at Mr. Gorman for not taking her back, after all her hard work over the past few years. She was mad at Doris, her so-called friend, for not sticking up for her. But most of all, she was mad at herself for all the stupid things she had done, all the bad decisions she had made. She opened the office door, charged through the kitchen, and stormed through the dining room. She almost bumped into Doris, who was taking a customer's order.

"So, you're back," sneered Doris. "I guess your mother wasn't sick after all."

Josie just glared at her and didn't answer.

Doris wasn't finished. "I lend you money because you tell me your mother's sick and then you run off to Montreal for a lark? You lied to me."

"I don't want to talk about this right now," said Josie.

"Well, *I* want to talk about it," said Doris, raising her voice. "I want my money back. Right now."

"I don't have the money right now to pay you back."

"No, you spent it all partying in Montreal."

"Doris, don't push it."

"Oh, I'm gonna push it. I want that money next payday."

"There's not going to be a next payday for me. Mr. Gorman just fired me."

"He fired you? Because you went to Montreal?"

"Not just that. Because he found out we had lied to him that time when we were in jail. Oh, and by the way, thanks for sticking up for me."

"What do you mean?"

"You get a 'stern warning' and I get fired. Some friend you are."

"Don't blame me for you getting fired. You're the one that didn't show up for work for four days. What did you expect him to do? And while we're talking about friends, what kind of friend lies to get money to go partying half way across the country. That's not the kind of friend I want."

"Fine, then I won't be your friend anymore."

"Fine with me!"

Josie pushed past Doris and flung open the restaurant door, leaving it to close on its own. Racing around to the side of the building and up the back stairs, she opened the unlocked door to her room and slammed it shut behind her. Then, throwing herself on her bed, she let it all come out. All the anger, all the shame, all the fear. She sobbed uncontrollably. Her world seemed to be coming apart at the seams. Her friends had deserted her, her family was angry with her, her boss had fired her.

She had no idea how long she cried, but eventually the sobbing subsided. She sat up on the side of her bed and wiped her eyes with the back of her hand. What was she going to do now?

For starters, she had to find a new job. But before she would even begin her search, something would happen that would shake the very foundation of her existence.

Chapter 27

Josie was awakened by a knock on her door. "Who is it?"

"It's me."

Becky? Josie glanced at her alarm clock. Ten to seven. What did Becky want at this time of the morning? She got out of bed, put on her housecoat, and opened the door. Becky was standing there in her waitress uniform.

"You woke me up," said Josie.

"I have to talk to you," said Becky, as she pushed past her sister and entered the room.

"About what?"

"Close the door."

Josie closed the door and turned to Becky. Her brow furrowed. "What's wrong, Becky?"

"I got a telephone call from Agatha last night. She was calling from Uncle Ted's."

"What did she want? Is something wrong?"

"Mom's very sick."

"You mean, like the flu or something?"

"No. Much worse." Becky stared at her sister. Her eyes moistened.

"Becky! Tell me. What is it?"

"It's cancer."

"Cancer?! Are they sure?"

"Agatha said Mom hadn't been feeling good for some time. But you know Mom. She never complains about herself, and she hates to go to the doctor. But I guess it got so bad that Dad started to notice. She'd get tired easily and have to sit down, and Dad could tell she was in a lot of pain. He finally convinced her to go to the doctor. They did some tests, and the doctor said it was cancer."

"What kind of cancer is it?"

"I guess it started in her female parts, then spread."

"But she's going to be okay, isn't she? They're going to operate or something, aren't they?"

Tears began trickling down Becky's face. She ran to Josie and threw her arms around her neck. "Oh Josie! We're going to lose our mother!"

The two sisters hugged each other tight. Becky's body heaved up and down as her tears dampened Josie's housecoat. Josie was in shock. Stunned. Could this be happening? Was her mother dying? It couldn't be. There had to be some kind of mistake. Doctors made mistakes all the time. Maybe they were wrong. Maybe the tests were wrong. Her mother couldn't die. Not now. What would her father do?

Josie broke her embrace with Becky. "I have to talk to Agatha. There has to be something they can do."

Becky wiped her face with her sleeve. "Agatha said the doctor told her there's nothing that can be done. The cancer is too far gone."

"I don't care what the doctor said," said Josie. "They have to do something."

Becky sniffed and rubbed her nose. "I have to get to work. My shift starts at seven. I'll talk to you later."

After Becky left, Josie got dressed and went downstairs to call Uncle Ted from the pay phone at Gorman's. When she reached him, she asked him to have Agatha call her at Becky's place at seven o'clock that night. Josie didn't discuss her mother's condition with her uncle. He didn't bring it up either. If he knew, he didn't let on.

Josie went over to Becky's after supper to wait for Agatha's call. Agatha called precisely at seven and she and Josie talked at length, while Becky sat nearby listening to Josie's side of the conversation. When Josie got off the phone, she turned to Becky.

"What did she say?" said Becky.

"The same thing she told you. The doctor says there's nothing that can be done."

Becky took a deep breath and exhaled. "I can't believe it."

Josie looked at her sister. "I'm going down. I'm going to talk to the doctor myself. There's got to be something they can do, with all the modern medicine these days."

"Maybe we should both go."

"Well, you're working, I'm not. You don't want to miss any time."

"I'm sure Mr. Gorman would give me a couple of days off. Maybe Albert could ask his boss if he could borrow his car and we could drive down. I can talk to Albert about it tonight. If Mom's that sick, I want to see her before it's too late."

"Don't say that, Becky."

"Well, if the doctor is right."

"He can't be right. Anyway, talk to Albert and let me know."

Josie gave her sister a hug and headed back to her place.

The next day, Becky came up to Josie's room during her break and told her that Albert had agreed to ask his boss to borrow his car, but they'd only be able to go down for the weekend because Albert was too busy at work to miss a weekday. They'd leave right after work Friday afternoon. Becky and Albert would return late Sunday afternoon. It would be a short visit, but at least Becky would get to see her mother. Josie would stay longer to try and see the doctor.

They left Halifax around two o'clock Friday afternoon. Albert's boss had loaned him his car and given him the afternoon off so they could leave early. His boss would use one of the Navy vehicles for the weekend. Albert just had to pay for the gas.

The trip took a little over six hours. They arrived at Josie's parents' house just after eight o'clock. They hadn't told anyone they were coming, not even Agatha, so their mother and father were quite surprised when the three of them walked in the door.

"What are you kids doing here?" said their mother.

"We came for a visit," said Josie.

"A visit? All the way from Halifax? Have you lost your mind?"

"We wanted to see you, Mom," said Becky. "To see how you were feeling."

Their mother seemed annoyed. "I'm feeling fine. Why shouldn't I be?"

Josie glanced over at her father. He lowered his eyes.

"Aren't you glad to see us, Mom?" said Josie.

"Well, of course, I'm always glad to see you, but…"

"Then give us a hug."

Josie gave her mother a hug. Becky then hugged her mother as well. Both girls then hugged their father.

"What have you got to eat, Mom?" said Josie. "We're starved. We didn't eat on the way down."

"Oh, of course. Where's my head? We have some ham left over from dinner last night, and some mustard pickles and homemade bread. Charles, boil the kettle for tea."

For at least the next hour or so, there was no talk of cancer, or sickness, or anything distressing. Josie and her family members enjoyed a meal together and some lively conversation about who made the best mustard pickles (Josie's mother or her grandmother), and whether tea was better for you than coffee. There were differences of opinion on both subjects but all in good fun. After the meal, Josie's mother suggested that the others play a game of cribbage while she washed the dishes. Josie insisted that she help her mother, so the others started into a three-handed game. As her mother washed and Josie dried, her mother leaned over to her and whispered so the others couldn't hear. "I know why you're all here."

"What do you mean?" said Josie.

"You came down because you think I'm dying."

The bluntness of her mother's words startled Josie. "Mom, don't be silly. We came down to visit you and Dad. Albert had his boss's car for the weekend, so we thought we'd come down."

"Josie, I know Agatha called Becky and told her about the cancer."

Josie wasn't sure what to say next. "Well, okay, we know about the cancer. We came down to see how you were feeling. Not because we think you're dying. Maybe the doctors are wrong. They can make mistakes too, you know."

"Josie, when the Good Lord thinks it's my time, he'll take me. Doesn't matter what the doctors say. In the meantime, I have to look after the house and look after your father. Nothing has changed."

Josie's mother never brought up the subject again for the rest of the weekend. Neither did anyone else. They just played cards, and talked, and ate. Agatha and Beatrice came over for supper on Saturday. Beatrice brought her kids. Agatha left hers with her husband Lawrence. Sunday morning, everyone went to mass. Outside the church after mass, they spoke with other members of the family, as well as several of the locals. Some asked Josie how her mother was feeling. Obviously, her mother's illness was no secret. That's the way it was in a small community. Everybody knew everybody else's business.

By three o'clock Sunday afternoon they were ready to head back to Halifax. Josie had warned Becky not to get too emotional when they left so as not to upset their mother. They couldn't make it seem that it would be the last time she would see her daughters, even though deep down they knew it might. Becky managed to hold it together fairly well, under the circumstances. She smiled, kissed her mother, told her to take care of herself, and said they'd visit the next chance they got.

Albert went out and started the car and waited in the vehicle. Josie's mother then turned to her daughter. "You better get going. Give me a kiss."

"I'm not going back with them," said Josie. "I think I'll stay for a few more days."

The announcement caught her mother by surprise. "What? Don't you have to get back to work?"

"I can take a few days off. Mr. Gorman won't mind. Right Becky?"

Josie looked over at her sister, hoping she would play along and not give her away.

"Sure," said Becky.

Their mother frowned. Josie sensed that she wanted to say something, but she remained silent.

"How will you get back?" said their father.

"I'll take the train or hitch a ride with someone going to Halifax," said Josie. "I'll worry about that later."

Just then, Albert beeped the car horn.

"You better get going," Josie said to Becky. "It's getting late."

Everyone went outside. Becky hugged her mother and father. She glanced at Josie, pursed her lips, but said nothing. She then got in the car. As they drove away, Becky stuck her head out of the window and waved.

Josie and her parents went back into the house. Almost immediately, her mother grabbed a broom and started sweeping the kitchen floor, not saying a word, not making eye contact with her daughter or her husband. Josie and her father looked at each other, then her father lowered his head and went out the back door. Josie stood watching her mother work. "Do you need any help?" she asked.

"No," said her mother, without looking up.

"I'm going for a walk, then."

Josie's mother didn't reply. She just kept sweeping.

Chapter 28

The end came peacefully enough. She took a breath, exhaled, and never took another breath. Josie had never seen someone die before, but she was glad she was at her bedside at the end. She kissed her mother on the forehead and went downstairs to give her father the news.

When Josie's eyes met her father's, she didn't have to say a word. He knew. He said he wanted to be alone with his wife and went upstairs. When he came back down, he hugged his daughter hard.

Her mother had gone downhill rapidly in the past few weeks. The doctor had been coming over every couple of days to give her a shot of morphine to deaden the pain. There was nothing else he could do. She had fought as hard as she could. Her fight was over. No more pain. She was now at rest.

Josie's father had maintained a brave front through it all. He served on his wife hand and foot, giving her everything she asked for and trying to make her as comfortable as possible. He told her not to give up hope and had knelt by her bed as they prayed for God's mercy. In the almost three months she had been home from Halifax, Josie had never once seen her father shed a tear. If he had indeed cried, he had done it secretly where no one could see him.

The body was waked at the house for two days and two nights, as per the local custom. Agatha had made all the arrangements. People flowed in continuously to pay their respects. Neighbours brought sandwiches and squares. The priest came to offer a blessing. The women from the CWL led everyone in saying the rosary.

Becky and Albert were down from Halifax. (Albert's mother wasn't able to join them.) All the rest of Josie's family were there, except George and Harry, and Beatrice's husband Cecil, who were all still overseas. Agatha had written to her brothers when the cancer was diagnosed, so they knew what was coming. Josie was sure their hearts were breaking that they couldn't be home to see their mother one last time. War was hell.

The daughters took turns staying up throughout the night for the two nights of the wake. That was another custom—the body was never to be left alone. Someone had to be with it at all times. Josie wasn't sure why, but that's the way it had always been done.

For two long days, Josie's father endured the steady parade of well-meaning visitors paying their respects. "Sorry for your loss," they would say to him, or "She was a wonderful woman," or "She's with God now." He would thank them, or politely nod, or engage in small talk. On the surface, he looked like he was holding up well, that he had prepared himself for this inevitable moment. But Josie knew better. She knew her father. She could see below the surface. She saw a shattered man, a man so deeply heartbroken that his very essence had drained out of him. His eyes were lifeless, staring into space, hollow and empty. He had lost his sweetheart, his companion, his tranquil harbour in the storm of life.

The church was packed for the funeral mass. The pews were all full, the balcony was overflowing, and men were standing in the aisles and at the back. Albert was one of the pallbearers, along with Agatha's husband Lawrence, Rose's husband Joseph, Margaret's husband Leonard, Uncle Ted, and Uncle Norman, another brother of Josie's mother. As the coffin was carried down the centre aisle to the foot of the altar, the women all cried and the men all looked solemn. That was the way it always was at funerals.

In his homily, the priest praised the deceased as a woman of faith, as a devoted wife, and as a loving mother who accepted God's gift of children with an open heart. He talked about the "immortality of the soul" and the "resurrection of the body", and how earthly death was not the end of life but, with God's grace, a new life in heaven with the "communion of saints." He commended "our sister" to God's merciful love and asked him to forgive her sins. Josie couldn't imagine that her mother had committed very many sins in her life.

When the mass was over and the coffin was being carried by the pallbearers back up the aisle, the women all cried again and the men all remained stoic. All the men except Josie's father. He finally broke down, sobbing unabashedly. Agatha and Rose put their arms around him to console him. Josie looked over at him from her spot further down the pew. It tore her apart to see him like that.

For Josie, the worst part of the funeral service was the gravesite ceremony. It was the finality of it. At the wake, it felt like her mother was still with them, sleeping peacefully in the coffin. Even at the mass, she was still among her family and friends. But once they lowered the coffin into that hole, it was over. She was gone. Alone in the cold ground.

From the cemetery, the immediate family and some close friends gathered back at the house. Agatha made some tea and put out some bread and molasses. Josie didn't feel much like eating. She kept looking over at her father sitting on the couch by himself. He hadn't said more than a few words all day. Agatha tried to get him to eat something, but he said he wasn't hungry. All he had was a cup of tea.

The afternoon was filled with small talk and reminiscences. Everyone was generally subdued, understandably so. Except the younger children, of course. They were behaving like you'd expect young children to behave—running and yelling and playing. They were too young to fully understand what had happened.

Josie thought that was a good thing. She wanted them to remain innocent to the heartaches of life for as long as they could.

Most of the family stayed for supper. After the table was cleared and the dishes washed and put away, the crowd began to thin out as mothers gathered up their children and headed home to prepare them for bed. Some of the men stayed a little longer to smoke and have a drink of rum. But before long they too headed home. By nine o'clock there was just Josie, her father, Becky, and Albert left at the house. Becky and Albert were staying overnight and leaving for Halifax in the morning.

Just before ten o'clock, Becky got up from her chair and stretched her arms above her head. "It's been a long day. I'm tired. I'm going to bed. Are you coming Albert?"

Albert nodded and went upstairs with his wife, leaving Josie and her father alone. Josie turned to her father. "You should get to bed too, Dad. You must be exhausted."

"I won't be able to sleep," he replied.

"Well, you need to at least try. You haven't slept much in the last few days."

He didn't respond. He just stared at the floor. Josie watched him for several seconds, then got up from her chair. She went into the kitchen and fetched a rum bottle from the cupboard under the sink. She found two clean glasses on the counter and poured roughly equal amounts of liquor in each one. She took the two drinks into the living room and handed one to her father. He looked up. "I don't want that," he said.

"Take it," said Josie. "It'll help you sleep."

Josie's father stared at the glass for a second or two, then took it. Josie pulled her chair next to her father on the couch. She raised her glass. "To Mom," she said.

He hesitated for a moment, then raised his glass and clinked it with Josie's. "To Sarah." He took a mouthful, then leaned back and sighed.

For the next hour or so, Josie and her father sipped rum and talked about Josie's mother. Her father recalled when he had first met her and had known right away that he would marry her someday. He talked about how nervous she had been on their wedding night and how nervous he had been when their first child, Rose, was born. He talked about her love of family, especially her children, and how proud she was of them. He talked about how she always liked to have the house full of people, how she loved cooking for a crowd, and how she loved to hear the local gossip. He talked about her strength, her stubbornness at times, and her faith in God to the end.

They drank, they talked, they laughed, and they cried. And as the time wore on, Josie could see her father growing tired, his eyes growing heavy. Before long he was asleep, with his head slumped back on the couch. Josie took the glass from his hand and placed it on the floor. She laid him down on the couch without waking him. She went upstairs and got a blanket and covered him with it. After picking up the glasses and putting the rum back in the cupboard, she went upstairs to bed. She buried her head in her pillow to muffle the sound and cried herself to sleep.

Chapter 29

The crowing of a rooster roused her from her sleep, as the early morning light pierced the room. She rubbed her eyes, stretched, and yawned. After lying in bed for a few minutes, she got up, put on a robe, and went downstairs. Her father was already up. Even though it was July, a fire was burning in the stove, just enough to take the chill from the ocean air.

"Good morning Dad."

"Good morning Josie."

"Did you sleep?"

"I slept a little."

Josie sat down on a chair at the kitchen table. She watched her father as he gathered the items for breakfast.

"Can you make the tea?" said her father.

Josie fetched the kettle, filled it with water from the boiler, and placed it on the stove. She then took the tea pot and dumped in two scoops of tea. When the water boiled, she filled the tea pot and placed it on the table to steep.

"Are Becky and Albert still sleeping?" said her father.

"I guess so," said Josie. "I didn't hear any movement."

Josie sat back down and continued to watch her father scurry about. She wondered if he was just trying to keep himself busy. Neither of them said anything for several minutes. Her father broke the silence. "Josie, I want you to go back to Halifax with Becky and Albert."

The request caught her off guard. About a week after she had first come down from Halifax, Josie had come clean with her parents. She had told them about Hector's marriage proposal, about her trip to Montreal, and about losing her job at Gorman's. They were upset at first, but as her mother's cancer progressed, there were more important things to worry about and the subject never came up again. Until now.

"Why?" said Josie.

"You need to get back to Halifax and find a job," said her father.

With her mother's illness, and then the funeral, Josie hadn't thought much about going back to Halifax, or getting a job, or anything at all about her future. But now her father's words brought her back to reality. What was she going to do? She couldn't leave her father alone. Not now. He needed her. And really, what was there for her in Halifax? She didn't have a job. Or a boyfriend. Or any female friends either, after her blowup with Doris. Was there any reason to go back? Everything had changed. Her whole world had been turned upside down. Maybe God was trying to tell her something. Maybe home was the best place for her to be.

"No, I'm not going back," said Josie. "I've decided that I'm going to stay with you. I'm going to move home for good."

"Josie, this is not the place for you. There's nothing for you here. You'd go crazy here. You're not like your older sisters. You're like a bird that needs to fly. You went to Halifax to get away from here. To make a new life for yourself."

"And look how that's turned out."

"You've had a bit of a setback, that's all. You'll bounce back. You're still young."

Josie pondered his words. As always, he was right. There wasn't much for her in Perch Cove. But she hated to leave her father alone, especially so soon. "But what about you?" she said. "You'll be all by yourself."

"I'll be fine. I can look after myself. Besides, Beatrice is here all the time. And the little ones. They'll keep me busy. Anyway, Josie, you have to look out for yourself. Make your own life."

Tears welled in her eyes. She got up from the chair and hugged her father. "I'll stay for two more weeks, then I'll go back."

"Good. Now pour us some tea. It should be nice and strong by now."

Josie filled their cups and they sipped their tea and talked about nothing in particular. Becky and Albert came down shortly after and they all had breakfast together. After breakfast, Becky packed their suitcase and Albert put it in the trunk. Josie told Becky she'd be going back to Halifax in two weeks on the train. Becky cried as she said her goodbyes to her father. They hugged each other long and hard.

Nine days later, Uncle Ted told Josie that one of his company's trucks was going to Halifax the following morning and she could hitch a ride if she wanted to. Her father told her to take him up on his offer. She accepted.

Their last evening together, Josie and her father went upstairs to her parents' bedroom to go through her mother's personal things—mostly her clothes, some religious articles, and a few keepsakes. Nothing had been removed since her mother's passing.

"Is there anything you want?" said Josie's father.

"Oh, I don't think so," said Josie.

"What about her wedding ring? You're our only daughter who isn't married. Your mother would probably want you to have it."

"No, you keep it, Dad. It'll help you remember Mom."

"Oh, I won't have any problems remembering her. I'll think about her every day. I can still feel her here in the house. She's with me every night when I go to bed."

Josie felt a lump in her throat. Her eyes watered but she held back the tears, for her father's sake. She kept rummaging through the items.

"Some of these clothes you should throw out, Dad," said Josie.

"I'll let the other girls go through them and take what they want," said her father.

"What they don't want, I'll give to the church. They send them to the needy."

When they were finished with the clothes, Josie's father pulled out the top drawer of a small bedroom dresser and dumped the contents on the bed. They were mostly religious items—a prayer book, a rosary, some religious medals. But then Josie came across a scapular. It triggered her memory.

"There is something I'll take with me, Dad," she said. "It's downstairs in the cupboard, unless Mom moved it."

Josie headed down the stairs with her father following behind. She went to the kitchen, climbed on a chair, and opened the cupboard door. The box was still there. She took it down, placed it on the kitchen table, and opened it.

"What's all this?" asked her father.

"It's something Mom wanted me to have," said Josie. "It's things from my childhood. She wanted to give them to me at Becky's wedding. She said I could show them to my little girl one day. I told her to keep them with her for the time being. I guess there's no reason to keep them here now."

Josie and her father leafed through the items—the scapular, a crucifix, Josie's first communion certificate, a photo of a dog.

"Is this King?" said Josie's father, holding up the photo.

"Yes it is," said Josie.

"He was a good dog."

"Yes he was."

Josie held up another item. "Look Dad, it's the gold star I won in a spelling bee in Grade 3. You were pretty proud of me."

Her father put his hand on hers. "I still am."

Josie wondered what he had to be proud of. She had given him many reasons to be ashamed of her instead. But that was a parent's love. Blind.

When they had finished going through all the items, Josie closed the box and put it aside to take with her in the morning.

For the rest of the evening, her and her father just talked. They talked about how she was going to get a new job when she returned to Halifax. They talked about how Josie's father would manage by himself. And they reminisced about their mother and their wife—about her strong will, her hard work, and her love of her family. Josie didn't want the night to end. She wanted to spend as much time with her father as she could. She wanted to soak up his spirit and his strength.

It was after midnight by the time they went to bed.

By seven o'clock the next morning Josie was on her way back to the big city. As she waved goodbye to her father, she recalled his words of encouragement from ten days earlier. "You've had a bit of a setback, that's all. You'll bounce back."

She appreciated her father's assurances. Only, she wasn't quite so sure.

Chapter 30

Finding another waitress job proved more difficult than Josie had imagined. She tried the Green Lantern, but when the manager there wanted to know why she had left Gorman's, she had no choice but to tell him the truth. He knew Mr. Gorman personally and told her he could check out her story. That killed her chances. The same thing happened at the Riviera, and at the Garden View, and at Lohnes'. It seemed that every restaurant manager in Halifax knew Mr. Gorman.

About two weeks into her search, Josie heard that Simpson's was looking for waitresses for their lunch counter. It only paid eleven dollars a week, and the tips would be a lot less than at Gorman's, but it was a job, so she went to see about it. They asked her about her experience and she told them she had worked at Gorman's, but they never asked her why she had left. Instead, they hired her on the spot. But that posed another problem. Simpson's was way out in the west end of the city and it took two tramcars to get there. Her very first day on the job, she arrived late, which didn't go over very well with her new boss. She started leaving for work earlier, but that didn't always help, especially when she was working the early morning shift, because the tramcar schedule was not always reliable. When one week she showed up late three days in a row, the manager let her go. She wasn't overly upset, though. With the low pay, minus the cost of travelling to work, and considering how few hours she was getting, it wasn't that great of a job anyway. Besides, she still believed she could find something closer to her place.

It didn't turn out that way. Even when she found a restaurant manager who didn't know Mr. Gorman, they weren't hiring. It seemed that as the war had dragged on, people were watching their pennies more closely and not eating at restaurants as much. Even the sailors were spending less. And when there *was* an opening, there were still so many girls looking for work that jobs were filled almost instantly. You had to be in the right place at the right time. It was just a matter of luck.

Josie had focused her search on waitressing jobs because that's what she knew, and she enjoyed the work. But she eventually realized she'd have to look for something else. She had no choice. She needed a job. She needed to pay her rent.

One day, while she was telling the Chinese man who lived across the hall about her difficulty finding employment, he mentioned that the hotel laundry where he worked was looking for people. Apparently, after Japan had entered the war, the hotel had stopped hiring Orientals, even though all of them were Chinese, not Japanese. They were now having problems filling vacancies because local people didn't want to work in a laundry room. Josie didn't much like the idea either, but she was getting desperate, so she decided to check it out. Hopefully, it would just be a stopgap until she could find something better.

The manager at the laundry was a greasy, balding, overweight man with huge hands. When Josie went to see him about the job, he scanned her up and down like he was choosing a side of beef, chomping down on an unlit stogie the entire time. After trying unsuccessfully to convince her that the laundry was no place for a girl like her, he gave her the job, promising to pay her more than what the Chinese were getting. "Just don't tell them," he had said, "or you're fired." When he told her how much she'd be getting, she couldn't believe that anyone would work for less than that.

The laundry turned out to be every bit the hellhole the manager had said it was. Steamy, hot, noisy, and back-breaking.

When Josie would get home after work, she'd be so drained and exhausted that she had no energy to do anything. She'd usually just take a bath and go to bed.

Her life was changing in other ways, too. Since being fired from Gorman's, she wasn't eating her meals there anymore because now she'd have to pay full price, like any regular customer. Besides, it would be awkward seeing Mr. Gorman after what had happened between them. So, she had found an old hotplate and was fixing her meals in her room. As a result, she was eating a lot less and was losing weight. Being worn out from her job didn't help either. Sometimes she'd come home and just have a slice of bread with peanut butter.

Her social life was changing as well—dramatically. Things were over between her and Hector. Right or wrong, she hadn't spoken with him since his proposal, and he hadn't tried to get in touch with her either. Even if he wanted to reconcile, she had no interest in getting back together, and had made that crystal clear to Becky. She assumed the message had been passed along.

And then there was the blow-up with Doris. She hadn't spoken to her since. Needless to say, they hadn't gone to any dances together either. In fact, Josie hadn't been to a dance at all since the Montreal "lark." With what she was getting paid at the laundry, money was tight. Rent and food were her first priorities. Besides, most of the time she was too tired to go dancing. But the main reason was because she didn't have anyone to go with. She wasn't going to ask Doris, and Becky was married to someone who didn't like to dance. Besides them, she didn't really have any other friends. For the first few years she had lived in Halifax, it had been her and Becky all the time. Then Doris had entered the picture. Now, there was no one. Even her relationship with Becky had changed. They still talked once in a while, but now that Becky was married they spent less time together. They were still sisters, of course, but it wasn't the same. Sadly, they were beginning to drift apart.

But where would she find new friends? It wasn't like she could make friends at work. Most of her co-workers couldn't speak English. And where could she meet new people? At a dance? No, not a good idea for a young girl to go to a dance alone. Instead, she stayed home. In her room. Go to work, go home, go to bed. That had become her life.

And then there was the drinking. One day after work, she decided to go for a walk instead of going straight home. She had just been paid and was feeling a little more buoyant than usual, and was even thinking about taking in a movie that night, even if she had to go by herself. As she walked along Hollis, she spotted the liquor store across the street. She thought maybe just a drink or two would help her relax and enjoy the movie. So she purchased a pint of lemon gin and took it home. She never made it to the movie. After a couple of drinks in her room, she felt so relaxed that she fell asleep and didn't wake up until the next morning.

In the weeks that followed, the trip to the liquor store became a weekly occurrence. She'd buy a pint of lemon gin, or sometimes rum, stop by a corner store for some mix, head back to her room, and drink. By herself. Sometimes she'd finish the whole pint, other times she'd fall asleep before the bottle was empty. She began telling the guys at the liquor store that it was her weekly "treat." But it soon became her weekly "re-treat," her escape from the real world. The one time each week when she was "feeling no pain," as she would say to herself. The one time each week when she didn't think about her lousy job, her bills, her deepening loneliness.

As the weeks wore on, the once-a-week trip to the liquor store became twice a week, then three times a week. Before long, she was spending so much money on booze that she was falling behind on her rent. Mr. Gorman had warned her that if she didn't keep up her payments, she wouldn't be able to stay there any longer. But she didn't care. The only thing she cared about was that feeling she'd get from the bottle, that feeling of exhilaration, of power, of invincibility—until she'd reach that threshold, that tipping point, when all she'd feel would be confusion and disorientation, until she'd pass out.

As she drank more, other parts of her life began to unravel as well. Her relationship with Becky worsened as Becky found out about her heavy drinking and admonished her for it, leading to several heated arguments. Her work suffered, as she began to show up late for her morning shift after an evening of drinking. Before long, she was missing entire shifts, drinking all night and sleeping all day. Her health suffered too, as she hardly took the time to eat. The booze consumed her, dictating her every thought and action. She worked just enough to pay for her habit, unconcerned, even unaware, of anything else. Her life spiraled out of control, like a runaway train on a winding mountain slope, unable to stop, barreling to an inevitable fiery crash.

The crash came one rainy October afternoon as she was returning home from the laundry. She had had a particularly rough week, with her boss on one of his rampages and her suffering from a bad hangover. To make matters worse, Mr. Gorman had informed her she had one week to pay her back rent or he was evicting her. That afternoon, she had felt nauseous and light-headed, and asked her boss if she could leave early. As she neared Gorman's, the light-headedness returned, only worse. Feeling faint, she stopped and leaned against a building. She began to see flashes of light, twinkling, like stars, blurring her vision. The sounds of the street grew dim, muffled, distant. She could feel herself swaying back and forth, spinning and spinning like a top. Her eyes grew heavy, her knees weak, her body limp. And then, blackness.

When she awoke, a man in a white coat was looking down at her. It took her a few moments to realize he was a doctor and that she was lying in a bed in a hospital.

"Welcome back, Miss Bourdeau," said the doctor. "How are you feeling?"

Josie didn't respond right away. She was still trying to gain her bearings. Then it dawned on her that the doctor had called her Miss Bourdeau. "How do you know my name?" she asked.

"The man who brought you in gave it to us," he replied.

"The man who brought me in? What was his name?"

The doctor checked his clipboard. "A Mr. Gorman. He said you had collapsed on the street near his restaurant."

Josie felt both embarrassed and grateful. The irony of being helped by the man who was about to evict her.

"So, how are you feeling?" repeated the doctor.

"Tired," said Josie.

"I'm not surprised. You're badly dehydrated and under nourished. When was the last time you had a good meal?"

"I…I can't remember."

Josie wasn't interested in discussing her eating habits. She was still thinking about her Good Samaritan. "Is Mr. Gorman still here?"

"Yes, he's waiting to see you. There are also a couple of other people out there who want to see you. Can I let them in?"

"Yes. Yes, please."

The doctor left the room. A couple of minutes later, the door flung open and in bolted Becky, followed by Albert and Mr. Gorman, then the doctor. Becky rushed to the side of Josie's hospital bed. "Oh my God, Josie!" said Becky, nearly in tears. "What happened? Are you alright? You look terrible."

"I'm fine," said Josie. "I just fainted."

"The doctor said you came in here in bad shape. He said you were very sick."

"I'm fine, really."

"It's the liquor. I'm telling you, Josie, you have to stop drinking. I told you that before. Look what it's doing to you. It's going to kill you."

"Becky, I don't need a lecture right now. I just want to get out of here and get back to my place."

Becky glanced at Mr. Gorman and Albert. Josie noticed they both had strange looks on their faces. Something was up. Becky turned to her sister. "Josie, you're not going back to your place, you're coming to stay with us. With Albert and me."

"What?"

"We all discussed it and we decided that it's the best thing for you."

"You…you all decided? You don't get to decide for me. I decide for myself. I'm not a child, Becky. I can make my own decisions."

Becky glanced again at Mr. Gorman. "Well, you have no choice, Josie. If you don't come and stay with us, Mr. Gorman is going to evict you anyway."

Josie couldn't believe what she was hearing. She stared at her former boss. "Mr. Gorman? Is that true?"

"Josie, you haven't paid me any rent in three months. I can't allow that to continue. What if my other tenants found out? I've already let this go much too far."

"But Mr. Gorman, I promise I'll make my payments as soon as I find a better job. I promise."

"Josie, you're drinking every cent you make. You have to get off the booze. This is the best thing for you. Go stay with your sister for a while, get yourself straightened out, get your life back on track."

Josie was crushed. Everyone was turning against her. Her whole world was collapsing. She lashed out. "I'll just go stay somewhere else! I don't need any of you!"

Becky pushed back. "Josie, don't be so stubborn. You need help. I'm your sister and I'm going to help you through this. That's what sisters do. You're coming to live with us and that's that. No argument!"

Josie was taken aback by Becky's forcefulness. She was angry with her, but she admired her strength. It weakened Josie's resistance. She knew deep down that Mr. Gorman was right. The booze was taking over her life and dragging it down to the gutter.

Part of her wanted to fight this battle herself, but part of her was comforted by Becky's support. She lowered her head. "I can't come and live with you guys," she said softly. "Albert and I will be fighting all the time."

Becky looked over at her husband. "Albert?"

Albert hesitated, then took Becky's cue. "I'd be happy to have you come and stay with us, Josie."

"Then it's decided," said Becky triumphantly. "We'll get you discharged from here, go over to your place to pick up your things, then get you settled in at our place."

Josie glanced over at Albert. She could tell he wasn't completely thrilled about the whole idea, but he had no choice. His wife called the shots. Anyway, she wasn't going to use Albert as an excuse to refuse Becky's offer. Becky had won. Josie had no defiance left in her. She was tired. Tired of arguing. Tired of resisting. Tired of struggling. Tired of feeling lousy all the time.

She was ready to give in.

Chapter 31

Becky converted a small reading room in their flat into a bed-room and borrowed a cot from Albert's mother to serve as Josie's bed. It was smaller than the bed she had at Mr. Gorman's, but it wasn't uncomfortable. Anyway, beggars couldn't be choosers.

Mr. Gorman had forgiven Josie's back rent. He had told her it was his contribution to helping her get back on her feet. With everything that had happened between them, between the firing and the eviction, she still liked Mr. Gorman. He was a decent man.

While Josie appreciated what Becky had done for her, living with her sister and Albert wasn't easy. As much as Becky tried to make her feel at home, she still felt like an intruder, imposing on their little love nest. Because there was no door to the read-ing room (Becky had hung a curtain to provide some privacy), at night Josie could often hear sounds coming from Becky and Albert's bedroom down the hall—sometimes muffled voices but occasionally, Josie assumed, the sounds of Becky and Albert making love. She was sure Becky had told Albert to keep the noise down, but Josie knew men couldn't always control themselves in the heat of the moment. After a few such awkward evenings, Josie started stuffing pieces of Kleenex in her ears.

Using the facilities was also awkward at times. The flat had only one bathroom, so the three of them had to share it. The biggest problem was in the morning when they were all getting ready for work. Albert got annoyed a few times when he felt Josie was taking too long, so she began getting up extra early to be finished before Albert got up. But then he'd still complain about all the strands of long, dark hair in the sink. After a while, Josie started brushing her hair in her room.

But the biggest problem for Josie was her loss of independence, of self-reliance. She was beholden to someone else for the roof over her head and the food on her plate. Yes, she had her own room, sort of, but it really wasn't hers. She wasn't paying for it. It had been given to her. It was charity. And even though Becky had said she could have the run of the house and do what she wanted, this was Becky and Albert's place, not hers. Ever since she had moved to Halifax, she'd had her own place, paid her own way, did what she wanted. Here, she felt restricted, confined, caged. Here she was a trespasser, a beggar.

At this point in her life, though, she had little choice. She had nowhere else to go. She was broke. Her escapade in Montreal and her heavy drinking over the past few months had used up what little savings she had. And with what she was getting paid at work, and the limited hours she was getting, she couldn't afford her own place anyway. At least, not until she could find a better job. For now, she'd just have to put up with it. Make the best of it. And try to stay out of Albert's way.

Her limited funds meant she didn't have much of a social life, either. No eating out in restaurants, no going to the movies, no dances even, although she'd rather lost interest in going to dances. Too many bad memories. And too much danger of falling off the wagon. Instead, she stayed home a lot with Becky and Albert. They didn't go out much either, except on weekends, when they'd sometimes socialize with couples that Albert knew through his work. Of course, Josie wouldn't be invited, and she wouldn't expect to be. During the week, Josie and Becky would chat a little after supper as they were washing the dishes, while Albert would have a smoke and read the newspaper in the parlour. Becky and Albert would usually go to bed early, although they didn't always go to sleep right away, since Josie could hear them talking (*probably Albert complaining about me*, she thought). Josie would then go to her room and listen to a small radio that Becky had given her. (On low volume, naturally, so as not to disturb Albert.) It made for a long evening, since Josie was accustomed to staying up late. So, that became her routine—getting up, going to work, coming home, eating supper, helping Becky with the dishes, retiring to her room, washing up, listening to the radio, then going to sleep. The next day, the same thing all over again.

As the weeks passed, not much changed. Each day was much the same as the day before. When the weather had been better, she and Becky would sometimes walk to the Public Gardens on a Sunday afternoon after mass. But as it turned colder, they stopped going. A couple of times they had gone shopping on a Saturday, but Josie didn't have any money to buy anything, so they discontinued that too. Josie knew that her sister was trying to spend as much time with her as she could, but her husband came first, and he often wanted them to do things just as a couple, or with other couples. Becky would occasionally ask Josie if she wanted to join them, but she'd usually decline. She always felt like an intruder.

By Christmas season, Josie was in a rut—lethargic, listless, with no energy. Not going anywhere, not doing anything other than working, eating, and sleeping. Spending hours alone in her little room, in her bed. Most nights she wouldn't even turn on the radio anymore. She'd just stare at the ceiling, almost in a trance, her mind blank. Even when Becky asked her to join her for something or another, Josie would pass, saying she was too tired. And she *was* tired. Tired physically, tired mentally, tired with her life.

One evening, about a week before Christmas, Becky pulled Josie aside as they were clearing away the supper dishes. "Albert's mother has invited us to her place for Christmas dinner this year."

"That's nice," said Josie.

"And you're invited as well."

"Oh, Becky, I appreciate you inviting me, but I'm sure Albert's family doesn't want me at their Christmas dinner."

"It's not me who's inviting you, it's Albert's mother who's inviting you. She insisted we bring you along."

"And what did Albert say?"

"He was fine with it."

"Really?"

"Josie, it's Christmas. My husband's not Scrooge."

An image popped into Josie's head, but she bit her tongue. "I don't know, Becky. I'll just be in the way."

"Don't be silly. Anyway, you can't stay here by yourself on Christmas Day. It wouldn't be right."

"I'll go down to the Navy kitchen. They always serve the bums at Christmas. I'll fit right in."

Becky rolled her eyes. "Now you're just feeling sorry for yourself. Anyway, you *have* to come. I need you there."

"Why?"

"Never mind, I just need you to be there. Trust me."

Josie wondered what Becky was being so mysterious about but didn't have the energy to question her further. "Okay, I'll go to Albert's mother's for Christmas dinner. Happy now?"

"Yes. Very happy."

Josie didn't think any more of the matter the rest of the week. When the day arrived, she dressed in her Sunday best, as Becky had insisted. Becky seemed particularly upbeat, although she always got excited at Christmas. So did Josie, normally, but this year was different. There wasn't much to get excited about, not for her. Not with her situation the way it was. But she'd try to put on a good show for her sister.

Even though Albert's mother's place was on Birmingham Street, close enough to walk, it was a cold and blustery day, so Albert had called a cab to take them there. Albert's mother met them at the front door, dressed all Christmasy and beaming from ear to ear. She gave Becky a big hug and kissed her son on the cheek. She then turned to Josie. "I'm so glad you're joining us, Josie."

"Thank you very much for inviting me, Mrs. Blanchard."

Once they had removed their boots and hung up their coats in the vestibule, Albert's mother led them into the parlour where they met the rest of the dinner guests. Josie immediately recognized Raymond, Albert's younger brother, who had made a pass at her at Becky's wedding. For one frightening moment, she wondered if that's why she had been invited, as Raymond's "date." But then Albert's mother introduced her to a woman named Lois, who she said was Raymond's girlfriend, much to Josie's relief. There were two other guests, Albert's Aunt Constance (his mother's sister) and his Uncle William, Constance's husband.

Albert's mother had prepared a traditional turkey dinner with all the trimmings, with a Christmas pudding for dessert. The conversation around the table had been lively and pleasant. Josie was placed at one end of the table, next to Becky, but spent most of the time talking with Uncle William, who was seated across the table from her. Becky's attention was mostly focused on Albert, sitting next to her, and Albert's mother, on his right. As Josie had noticed earlier, Becky was highly animated, almost bubbly. She studied her sister more closely. Becky's face appeared to be glowing. She was definitely happy about something.

As the dessert course was ending and the guests were enjoying their tea or coffee, Becky and Albert suddenly stood up. Albert tapped his water glass with a spoon. All conversation around the table abruptly stopped and everyone looked up. He waited until he had everyone's attention. "Rebecca and I have an announcement to make. Darling?"

Albert gestured to Becky, grinning widely. Becky seemed ready to explode. She paused for effect, then blurted it out. "I'm expecting! We're going to have a baby!"

The room went deathly silent for a split second, then erupted like a volcano. Aunt Constance squealed with delight and Uncle William shouted "Bravo." Albert's mother hugged Albert and Becky, tears of joy streaming down her face. Raymond gave Albert an "I didn't think you had it in ya," then went around the table to shake his brother's hand. Raymond's girlfriend shrieked and clapped. Everyone was joyous and jubilant, congratulating the couple.

Josie sat stunned. Becky was expecting? She had no idea. She hadn't seen it coming. She hadn't noticed anything different about her sister. How could she have not known? She should have been able to tell.

Josie went to congratulate Becky but couldn't get near her. Everyone was all over her, hugging her, kissing her on the cheek, touching her belly. Josie would have to wait her turn. As she watched the celebration, conflicting emotions swept through her. She was thrilled for her sister, of course. She seemed so happy. This was obviously something she wanted very much. But she was also hurt, hurt because she hadn't been the first to know, that Becky hadn't told her as soon as she had found out, that she had announced the news in front of Albert's family instead of to her first. Her sister, her best friend. After everything they had been through together. She realized she was being selfish, that she should be thinking of Becky right now, and she hated herself for it, but that's how she felt. That's how she honestly felt.

The crowd around Becky finally dispersed a little and Josie moved in. "I'm so happy for you," she said, hugging her sister.

"Thank you," said Becky. "That's why I wanted you to come with us, to hear the news."

Josie smiled a half-hearted smile, her feelings still bruised. Before she could say anything else, Becky's attention was diverted by Albert's mother who began dragging her daughter-in-law into the parlour. "You're going to need your rest now, dear," she said. "Come and sit down."

Albert asked everyone to take their tea or coffee and join Becky and his mother in the parlour. For the remainder of the evening, Becky's pregnancy was the sole topic of conversation. Albert's mother and Aunt Constance talked about their experiences when they were expecting, and overwhelmed Becky with advice and suggestions about what she should do over the next few months to ensure a healthy baby and a successful delivery.

"Do you want a boy or a girl?" asked Lois, Raymond's girlfriend.

"It's best if the first child is a boy," said Uncle William.

"Why is that?" asked Lois.

"Because one day he might have to become the man of the house if something happened to Albert," explained Uncle William.

"It doesn't matter to me," said Becky. "We'll take what God gives us. As long as the baby is born healthy. And nothing is going to happen to Albert for a long time."

Everyone nodded in agreement.

"Do you have names picked out yet?" asked Lois.

"It's unlucky to choose a name before the baby is born," said Aunt Constance.

"Oh, that's just an old wives' tale," said Uncle William.

"Well, I'm an old wife," said Aunt Constance proudly. "So there."

Everyone laughed.

Raymond decided to enter his two cents worth. "All I can say is that it took Albert long enough to prove that he's a real man."

"Oh, I can assure you he's a real man," piped in Becky.

Everyone laughed even harder. Except Raymond. Even Albert's mother chuckled just a little.

Through it all, Josie sat quietly, half-listening to the chatter, smiling when appropriate, but mostly absorbed in her own thoughts. She thought about how different Becky's life was from hers. Becky had a husband with a good job, a child on the way, and a place of her own. Not only that, but she had a whole new family, Albert's family, to love her and care for her. She, on the other hand, was alone, working at a job she hated, living under someone else's roof, with her closest sister—*her* family—slowly drifting away.

In the middle of a lively discussion about morning sickness, Josie decided she had heard enough. She had to get out of there. She stood up and headed for the front door. Albert's mother was the only one who noticed her leaving. "Where are you going, dear?"

"I'm just going out to get some air," said Josie.

"Well, dress warmly. It's cold out there tonight."

Josie slipped on her winter boots, put on her coat and hat, wrapped her scarf around her neck, and went outside. It was indeed a cold night—cold and blustery, with flurries swirling about. The rooftops and postage-stamp lawns were covered in snow from a storm earlier in the week, but the sidewalks and streets were mostly clear. She started walking, with no particular destination in mind. She walked along Birmingham to Morris, then down Morris to Queen. At Queen, the wind howled down the street from the north, stinging her flesh, so she wrapped her scarf over her face and tied it at the back. Past Queen, the buildings provided shelter, so she kept walking down Morris to Barrington. At Barrington, the shops were all closed and the streets practically deserted, with hardly another soul in sight. From Barrington, Josie kept going down Morris to Hollis. Gorman's was closed, but she stopped and peered into one of the windows, remembering when she used to work there, remembering the good times, remembering her old friends.

She kept going, right down to Lower Water Street. From there, she could see the harbour—black and murky in the distance. Strangely, it seemed to beckon her. She crossed Lower Water and wended her way down a lane between two warehouse buildings, then through a small parking lot onto a pier. She stopped. She shivered from the cold. She thought about turning around and going back, but something seemed to be drawing her, pulling her, like a magnet. She trudged on, fighting the strong wind and bitter cold, farther and farther out on the pier, closer and closer to the water's edge. The force that had been pulling her eased, then released. She was at the very end of the pier—the angry, rough seas before her. She could hear the roiling waves crashing like thunder against the pillars, splashing salty spray high into the night sky.

She gazed out into the darkness. Her mind fixed on the evening's big event. Becky was going to have a baby. She was going to bring another human being into the world. Her life would now mean something. She would have a child to raise, a child that might grow up to be someone important someday. Her life now mattered—to her child, to her family, to the world.

Josie reflected on her own life. Did it matter? Did it mean anything? What had she accomplished? What difference was she making to the world, or even to her own family and friends? What difference would it make if she wasn't there? Would anyone miss her? Becky would surely be missed—by Albert, by Albert's family, by her unborn child. It would change their lives. But her? Sure, her father and her siblings would be upset, but they'd get over it. Like everybody else does. Like every parent or sibling who has lost a loved one in this lousy war. They'd move on. It wouldn't change their lives, not a bit. No, it wouldn't mean that much to anyone if she wasn't here. Except to her. It would mean the end. The end of her pain, her hurt, her loneliness.

Josie took a deep breath. She stepped up on the raised wooden beam at the edge of the pier. She looked down at the churning, raging water below. A calmness came over her. A quiet. Her mind stilled. It would soon be over. All over. Everything. She no longer felt the cold wind lashing her face. Instead, she felt a warmth ooze through her. She lifted her right leg.

All of a sudden, she heard a voice.

"No Josie. Don't do it."

It was a woman's voice. Soft, but clear. Coming from directly behind her. Almost in her ear. She could sense her presence. She was standing right behind her. She turned quickly. What? There was no one there! She strained through the darkness but saw no one. "Hello? Who's there?" she shouted out loud.

But there was no answer. No one was there. "*But that's impossible,*" she told herself. The voice came from right behind her. She heard it plain as day. She played the voice again in her head. It sounded familiar. She had heard that voice before. Yes, she recognized it. She knew that voice. Was it…was it her? It couldn't be.

Or could it?

A chill ran through her. She felt the ocean spray on her face. She turned back toward the water and looked down. *Where am I? What am I doing here? Why am I standing on this ledge? Oh my God!* She jumped back off the beam. Her heart started pounding, pounding, faster and faster. Her consciousness flooded with realization. What was she thinking? What did she almost do? Was she crazy? Had she lost her mind? Who is she? This is not her. This is not Josie. What has she become? Who is this person? This person she doesn't recognize. It's not her. No, it must be someone else. Someone forcing her to do terrible things. She must escape! Escape from this madwoman who has taken control of her.

She raced back up the pier as fast as she could, stumbling and floundering but determined to get away. She leapt off the pier, through the parking lot, past the warehouse buildings, and across Lower Water to Morris. Oblivious to the wind and cold, she dashed up Morris, past Hollis and Barrington and Queen, struggling but never stopping. Finally, she turned the corner onto Birmingham and reached the house. Throwing open the door, she bolted through the vestibule and into the parlour without undressing. Everyone was still there, still chatting about babies. When they spotted her standing in the parlour doorway, they interrupted their conversation.

"Did you go outside?" asked Becky, obviously unaware of Josie's absence from the group. "You look frozen."

Gasping for air, Josie smiled a huge smile. She walked over to Becky, kissed her on the cheek, told her she loved her, and gave her a huge hug—the biggest hug she had ever given her. So big that Albert's mother shouted out "Watch the baby!" She then walked over to Albert, grabbed his head with her two hands, pulled it towards her, and gave him a long kiss right on the lips—much to Albert's astonishment, his mother's embarrassment, and Raymond's hooting and hollering. As she broke off the kiss, she looked him straight in the eyes. "Congratulations. You'll make a great father." From there, she went around the room, hugging everyone, wishing everybody a Merry Christmas. She even let Raymond kiss her, right on the lips, although his exuberance with the task didn't sit well with his girlfriend. He didn't seem to care.

For the remainder of the evening, Josie was buoyant and engaging, participating enthusiastically in all the discussions about babies and motherhood. She talked about how excited she was to be an aunt again, and how she was going to help Becky out as much as she could, both before and after the birth. She even had some eggnog which Raymond had secretly spiked with a little rum.

She was back. Back to herself. Back to the old Josie. Back from the abyss.

That night, she slept like a baby.

And dreamt of her mother.

Chapter 32

Over the next few days, Josie devised a plan to change her life; and the day after New Year's, she began putting that plan into effect. The first thing she did was to go see her former boss, Mr. Gorman, about getting her old job back. While he didn't have anything for her at the moment, he told her that the Green Lantern was looking for a waitress and promised to contact the manager there, who was a friend of his. Two days later, on a Friday evening after supper, she received a call from the manager. She started at the Green Lantern the following Monday, after quitting her job at the laundry.

Landing the new job was the break she needed. She was now making more money, was doing something she enjoyed, and was good at it. And she was making new friends, too. Within a few weeks of starting at the Green Lantern, she went to a dance at the Masonic Hall with two girls from the restaurant.

The second major change she made was in her living quarters. While Becky wanted her to stay with them at least until the baby was born, Josie insisted that she needed to find her own place and not sponge off them anymore. Besides, Albert wanted to turn the reading room into a nursery. It was best for everyone. On a tip from a girl at work, she found a place on Grafton Street, right across from St. David's Presbyterian Church. It was an old, rather musty house, but the husband and wife owners, a Mr. and Mrs. Walsh, were very nice, and meals were included in the rent.

And the third thing she did was patch things up with her old friend, Doris. One day, during her lunch break, she walked down to Gorman's and paid Doris the ten dollars she still owed her. Doris was surprised but clearly pleased. They chatted for a minute or two before Josie went back to work. While they never did chum around again like they had before, mostly because Doris rarely went out anymore, they were always friendly with each other whenever they would meet. Josie was happy she had made things right between them.

By the spring of 1945, Josie's life was going in the right direction—new job, new place, new friends. Back to the dances, enjoying herself, having a good time. Having the occasional drink but never over-indulging.

The mood in the city was better, too. By mid-1944, Halifax had become war weary, with continual reports of local boys lost in battle, mounting conflicts between sailors and townspeople, and frustrations over wartime rules and restrictions. But now, with news from Europe that the Germans were in full retreat, optimism grew that the war would soon be over; that everything would return to normal, whatever that meant. Against this atmosphere of anticipation, Josie went to work each day happy, and hopeful for the future. Soon, though, she would get a glimpse of what that future would look like. And it wasn't at all what she had expected.

It was a mild, sunny day, the first real day of spring-like weather. It had been a good morning. The restaurant had been busy for breakfast, and everyone, customers and staff alike, seemed in good spirits. Including Josie.

Shortly after noon, the lunch crowd started pouring in, bigger than normal, drawn by the good weather. The girls worked feverishly to keep up. Josie finished serving a customer and moved to the next table where a man was seated by himself, his back turned to her. She came alongside him, not looking up, jotting the table number in her order pad. "What'll it be today, hon?" she asked.

"Hi Josie," came the gentle reply.

Josie looked up. She had recognized the voice instantly. "Hector!"

She hadn't seen him since that fateful day. She felt awkward. What should she say to him? She struggled to find the right words. "How have you been?"

"Fine. And you?"

"Good. I'm working here now."

"Yes, I see that."

Josie realized how dumb it was for her to state the obvious. Of *course* she was working there. Why else would she be taking his order? But she couldn't think of anything else to say. She stared at him in painful silence for a few seconds, then blurted out the first thing that popped into her head. "Becky's expecting."

"Yes, I know. Albert told me."

Of *course* Albert would have told him. They work together. He'd certainly tell him something as important as that. He'd probably told him a lot of other things, too. Things about her, no doubt. He'd probably told Hector that she'd run off to Montreal after his proposal, and that she'd lost her job at Gorman's, and that she'd started drinking heavily and had ended up in the hospital after collapsing in the street, and that she'd moved in with Becky and him as a result. He'd probably told Hector everything—every sordid detail. She flushed with embarrassment at the prospect.

"What's your special today?" asked Hector, mercifully breaking Josie's train of thought. She told him about the soup and sandwich deal, which he ordered. She smiled at him and went to place his order, relieved that their conversation hadn't gone beyond small talk. When she brought him his order, she smiled at him again but said nothing. When he was finished eating, she brought him the bill. He looked at it briefly, stood up, pulled out his wallet, and placed a few bills on the table. He then took a one-dollar bill and handed it to Josie. "This is for you," he said.

She smiled, thanked him, and turned to leave. He called out to her. "Josie?"

She turned. "Yes, Hector?"

He looked down at the floor. Josie could tell he wanted to say something but was having trouble getting it out. "What is it, Hector?"

"You still haven't answered my question."

Josie was confused. "What question?"

"The question I asked you exactly one year ago today. You still haven't given me an answer."

Josie tried to think back. One year ago today. What day is today? April 16th. One year ago today. What happened on April...? Then it hit her. Like a sledgehammer. *Is that what he meant? Is that the question he wants me to answer?*

"Are you serious?" she said.

His voice trembled. "Yes, Josie. I've never been more serious in my life. One year ago today, I asked you if you would be my wife. You never gave me an answer. I'm still waiting for your answer."

Josie couldn't believe what she was hearing. Was he crazy? She had bolted, left him hanging, disrespected him, hurt him. Why would he still want to marry her? "Hector, you don't want to marry me. You can find someone much better than me. Someone who'll treat you better than I treated you."

"I don't want someone else, Josie. I want you. I wanted you then, and I want you now. Ever since I proposed to you, I've been thinking, she hasn't said no, so maybe there's still a chance she'll say yes. So, I've been waiting. Waiting for the right time for your answer. Albert told me about what's been going on in your life, the difficulties you've had. I assumed you needed some time to deal with them. But now you've dealt with them, like I knew you would. So now is the right time to get your answer. One year exactly from the first time I asked you. So, I'll repeat the question."

Hector got down on one knee. He took Josie by the hand. "Josephine Bourdeau, will you marry me?"

Josie gasped. Her mouth opened wide. "Hector, are you sure you want to do this?"

"I've never been more sure of anything in my life."

"What if I say no?"

"Then, at least I'll have your answer."

A number of people in the restaurant had noticed Hector down on one knee and were alerting others to the unfolding drama. Before long, everyone in the place was watching, waiting for Josie's response. Her co-workers had gathered as well, smiling excitedly, nodding and spurring her on. The whole place was at a standstill. Josie looked around at all the faces staring at her—familiar faces, unfamiliar faces. She saw excitement in their eyes. Anticipation. Hope. She turned and looked at Hector staring up at her, his eyes pleading with her like a child pleading for its mother's love. Was this the man she was destined to marry, the man with the small ears? She looked at him closer. She saw something else. Sincerity. Honesty. Trust. Good things to have in a husband. Important things. More important that the size of one's ears. Maybe this was meant to be. Maybe everything she had gone through for the past year was to prepare her for this moment; to make her realize what was really meaningful in life. She swallowed hard. "I don't want to get married until the war is over. I want my brothers to be able to come to the wedding. And I can't get married until Becky has her baby. She has to be my maid of honour."

A collective buzz went through the crowd. Albert's eyes bulged wide. He started to shake. "Is that a yes?" he asked excitedly.

Josie hesitated. She looked around the room. Everyone was silent, awaiting her response. She looked back at Hector. "Yes. Yes, I'll marry you, Hector."

The place erupted. People cheered and clapped, hooted and hollered. Hector leapt to his feet, embracing Josie and kissing her passionately. He looked like he was in a state of shock, of disbelief. "Thank you, thank you," he blubbered. "I promise you I'll be the best husband you could ever have."

Before he could say another word, Josie's co-workers were all over her, hugging her and congratulating her. Total strangers were coming up to Hector, shaking his hand and patting him on the back. It seemed that in these times of hardship and heartache, people latched on to every bit of happiness and hope they could find, even if it was through others.

After a few minutes of jubilation, customers went back to their meals and the workers back to their tasks. Even Josie had to get back to work. She and Hector agreed to get together on the weekend to begin making plans. When Hector left, he looked like a man on cloud nine.

As Josie watched him head out the front door and disappear past the restaurant window, she reflected on what had just happened. She had agreed to get married. To Hector. Hector with the small ears. She wiped a table with her cloth.

"Now what have I done?"

Chapter 33

Becky was ecstatic when she heard the news and thrilled that Josie wanted her to be maid of honour. But they both agreed the wedding would have to wait until the baby was born, which wouldn't be until late July. Becky would also need a few weeks after the birth to recover, so they concluded the wedding couldn't take place until at least late August or early September.

Josie's second condition for the wedding date—to wait until the war was over—proved not to be a problem. By the third week in April, everyone was predicting the war would end in a matter of days. The Allies had reached Berlin, and rumours were circulating that Hitler had committed suicide. The end finally came on Monday, May 7 when the Germans surrendered unconditionally. The news hit Halifax that morning. Despite heavy fog and rain, the streets filled quickly with jubilant crowds cheering, shouting, singing, and dancing. Drivers honked their horns, office workers threw toilet paper streamers from buildings, couples kissed, children ran wild, and flags flew everywhere. A city exhausted from war was letting off steam.

By noon, the rain stopped and the fog cleared, so it turned out to be a lovely sunny day. It was as if Mother Nature was also rejoicing. The Green Lantern closed their doors at one o'clock, and Josie and her co-workers poured onto Barrington to join in the celebrations. By then, the streets were overflowing with revellers. Most businesses had already closed, so store clerks and secretaries, waitresses and salesmen, all joined in the party. The festivities continued all afternoon and into the evening, with the crowds only increasing in size. It seemed that everyone in the city was there.

Around five thirty, Josie decided to head back to her boarding house for supper. She hated to leave all the fun, but with every downtown eating establishment closed, if she missed the six o'clock sitting at the house, she'd be hungry all night. And she was starving. It had been so busy at work that she hadn't had a chance to have any lunch before they closed.

After supper, Josie went back downtown. Another girl who lived at the Walsh house, Irene, joined her. In the few months that Josie had been at the Walsh house, she and Irene had struck up a friendship. Irene was a few years younger than Josie and tended to look up to her, like an older sister. She'd ask Josie advice about things, like how to meet boys or what to wear to a dance. It reminded Josie of the kind of relationship she once had with Becky.

Josie and Irene followed the noise of the crowds down to Barrington, which seemed to be the centre of all the hoopla. The street was so packed with people that you could barely move. There were now hundreds of sailors about, which was a change from the afternoon when it was all civilians. They were definitely in a joyous mood, hooting and hollering, cheering and clapping, often in groups of four or five with their arms around each other's necks. Some of them were climbing telephone poles or standing on top of parked cars, bouncing up and down. Josie felt sorry for the owners of those cars. They weren't getting them off the street tonight.

There was also a lot of drinking going on, especially by the sailors. During the afternoon, they hadn't seen anyone with liquor. Now, many of the sailors had bottles of beer or rum and were drinking them openly in plain sight. Nobody was stopping them. The atmosphere everywhere was exciting, electrifying, wild!

Josie heard someone in the crowd say that the City was putting on a fireworks display on Citadel Hill after dark. The sun was already beginning to set, so Josie and Irene decided they should make their way up to the Hill to find a good vantage point. When they arrived, hundreds, even thousands of people were already there, all jockeying for a good location. Josie and Irene found a decent spot and sat down on the grass to wait for the spectacle to begin.

The fireworks started shortly before ten o'clock and lasted until almost midnight. Irene said it was the most amazing thing she had ever seen. Josie had to agree. When it was over, they decided to head back to the boarding house rather than return to Barrington, where the party was still going strong. Besides, someone at the fireworks had told them that the government had declared Tuesday, the following day, "Victory in Europe Day," and there would be events and festivities all over the city.

As they made their way home, however, they noticed a change in the behaviour of the crowds, particularly among the sailors. Small bands of them were wandering about, throwing empty liquor bottles through store windows, setting fires in garbage bins, even overturning cars. Police sirens wailed in the distance, and Josie heard loud bangs that sounded like gunfire. The mood had definitely changed. No longer joyous and celebratory, it was now growing violent and ugly. Irene became concerned for their safety, but Josie assured her they had nothing to worry about. Some of the sailors whistled and made comments, but they didn't bother them. They were too busy fighting with each other. But just to be on the safe side, they stayed close to other people also leaving the fireworks. They arrived at their boarding house without incident. Later, as Josie lay in bed trying to get to sleep, she could still hear sounds coming from the downtown area—people shouting, horns beeping, sirens wailing. She assumed the party would continue all night.

The next morning, Josie got up at her usual time to go to work. When she went downstairs for breakfast, Mr. Walsh told her he had heard over the radio that everything—stores, shops, restaurants, offices, literally every workplace—was closed for V-E Day, and city officials were encouraging people to participate in all the planned activities. Josie went to find Irene to tell her the good news. They made plans to join the party later that morning.

They left the house about eleven o'clock in high spirits, ready to have some fun. But as soon as they stepped onto the sidewalk, they could hear some kind of commotion coming from the downtown area. When they turned the corner at Grafton and Blowers, they were shocked at the scene before them. Smashed store windows. Broken beer bottles. Glass and garbage all over the street. And people running in all directions—sailors and civilians—with clothes, and shoes, and all sorts of items in their arms. As they walked farther down Blowers to Argyle, they saw even more destruction. More broken windows, more debris, and more people running with stuff in their arms. Irene wanted to go back to the house, but Josie had to find out what was happening. They kept walking. As they passed Argyle, they spotted a woman running up the street toward them carrying two full-length fur coats. Josie stopped her. "What's going on?" Josie asked her.

"It's all free!" shrieked the woman. "They don't care. The police don't care. They're not arresting anyone. They're letting everybody take what they want."

The woman pushed past Josie and continued running up the street, clutching her booty tightly, giggling as she went. Josie raced down the hill to Barrington, with Irene following her. As she turned the corner, Josie could not believe what she was seeing. Total devastation. It looked like a war zone. Every storefront window smashed. Glass and debris everywhere. Crumbled clothes racks and broken shelving littering the street. Overturned and demolished cars. She even saw a burned-out police car. And the people! People everywhere. Climbing into the stores through the shattered windows or kicked-in doors, taking things out. Everything. Anything. Clothes, shoes, boots, hats, jewellery, watches, toasters, dishes, chairs, boxes of chocolates, bags of coffee, sacks of potatoes. Everything and anything you could imagine. Josie even saw two burly men carrying out a big desk. And all types of people. Sailors and civilians. Young and old.

Men and women. Adults and children. Men in suits. Women in fancy dresses. Bums and vagabonds. Everyone. And the woman Josie had stopped on the street was absolutely right. No one seemed to care. There was not a policeman in sight. Not one. No security guards. No one protecting the stores. Everyone free to take whatever they wanted. But the strangest thing was the mood of the crowd. No one was angry or enraged or incensed. On the contrary, everyone was festive, jubilant, even playful. It was one big party.

Josie and Irene trudged along the sidewalk through the broken glass, sidestepping debris as they went. They stopped in front of Gordon & Keith Furs. Like every other shop, the front windows were completely smashed. Josie peered in through the opening. There didn't appear to be much left inside. "Do you want to go in?" she asked Irene.

"What for?" said Irene.

"To get something," said Josie.

"Wouldn't that be stealing?"

"Everybody's doing it. If we don't take it, somebody else will."

Josie walked in through the open store door with Irene close behind. They looked around. The place was a mess—coat racks knocked over, fixtures demolished, boxes strewn about, glass everywhere. But no fur coats. It looked like it had been completely cleaned out. Then Josie spotted something on the floor behind the main counter, partially hidden under a gift box. She went over and pulled it out. It was a woman's fur hat. "Do you like this?" she asked Irene.

"I don't know," said Irene.

"Try it on."

Irene frowned.

"Try it on!" insisted Josie.

Irene took the hat from Josie's hand, shook it to remove a few shards of glass, and put it on her head. It went down over her ears. "It's too big," she said, as if relieved.

"You can take it in."

Irene moaned. "Josie, just leave it. Let's get out of here."

"We're taking it," insisted Josie. "We're taking it for you. Now I need to find something for me."

Josie left the fur store and went back out into the street. Irene tagged along, holding the hat behind her back as if she were afraid someone would see her with it. They continued to walk north along Barrington, Josie checking out the various establishments for something she liked. Most of the stores had already been completely looted or only had items that wouldn't be of much use to Josie, like men's ties or handkerchiefs. She considered taking something for Hector, but then figured he wouldn't be too happy when she told him where she had got it.

At Prince, they crossed the street to the other side and started walking south. It was the same on that side; every store broken into and most of the merchandise gone or destroyed. When they got to Zellers, Josie went in. "Maybe I'll find something here."

There were several people inside, scrounging through what was left, which wasn't much. The better items were gone, with mostly knick-knacks or trinkets remaining. Many items, like glasses and dishes, had been smashed and broken in the looting.

Josie wandered about, sifting through the merchandise, checking shelves, under counters, even in the back rooms, which were completely empty. Then she found something that apparently had been missed by everyone—a pair of yellow baby booties with white pompoms, sitting alone on a shelf against a far wall, like an outcast, abandoned, unwanted. This would be her souvenir from VE Day. She'd give it to Becky for the baby.

Satisfied with her treasure, she found Irene and they left the store. They were done. They each had something, so they could now go home. As they reached Blowers, Josie looked back down Barrington before they headed up the hill. *Wow! Unbelievable*, she thought. She turned to Irene. "Look at that mess. In one day, our own sailors and citizens have done more damage to Halifax than the enemy did in six years of war."

"Sad. Very sad," said her friend.

Chapter 34

The wedding date was set for Saturday, September 8—three months away. Becky's baby would be more than a month old by then, so Becky should be strong enough for her maid of honour duties. Hector's brother, Clarence, would be the best man. His mother and father would be coming down from Truro. He hoped some of his sisters could make it as well. Josie had assumed none of her family would be able to attend because they couldn't afford the trip, but since Hector had offered to pay two bus fares, her father and her sister Beatrice were now planning to come.

Josie hoped her brothers George and Harry would be home by then, although no one seemed to know for sure when the troops would be returning. Josie had no idea where Harry's ship was. He could be anywhere in the world and it might take him a while to get back to Halifax. George was still in England, as far as Josie knew.

Josie and Hector weren't seeing a lot of each other these days. Hector was even busier at work now than he had been during the war, with mounds of paperwork processing returning servicemen, so he often worked late. Josie took some extra shifts to make some additional money. They'd usually get together on the weekends, sometimes going to a movie or just back to Hector's flat. Like Albert, Hector wasn't much for dancing, but one Saturday Josie convinced him to go. He sat there most of the evening, too embarrassed to get on the floor, so Josie sat with him. After that, she would occasionally go without him, usually with Irene or one of the girls from the restaurant. He didn't much like that, but Josie told him he had a choice: go with her and dance, or let her go without him. Truth be told, she was glad he didn't want to go. At least this way she'd actually get to dance.

On the evenings that Josie would go to Hector's, they'd play cards or just sit on the couch and listen to the radio. Hector would sometimes get a little frisky, so Josie would let him kiss and fondle her, like they had done when they were dating previously. But when he'd try to go further, she would tell him he'd have to wait until they were married.

May turned into June, and June into July. Josie didn't think about the wedding very much. All the plans were made, so it was just a matter of waiting for the big day. Instead, a lot of her attention was focused on Becky's impending motherhood. By June, Becky was quite large and feeling uncomfortable. The pregnancy had gone well, except for some morning sickness in the early stages, but everyone was telling her that the last two months were the worst. Albert's mother was spending a lot of time with her, cooking and housecleaning, but Becky was finding that a mixed blessing. She liked the help, but she could only take so much of the constant "advice" about how she should care for the new baby. It got on her nerves. So Josie would try to give her a break by visiting her as much as she could. She'd drop over after work or spend Saturday afternoons with her before going over to Hector's. They'd just sit and talk, or sometimes go for short walks to give Becky an outing. They'd stroll along arm in arm, discussing plans for the future, or just gossiping. It reminded Josie of when they were younger.

As Becky's due date approached, she became increasingly uncomfortable but seldom complained. The joyful event came on July 26 at the Grace Maternity Hospital with the birth of a healthy seven-pound eleven-ounce baby girl. They named her Gwendolyn, after Albert's grandmother. Becky said they'd call her Wendy, for short. As the doctor proclaimed at the time, "Mother and baby are doing well."

With the birth of Becky's baby now behind them, Josie and Hector's attention turned to their impending nuptials, which were now just a little over a month away. Hector had already bought a ring and had even purchased a new bed for their "love nest." He was busy getting his flat ready for his bride-to-be.

Hector had also arranged a short honeymoon. He'd borrow a friend's car, they'd drive to the Valley (now that gas rationing had eased), and stay overnight in a hotel. Josie had to decide on a dress and a going-away outfit for the honeymoon. They'd have to be simple; she couldn't afford much.

As the big day approached, Josie began thinking a lot about how her life was soon to change. She'd have to notify her landlord that she would be giving up her room. She'd have farther to walk to work because Hector lived over on Church Street. She'd be a wife now, so she'd have to cook for her husband and keep his house clean. And she'd have to perform her wifely duties; no more putting that off. She figured she could handle all that. What she wasn't sure about was whether she could spend the rest of her life with a man she didn't truly love.

But maybe she was expecting too much. He was a decent man. He was good to her. Kind and considerate. He'd make a good husband. And a good father, because she'd decided she wanted to have children one day. Seeing Becky's baby had triggered the mother instinct in her. No, it was the right decision. A sensible decision. She could do a lot worse.

Josie and Hector had agreed not to see each other for a week before the wedding. Hector had said it was because he wasn't sure if he could contain himself and he didn't want to spoil their wedding night. Josie just wanted some time to herself. On the Saturday before Josie was to walk down the aisle, she and Irene went to the dance at the Strand. Being a long weekend, the place was packed, and Josie had a great time, dancing all night. Irene told the band that her friend was getting married, so they brought her up by the stage. They played a few bars of "Here Comes the Bride," then Benny Goodman's "Taking a

Chance on Love," dedicating it to Josie. She had to agree it was an appropriate choice.

As Josie and Irene walked back to their boarding house after the dance, Josie was in a good mood. She had enjoyed herself. "Thanks for joining me," she said to Irene.

"Hey, I had to help you celebrate," said her young friend.

"Celebrate?"

"Yeah, your last dance as a single woman."

The comment jolted her. *That's right, my last dance as a single woman.*

A chill ran through her.

Chapter 35

Tuesday. Four days to go. The day started like most others. Josie arrived at work just before the restaurant opened for business at seven. It was a normal breakfast crowd for a Tuesday, not too busy, mostly the regulars. The rest of the morning was slow. Josie was tidying up around the counter in preparation for the noon rush when Jean, one of her co-workers, approached her.

"Josie, there's a lady over there asking for you." Jean pointed to a table in the far corner where an older, well-dressed woman was sitting, nervously looking around. Josie didn't recognize her.

"What does she want?"

"I don't know. She didn't say."

"Who is she? Is she a customer?"

"I have no idea. She didn't ask for a menu or anything, she just asked for you. She said, 'Is there a Josephine Bourdeau here?' I said, 'Yes.' Then she said, 'May I speak with her?' So I told her I'd go get you."

Josie found it odd that someone would ask for her by her full name. Not many people knew her last name. And no one ever called her Josephine. Josie wondered if it had anything to do with the wedding. *Maybe somebody from the church*, she thought.

"Can you cover my tables for me for a minute, Jean?"

"Sure."

Josie made her way over to the woman. "You wanted to speak with me?"

"Are you Josephine Bourdeau?"

"Yes."

"Oh, thank goodness. The manager at Gorman's said I would find you here. Please, have a seat."

The woman appeared to be in her sixties. Her short, mostly grey hair was neatly gathered up and away from her face, and she wore a stylish hat. Her elegant knee length dress was dark blue in colour, with a white collar. She had a sophisticated way about her. But she seemed anxious and uneasy.

"We've never met before, Miss Bourdeau. My name is Margaret O'Reilly. I'm Anna Bennett's sister."

Her tone gave the impression that Josie would know who Anna Bennett was, but it didn't register with Josie right away. "Anna Bennett?"

"Yes, Anna Bennett. I understand you stayed at her boarding house a few years ago?"

"Oh, Miss Bennett!" blurted out Josie, finally making the connection.

"Yes, Miss Bennett."

Until that very moment, Josie had no idea what Miss Bennett's first name was. In all the time she had lived at the boarding house, she had never heard anyone call her by her first name. She was always just "Miss Bennett."

"So, you're her sister?"

"Yes."

"Why do you want to speak with *me*?"

The woman paused. She leaned forward. "My sister is dying. She's on her deathbed. She doesn't have long to live."

"Oh, I didn't know. I'm very sorry to hear that."

"Thank you for your kindness."

"Is that what you wanted to tell me?"

"There's more. She's asked to see you before she dies."

"Me? Why me?"

"She has something very important to tell you."

"Something important to tell *me*? What?"

"Honestly, I do not know. She would not tell me. All she said was that it was imperative that she speak with you before she dies. She was very adamant about it."

Josie was baffled. What could Miss Bennett possibly want to talk to her about? She hadn't seen her in almost three years. Not since she had kicked her out of the boarding house. Was that what she wanted to speak with her about; to apologize for putting her out on the street? Was this some type of deathbed act of contrition to atone for her sin? Was she trying to cleanse her soul before meeting her maker? Josie was sorry that she was dying—she didn't want to see anyone die—but she wasn't inclined to grant her wish just so she could ease her conscience. If Miss Bennett had treated her better in the first place, she wouldn't have to be asking for forgiveness now. "I don't know, ma'am. I'm very busy this week. I'm getting married on Saturday. I've got a lot of things to do. I'm very sorry about your sister, I really am, but I don't know if I'm going to have time to see her."

Miss Bennett's sister lowered her head and sighed. After a few seconds, she looked up at Josie. She smiled softly. "Miss Bourdeau, my sister is on her deathbed. This is her dying wish. If you could find it in your heart to grant her this one last request, she can die in peace."

Josie was torn. She didn't want to appear heartless. "Well, maybe I could drop by to see her for a few minutes."

"Thank you so very much. You're very kind. She's at the boarding house. I'm staying with her. But please don't wait too long. I don't know how much more time she has."

With that, Miss Bennett's sister left the restaurant. No sooner was she gone than Josie started to regret what she had promised. Why *should* she go see Miss Bennett? She didn't really owe her anything. Miss Bennett had been nothing but mean and nasty to her, the old witch. Why should she be nice to her now, even if she *is* dying? Miss Bennett's sister had made her feel guilty, that's all. Anyway, she didn't *promise* that she'd go, she just said *maybe*. Or maybe not.

For the rest of her shift, Josie wrestled with her dilemma. When she left the restaurant at the end of the day, she still had not made up her mind. But as she walked down Barrington, instead of continuing to Miss Bennett's, she turned up Blowers and went home. All during supper, Josie thought of nothing else. Should she go or shouldn't she? Part of her was annoyed that Miss Bennett would have the gall to ask to see her, but part of her was curious to find out what the old woman actually wanted to say to her. She decided to run it by Irene who was sitting next to her at the dinner table.

"You'll never guess what happened to me today."

"What?" said Irene.

"A woman came to see me at work. She said she was the sister of my former landlady, Miss Bennett. She said Miss Bennett was on her deathbed and wanted to see me to tell me something before she died."

"What did she want to tell you?"

"The woman didn't know. She said her sister hadn't told her. She just told her that she absolutely had to see me."

"So, did you go see her?"

"No."

"Are you going to?"

"I don't know."

"Why not?"

"Irene, this woman kicked me out of her boarding house three years ago. Out on the street. I had no place to go. I ended up staying at the Sisters of Service until I found my own place. She was a real witch. We never got along. Now she wants to see me because she's dying? She probably wants to apologize for what she did to me."

"So, let her apologize."

"And give her the satisfaction? Like I told her sister, I was sorry she was dying, but I really don't want to see her."

"Did you tell her sister you wouldn't go?"

"Well, at first I told her I was too busy because I was getting married and had things to do for the wedding. But she kept begging me, so I said I'd try to go. Now I'm starting to wish I hadn't said that."

"I'd go if I were you," said Irene.

"Why?" said Josie. "Why should I forgive her?"

"Maybe that's not the reason she wants to talk to you."

"What else could it be?"

"Maybe she wants to leave you some money in her will."

Josie laughed. "Oh, I don't think she'd leave me anything in her will. Unless it was a smelly pair of old socks. She hates me. She kicked me out of her boarding house, remember."

"And that's exactly why she might want to give you some money. She's feeling guilty about what she did and now she wants to make amends before she dies. That's what these rich, eccentric people do. They think they're buying their way into heaven by doing some good deed. Anyway, what have you got to lose? If you go and it's not that, then you've just lost a bit of your time. If she wants to leave you something in her will and you don't go, she might change her mind, and you'll get nothing."

Irene made a lot of sense. What did Josie have to lose? Nothing, really. But potentially, she had a lot to gain. The girl was wise beyond her years. "How'd you get so smart so young?" she said to her friend.

The next day after work, instead of going home, she went to Miss Bennett's. When she reached the boarding house, she hesitated for a second, then climbed the steps and rang the doorbell. Miss Bennett's sister came to the door. Her eyes seemed swollen and red, but she maintained her dignified air.

"Hello, Miss Bourdeau," she said solemnly. "Please come with me."

Josie followed her into the hall, glancing to her left into the dining room and then to her right into the parlour. Nothing had changed. It was exactly the same as when she had lived there. Miss Bennett's sister led her down to the end of the hall and into

Miss Bennett's office. Josie recalled the last time she had been in this room, on her last day at the boarding house.

"Please, have a seat," said Miss Bennett's sister, gesturing for Josie to take one of two chairs by the fireplace. Josie sat down. Miss Bennett's sister sat down in the other chair, facing Josie. She looked at Josie and smiled. "I'm afraid my sister passed away early this morning. She tried to hold on as long as she could, but she was very sick. She prayed you would come to see her because she so desperately wanted to speak with you. But she couldn't hold on any longer."

A single tear ran down the elderly woman's face, though she was still smiling. Josie didn't know what she should say. She was sorry to hear that Miss Bennett had passed away, of course, but she could not pretend what she did not feel. There was no great swell of emotion rising inside her. She felt nothing. But she recalled the words several people had said to her father at her mother's funeral. "I'm sorry for your loss."

"Thank you," said Miss Bennett's sister.

Josie squirmed in her chair, uncertain what to say next. She still wanted to find out if Irene was right, that maybe Miss Bennett wanted to leave her some money, but she didn't want to appear insensitive or greedy. She had to proceed cautiously. "Miss O'Reilly…"

"It's Mrs. O'Reilly, dear."

"Sorry. Mrs. O'Reilly…I was just wondering…I know I got here too late, but…did she tell you why she wanted to speak with me?"

The woman inhaled deeply, her breath fluttering, as if she were struggling not to cry. "Yes, she did. Just before she died."

"What did she want?"

The woman rose from her chair and walked over to Miss Bennett's desk. She opened a wooden box sitting on top of the desk and took something out, which she handed to Josie without saying a word. Josie was puzzled. The woman had given her four separate letters in sealed envelopes. Each letter was addressed "Josephine Bourdeau, 69 Hollis Street, Halifax, Canada."

"What's this?" asked Josie, still completely confused.

The woman hesitated, clearly fighting back tears. "My sister's last words were, 'Tell Josie I'm so very sorry.'"

It was then that Josie noticed the return address in the top left hand corner of each of the envelopes. A shiver ran up her spine. Was she seeing clearly? She squinted to focus her eyes in the dim light. Yes! She had read it right! They were from Peter. Her Peter. The Peter she had fallen in love with that magnificent weekend. The Peter who hadn't written to her as he had promised. The Peter who had abandoned her, who had lied to her, who had torn out her heart, who had doomed her to a life unfulfilled.

Josie frantically scanned the stamps to find the earliest date, tore the envelope open like a madwoman, and began to read.

My Beautiful Darling,

How could I have been so fortunate to have found someone as wonderful as you? Someone so beautiful, so caring, so full of life. I know our time together was short, but you have already stolen my heart. I have never felt this way before. Ever. From the moment I met you I knew this was different, this was something special. And from the moment we said goodbye, I have longed to return to you, to hold you in my arms, to kiss you again like we kissed before. It would be madness for sure, but I want to seize control of this ship, turn it around, and sail back to you.

I hope you feel the same way. You must. I know you do. I saw it in your eyes, I sensed it in your touch, I felt it on your lips. Please don't tell me I'm wrong. I would be devastated.

Write to me as soon as you receive this letter. I need to know how you feel. Do you feel what I feel? Have I captured your heart too, or am I just a lovesick fool?

Your Loving Peter

Josie began to shake. Her hands trembled as she fumbled through the other envelopes, searching for the one that was dated next. She ripped it open.

My Darling,

I have waited patiently for your response to my letter but have not received it yet. I am assuming it is because of the war. I know that it takes a long time for letters to arrive to our ship. They must go to Navy Command first, then through the censors, then on to the ships. And sometimes they get mislaid. I have heard of letters arriving four months after they were sent. And sometimes they get lost altogether.

At least I am hoping that is what happened. Because the alternative is too painful to contemplate, that you received my letter and chose not to respond. That you don't feel the same way I do. That your heart is cold towards me. That I am indeed a fool. No, I cannot accept that. I know you feel the same way. I am sure of it. I am sorry for even doubting you. I shouldn't have said that. I'm sorry.

I must sound like a babbling idiot, but I so want to hear from you. Write to me as soon as you can. If you have already written by the time you receive this letter, then write to me again. I want to imagine your sweet voice as I am reading your words.

Your Peter

Josie gasped for air. Emotions raged through her. She *had* to read on. She tore open the next envelope.

Darling?

I am beginning to grow despondent. It has been months now since I first wrote to you and still have not received a reply. It you had indeed written, I should have received your letter by now. If the first one was mislaid or lost, surely the second one would have made its way through.

What I am to think? Perhaps something has happened to you. Perhaps you are unable to write. I perish the thought, but at least it would be a justifiable excuse. I know it is a terrible, selfish thing to say, but I might prefer that explanation to the other possibility. Because that other possibility is that I mean nothing to you, that I am just another sailor that you met for a weekend during this dastardly war.

I find it hard to believe that. My heart won't accept it. But perhaps my heart is deceiving me. Please, I need to know. Please do not leave me blowing in the wind. If you do not feel the same way I do, please tell me. Please release me from these chains. Because, as long as there is a hope that my love for you will be returned, I will hold on to that hope.

Your Still Hopeful Peter

By now, Josie was sobbing, her eyes full with tears. But there was one more letter to read.

Josie,

How could I have been so foolish to have given you my heart? Now you have ripped it to shreds. Tossed it aside like a pile of trash. Without even the kindness of being honest with me, of telling me the truth.

I loved you, Josie, I truly did. Maybe you can't understand that. Maybe you think I am just some naïve fool who made too much of a chance encounter in the middle of a war. But my feelings were real. My heart was true. I loved you. And maybe I always will.

Have a good life, Josephine Bourdeau.

Peter

Josie was stunned. Dumbfounded. Confused. Angry. She looked up through her tears at Miss Bennett's sister.

"I don't understand. Miss Bennett had these letters?"

"Yes," Mrs. O'Reilly replied, bowing her head.

"All these years?"

"Yes."

"Then…then…why didn't she give them to me?"

Without answering, Mrs. O'Reilly got up from her chair and went over to Miss Bennett's desk. She opened the top right drawer and took out a framed photograph. She returned to Josie and handed her the photo. It was of a young man in uniform.

"Do you know who this is?" she asked.

Josie wiped her eyes. She recognized the photograph right away. It was the same one she had taken out of that same drawer the time she was searching for some paper to give Peter her mailing address.

"I've seen this before," said Josie, "but I don't know who it is. Miss Bennett didn't tell me."

"It's a picture of her son."

"Her son? I didn't know she had been married."

"She never was."

Josie looked up at Mrs. O'Reilly. She couldn't believe what she was hearing. Miss Bennett had a son? She had conceived a child out of wedlock? The news shocked her.

"We never knew," said Josie. "She never told us. She never told us anything about herself."

Mrs. O'Reilly took the photograph from Josie's hand and stared at it. "She told very few people. Only the family knew the whole story. It was quite a scandal."

"What happened?" Josie asked.

"Well, she was living in Boston at the time, with our parents. That's where our family home is. She met a young sailor and fell deeply in love. After they had been courting for about two weeks, he left to go to sea. Shortly after, she found out she was expecting. So, naturally, she tried to contact him to give him the news. She knew what ship he was on, so she sent him a telegram. But she received no reply. She tried again. Still no reply. She decided to send a telegram to the ship's captain, telling him that she needed to contact one of his crew on an urgent personal matter. She received a reply from the captain telling her that he had passed along the message. But after several days, she still had not heard from the young sailor. She then wrote letter after letter to him, telling him that he was going to be a father and that he should contact her right away. He never answered any of her letters, and she never saw him or heard from him again. She had the baby and raised it herself, with help from our parents."

Josie was fascinated by the tale. Maybe it helped explain why Miss Bennett was so miserable all the time. But it didn't explain why she had kept Peter's letters from her. "It's a very sad story," said Josie. "But what does it have to do with me?"

Mrs. O'Reilly smiled, then continued.

"When America entered the Great War in 1917, her son, who was nineteen at the time, wanted to join the Navy, like his father. My sister had never told her son that his father had abandoned them. Instead, she told him that he had died at sea in a storm. So, her son had developed this romantic notion of his father as a sailor and wanted to follow in his footsteps. My sister was vehemently opposed to the idea, for obvious reasons, but he wouldn't listen to her and signed up anyway. Just four months after he shipped out, my sister received a telegram from the Navy that her son had been lost at sea in a battle with the enemy. Devastated, she swore she would never marry and never have another child. After our parents passed away, she moved to Halifax and used her part of the inheritance to open the boarding house."

Josie was trying to be patient, but Miss Bennett's sister still hadn't answered her question. "Your sister had a very hard life. Terrible things happened to her. But I still don't understand. Why did she keep these letters from me?"

Mrs. O'Reilly seemed surprised by the question. "Don't you see, dear? She was trying to protect you."

"Protect me? From what?"

"From getting involved with a sailor."

"What?!"

"Yes. When she heard you had fallen for a sailor, she didn't want the same thing that happened to her to happen to you."

Josie couldn't believe what she was hearing. She flew into a rage. "She had no right to do that! It was none of her business! Those were *my* letters!"

"But she was only trying to protect you, my dear."

"I don't *need* protecting. I can look after myself. Just because some sailor abandoned her didn't mean Peter would abandon me."

"Well, I'm very sorry, dear. But she believed she was doing the right thing."

"No, no she didn't. She lied to you. That's not why she kept the letters. She kept them because she hated me. She always hated me. She wanted to ruin my life. And now she has. I hate her. I hate her! I'm glad she's dead! She was nothing but a mean old bitch!"

With that, Josie threw herself on the floor, sobbing. Mrs. O'Reilly tried to console her, caressing her back. But there was no consoling her. She pushed Mrs. O'Reilly away and howled in agony, her body convulsing. She stayed on the floor, crying, for almost ten minutes. Eventually, she sat up, her body still shaking.

"He loved me. He really did love me. I knew he did," said Josie. "She shouldn't have done that. She had no right."

"No, she shouldn't have," said Mrs. O'Reilly. "She made a huge mistake and she realized it at the end. She tried to make it right."

Josie was too consumed with her own grief to even hear what Mrs. O'Reilly was saying. Still sobbing, she thought about how Miss Bennett had destroyed her chance at true happiness. About how Peter must have felt when his letters went unanswered. How heartbroken he must have been.

Mrs. O'Reilly fetched a handkerchief from her purse and passed it to Josie. Josie took it and blew her nose. Mrs. O'Reilly then went over to her sister's desk, opened a drawer, took out an unsealed envelope, and held the envelope out to Josie.

"What's that?" said Josie.

"My sister wanted you to have this."

Josie took the envelope and lifted the flap to look inside. It was filled with money. Josie stared at it, then glared angrily at Miss Bennett's sister. "Did she think this was going to make up for what she did to me? I don't want her filthy money."

Josie threw the envelope on the floor, scattering the bills. Mrs. O'Reilly calmly retrieved them and placed them back in the envelope. "Take the money, dear. If I recall, you said you were getting married this weekend? This will help you get a head start in your married life. Take the money, please." She stuffed the envelope into the pocket of Josie's uniform.

The wedding! It was only three days away. In three days she'd be married to Hector. Imagine. If Miss Bennett had given her those letters over three years ago, she might be married to Peter by now. The man she truly loved. The man she was meant to be with. She slowly climbed to her feet, then wiped her eyes with her sleeve. She stuffed Peter's letters in her uniform pocket, next to the money.

"I have to go," she said quietly, then turned and left the room. Mrs. O'Reilly watched her leave without saying a word. Josie descended the steps of the boarding house to the sidewalk below, then stopped. It occurred to her that she was standing on the exact spot where she had last seen Peter. She could still picture his cab disappearing down the street.

She walked back to the Walsh house feeling numb. Dazed. Distraught. Had this really happened to her? That her chance at true love had been stolen from her? And she was only finding out now, three days before she was about to marry another man? Why hadn't Miss Bennett died sooner? Before she had accepted Hector's proposal. Before she even knew Hector.

She couldn't back out now. She had made a commitment. The date was set. The plans were made. It was too late.

Or was it?

Chapter 36

Josie was unusually quiet at supper. Distant. Like her mind was somewhere else. In another world. She barely said a word. And she was hardly eating anything. Just picking at her food. Irene noticed. "Are you alright, Josie?"

"What?"

"Are you alright? You look like you're daydreaming."

"Oh…no, I'm fine. Just, uh, just thinking about something."

"About your wedding?"

"The wedding? Uh, yes, about the wedding."

"Are you getting excited?"

"What?"

"Excited. Are you getting excited about the wedding?"

"Oh. Yes. Sure."

"It's coming soon."

"Yes, it is."

"Just think. In three days, you'll be a married woman."

A married woman. Mrs. Hector MacIsaac. Josie tried to imagine it. She tried to picture her and Hector walking down the aisle. But Peter's face kept popping into her head.

"So," continued Irene, "did you go see that old lady?"

"What old lady?" said Josie.

"The old lady that was dying and wanted to talk to you before she died. What was her name again?"

"Miss Bennett."

"Did you go see her?"

"Yes, I did."

"And did she give you any money?"

The money in the envelope. Josie hadn't even counted it. She had just stuffed it in her dresser, along with Peter's letters. "No, no she didn't. Not a penny."

"What did she want?"

"What did she want?" Josie repeated.

"Yeah, what did she want to talk to you about?"

"Oh, um, she wanted me to forgive her for kicking me out of the boarding house."

"Just as you suspected. You said that's what it was probably about. So, did you?"

Josie considered how best to answer. "Yes, I did."

"And then what did she say?"

"Nothing. Then she just died."

"Wow. I guess you were right. She just wanted to clear her conscious before meeting Saint Peter at the pearly gates. What was it like to watch someone die?"

"Um, I didn't really see her die. Her sister was with her. I was in another room when it happened."

"I guess it's something you never forget. It never happened to me, but Mrs. Walsh once told me that a friend of Mr. Walsh's died in his arms when he was in the Navy, and it bothered him for a long time."

Josie's ears perked up. It was something Irene had said. "Mr. Walsh was in the Navy?"

"Yeah. For quite a while, I guess."

"Hmm, interesting."

"Why's that?"

"Oh, no reason."

There *was* a reason, of course. She waited until after supper, then approached Mr. Walsh as he was sitting alone in the parlour reading the paper. "Mr. Walsh, can I talk to you for a minute?"

"Sure, Josie. What is it?"

"I heard you were in the Navy?"

"Yes I was."

"The Canadian Navy?"

"Yes, the Canadian Navy."

"For quite a while?"

"Quite a while. Thirty-two years, to be exact. Joined when I was eighteen. Retired as a senior officer."

"So, you know quite a bit about the Navy, then."

Mr. Walsh chuckled. "Yes, I suppose I do."

"Do you know anything about the British Navy?"

"Well, uh, a little. We used to do some joint exercises at times. I spent some time over in England doing some land-based training. I was on a few Royal Navy vessels. Why do you ask?"

"If I wanted to find someone who was in the British Navy, how would I find them?"

Mr. Walsh put down his newspaper and leaned forward, resting his arms on his thighs with his hands folded. He gazed intently at Josie.

"A sailor, I suppose?"

"Yes."

"I assume you know his name?"

Josie blushed. "Yes."

"First and last name?"

"Yes."

"Are you sure he gave you his real name?"

"What do you mean?"

"Well, some of these fellows don't always give the girl their real names, so they can't be tracked."

Josie frowned. She had never even thought about that possibility. No, Peter had given her his real name, for sure. It was on the letters that Miss Bennett's sister had given her.

"Yes, I'm sure. I'm absolutely sure."

"So, he's in the British Navy?"

"Well, he was when I met him, but that was three years ago. I don't know if he's still in the Navy now. Or even if he's still alive."

"Wow, three years ago. Why do you need to get in touch with him now?"

Josie squirmed. "It's personal, Mr. Walsh. I'd rather not say."

"Oh, I'm sorry. I didn't mean to pry. Do you know what ships he sailed on back then?"

Josie recalled the return addresses on Peter's letters. "I know some of them."

Mr. Walsh paused, then leaned back in his chair. "Okay, we have his name. We have some of his previous assignments. That's a good starting point. Well, uh, the Naval staff office is in London. That's where all the personnel files would be, I would imagine. You would have to write a letter or send a telegram to the Naval staff offices and tell them you're trying to contact this particular person. They wouldn't give you the person's whereabouts or mailing address, for security reasons. Instead, they would then contact the individual and let him know that someone was trying to get in touch with him."

"How long would that take?"

"I don't know. A week or two. Maybe more. If the Royal Navy is anything like the Canadian Navy, they don't move very fast."

A week or two. Josie didn't have that much time. Dejected, she turned to leave. Then a thought occurred to her. "Mr. Walsh, can I ask you something else?"

"By all means."

"If I wanted to send a parcel to England, how would I get it there?"

"Well, you could send it by air mail or by sea."

"If I sent it by sea, how long would it take to get there?"

"Mmm, two weeks or so, depending on the ship and where it's going in England."

"Two weeks. And how do I find out what ships are sailing from Halifax to England in the next while?"

"You could contact Cunard-White Star. They have an office down on the corner of George and Granville."

Josie's spirits lifted slightly. "Thank you so much, Mr. Walsh."

Mr. Walsh smiled. "Not at all."

Josie went up to her room, plopped herself on her bed, and stared at the ceiling. Her thoughts raced. Was she crazy? Going to England to find Peter? To find out if he still loved her? And where would she look? She had no idea where he lived. Was he even in England? Maybe he was at sea. Or maybe he had moved to Australia, or India, or Tahiti, sipping coconut juice with some young maiden hanging all over him.

And what about her wedding? What would she tell Hector? That she wanted to postpone the ceremony for a few weeks while she sailed off to England to find out if a sailor she had fallen in love with three years ago still wanted her? And if he didn't, then she'd come back and marry him? What man in his right mind would agree to that?

No, it was madness, sheer madness to even think about it. It made no sense at all. Peter could be dead, for all she knew. Or worse, married. And anyway, how could she do that to a decent man like Hector just days before their wedding? No, Peter was the past—the romantic, passionate past. A never-to-be-forgotten past, but the past, nonetheless. Hector was her "here and now." Her future. Her fate.

She tossed and turned all night.

Chapter 37

Josie heard a knock on the door. She went to open it, but her feet wouldn't move. It was like they were glued to the floor. "Come in," she called out.

The door opened slowly. A shadow stood in the entranceway, shrouded in darkness. Josie strained to see who it was. The figure moved forward, emerging in the light. It was Peter. Her Peter. He was reaching out to her, arms fully extended, anguish in his eyes, suffering on his face. She tried to go to him, but her legs were heavy, like lead. "Peter!" she cried out.

"Josie!" he wailed.

He took a step towards her, then stopped. Something was holding him back, pulling him away from her. He tried to break free but couldn't. It kept drawing him back toward the door, back to the darkness, farther and farther from Josie. Then Josie saw it, the force controlling Peter, the creature dragging him away. It was Miss Bennett! Grotesque, hideous Miss Bennett, with her hair aflame and evil in her eyes. She was laughing, cackling, taunting Josie, as she pulled Peter away. "You can't have him," she snickered. "You can never have him!"

Josie struggled and fought to free herself from her chains, but it was no use. Her feet would not budge. She watched helplessly as Peter grew smaller and smaller as he slowly disappeared into the blackness. Miss Bennett's laughter rose louder and louder as Peter faded out of sight.

"No! No! Peter, come back! Come back!" wept Josie.

"Josie! Josie! Help me! Help me!" cried Peter.

"Peter! Peter!"

"Josie! Josie!"

"Peter! Pe-"

Josie woke with a start. She looked around. She was in her room, in her bed, alone. It had been a dream. A bad dream. A very bad dream. She turned on the lamp on her night table and glanced at her alarm clock. Twenty-five past four. She fell back onto the pillow.

Sleep eluded her for the rest of the night, as images of Peter and a grotesque Miss Bennett continually popped into her head. The alarm went off at six, but she didn't need it. She was already awake. She got up, washed and dressed, had breakfast, and went to work.

Thursday. Two days to go. She was going to Becky's after work to make any necessary last-minute alterations to her wedding dress. But before that, Josie had one other thing she needed to do. Shortly after four, she left the restaurant and walked over to the Cunard-White Star offices. She walked in and went up to a middle-aged gentleman sitting at a desk.

"Can I help you, Miss?"

Josie hesitated. She was having second thoughts. Maybe she should just leave and go home.

"Miss?"

"Yes, I'm looking for passage to England. I was wondering if you have any ships sailing to England in the next two days?"

"Not in the next two days, Miss. Our next passenger ship heading for England wouldn't be for another four weeks."

"Four weeks? But I see ships coming into the harbour every day. Aren't any of those going back to England?"

"Most of those are troop ships, Miss, bringing soldiers back from the war front. From here they might go to North Africa or Cape Town to pick up more troops. Not all the ships go back to England. Besides, civilians are restricted from these ships right now until we get all the troops back, unless they're wives or children of servicemen."

"Are there any other types of ships going to England that are not troop ships?"

"Well, there's always cargo ships and tankers leaving from time to time, but we don't have any of those in our fleet."

"Where would I find them?"

"They're strewn along the docks in different locations. Some of them are Navy vessels, some owned by private operators. In any event, Miss, you wouldn't be able to get on any of those ships. They don't take passengers, just their crews."

Josie groaned. "Isn't there any other way to get to England?"

"Not unless you want to wait four weeks for our next passenger liner."

"That's too late."

"I'm sorry I couldn't be of more help."

Josie left the office disheartened. It looked like her trip to England to find Peter wasn't going to happen. She couldn't wait four weeks. She'd be married by then and it would be too late to turn back. Once again she considered asking Hector to postpone the wedding, but what excuse would she give him? That she was sick? Then how would she explain her trip to England? That she had to go to visit a sick relative? He'd know that wasn't true. Certainly, Becky would. No, it wasn't to be. The timing was all wrong. If the wedding was later in the year, she might have had time to go to England and get back. Come up with some other excuse. Or if Miss Bennett had given her Peter's letters earlier. If she hadn't waited until she was on her deathbed. But those were all "ifs." They hadn't happened. There was nothing she could do about it now. She was getting married. To Hector. In two days. Plain and simple.

The thought made her nauseous.

Chapter 38

Friday. One day to go. Josie's father and her sister Beatrice arrived by bus around three in the afternoon. Josie went with Albert to pick them up at the station in his new second-hand Nash Rambler. She had worked all morning, but her boss had given her the afternoon off. Her father and Beatrice were staying at Albert's mother's place. They'd sleep there Friday and Saturday night, then head back home by bus on Sunday.

George and Harry would both be at the wedding. George had returned from England a month earlier and was stationed in Debert. He had taken the bus down to Halifax the day before. Harry had taken shore leave for the wedding, then was rendez-vousing with his ship in New York the following week. It looked like he was going to stay in the Navy. Both George and Harry were staying at Becky's.

Everyone gathered at Becky and Albert's that night for a pre-wedding party—Josie, her father, Beatrice, George, Harry, Albert's mother, Albert's brother Raymond and his latest girlfriend (he had a new one every time Josie saw him), and, of course, Becky and Albert. Everyone except Hector. Josie had told him she didn't want to see him before the wedding. Bad luck, she insisted.

They enjoyed a hearty meal, prepared mostly by Albert's mother with some help from Becky. Josie ate very little. While the evening was supposed to be about Josie and her impending nuptials, the real centre of attention was little Wendy, just six weeks old to the day. Josie's father was seeing his grandchild for the first time, so the little one spent a lot of time in her grand-father's arms. He mentioned how he wished Josie's mother were still alive to see her new granddaughter.

Everyone, of course, remarked how beautiful the baby was. The prevailing opinion was that she looked more like Becky, although Raymond said she looked more like *him*. Becky gave him a dirty look for that remark.

After the baby was put to bed, everyone gathered in the parlour with their tea or coffee. Before long, three separate conversations were taking place at the same time. The three mothers—Becky, Albert's mother, and Beatrice—were talking about babies. Harry, George, and Albert were talking about the recent news of Japan's surrender while Josie's father listened in without comment. And Raymond and his girlfriend were arguing about who was the best Hollywood actor.

While all this was going on, Josie sat uncharacteristically silent, absorbed in her own thoughts—thoughts about Peter, about Hector, about her future. Would she ever be able to forget her handsome Brit now that she knew he had loved her? Would she ever be able to love Hector the way he deserved to be loved? What kind of a wife would she be for him if she held someone else in her heart? Was she doomed to a lifetime of unhappiness, married to one man but in love with another?

As she struggled to find answers to her questions, the nausea she had experienced the day before returned. Her insides churned and her breathing grew laboured. She was feeling sick to her stomach. She tried to control it, but she couldn't. It was getting worse by the second. The sensation rose to her throat. She began to gag. Her body wretched forward. She needed to get to the bathroom.

She got up from her chair and slowly left the room, not want-ing to draw attention to herself. As she walked down the hall to the bathroom, her body convulsed again and again. She had to hold on just a little longer. Finally, she made it. She pulled on the light chain, closed the door behind her, knelt in front of the toilet, lifted the seat, and let it go. Vomit spewed like a gusher, splashing in the bowl. For a moment or two, she felt relief. Then the sensation returned, rising from her gut, travelling up to her throat. She vomited again, unable to hold it back. The foul liquid erupted from her like fiery lava from a volcano. This time, the relief lasted a little longer, giving her a moment to catch her breath and wipe her mouth with a tissue.

She heard a knock on the door.

"Josie? Are you alright?"

It was her father. She didn't answer him right away.

"Josie, are you okay? Can I come in?"

"No! No, I'm fine. I'll be out in a minute."

Josie still felt nauseous, but the vomiting had stopped. She lifted her head gingerly from the toilet bowl and sat up, giving her head a few seconds to clear. She stood, flushed the toilet, wiped the sweat from her forehead, and took a deep breath. Then she washed her hands, splashed some water on her face, and opened the door. Her father was standing there. "Are you okay?" he said.

"I'm fine, Dad."

Josie's father stuck his head in the bathroom. His nose picked up the unmistakable odor. "Were you sick?"

"It's nothing, Dad. I just felt a little queasy for a minute. I'm better now."

"Are you sure? You look white as a ghost."

"Yes, I'm sure."

"Are you coming back to the parlour?"

"Just give me a minute."

"Okay."

Josie went back into the bathroom and checked herself in the mirror. Her father was right, she *did* look like a ghost. She found a hair brush and some lipstick in the medicine cabinet and spruced herself up, tidied her dress, and headed back to rejoin the others. When she entered the parlour, everyone looked up.

"Are you alright, Josie?" asked Becky. "Dad said you threw up."

"I'm fine," said Josie. "My stomach was just a little upset. Maybe something I ate."

Albert's mother piped in. "Wedding jitters, my dear. We all had them."

"Or morning sickness," laughed Raymond.

"Raymond!" scolded Albert's mother.

Josie didn't take the bait. Raymond wasn't worth it. "I think I'll just go outside and get some air."

"That's a good idea," said Albert's mother. "It'll make you feel better."

Josie left the flat, proceeding down the stairs and out the building to the sidewalk. She leaned against a telephone pole and took a deep breath. Her stomach was still a little unsettled, but the fresh air felt good. Seconds later, the front door opened and out stepped her father. "Feeling any better?" he said.

"A little."

"Is there anything I can get you?"

"How about a cigarette?"

The request surprised Josie's father. "I didn't know you smoked."

Josie looked up at her father and smiled. "There's a lot you don't know about me, Dad."

He reached into his pants pocket, pulled out a small tin case, and offered his hand-rolled cigarettes to his daughter. She took one. He then took one for himself and lit both cigarettes. For the next minute or so, father and daughter blew smoke rings in the air, arguing about who had made the best one. Eventually, Josie's father turned the conversation to a more serious subject. "So, Raymond wasn't right, was he?"

Josie glared at her father. "Dad! Of course not. How could you think that?"

"Well, you said there was a lot about you I didn't know."

Josie laughed. "Yes, I did say that, didn't I. But I would have told you about that."

"So, it's the jitters, then?"

"What?"

"The reason you got sick to your stomach. Are you nervous about getting married?"

"Nervous? About getting married? No, not really."

"Are you nervous about your wedding night? You could talk to Becky or Beatrice about that."

Josie chuckled. "No, Dad, it's not that."

"Well, what is it, ma petite fleur? Something is bothering you. I can tell."

Ma petite fleur. His pet name for her when she was a little girl. My little flower. And he'd usually call her that when something was troubling her. He always seemed to know, somehow. And he'd always get it out of her, eventually. When she was growing up she'd tell her father things that she could never tell her mother. When she'd tell her mother about her problems, her mother would always make light of them, like they weren't important, like she was just being silly. Her father would always listen to her, always take her seriously, never tell her she was being silly, even if he thought she was. And he would never tell her what to do the way her mother would. Instead, he'd find a way to help her come up with her own answers, her own solutions. He might have had his own ideas about what she should do, but he'd never force them on her. He might gently suggest or nudge, but he'd allow her to decide on her own. And she'd always feel better after their talks. He had a gift. It had taken Josie years to realize it.

But she was an adult now. Not a little girl anymore. Should she tell her father what was really bothering her? Should she confide in him? Could he help her solve her problem? She had wanted to tell *somebody*. Get another opinion, another viewpoint. Reassure her that what she was thinking made sense—or make her realize it was utter madness. She had to get it off her chest. She couldn't keep it bottled inside any longer. It was driving her crazy.

"If I tell you, Dad, you can't tell anyone else."

"Okay."

"No one, Dad. Not Becky, not Beatrice, absolutely no one. If you do, I'll never forgive you. I'm serious"

"I understand. I won't tell anyone."

"Promise?"

"Promise."

"Swear to God?"

"Josie, I won't tell anyone. I promise."

Josie was satisfied. She trusted him. He would keep his promise. She paused briefly to collect her thoughts, then proceeded to tell him the entire story. She told him about Peter, about Miss Bennett, about the letters. Everything. She told him how she had thought about going to England to find Peter. She told him how she was torn between her love for Peter and her promise to Hector. She told him she didn't truly love Hector, but she didn't want to hurt him, because he was a decent man. And she told him that the conflict inside her was making her sick. When she was finished, she looked at her father to gauge his reaction, to see what he might say. She felt like a little girl again. "What should I do, Daddy?"

Josie's father dropped his cigarette butt on the sidewalk and crushed it with his shoe. He folded one arm across his chest and stroked his chin with the other. "So, this Peter fella. You knew him for one day?"

"Basically."

"And how long have you known Hector?"

"Uh, about two years, I guess."

"And you're trying to decide if you should marry Hector or go to England to find Peter and see if he wants to marry you?"

"Well, yes, I guess that's what I'm trying to decide."

"So, you *do* want to get married, then, to somebody."

"Yes, I guess so."

"You guess so?"

"No. No, I want to get married."

"But you don't know if you want to marry Hector or Peter?"

"Right."

Josie's father paused for a moment. He seemed to be deep in thought. "Do you know what type of husband Peter would be?"

Josie looked down at the ground. "No, not really."

"Do you know what type of husband Hector would be?"

"I have a pretty good idea."

"What type of husband would he make?"

"He'd make a good husband."

"Would he take care of you and be good to you?"

"Yes, he would."

"Would he be a good father to your children?"

"Yes, he'd be an excellent father to my children."

Josie's father paused again, then continued. "Why do you think you feel the way you do about Peter?"

"I guess he just swept me off my feet. He was so handsome, with his blue eyes and his smile. And I loved his English accent."

"So, you fell in love with his eyes and his smile and his accent?"

It sounded so shallow the way her father said it. "I guess so."

"And not with *him*, because you admitted you really don't know him."

Josie was beginning to see what her father was getting at. "I suppose. But those letters, Dad. If you read them, you'd see that he really loved me."

"After knowing you for only one day."

"It can happen."

"Okay, fine. You're right, it can happen. So, if you went to England and found this Peter, what would you say to him?"

"I'd ask him if he still loved me and wanted to marry me."

"And what if he said he didn't love you anymore or was already married?"

"Well, then, I guess I'd have to come back to Canada."

"And would you then marry Hector?"

"He wouldn't want me then. I couldn't blame him."

"But if he *did* still want you, would you marry him?"

Josie considered the question. "Yes, I suppose I would."

"So, you have a decision to make. Either go to England to try and find a man you met one day during the war and who you barely know, and see if he wants to marry you, if he's not already married. Or marry a man you've known for two years, who you know wants to marry you, and who you know would make a good husband."

Josie smiled at her father. "I know what you want me to do."

"I'm not telling you to do anything. It's your decision. What do you think you should do?"

Josie sighed. Her father made sense. She didn't really know Peter at all. Maybe she had just fallen in love with an idea, the idea of being in love, a wild romantic notion. Reality was a lot different. Reality was Hector. Caring, kind, loyal.

"You think I'm crazy, don't you?" she said to her father.

"No, I don't think you're crazy. I think you're headstrong sometimes. You don't always think things through."

Josie smiled. "I love you, Father."

"I love you too, Josie."

Josie hooked her arm under her father's and leaned her head against his shoulder. She felt so comfortable, so safe by his side. She could see why her mother had fallen in love with him.

They went back into the house. Everyone was still in the parlour, chatting up a storm. Albert had brought out a small decanter of sherry, which seemed to lubricate the conversation. Albert's mother was particularly talkative. "Are you feeling better, my dear?" she said, as Josie and her father entered the room.

"Yes, much better," said Josie. "Thank you."

"You were gone quite a while," said Becky.

Josie gazed lovingly at her father. "We had a good long talk, didn't we, Dad."

"Yes, we did. Yes, we did."

Chapter 39

Saturday. Wedding day. It was literally a two-minute walk from her boarding house to St. Mary's Cathedral, so Josie had wanted to get dressed in her room, then walk over to the church in time for the ceremony, which was at eleven. But Becky wouldn't hear of it. "How would it look, a bride in her wedding dress walking on the street?" she had said. So, Albert was picking Josie up around nine and taking her back to Becky's to get dressed. He would then drive her and Becky to the church. It would be a busy morning for Albert and his Nash. He also had to drive his mother, Josie's father, and Beatrice.

Josie and Hector were expecting about twenty-five people for the ceremony. On Josie's side there would be Becky and Albert and their baby. (Since Becky was the maid of honour, it would be up to Albert to keep the baby quiet during the mass.) There would be Josie's father, her sister Beatrice, and her brothers George and Harry. They had also invited Albert's mother, his brother Raymond, and Raymond's girlfriend. Josie had invited Irene and a couple of her friends from work, as well as Mr. Gorman and his wife. She had also invited Doris and her husband, although she wasn't sure they would attend, given her husband's condition. On Hector's side, there would be his brother Clarence as the best man, his parents, and his two sisters. He had also invited three of his co-workers, who could each bring a guest.

Josie had a restful sleep and woke to the alarm at seven. She washed, dressed, and had breakfast. After breakfast, she went back to her room to wait for Albert. As she waited, she checked to see if she had everything ready for her wedding night and honeymoon. Becky had given her a small suitcase so she wouldn't have to use her big one, and she had packed it the night before. Just to be sure, she opened it to see if she had everything she wanted. She then checked her going-away suit which she had hung in the closet. She remembered that she had wanted to pin a brooch on the lapel, the one Becky had given her for Christmas a few years earlier. She kept it in a small jewellery box in the top drawer of her dresser.

It was when she opened the drawer that she saw them. Staring up at her. The letters. Peter's letters. She reached in and picked them up. She shuffled through them to find the one with the earliest postmark. She stared at it for several seconds, trying to decide. Should she? Should she torture herself again? What was the point? But she couldn't help herself. She had to. One more time. She took the letter out of the envelope, unfolded it, and began to read.

My Beautiful Darling,

How could I have been so fortunate to have found someone as wonderful as you? Someone so beautiful, so caring, so full of life. I know our time together was short, but you have already stolen my heart. I have never felt this way before. Ever. From the moment I met you...

Stop! This was craziness. What was she doing? Her father was right. She had to forget Peter. She was marrying Hector. Hector was her future. Peter was her past. A fleeting moment in time. A fantasy. Hector was real.

She folded the letter, stuffed it back in the envelope, and placed all four letters back in the drawer. But as they lay there, she couldn't take her eyes off them. They seemed to be calling her.

She felt an urge to reach back and take them. But she resisted. She defied them. She looked away.

As she did, she spotted another envelope. It was the envelope of money that Miss Bennett had left for her. The money. She hadn't even counted it. She picked up the envelope and removed the wad of bills. They were all twenties. She began counting. Twenty, forty, sixty, eighty, one hundred, twenty, forty, sixty, eighty, two hundred, twenty…. When she had finished, she had counted five hundred dollars. Five hundred dollars! A fortune! More than eight months of wages at the Green Lantern. She couldn't believe it. Miss Bennett had left her five hundred dollars. She had never had that much money in all her life. She had never even *seen* that much money in all her life. Miss Bennett's sister had told her it would give her a good start on her married life. Yes, it would. But Josie was thinking of something else it would do.

There was a knock on the door. Josie hurriedly jammed the money back in the envelope and tucked the envelope next to Peter's letters. She grabbed the brooch from the jewellery box and closed the drawer. "Who is it?"

"It's me, Josie. There's a gentleman downstairs asking for you."

Josie's heart skipped a beat. Could it be…? Then she realized it would be Albert, coming to pick her up. "I'll be right down, Mr. Walsh."

Josie went to the closet and pinned the brooch on her outfit. Gathering the items she needed for getting dressed, she went downstairs. It was indeed Albert who had been asking for her. He was right on time. Nine o'clock on the button.

When they got to the flat, Becky was buzzing about, tending to the baby and tidying up in the kitchen. As soon as they walked in, she had orders ready for her husband. "Albert, you look after the baby. She needs to be fed and dressed. Her clothes are on the bed. Josie and I have a wedding to get ready for."

Becky fixed Josie's hair and helped her get dressed. When they were done, Josie examined herself in the bathroom mirror. This was it. She was really getting married. Today.

"You look beautiful," said Becky.

"Thank you, Sis."

As was the custom, they arrived at the church just a few minutes before the ceremony was scheduled to begin to allow all the guests to arrive first and take their seats. Albert parked the car in the lot next to the church. He helped Becky out of the front seat first and took the baby from her. He then opened the back door and helped Josie out. They all walked around to the main doors of the church, with Becky holding up Josie's dress at the back. When they entered the church, Josie's father was waiting in the foyer to escort his daughter down the aisle. He gave her a big hug, then looked at her and smiled. "Are you ready?"

Josie paused for a moment to calm herself, then nodded.

"I'll tell them," said Albert.

Albert proceeded to the front of the church, stopping where his mother was seated to hand her the baby. He went to the bottom of the altar steps and nodded to the priest, who was standing at the top of the steps, then joined his mother in the pew. The priest motioned to the organist in the choir loft. Instantly, the church filled with sound, echoing in the cavernous structure. Becky took her cue, exiting the foyer and entering the main body of the church. Flowers in hand, she began her procession down the aisle, slowly and methodically, just as she had rehearsed. In the foyer, Josie stood alongside her father, her hand under his arm and his hand on hers. He moved to walk, but Josie didn't budge. He looked over at her and frowned, then tugged her slightly. She started walking, out of the foyer and into the church. As she began to make her way down the long aisle, she looked at the scene before her—rows of empty pews, people in the distance staring back at her, a tiny figure in a robe standing at the altar, dwarfed by the imposing backdrop. Her heart started beating faster and faster. Her breathing quickened. Her mouth went dry.

Suddenly, she froze in her tracks. The organist stopped playing. A murmur went through the guests.

"I can't," said Josie.

"What?" said her father.

"I can't."

"Josie!"

"I'm sorry, Dad. I just can't."

She pulled her hand from under her father's arm and ran for the door, lifting her dress above her ankles. Pushing the heavy doors open with her shoulder, she stumbled down the church steps to the sidewalk, then scurried around the side of the church, almost losing her balance. Gasping for air, she threw herself on the ground next to a tree. Within seconds, her father had found her.

"Josie, what's wrong?" he asked her calmly.

"I can't go through with this, Dad. I just can't."

"Josie, it's just nerves. You'll be okay. C'mon back inside."

"I can't."

"Yes, you can. I'll be with you. We'll walk down that aisle together."

Just then, Harry arrived on the scene. "What's going on?" he said. "Everyone's waiting inside."

Josie's father looked up at Harry. "She's just feeling a little faint, that's all. It's just nerves. She'll be alright. Just go back in and tell them to give her a few minutes."

"But…"

"Son, just do what I ask, please."

Harry headed back to the church. Josie's father turned to his daughter. "Okay, Josie, let's go. Hector's waiting to make you his wife."

Those words. *Hector's waiting to make you his wife.* Her heart raced faster.

"Dad, I don't know if I love him. What kind of a wife would I be if I married a man I didn't love? It wouldn't be fair to him. He's better off finding someone who truly loves him."

"Josie, we talked about this. You said that Hector would make a good husband and a good father, didn't you?"

"Yes, I did."

"Josie, love happens over time. It did with your mother and me."

Just then Becky came around the corner of the church and headed over to them. "What's going on here, Josie? Everyone's waiting."

"Everything's fine, Becky," said Josie's father. "She was just feeling a little faint. We'll be there in a second."

"Well, you better not take too long. The priest is starting to get annoyed."

"Tell him to relax. We'll be right in."

Becky went back inside. Josie's father placed his hand on her shoulder. "Are you ready? Let's go."

Josie rose to her feet. "You go ahead, Dad. I'll be right in. I just need a minute to myself."

"Are you sure?"

"Yes, I'll be right in."

Josie's father kissed his daughter on the forehead and started to head back to the church. Josie called out to him. "Dad?"

"Yes, Josie?"

"I love you."

"I love you too. Now, don't be too long."

As soon as her father was out of sight, Josie started running as fast as she could—through the parking lot, on to Grafton, and back to the Walsh boarding house, almost knocking over a startled couple on the street as she ran. She was at the boarding house in no time, racing up the stairs and into her room. She kicked off her high heels and frantically removed her wedding dress, tossing it on the chair in the corner. She had no time to lose. They'd soon discover she had fled and would come looking for her. She grabbed one of the dresses hanging in her closet and slipped it on. She hauled her big suitcase out from under her bed, flung it on top, and opened it. Darting like mad from the dresser to the bed, she snatched pieces of clothing and threw them haphazardly into the suitcase. Toiletries. She needed toiletries. She fired her hairbrush, lipsticks, powder, a bottle of perfume, and a bar of soap in with her clothes. Shoes. She needed a sturdy pair of shoes. She went to her closet and put on a pair she wore to work. She spotted the suit she had bought for the honeymoon. Should she take it? She had to decide quickly. She tore it off the hanger, folded it, and stuffed it in the suitcase. She'd need an extra pair of shoes as well. She grabbed a pair and hurled them into the case. Oh, what about the clothes in the small suitcase that Becky had given her? She flipped it open. Pajamas, lingerie, mostly frilly stuff. She plucked out a few pieces and tossed them in. And finally, the last items. She grabbed Peter's letters and her money out of her top drawer and jammed them in her purse.

Time to go.

She took one last look around to see if she had everything she needed. Satisfied, she threw her purse strap over her shoulder, snapped her suitcase shut, and yanked it off the bed. She opened her door and peeked outside to see if anyone was in the hall, then closed the door behind her and locked it, calculating that if they came looking for her, they'd check her room first. If it was locked, at least it would slow them down a little.

She headed down the hall to the stairs. Then, all of a sudden, she heard voices coming from the main floor. She strained to listen. "Oh my God!" she gasped. It sounded like her father and Harry talking to Mr. Walsh. She had to get out of there right away. But how? There were no back stairs. The fire escape! She could use the fire escape.

She ran to the end of the hall to the rear window. She dropped her suitcase on the floor and pushed up the window with both hands. She picked up her suitcase and shoved it through the opening and onto the fire escape. Climbing through, she shut the window behind her, snatched her suitcase, and scampered down the fire escape, jumping to the ground at the bottom. Righting herself, she scrambled through the backyards of the buildings, down lanes, through gates, climbing over stone fences, trying to stay off the main thoroughfares. She got as far as Barrington but couldn't find a way through. She'd have to cross the street and risk being seen. She peeked out from the side of the building to see if the coast was clear, then darted to the other side. She was at Salter. She tore down Salter as fast as she could, past Hollis to Lower Water, then to the waterfront.

Once on the docks, she stopped to catch her breath, then looked back to see if anyone was following her. All clear. But she couldn't rest for long. She wasn't out of the woods yet. She quickly made her way up the docks, desperately searching for a ship about to sail. It was a busy day on the waterfront, with several ships in port, tied up at their berths. Crewmen were everywhere, civilians and sailors alike, some loading and unloading cargo, others just milling about. As she made her way, she approached as many men as she could find and asked for help. Some completely ignored her, others said they weren't sailing for a few days, a few couldn't even speak English. She was just about to give up hope when she spotted a man barking orders at some men carrying barrels onto a small ship. He was wearing what looked like a captain's hat. She came up to him. "Excuse me, sir. Are you the captain of this ship?"

"That I am," he shot back, without looking at her.

"Are you sailing today?"

"As soon as we get this cargo loaded. You over there, grab that barrel."

"Are you going to England?"

"Eventually. Newfoundland, then Holland, then England."

"I'm looking for passage to England."

"Can't help you," he replied curtly. He then hollered at one of his men. "You there, get a move on. We have to get her loaded today."

"I can pay you," said Josie.

"Doesn't matter, Miss. We don't take passengers. Only crew. This is a cargo ship."

"I can pay you a hundred dollars."

The man looked at Josie for the first time. She now had his attention. "A hundred dollars?"

"Yes."

He eyeballed Josie intently. She could tell the wheels were turning in his head.

"Hmm. No, it's tempting, but I can't. We never take passengers. Besides, a pretty girl like you? You wouldn't be safe on this boat with these men."

"I can take care of myself."

"Not with these hooligans you couldn't."

Josie realized she had to pull out all the stops. "What if I gave you *two* hundred?"

"Two hundred! You have two hundred dollars?"

"Yes, I do."

"Two hundred dollars. Hmm. That's a lot of money. But how would I keep the men away from you? And where would I put you? Unless…"

"Unless what?"

The man seemed to be talking aloud to himself. "Unless I told them you were my daughter…and I was taking you to England to meet up with your husband…who was an officer in the British Navy. Then they'd keep their hands off you."

"Would they believe that?"

"Well, I actually have a daughter about your age. Some of them know that. But none of them have ever met her. Anyway, most of them are too dumb to ask any questions." He paused. "But there's one other thing."

"What's that?"

"You'd have to sleep in my cabin. There's no way they'd believe I'd bunk my own daughter with them."

Josie examined the man closely. He had kind eyes. She trusted him. "That would be fine."

"There's not much room in there. It's quite cramped. There's a bench you could sleep on. We'd find you a bunk mattress from somewhere."

"I don't care. I just need to get to England."

Josie glanced over her shoulder. The man noticed. "Someone following you?"

"No," mumbled Josie. "So, do we have a deal?"

"Two hundred dollars?"

"Two hundred dollars."

"Then we have a deal."

The man reached out his hand and Josie shook it.

"By the way," the man said, "what's your name?"

"Josie."

"It's now Anna. That's my real daughter's name. As long as you're on my boat, you're Anna."

Anna, thought Josie. The same as Miss Bennett. She didn't know if she liked using the same name as that nasty old woman. But she had no choice. She was now Anna.

The man waved to one of his crew who had been directing the loading. The crew member quickly came over.

"Barney, this is my daughter Anna. She's going to be sailing with us to England to join her husband, who's in the British Navy. I'm putting her up in my cabin. I want you to take her there now, get her settled, make sure she's comfortable."

"Yes, sir," said Barney.

Barney turned to Josie and took off his hat. "Pleased to meet you, Ma'am."

Josie smiled for the first time all day. "Pleased to meet you too, Barney."

Barney picked up Josie's suitcase and motioned to her to go ahead. Just before they reached the gangway, the captain called out, waving Josie over. "Oh, Anna, there's one other thing we need to discuss. Privately."

Josie went over to the captain while Barney waited at the bottom of the gangway. "Anything wrong?" Josie asked.

"You need to pay me the two hundred dollars before you get on the ship," said the captain. "I don't mean to offend you, but I have to be sure you actually have the money before I let you board. I hope you understand. Once we set sail, I can't throw you into the sea."

Josie thought about the Captain's demands for a second. She had another idea. "I'll pay you one hundred dollars now, and another one hundred dollars when we get to England."

The captain smiled. "Fair enough."

Josie returned to Barney and followed him up the gangway to the deck of the ship. He escorted her to the captain's quarters. As she entered the cabin and looked around, she could see what the captain had meant. It was indeed a little cramped. But that didn't matter. Only one thing mattered to her at this moment—one thing and only one thing.

She was going to England.

Chapter 40

The seas between Halifax and St. John's were relatively calm, so Josie didn't mind the first leg of her voyage at all. She had been on her father's fishing boat many times when she was a young girl and never got seasick. And this was a much larger vessel.

Her makeshift bed in the captain's cabin was small but functional. The only complication arose when she'd get ready to retire for the evening. The Captain had to leave his quarters while Josie changed into her nightclothes. It was a bit awkward, but he took it in stride. All in all, Josie felt he was treating her very well, trying to make her as comfortable as possible. And she now knew his name. Bill Stewart. Captain Bill Stewart. Of course, in front of the crew she had to refer to him as "Father." He suggested she also call him that when they were alone, to lessen the chances of her slipping up.

The crew were nice to her as well, for the most part. They'd usually tip their hats and say "Good morning, Ma'am" or "Good afternoon, Ma'am" when she passed by. She knew some of them stared at her shapely figure when they thought she wasn't looking, and a couple even made suggestive gestures, but it was nothing she couldn't handle, and not worth reporting to Captain Stewart. She didn't want to turn the crew against her. In any event, Barney became her unofficial protector, her gallant knight, admonishing any of his fellow crew members when they stepped out of line.

The trip to Newfoundland took almost three days. And except for meals, which she took with the captain, she spent much of the time in her cabin, sleeping. The strain of the previous few days had left her completely exhausted. Discovering Peter's letters, bolting from the church, catching a boat for England before they stopped her—it was all too much. Now that she was safe, her body just collapsed.

But she did take the time to do one important thing—write some letters. She wrote separate letters to Hector, to her father, and to Becky, trying to explain why she had run away. And she begged them to forgive her, although she told them she'd understand if they couldn't, especially Hector.

Hector. Poor Hector. How could she have done this to him? Leaving him standing there at the altar, in front of his family and friends. How embarrassed he must have been. How angry with her. He must feel she's a terrible person. Selfish. Wicked, even. But she had to do it. She had to find out. For her own future happiness. And his as well. Hopefully, one day he'd understand.

The ship arrived in St. John's just after ten o'clock in the morning on Tuesday. They'd encountered heavy coastal fog as they approached Newfoundland, but by the time they reached St. John's the fog had lifted, and it was a bright, sunny day. Josie went out on the deck. She had never been to St. John's. As they entered the harbour, her mouth opened wide. It was as if they were in a bowl, with high hills all around and the city to their right. It was beautiful. Barney had told Josie they were unloading goods from the mainland for local merchants, then loading barrels of salt cod for transport to Europe. They'd also be topping up their fuel and other supplies. The work would take all day and the captain had decided to wait until the next morning to set sail. It would give the crew their last bit of shore leave before crossing the Atlantic.

It was also a welcomed break for Josie. She'd get a chance to go ashore, get her land legs, and do a little sightseeing. She'd also mail her letters. And that evening, she was going to supper with Captain Stewart. Apparently, it was his custom, time permitting, to dine at a local restaurant whenever he was in port overnight.

And, as he had said, it wouldn't make sense to the crew if he didn't take his daughter along with him. So, Josie was in for an unexpected treat.

She had also considered taking a room at a hotel for the night. She certainly could afford it, and it would give her a chance to have a nice hot bath and sleep in a big, comfy bed. But how would it look if the captain's daughter spent the night at a hotel instead of on the ship with her father? So she hadn't mentioned it to the captain. Besides, she was a little worried that she might be giving him ideas, and he'd want to stay at the hotel with her. She trusted him—but only to a point.

So she spent the day walking around the downtown, taking in the sights, doing a little shopping. She bought a woolen sweater because she hadn't packed a sweater in her haste to flee the boarding house. Captain Stewart had told her that England could be damp and cold in the fall, so she'd need something warm.

She hadn't taken all her money ashore, just one hundred dollars. The rest of it was in the safe in the captain's cabin. When he had suggested that she keep it there, she was reluctant at first, concerned that he might steal it. But when he explained that keeping it in her purse or on herself was a lot riskier, she had agreed. Besides, he said, if someone ashore robbed her, he wouldn't get his final one hundred dollars. But just to be on the safe side, she had kept one hundred dollars on herself, then made him sign a note that she had placed three hundred dollars in his custody in his safe. As a further safeguard, she put a twenty-dollar bill in each of her socks, leaving just sixty dollars in her purse.

She returned to the ship just after five o'clock to get ready for her dinner with the captain. She changed her dress, brushed her hair, put on some lipstick, and even dabbed on a little perfume. He spruced up, too. He shaved, put on a sharp-looking double-breasted pea coat, and topped it off with a navy-blue sailor's hat which he called a Breton. They left the ship around six, marching down the gangway arm-in-arm like a loving father and daughter. They played the part to the hilt.

They had a lovely meal at a nice restaurant. The captain even picked up the bill. But as he was paying, he surprised Josie with a suggestion. "Why don't you get a room at a local hotel for the night? I know you can afford it. It'll give you a break from the cabin. Have a nice hot bath. Sleep in a comfortable bed. I know a nice, small hotel near the waterfront. We'll go back to the ship so you can pick up what you need. I'll then get Barney to take you over there. He'll pick you up in the morning. You'll have to be up early, though. We're leaving at the crack of dawn."

Josie smiled to herself. What a coincidence. She and the captain with the same idea. "Won't the crew find it odd that the captain's daughter is spending the night in a hotel by herself?"

"Not at all. They might be surprised if she didn't. They'd think that her father was a cheapskate for not putting her in a nice room for a night."

"Wouldn't they expect the captain to accompany his daughter?"

Captain Stewart frowned and shook his head. "The captain always sleeps on his ship during a voyage, even when in port."

Reassured that she had nothing to fear, Josie agreed to his suggestion. They went back to the ship and she put her night-clothes and a few toiletries in a knapsack the captain gave her, then Barney took her to the hotel.

Her room was small but certainly bigger than the cabin on the ship. And clean. She had a wonderful hot bath in the bath-room down the hall and washed her hair. The bed was soft and comfortable. It was the best sleep she had had in weeks.

The alarm went off at five thirty. Barney was picking her up at six and they'd be sailing at six thirty. The bed was so comfortable that Josie hated to get up. But Barney would be there in thirty minutes, so she dragged herself to her feet, went to the bathroom to freshen up, changed, packed her knapsack, and went down to the lobby to wait for him. She'd eat breakfast back on the boat. Barney was right on time, and they returned to the ship immediately. The ship left the dock at six forty.

Josie went out on deck for the departure. The cool ocean breeze on her face refreshed her. As they left the harbour and picked up speed, Josie felt upbeat.

She was one step closer to finding her prince.

Chapter 41

While the waters of the Gulf of St. Lawrence had been rather tranquil, the seas of the North Atlantic proved to be anything but. Huge waves, whipped up by gale force winds often accompanied by heavy rain, battered the ship for parts of the journey. At times, deep ocean swells would lift the boat up and slam it back down with so much force that Josie was sure the ship would break apart. During these rougher patches, she spent most of the time in her cabin as it was too dangerous to be out on deck.

The biggest problem for Josie, however, was the boredom. There wasn't much for her to do. During calmer seas, she would sometimes go up to the wheelhouse and the helmsman would let her steer the ship. At first, she found the experience exhilarating, but the novelty soon wore off. She even suggested to the captain that she could help the cook prepare and serve meals for the crew, given that she was a waitress and knew her way around a kitchen. At least it would help pass the time. But the captain scuttled that idea. He said it wouldn't be appropriate for his "daughter" to be slogging away in a ship's galley. So, for a while, Josie seemed destined to spend most of the trip lying in her bunk looking up at the ceiling, or out on deck staring at the blackness of the endless ocean. Until, one night at dinner, Captain Stewart had a suggestion.

"Do you like to read?" he asked her.

"I did when I was a little girl in school," she said.

"I have a book you might like. I bought it for my daughter. She loved it. It's in my cabin. I'll give it to you once we're done."

After they had finished eating, they went back to the captain's quarters. He opened the door of a cabinet behind his desk, took a book off the shelf, and handed it to her. "It's *Sense and Sensibility*, by Jane Austen," he said. "Have you heard of it?"

Josie had never heard of the book, or the author for that matter. She hadn't really read any books since she'd left school. She felt embarrassed. "No, I haven't."

Captain Stewart told her it was a well-known "work of literature." A classic, he called it. She was a little surprised that the captain of a cargo ship would know so much about books. "People can surprise you sometimes," she remembered her father telling her.

That night, she took a kerosene lamp over to her bunk and began reading, while the captain sat at his desk writing in his log. It wasn't long before she began to struggle. She hadn't gone very far in school, only Grade 8, and many of the words she didn't understand. And even when she knew the words, she had a difficult time following the story. After battling through two chapters, she was totally lost. She put the book down, turned off the lamp, and slid under the covers.

"Is that all the reading you're going to do tonight?" asked Captain Stewart.

"I'm just tired," said Josie.

The next day, the seas were rough, so after breakfast Josie returned to her cabin. She had nothing else to do, so she decided to give *Sense and Sensibility* another try. Starting again from the beginning, she concentrated on every word, trying to piece them together to make some sense of what she was reading. But it didn't help. Just like the evening before, she soon became lost, and this time, frustrated. She didn't know anyone who talked the way the characters in the book talked, and most of the time she couldn't make heads or tails of what they were saying. She had thought she knew how to read, at least a little, but apparently she couldn't read "classics."

That night, the captain noticed that she had gone to her bunk without the book. "You're not reading tonight?" he asked from behind his desk.

"No, not tonight," she answered.

"If you don't read every chance you get, you're not going to finish it before we get to England."

Josie didn't respond. Captain Stewart looked at her intently and frowned. "Don't you like the book?"

Josie hesitated. She was embarrassed to admit she was having difficulty understanding it, but she didn't want to say she didn't like it, in case that sounded ungrateful. "It's not that. It's…it's just…I have a hard time reading at night. It makes me sleepy."

"Did you read some today? You spent a lot of time in the cabin."

"Um, a little."

"How far did you get?"

"Uh, I don't know. I…I forget."

He stared at her for several seconds without speaking. Then he leaned forward. "You *can* read, can't you?"

"Of course I can read. I'm not stupid."

"I didn't say you were stupid. It's just that those types of books are written in an old style, and they're sometimes hard to follow if you're not used to that type of writing. They use a lot of words that people today don't use very much anymore."

He seemed to be waiting for Josie to respond, but she said nothing. "Do you want me to help you?" he asked her.

"Help me? How?"

"Well, you go ahead and read, and if you get stuck on a word, you can ask me about it and I'll try to tell you what it means."

Josie realized there was no sense hiding it any longer. The captain knew she was having difficulty with the book. Even though she was embarrassed, she really *did* want to find out what the story was about. So she took him up on his offer. They started right away, from the beginning. Josie would read, then stop on a word she didn't understand. She'd show it to the captain and he'd explain what it meant. He always knew. After a few sentences, she'd ask him what they were talking about because most of the time she couldn't figure it out. He'd then explain their conversations and tie everything together. Then she'd move on to the next few sentences. As they went, Josie grew more interested in the story, now that she better understood what was going on. But the process was slow. It was taking them so much time just to get through a few pages because there were so many words that Josie didn't know, and so much of the story that the captain had to explain. At this rate, it was obvious to both of them that they'd never finish the book before the ship arrived in England. Captain Stewart offered a solution. "How about if I just read it to you. It'll go much faster. I used to read to my daughter when she was a little girl."

Josie didn't like being compared to a "little girl," but she had to admit she liked the captain's suggestion. The way they had been doing it to this point was painful. So much stopping and starting. This way, she could just relax and enjoy the story. So, that's what they did. Captain Stewart read the story aloud to Josie and explained as he went, and Josie just sat back and listened, and occasionally asked a question if she didn't understand something. Things moved along much quicker as a result. That night, the captain read until Josie fell asleep.

For the next few days, Captain Stewart would read to Josie every chance they got; at night before they went to sleep, and during the day whenever the captain could free himself from his duties. They even started taking their meals in the captain's cabin, so he could read while they ate. As a result, it didn't take long before Josie became totally engrossed in the story. She was fascinated by the lifestyle of the characters, how they were always entertaining or having parties or going to balls. She wondered if anyone actually lived like that, even then. She assumed that's what life was like when you had lots of money and didn't have to work. She imagined herself living that kind of lifestyle. Would it be for her?

She also became completely captivated by the characters themselves, and began drawing parallels in her mind between the characters in the book and the people in her own life. She, Josie, was Marianne; lively, fun-loving, romantic, emotional. The "sensibility" in the title, as the captain had explained it. Becky was Elinor. Even though Elinor was older than Marianne, and Becky was younger than Josie, Becky was more like Elinor; sensible, practical, reserved. The "sense" in the title. Edward, who married Elinor, was Albert, who married Becky. Not handsome, quiet, a bit dull. Just like Albert. In the book, Marianne felt Edward lacked "spirit," exactly the way Josie felt about Albert.

Willoughby. Was he Peter? They're both dashing and handsome. And Marianne falls for Willoughby just like Josie fell for Peter. But would Peter turn out to be the bastard that Willoughby was? Was she being fooled by Peter the way Marianne was fooled by Willoughby?

And what about Miss Bennett? Was she Eliza, the young girl who Willoughby fathered a child with and then abandoned? Josie remembered how bad she had felt for Eliza when Captain Stewart read that part of the story. A young girl with a baby and no husband. No father for her child. She began to understand how Miss Bennett must have felt. Abandoned. Rejected. Alone. How bitter she must have been. Maybe she really did think she was doing the right thing by keeping the letters. Maybe, in her own way, she really was trying to protect her. Josie felt a touch of guilt.

So, who did that leave? Hector. Hector was obviously Colonel Brandon; steady, reliable, not as dashing as Willoughby. Just like Hector was not as dashing as Peter. But Marianne ends up marrying Brandon. Coming to her "senses." Josie wondered if God was sending her a sign. Through the captain. Through the book. Come to your "senses" and marry Hector. Listen to your head. Or maybe it was an entirely different message. Maybe he was saying "Follow your heart." Sensibility.

But Peter wasn't Willoughby. Willoughby was just a character in a book. Peter was real. The letters were real. His love was real. She had to find him. She had to follow her heart. After all, the characters in the book all eventually married for love—not money, or security, or because someone wanted them to marry someone else. Elinor married Edward because she loved him. He had no money. Marianne married Brandon because she loved him. Eventually. They all followed their hearts. That was the lesson to be learned from the book. Follow your heart!

Peter. What would she say to him when she finally found him? *Hi, I'm Josie, remember me?* No, he'd remember her. She'd tell him about the letters, about why she hadn't answered them, about what Miss Bennett had done. He'd understand. She'd tell him how much she loved him and that he was the only man she'd ever love. That she wanted to be with him forever, and have his children, and die old in each other's arms.

What would he say to her? Would he tell her that he had never stopped loving her and never stopped hoping that he would find her? And what would he do? Would he take her in his arms and kiss her the way he had kissed her the last time they were together? Josie was sure that he would. It would be magical. It would be the most wonderful moment in her life. It would make everything she had gone through worthwhile.

When Captain Stewart finished reading the last page of the book, Josie felt sad. She had enjoyed it so much that she didn't want it to end. It was like leaving a friend. She had come to feel she knew the characters personally—like they were real people. Yes, maybe people who had lots of money and who lived a fancy life, but people who had problems and suffered heartache and felt pain. Just like she did. She'd miss them.

There was something else she'd miss. She'd miss the captain reading to her. He made the story so interesting, so alive. She'd miss listening to his voice, watching his expressions, how his mouth moved, how his eyes would light up when he came to an exciting part of the book. And how patient he was with her, defining words or explaining the story. Most of all, though, she'd miss him. Just being with him. They'd spent a lot of time together the past few days. The book had brought them closer. As they became more comfortable with each other, more trusting, they talked more. Not just about the book, but about themselves and their lives. They learned a lot about each other. Especially the night Captain Stewart began talking about his daughter.

"You remind me a lot of her," he said to Josie, "although she's a little older than you, I suspect."

"How old is she?" said Josie.

"She's thirty-two."

Josie told him she was twenty-five. Twenty-six in December.

"Is she married?"

"Yes. Her husband has a high-level job with the government in Ottawa."

"So she lives in Ottawa?"

"Yes."

"Do you get to see her at all?"

"Not very often. Hardly ever, anymore. She used to come down to Halifax when her mother was living and I'd try to make sure I was in port at the same time. But it's been difficult to get our schedules to match, especially when the war was on. Besides, she's so busy with the children."

"How many children does she have?"

"Three. Two girls and a boy. The boy is only a year old."

"So you're a grandfather! Have you seen them?"

"Just the oldest girl. Once."

Josie thought how sad it must be for him to have grandchildren he'd never seen.

"When did your wife die?"

"Five years ago."

"That must have been hard for you."

"She had been sick for a few years. She probably welcomed death."

Josie remembered her mother hinting at the same thing during her cancer. At the time, Josie couldn't imagine anyone wanting to die. But as she saw her mother in pain during the final days, she began to understand.

"Do you have any other children?"

"No, just Anna. My wife had a difficult time when Anna was born and she wasn't able to have any more children."

"Have you remarried?" Josie hadn't seen a ring on his finger, but decided to ask anyway.

"No, just one wife for me. The sea is my wife now."

"How long have you been at sea?"

"Most of my life. Sailed on my first ship when I was twenty-two. I'll be sixty my next birthday."

"Do you come from a sailing family?"

"Actually, no. Not at all."

Captain Stewart then proceeded to tell Josie that he had come from a fairly well-to-do family. His father had been a lawyer, then a judge, and had wanted his son to follow in his footsteps. So, he had gone to college for a couple of years. But he dropped out to join the Navy, against his father's wishes. He told Josie that even as a small boy, he loved boats and the ocean. He couldn't see himself working in an office.

"Why did you leave the Navy?" she asked.

The captain lowered his head for several seconds, then looked up at Josie. He had a serious expression on his face. "If I tell you something, you must promise not to say anything to anyone, especially my crew. None of them know about this. Do you promise?"

"Yes, I promise."

He took a deep breath. "In the Navy, I moved through the ranks quickly. I don't know if it was because of my education or because of my love for the job, but I soon became an officer. And before long, I was commanding my own ship. Keep in mind, the

Navy was a lot smaller then than it is now, so there weren't many openings. But I excelled so much that I became the youngest commander in the fleet."

Captain Stewart took another deep breath. "Then, one night, during manoeuvres off Halifax, I did something very foolish. I got drunk and ran the ship aground on some rocks. One of my crew was killed. I was dishonourably discharged. After that, I didn't sail for a few years. But I missed it. I had to get back to sea. So, I got a job as a deckhand on a tanker. When the war broke out, they were short of experienced men to captain cargo ships. I was soon at the helm of this bucket of bolts. No one bothered to check my background. I've been sailing her ever since."

The captain smiled. "That's my story."

Josie felt bad for him. He'd been through a lot in his life. Her own problems seemed insignificant in comparison.

"So," he continued, "I've told you everything about me. Now it's your turn. Tell me about yourself."

Josie protested that her life story wasn't nearly as interesting as his, but he insisted on hearing it. So she told him where she was from, and her upbringing, and how she had come to Halifax during the war to find work, and about her job at Gorman's. But she stopped there. "See, I told you it was boring."

Captain Stewart peered at her intently. "I have a feeling there's more."

"What do you mean?"

"I've told you everything about me, but I don't think you've told me everything about yourself."

"There's nothing more to tell."

"I think there is."

"Like what?"

"Well, for starters, you haven't told me why you're going to England."

The captain had been open with her, but she wasn't sure she wanted to be open with him. Not about that. He'd probably think she was crazy, travelling halfway across the world chasing after some man she hardly knew. He'd probably tell her to come to her senses, go back home, and marry Hector, like Becky and everyone else had told her. He'd probably think she was a terrible person for leaving poor Hector at the altar. She didn't want him to think she was a terrible person.

"Can I ask you something?" said the captain. "When you approached me on the dock, you were looking over your shoulder, as if you were afraid someone was following you. Are you running away from something?"

Josie didn't respond.

"It's okay, Anna, trust me. Your secret is safe with me."

Josie smiled to herself. He had called her Anna. Her resolve weakened. "You'll think I'm terrible."

"No I won't. I won't judge you. How can I judge you? I was responsible for a man's death."

Josie swallowed, then proceeded to tell the captain the whole story—about Peter, about Hector, about Miss Bennett, about the letters, about her wedding, about her decision to go to England. When she was done, she bowed her head. "You think I'm a wicked person, don't you," she said.

"No, I don't think you're a wicked person," he replied.

"But you think I'm crazy, going to England to find him."

"No, I don't think you're crazy. Crazy would be marrying someone you don't love. Life's too short for that."

The two new confidantes sat silently for several moments.

"What will you do if you can't find him?" asked Captain Stewart. "Or you find him, but he doesn't feel the same way anymore? Or, heaven forbid, you know..."

Josie hadn't wanted to even think about it, but the captain's questions were forcing her to consider those possibilities. She had to prepare herself. Prepare herself for a life without Peter. "I don't know. I guess I'll have to go back to Halifax. Back to my boring life."

"But at least you'll know."

He was right. Absolutely right. At least she'd know.

Chapter 42

Shortly after breakfast on the tenth day since they'd left St. John's, Josie spotted land as she stood on deck breathing in the salt air. She raced up to the wheelhouse to find the captain. He was standing by the wheel, peering straight ahead through a pair of binoculars. He saw her as she approached. "Have a look," he said, offering her the binoculars.

Josie put them to her eyes. "Is that...?"

"Yes, it is. That's England."

Josie beamed. *Almost there*, she said to herself. It wouldn't be long before she and Peter would be reunited. But she'd have to wait a little while yet before she reached her ultimate destination. They still had another day's sailing to Rotterdam, and then almost a day's sailing back to Southampton where they'd be docking.

They arrived in Rotterdam just after midnight on September 23. After breakfast, Josie went out on deck to catch a glimpse of the city. The captain told her Rotterdam had been heavily bombed by the Germans during the war, and she could see some of the damage, but it looked like a busy place nonetheless, with ships coming and going in the harbour and the docks bustling with activity.

They left the Dutch port about five in the afternoon later that day. As they passed the white cliffs of Dover on their way back, Josie grew more anxious to begin her search for Peter. Mr. Walsh had told her the British Navy's offices were in London, but she had no idea where Southampton was in relationship to London.

Was it close? Could she take a cab there? Or would she need to take a bus or a train, or even another ship? She had absolutely no idea. All she knew was that she'd be in England. She'd just have to figure things out once she got to Southampton. Or maybe ask the captain. He might know. He'd been to England before.

The ship arrived at the pier in Southampton at around seven in the evening the next day, after an uneventful twenty-six hours. Josie had packed her suitcase earlier that afternoon and was ready to go. As she was packing, Captain Stewart came into the cabin. "Do you have everything?" he asked.

"Yes," said Josie.

"You're all set then?"

"Yes. There's just one more thing."

Josie reached into her purse and took out five twenty-dollar bills, and offered them to the captain. "Here's the rest of the money I owe you."

The captain smiled. "You keep it."

"No, a deal is a deal. We agreed on two hundred dollars."

"Well, the price is now one hundred dollars. Take it or leave it."

"Are you sure?"

"I'm sure. You're probably going to need it to find this sailor of yours."

Josie smiled. "Thank you."

Josie disembarked around seven-thirty, but not before saying goodbye to the crew, especially Barney, who had been so kind to her the entire voyage. She gave him a big hug. Captain Stewart escorted her off the ship and stayed with her until she had exited the docks and found a taxi. They had to keep up the charade till the last minute. As he opened the door of the cab, he wished her luck. "You're Josie again."

She kissed him on the cheek. "Thank you for everything. I'll never forget you." As he turned to leave, she thought she saw tears in his eyes.

Josie slid into the back seat of the cab while the driver put her suitcase in the trunk. Once he was behind the wheel the cabbie turned to her. "Where to, Miss?"

The captain had told Josie he was familiar with all the major English ports but had never been to London and wasn't sure how far it was from Southampton. She asked the cabbie. The driver seemed surprised by the question. "London? About eighty miles, I guess," he said.

"How long would it take to get there?" asked Josie.

"Depends how you've travelling, Miss. By car, about two hours. By train, longer, because they're making several stops."

It was after eight o'clock and almost dark, so Josie thought it best to get a hotel room in Southampton for the night and strike out for London in the morning. Besides, she was exhausted from the long ocean voyage. She also needed to find her land legs after being at sea for over two weeks. Yes, she was anxious to find Peter as soon as possible, but a good night's sleep right now was her first priority. She asked the driver to take her to a nice hotel. Not the priciest but something comfortable and clean, and in a safe part of town. The cabbie said he knew exactly the place. As they headed for the hotel, Josie asked the cabbie, "Could you take me to London in the morning?"

"Can't, Miss. The company only allows us to service the Southampton area. Besides, a cab drive to London would be quite dear. You're better off to take the train."

Josie figured she probably had enough money to go by cab, but there was no sense spending more than she needed to. The train would be fine.

Within a few minutes, they arrived at the hotel. Josie opened her purse. "How much do I owe you, sir?"

"Fifty pence."

"How much is that in Canadian dollars?"

"Canadian dollars? We don't take Canadian dollars. We can take *American* dollars."

"I don't have any American money. I only have Canadian money."

"Sorry, I can't accept it. You'll have to come up with English money or American money."

Josie hadn't even thought about changing her Canadian money into English money. She had no idea how or where to do it, or even if she could. Maybe nobody would take her money. Maybe it was worthless. She had come all this way and now she couldn't even pay for cab fare? How was she ever going to make her way around England and find Peter? She wouldn't be able to go anywhere without money. How could she be so stupid? What was she going to do now? What if her whole trip was for nothing?

The strain of the voyage and the stress she was under got the best of her. "I told you I don't have any English or American money," she shouted. "If you won't take my money, then…then just call the police and have me arrested!"

"Lady, lady, relax," said the cabbie. I'm not calling the Bobbies. Look…how much would this cab ride cost you in Canada?"

Josie regained her composure. "Fifty or sixty cents, probably."

"Then just give me sixty cents in Canadian money and we'll call it square."

Josie took a one-dollar bill out of her purse and handed it to the cabbie. "I'll give you one dollar. That's more than sixty cents."

"That will be fine."

"Thank you so much. I'm sorry I lost my temper. It's just that I came all the way from Canada to find someone, and I guess I'm a little cranky."

"Not to worry, Miss. But you'll want to change your Canadian money into English money if you're going to travel around the country."

"How do I do that?"

"Just ask them at the hotel. They'll be able to help you."

The driver got out, opened Josie's door, took her suitcase out of the trunk, and brought it into the lobby of the hotel, with Josie following behind.

"Thank you again," said Josie.

"You're welcome, Miss. Have a pleasant evening."

Josie fluffed her hair, straightened her dress, and went over to the front desk. The hotel had an available room, so she checked in. As luck would have it, they accepted Canadian money, though they advised Josie to visit a bank in the morning and convert her Canadian currency to English pounds.

Her room was small but very clean. And it had its own bathroom with a tub. The mattress was a little firm, but she wasn't about to complain. It was better than the bunk on the ship. After she bathed, she changed into her nightclothes and slipped under the covers. As she lay in bed reflecting on her situation, she felt hopeful. Tomorrow would be the most important day of her life. The day she would find Peter. The day all her dreams would come true. The day she would find true love.

Sleep came quickly.

Chapter 43

The clerk at the front desk informed her there was a bank just around the corner. It would be open at nine. She had breakfast in the hotel dining room then went to the bank, arriving just as they were opening. After exchanging one hundred of her Canadian dollars for English pounds, she went back to the hotel and packed, removing Peter's letters from her suitcase and putting them in her purse in case she needed to show them to someone at the Navy office. She checked out and asked the front desk clerk to call her a cab to take her to the train station.

The drive to the station took no more than fifteen minutes. She purchased a one-way ticket to London and boarded the eleven fifteen. The trip took over two and a half hours, with several stops along the route. Josie spent most of the time gazing out the window at the English countryside, with its rolling hills of green farmland, patches of forest, and herds of cows and sheep. It reminded her a little of the time she went with Becky, Albert, and Hector to the Annapolis Valley. Hector. She wondered how he was doing. She hoped she hadn't hurt him too much.

The train arrived at Waterloo Station in London at about one thirty in the afternoon. When Josie stepped off the car and onto the platform, she was amazed at the sight before her. Rows of trains lined up at platforms to both sides of her; hordes of people rushing everywhere; conductors and attendants in spiffy uniforms blowing whistles and directing passengers here and there; happy children greeting their fathers; tearful lovers saying goodbye. She had never seen such a busy place in all her life.

Hauling her suitcase, she pushed her way through the huge crowds and out the station's main doors to hail a taxi. She'd ask the cab driver to take her to the Navy offices. They seemed to know where everything was. As she exited the station, she noticed that people were standing in a line waiting for cabs, so she joined the line. Before long, she was at the front. Seconds later, a car pulled up. The driver got out, opened the back door of the cab for her, put her suitcase in the trunk, and jumped back in the car.

"Where to, Miss?"

"Do you know where the Navy Offices are?"

"Surely do, Miss. I'm a Navy man myself. Retired now. They're in Whitehall."

"Can you take me there?"

"Quite."

Josie assumed that "quite" meant "yes" and leaned back in the seat, relieved. She had worried the Navy offices might be harder to find. As they proceeded to Whitehall, the cabbie struck up a conversation.

"Is that an American accent, Miss?"

"Canadian."

"Ah, a Canuck. Where in Canada?"

"Nova Scotia. Halifax."

"I've been there. When I was in the Navy. We stopped there on the way to New York once. Nice little town."

As Josie stared out the window of the cab, she could see why the driver had called Halifax a "little town." London was a big city. And busy. But she could also see some of the effects of the war, the buildings damaged and destroyed by German bombs. Fortunately, nothing like that had happened in Halifax.

The cabbie crossed a bridge, then turned left and followed a street running alongside the river.

"What's that river?" Josie asked the driver.

"That's the famous Thames, Miss."

A few minutes later the cabbie made a right turn onto a smaller street, then another right onto a much wider street. He pulled up to the curb in front of a ten-story grey concrete building.

"The offices of the Royal Navy, Miss," announced the cabbie.

Josie peered out the window at the imposing structure. Rows of windows ran the full length of each floor. Four twenty-foot high stone columns protected the front entry. Two imposing statues sat atop huge concrete pillars on each side of the entrance. It was an intimidating sight.

"This is the main entrance here," the cabbie told her. "What particular office were you looking for?"

"I'm not sure. I'm trying to locate someone who was in the Navy during the war."

"That would be the Naval Staff Office."

That was it! The Naval Staff Office. That's exactly what Mr. Walsh had called it. She got out of the cab and started to walk towards the building. The cabbie jumped out of the vehicle and hollered to her. "Miss! You forgot your suitcase."

Josie stopped and looked back. She didn't really want to drag her suitcase along with her. Besides, she would need a cab ride to wherever she needed to go next in her search for Peter.

"Can you wait for me here?"

"How long will you be?"

"Not long, I hope."

"Not a problem. I can wait for you. I'll have to keep the meter running, though."

"That's fine."

Josie turned and walked towards the building. As she ascended the front steps, she glanced up at a uniformed guard standing at the top, staring straight ahead with his hands behind his back. As she walked past him, he didn't seem to notice her, continuing his stare, motionless.

People in uniforms and business attire were coming in and out of the building, mostly men but a few women as well. As Josie approached the mammoth main doors, a man in a suit nodded to her and held the door open. She smiled at him and entered. Inside, she stopped and stared at the sight before her—high ceilings, ornate furnishings, oil paintings on the walls, intricately tiled floors. It made her nervous. But she had to push on.

She proceeded down the wide foyer to an enclosed booth where a man in a uniform was seated behind a glass window with his head down, writing on a sheet of paper. Josie stood in front of the window. After a few seconds, he looked up and slid open the window. As he did, a group of three men, two in uniform and one in civvies, passed behind Josie and flashed some type of card at him. He nodded to them, then turned his attention to Josie. "Can I help you?"

Josie was hoping for a friendlier reception. The man in the uniform looked serious, even stern. There was no smile on his face. "Yes. I'm looking for the Naval Staff Office."

"Do you have an appointment?"

Josie hadn't thought about making an appointment. She hoped that wasn't going to be a problem. "No, I don't."

"What is the purpose of your visit?"

"I'm trying to locate someone who was in the British Navy during the war."

The man pulled out a sheet of paper from a tray on his right, slid it toward her, and placed a pencil on the sheet. "Fill in your name and address, then sign on the bottom."

Josie filled out the form and slid it back to him. He swirled his chair around to face his typewriter, typed out an ID card, fastened some string to it, and handed the card to Josie. Josie looped the string over her head and around her neck.

"The Naval Staff Office is on the fourth floor, room 406," he said, again without a smile. "Elevators are just ahead to your left."

Josie proceeded up the elevator to the fourth floor and soon found room 406. She opened the door and walked in. To the left, seated behind a desk, was an older lady wearing glasses, speaking to a younger woman who was sitting in a chair on the other side of the desk. To the right, seated on a long wooden bench, were two sailors in uniform and a woman. Straight ahead was a three-foot-high wooden railing separating the front of the office from the back. A gate in the railing led to a larger area of filing cabinets and more desks.

Josie sat down on the bench beside the woman. After more than a half-hour wait, it was finally her turn. She sat down in the chair opposite the older woman. The woman glanced at the ID card around Josie's neck.

"Josephine Bourdeau is it?" asked the woman, peering over her glasses. She gave Josie a welcoming smile. Josie was encouraged. At least she was friendlier than the man in the booth.

"Yes," replied Josie.

"How may I help you, dear?"

"I'm trying to locate a sailor who was in the British Navy during the war."

"And what was this sailor's name?"

"Peter Harris."

"Is he a relative of yours?"

Josie wondered how she should answer the question. She could just say yes, but what if they asked for proof. She had to tell the truth. "No. A friend."

The woman took off her glasses and placed them on her desk. She leaned forward and crossed her arms, resting them on the desk. She looked at Josie intently. Her demeanour was still pleasant but more businesslike. "What type of friend, dear?"

Josie proceeded to tell the woman about her and Peter and his letters, and how she had travelled all the way from Canada in hopes of locating him and finding out if he still loved her. When Josie had finished recounting her story, the woman looked down as if deep in thought, then looked back up at Josie.

"Miss Bourdeau, during the war a lot of sailors met a lot of girls in a lot of different ports. And they all thought they were in love. The sailors and the girls alike. It was wartime. But then those sailors went back home and forgot about the girls they had met in those distance lands. They came back to their sweethearts who lived next door in their home villages and towns. It's unfortunate for girls like yourself, I know, but it's a reality of war."

"But this is different," insisted Josie. "I can show you his letters."

Josie reached into her purse and pulled out Peter's letters. She opened the first one and offered it to the woman. The woman shrugged and shook her head. "Miss, I don't need to read the letters."

"Please," Josie pleaded. "Please read it. You'll understand what I'm saying."

"I'm sorry, I really don't have time to read letters. I'm very busy here."

"I beg of you, please read it. I've come all this way. Surely you can spare just a few minutes."

The woman sighed. She took the letter from Josie, slipped on her glasses, and scanned the letter quickly. When she was finished, she peered at Josie over her glasses.

"It's a beautiful letter, dear, but..."

Josie took out the second letter and shoved it toward the woman.

"Please. You have to read this one. It will show you how true his love was."

The woman exhaled heavily, then took the letter and read it, again quickly. When Josie attempted to give her the third and fourth letters, the woman put up her hand. She took off her glasses and stared at Josie. This time her look was more one of pity, and sadness.

"Dear, I understand how you must feel. But that was three years ago. A lot can change in that time. He might be married. Or deceased, God forbid. Besides, even if I wanted to help you, I couldn't. Unless you're a relative, I cannot reveal personal information about any of our service personnel. It's contrary to our policy."

"Then just pretend I'm a relative. Nobody will find out. I won't tell them."

"What if I were to tell you where to find him, and you go see him, but then he doesn't want to see you? And he complains to the staff office that, against policy, someone has given out his personal information. I could lose my job."

Josie slumped back in the chair. "Instead, I lose the love of my life. What's worse?"

The woman handed the letters back to Josie. "I'm sorry dear, I really am. There's nothing I can do for you. Now, if you'll excuse me, I have to serve the next person."

Josie stared at her. She wanted to tell her off, tell her how heartless she was, how she was ruining her life. But she knew there was no point. The woman wasn't going to change her mind. Josie stuffed the letters back in her purse, rose slowly from the chair, and turned to leave. But then she stopped and looked back at the woman.

"Can you tell me one thing? Just one thing."

"What's that?" said the woman.

"Is he still alive?"

The woman stared at Josie for a second or two, then stood up. "Wait here," she said. She went into the back part of the office, disappearing behind a row of cabinets. She returned about five minutes later. "We have four Peter Harris's in our records. One was lost at sea. The other three are still living."

"The three that are still alive," said Josie, "can you tell me where they live?"

"Miss, I already told you I can't give out any personal information."

"Then how do I know which Peter is mine?"

"Do you know his middle name?"

Josie lowered her head. "No."

"Then I can't help you."

The woman looked past Josie to the people waiting on the bench. "Next."

"Wait!" said Josie. "I know the ships he was on. The names are on the letters he wrote. Here," said Josie, offering the letters again to the woman. "Can you check what ships they sailed on?"

"Miss, I have people waiting. You've already taken up much too much of my time."

"Please," said Josie. "If my Peter is dead, I can go home. Don't make me search all over England for someone who is dead."

The woman stared at Josie, exhaled loudly, took the letters from her, got up from her chair, and went back to the row of cabinets. She returned a few minutes later. "Your Peter is still alive. But that's all I'm telling you."

Josie let out a huge sigh of relief. At least he was alive. That was the good news. Now she just had to figure out a way to find him, without the Navy's help. That was the bad news. She had no idea where to start. She thanked the woman, took the elevator down to the main floor, and dropped off her ID card at the booth. When she got outside, the cab was in the exact same spot where she had been dropped off. She opened the back door and got in. "Sorry that took so long," she said.

"Not to worry, luv," said the cabbie. "How did you get along?"

"Well, so-so."

"I remember you saying you were trying to locate someone who was in the Navy. Didn't they know where he was?"

"They knew, but they wouldn't tell me. They said it was personal information and they couldn't give it to me unless I was a relative."

"And you're not a relative of this person, I take it."

"No, just a friend. More than a friend, actually."

Josie proceeded to tell the cabbie the whole story—everything she had told the woman in the Naval office. The cabbie shook his head.

"Oh, the damn Navy. I'm very sorry, Miss. What are you going to do now?"

"I don't know. I haven't come all this way to give up now. At least I know he's still alive. They told me that much. They said there were three sailors with the same name that survived the war. I had the names of some of his ships, so they were able to tell me he was still living. But they wouldn't tell me anything else. Now I just have to find mine. But I don't know how I'm going to do that. I don't even know where to start looking."

The cabbie shrugged. "Blimey, I wish I could help you."

"I wish you could too."

"Well, I can take you wherever you'd like to go."

Josie thought for a second. "What time is it?"

The cabbie glanced at his dashboard clock. "Just after three thirty."

It had been a stressful day. She was tired and hadn't eaten a bite since breakfast. The business day was almost over and there wasn't much time to visit other offices. Besides, she didn't know where to go, who to see, who to talk to. She needed some time to relax, clear her mind, and come up with a plan. A plan to find Peter.

"I may as well check in to a hotel for the night," she said. "Then decide what I'm going to do and start fresh in the morning. There has to be some way of finding him."

She asked the cabbie to recommend a hotel, something not too expensive but clean and safe. She certainly could afford a fancy hotel but decided she should be a little frugal for now, not sure of what other expenses she might incur in her search. She certainly didn't want to run out of money.

"Do you want to stay in central London or on the outskirts?" asked the cabbie.

"What's the difference?" said Josie.

"Well, the hotels on the outskirts are going to be cheaper."

"I don't want something too pricey, but I need to be close to the government offices, and to the train and bus stations."

"I know just the place."

The driver selected a small, quaint hotel in the heart of the city, within sight of the Thames. He said it would be handy to Waterloo train station and to the Navy offices in case Josie decided to go back there again. They arrived at the hotel in fifteen minutes. Josie paid the fare and the driver carried her suitcase into the lobby.

"Thank you for all your help," she said.

He doffed his cap. "My pleasure, Miss. Oh, by the way, what's the name of your sailor friend?"

"Peter Harris."

"Peter Harris, eh? I'm sure you'll find him, Miss."

Josie hoped he was right.

Josie checked in to the hotel and went up to her room. She undressed and went to bed for a nap, setting the alarm for six to wake herself for supper. When the alarm went off, she jumped out of bed, washed, dressed, went downstairs to the lobby, and asked the desk clerk to recommend a nice restaurant within walking distance. He suggested a place just two blocks from the hotel. After receiving his assurances that it was safe for a young lady to walk in that neighbourhood in the evening, she set off for the restaurant. She had lamb chops (something she never ate back in Canada), with a baked potato and string beans, plus a delicious plum pudding for dessert. Her eyes bulged when she saw the bill; London was certainly more expensive than Halifax. She was thankful for Miss Bennett's deathbed generosity, whatever her motivation.

It was eight thirty by the time she got back. The hotel had a small sitting room off the lobby with four wingback chairs, a coffee table, and a fireplace. The fireplace was lit and there was no one in the room, so Josie sat down to collect her thoughts and come up with a plan to find Peter. What would she do if she was back in Halifax and was trying to locate someone? Where would she go? Who would she talk to? The ideas weren't coming to her. Despite her earlier nap, she was still feeling quite tired, especially with a full belly. The best thing was to have a good night's rest and start fresh in the morning.

As she lay in bed searching for sleep, she fought back doubts about her decision. She had to stay positive. There had to be a way to find him.

Tomorrow would be another day. The day, she prayed, she would find what she was looking for.

Chapter 44

Josie awoke around six o'clock the next morning. She took a leisurely hot bath, and dressed. The hotel didn't offer a full breakfast, but they served tea and raisin biscuits in the sitting room. As she was eating, an idea popped into her head. Maybe the front desk clerk would have some ideas about how to find Peter. There was no harm in asking. She gulped down her last mouthful of tea and went over to the counter.

"Excuse me," she said to the clerk, "can I ask you a question?"

"By all means, Miss," he said.

"If you were trying to find someone, say, someone you had met three years ago, but you didn't know where they lived, how would you go about finding them?"

"Is it a gentleman?"

"Yes."

"Do you know where he works?"

"No."

"Do you know any of his relatives or friends?"

"No."

"Hmm, no relatives or friends. Let me think. You might want to check the telephone directory. He may be listed there."

"Do you have one?"

"We have one for London. Do you know if he lives in London?"

"No, I don't. I think he's somewhere in England."

"There's a lot of places in England, Miss, and a lot of people."

"I know, but that's all I've got to go on."

"Well, I can give you the London directory to have a look. Keep in mind, though, most regular folks don't have telephones. It's mostly government offices and businesses, and the well-off. But you're welcome to try."

He reached under the counter for the book and passed it to her. She opened it. Thankfully, it was in alphabetical order by surname, so it would be easy to find him if he were there. She flipped the pages until she came to *H*, then scanned down for Harris. There were a few Harrises: Adam, George, Milton… Then she saw it! In black and white. Peter Harris. Kensington. Could it be? Could it actually be him? Right here in London? Could it be that easy? Her heart fluttered. Her breathing quickened. What should she do? Should she call him right now? What would she say? Would she recognize his voice? Would he recognize hers? What if it was a different Peter Harris? What if it was the real Peter Harris, her Peter Harris, but he pretended to be a different Peter Harris because he didn't want to speak to her? No, she had to see him in person. Face-to-face. To know it was really him. To find out for sure if he still loved her.

"Did you find his name?" asked the clerk.

"Uh, well, I found *a* Peter Harris. It says he's in Kensington. I don't know if it's the same one."

"Would you like to ring him up? You can use our telephone."

"I don't want to call him right now. I'll write down his number and call him later. Do you have a piece of paper and a pencil?"

The clerk grabbed a sheet of paper from a shelf on the back wall and a pencil from under the counter. Josie scribbled down the telephone number and handed the pencil back to him. "How far is it from here to Kensington?" she asked.

"About thirty minutes by taxi."

"Thank you."

Josie went back to her room to think about what she should do. She *could* call him. If it wasn't him, it would save her wasting time going out there. If it *was* him, and he was overjoyed to hear from her, her mission would be accomplished. They'd get together, renew their love, and her dreams would be fulfilled. If it was him and he *didn't* want to see her, she'd be devastated. If she called and a woman answered, it would mean he was married. Or maybe not. It could be his mother or a housekeeper or anyone. Josie's head was spinning. There were too many ifs. She decided she had to go to Kensington. She had to find out for sure.

She changed into the suit she had planned to wear on her honeymoon. If it was indeed her Peter, she wanted to look her best. She checked her purse to make sure the letters were still there. She then went downstairs and approached the desk clerk.

"Can you call a taxi for me?"

"Certainly, Miss. For where?"

She hesitated, feeling slightly embarrassed. "Kensington."

The clerk smiled but said nothing. He picked up the phone and dialed. The cab arrived about ten minutes later.

"Where to, Miss?" asked the cabbie.

"Kensington."

"Any particular spot in Kensington?"

"Is Kensington a big place?"

"It's a fair size, Miss."

"Then, just drop me off somewhere in the middle."

"Very well, Miss. I'll drop you off on Kensington High Street near the shops."

As the clerk at the hotel had said, it took about thirty minutes to get there. As soon as Josie got out of the cab, she could tell she was in a very ritzy part of town. *If Peter lived here,* she thought, *he'd done very well for himself.* Standing on the sidewalk in front of a dress shop, she wondered what her next step should be. She hadn't planned this far ahead. Perhaps she should just start going into the shops and asking the clerks if they knew Peter Harris. If he lived in the area, they might know him. It might take all day, but she had lots of time.

So that's what she did. She went from shop to shop and asked the clerks if they knew a Peter Harris. The reactions were mixed. Some tried to be helpful, others were suspicious of her intentions. After a few such encounters, she realized she needed to come up with a reason why she was asking. She started telling people she was a long-lost relative from Canada separated by the war, that she had been told by her mother back home that Peter lived somewhere in Kensington, and that she wanted to surprise her "cousin." She actually surprised herself how good she was at lying. But the ruse didn't seem to help. After three hours, she still had not found anyone who knew Peter Harris, or at least anyone who would tell her they knew him.

It was almost one in the afternoon, so she decided to drop in to a small café for some lunch. As she picked away at her sandwich, she felt discouraged. How was she ever going to find him this way? It was like looking for a needle in a haystack. Maybe she should just call the telephone number and be done with it, one way or the other.

The waitress came to her table. "Anything the matter with your sandwich, luv?"

"No, I guess I'm just not hungry. I've had a bad morning."

"You do look a mite glum, I must say. You need to cheer up."

"I'll cheer up when I find the person I'm looking for. He's supposed to live in Kensington, but I can't find him."

"You're looking for someone? What's his name?"

"Peter Harris."

"Peter Harris the accountant?"

Josie perked right up. "You know him?"

"I don't know him personally, but I see his name every morning when I get off the bus, and every day after work while I'm waiting for the bus to take me home. It's on a sign in front of the building right by the bus stop. It's a firm of accountants. I've read those names so many times, I have them memorized. He's the third one on the list. Peter Harris."

Josie was so excited, she wanted to hug the waitress. "Where is this bus stop?"

"It's just up the street about a block. You turn right when you leave here. You can't miss it."

Josie paid for her sandwich and hurried out of the café. She turned right and headed up the street. Within moments, she could see the bus stop marker up ahead. She rushed to the spot, then looked to her right. There it was, the sign, on the stoop of a rather important looking building. And there was his name, plain as day. Peter Harris. Third on the list.

Could this be him? An accountant? Could he have been an accountant in the Navy when she met him? He never said anything about what he did. Or could he have left the Navy since '42 and become a civilian accountant? Maybe he had been injured and couldn't serve anymore. She knew so little about him, anything was possible.

Her heart started beating a mile a minute. She felt slightly nauseous. *Oh my God*, she thought. *Am I actually about to meet him? After all these years? What am I going to say? What is he going to say? What if he doesn't love me anymore?* A sense of confusion engulfed her. She began having second thoughts. Was this the right thing to do, showing up unannounced? Should she have called first? Should she have stayed in Canada? Should she have listened to her father? Should she have married Hector? Or was she just getting cold feet? No, she had to find out one way or the other. Whatever happened, happened. She had to accept it, good or bad. One thing she knew for sure—she couldn't keep on like this. This was craziness. It had to be settled.

Steeling herself, she walked up the three steps to the landing, opened the door, and entered the building. She was in a large foyer leading to several rooms with open archways. She spotted a middle-aged woman sitting at a desk in the room to the right, and approached her. The woman looked up almost immediately.

"May I help you?" she said with a warm smile.

"Yes, is Peter Harris in?"

"He's not here at the moment. Did you have an appointment?"

"No. I...I...I just wanted to see him on a business matter."

"I can have someone else help you."

"No!" said Josie abruptly, then realized she had reacted too quickly. "I mean, no, I'd prefer to see Mr. Harris. He came recommended."

"Very well. He'll be back by four o'clock. Would you like to come back then?"

"What time is it now?"

"It's almost two o'clock."

Josie was worried that if she left she might not have the nerve to come back. "Is it all right if I stay here and wait?"

"By all means. You can have a seat in the waiting room on the other side of the foyer. When he arrives, I'll let him know you're here."

Josie smiled, thanked the women, and took a seat in the waiting room. The wait seemed like an eternity. From time to time she'd catch glimpses of people passing through the foyer, entering or leaving the building, but none of them resembling her Peter. Finally, at ten after four, a man in a blue suit entered the waiting room and came up to her. "Excuse me, Miss. You were looking for me? I'm Peter Harris."

Josie's heart sank. It was not her Peter. It was an older man, greying at the temples. Distinguished looking, even handsome, but not her Peter. She rose from her chair. "I'm sorry, I've made a huge mistake," she said.

"I beg your pardon?" said the man politely.

"I was looking for someone else. A different Peter Harris. I was hoping you might be him. I'm really sorry if I wasted your time."

The man was clearly perplexed but remained polite. "No harm done," he said with a smile. "I'm sorry I'm not the Peter Harris you were looking for. It's not an uncommon name."

Josie excused herself and slinked away, out through the lobby and onto the street. She was crushed. Her hopes had been so high that this was the one. Now they were completely dashed. She began to wonder if she'd ever find her Peter, no matter how hard she looked. If he wasn't in London, he could be anywhere in

England. It might take her forever to search the whole country. She'd run out of money and have to return home. If only that woman at the Navy office had helped her.

There was nothing for her to do now but return to her hotel. The Kensington lead hadn't panned out and she had no idea what to do next. The quest seemed doomed. She was losing hope. She stood on the curb and flagged down a cab. On the ride back, the cabbie tried to strike up a conversation, but she didn't want to talk to anyone. She just wanted to be left alone. Alone. As she now seemed destined to be for the rest of her life.

It was five o'clock when she got back to the hotel. Even though it was still early, Josie just wanted to go up to her room, get in bed, and pull the covers over her head. As she trudged through the lobby on her way to the elevator, the front desk clerk called out to her. "Oh Miss Bourdeau, there's a message here for you."

Josie stopped abruptly. A message for her? From who? Nobody knew she was here. She walked over to the counter. "A message for me?" she asked.

"Yes, I have it right here."

He handed her a small piece of paper, folded in two. She unfolded it and read the message that had been scribbled in pencil.

Peter Harris
32 Harlech Road
Crosby, Sefton
England
(Your Navy friend)

Josie's pulse quickened. She looked up at the clerk. "Who left this message?"

"I don't know. I just came on at four and the bloke on the previous shift told me to give to you."

"He didn't say who left the message?"

"No, he didn't."

"Where is he now?"

"He's gone home for the day."

"Is there a way to get in touch with him? Can we call him?"

"I don't believe he has a phone. He's in again tomorrow morning."

Josie read the message again. Could it be? Could it really be Peter's address? Her Peter? And what did "Your Navy friend" mean? Did that refer to Peter or to the person who left the message? Could it be the woman at the Navy office? Did she have a change of heart? But how did she know where Josie was staying?

In any event, it didn't really matter. The only thing that mattered was finding Peter. She now had another lead. An actual street address. She now had hope. She looked up at the clerk. "Where is Crosby?"

"Crosby?"

"Yes, Crosby, Sefton."

"There's a Crosby near Liverpool, I believe."

"Where's Liverpool?"

"It's in the North. Lancashire."

"How far is that from here?"

"I would say, six or seven hours by train."

Six or seven hours by train. There'd be no going to bed just yet. Josie had a trip to plan.

Chapter 45

Josie rose early for what she hoped would be the greatest day of her life. The hotel manager had a map of England in his office that confirmed Crosby was indeed near Liverpool, about ten miles to the north of the city. She'd have to take the train to Liverpool, then either another train or a bus to Crosby. The manager estimated the whole trip would take at least six hours. It was a Wednesday, and Peter might be at work during the day, so she wanted to time her arrival for after supper when he would most likely be home.

After eating breakfast at the restaurant down the street, she returned to the hotel, bathed, and changed into her suit. She packed her suitcase, double-checked that she had Peter's letters and his address in her purse, and went downstairs. The first item on her agenda was to speak with the desk clerk.

"I'm Miss Bourdeau," she began. "Were you the one who took the message for me yesterday afternoon?"

"Yes I was," said the clerk.

"Who gave you the message?"

"It was a taxi driver."

Oh my God! thought Josie. The cabbie who took her to Whitehall yesterday and dropped her off at the hotel. He said he was in the Navy. Did he go back to the Navy office? Did he convince the woman to give him Peter's address? Maybe he had connections. Maybe he pulled some strings. She then remembered what he had said to her as he dropped her off. *I'm sure you'll find him.*

The manager had informed her that the trains to Liverpool left from Euston Station, to the north of the city across the Thames, so she arranged for a cab to take her there. She checked out and went to the sitting room to wait for her drive. The taxi took a while to arrive, but she wasn't concerned, she had plenty of time. The ride to the station took about twenty minutes. It was a beautiful, sunny early-autumn day. Josie hoped it was a good omen. She gave the cabbie a nice tip and entered the station. There was a long lineup at the ticket counter, but she waited patiently and purchased her ticket. The train was departing at ten fifty-five and was scheduled to arrive in Liverpool at four forty-five in the afternoon. That would give her plenty of leeway to get to Crosby at the time she wished.

The train was fifteen minutes late leaving but eventually got underway. Josie settled in for the long ride. She passed the time by chatting with some of the other passengers, taking an extra-long lunch in the dining car, and staring out the window at the countryside. She read and reread Peter's letters and rehearsed what she was going to say to him. But it never sounded right. She'd just have to wait until she saw him.

She started to worry if she had the right address. What if it was the wrong Peter Harris again, and she'd be going on another wild goose chase? No, it couldn't be. This was the right Peter. Surely her cabbie had the right address, however he got it.

The train was more or less on time at all the stops along the way. Until they got to Stafford. They'd been on the platform there for about fifteen minutes when the conductor came around and informed everyone the train would be delayed for another thirty minutes. Some type of mechanical problem. The new arrival time in Liverpool was five thirty. Josie was getting anxious. She wanted to get there as soon as possible.

The train pulled into the Moorfields station in Liverpool at five twenty-five. Josie disembarked and went to the wicket to ask for directions to Crosby.

"There's a bus to Crosby," said the agent. "What station do you want to be dropped off at?"

"Harlech Road," said Josie.

"There's no station at Harlech Road, Miss. I've never even heard of Harlech Road. Are you sure you have the right address?"

Josie looked at the note again. No, it said Harlech Road. Why hadn't the ticket agent ever heard of it? Could her Navy friend have given her the wrong street name? Not another setback. Would she ever find Peter?

An elderly gentleman standing behind her in the ticket line touched her on the arm. "I overheard your conversation, Miss. You're looking for Harlech Road?"

"Yes," said Josie.

"Take the bus to Crosby and get off at Blundellsands. Harlech Road is just a five-minute walk from there."

Josie thanked him and purchased her ticket. The bus departed ten minutes later and arrived at the Blundellsands station about thirty minutes after that. As Josie prepared to depart the bus, she asked the driver for directions to Harlech Road.

"We drove right by it, actually, just a minute ago," he said. "We're on Agnes Road. When you get off the bus, just turn to your left and go down Agnes to the Mersey Road. Turn right on Mersey. You'll see a church on your left. Turn left on Bridge Road, then left again onto Harlech."

"How long will it take me to walk there?"

"Five or six minutes."

"Thank you very kindly. Oh, do you have the time?"

"Twenty-five past six, Miss."

"Thank you again."

"You're more than welcome, Miss."

Josie got off the bus, turned left and walked down Agnes Road to the Mersey Road. She saw the church just ahead on the left. A short distance later she reached Bridge Road, where she turned left. Then, almost immediately, she spotted the street sign. Harlech Road. This was it. The moment of truth. There was no turning back now. Her heart started beating faster. Her breathing quickened. Her palms felt sticky. Her mouth went dry.

She turned onto Harlech. It was a short, dead end street of small row houses, all connected together, each with its own tiny front yard bordered neatly by hedges. Short walkways ran from the sidewalk to each door at ground level. The sun was beginning to set. Josie strained in the remaining light to see the numbers on the doors. The even numbered were on the right, so Josie crossed the street to the other side. She walked slowly, looking for number 32. It was farther up. 20, 22, 24. Still farther. 26, 28, 30. There it was. Number 32. The last house on the street.

She stopped and stared at it from the sidewalk. Her heart was beating even faster now, her breathing more laboured. She had to get control of herself. *Relax*, she told herself. *Breathe in deeply, breathe out slowly. Again. Breathe in deeply, breathe out slowly.*

She was ready. She moved along the walkway, step by step, one foot in front of the other. And then she was there. Standing in front of the door. She put her suitcase down beside her, brushed back her hair, straightened her suit jacket, braced herself—and knocked.

Nothing. She could see through the frosted glass in the door that there were lights on inside. She knocked again. Then, seconds later, the door opened. And there he stood. Peter. Her Peter. She recognized him immediately. He hadn't changed. The wavy blond hair, the caring face, the hypnotic blue eyes. Her handsome Englishman. She couldn't believe it.

"Peter!" she blurted out, overcome with joy.

"Yes?" he answered, frowning.

Something was wrong. He didn't seem to know her. There was no sense of recognition at all on his face. "Peter! It's me! Josie!"

Peter shook his head. "I'm sorry. Josie who?

Josie couldn't believe what she was hearing. "Josie. Josie Bourdeau. From Canada. From Halifax. Don't you remember?"

"Have we met before?"

"We met in Halifax. Three years ago. During the war. We met at a dance, and we went to the Dingle, and we…. Don't you remember? You *must* remember."

"I'm sorry, Miss. I met a lot of girls during the war. In a lot of different ports. It's difficult to remember them all."

Josie was in shock. This couldn't be happening. "You said you loved me!"

Peter sighed. "Miss, we told every girl we loved them. I'm not proud of it. But it was wartime. Things like that happen during wars."

"But your letters. You wrote me letters."

Josie frantically rifled through her purse and retrieved the letters. "These letters," she said. "You wrote four of them. And you said you loved me. Truly loved me. And… and…you said that you couldn't wait until we were together again. But I never received the letters. My landlady kept them from me because a sailor had abandoned her with a child, and she didn't want the same thing to happen to me. But then on her deathbed three years later, she gave them to me. And…and…I read them for the first time. And, and … I was supposed to get married to someone else. But I didn't love him. I still loved you. So, I left Canada and came to England to find you. And I looked for you in London. And then somebody told me you lived in Crosby. So I took the train to Liverpool and then the bus here. And now I've found you!"

Josie realized she had been rambling. She stopped to catch her breath. "These are your letters."

She handed the letters to Peter. He hesitated for a second, then took them and began to read. He read the first one, then the second and the third more hurriedly, stopping before finishing the third. "Miss, I didn't write these letters. These are what we used to call "Dear Jane" letters. One of the chaps on the ship would write them for all the guys. It was an easy way to dump girls we had met in port. All the boys did it."

Peter handed the letters back to Josie.

"I don't believe you!" she shouted through her tears. "You wrote these letters! You loved me!"

Just then, a woman's voice came from inside the house. "Peter, who is it? Is everything alright?"

"Everything is fine, dear. It's just someone looking for directions."

A pain shot through Josie's chest as though someone had stabbed her with a knife. Peter was married. He loved someone else. She meant nothing to him. Maybe he actually had forgotten about her. Maybe they really were "Dear Jane" letters. Maybe she had been taken for a complete fool. Maybe she was just like so many other girls in so many other ports during that hateful war.

The woman called out again. "Peter, your dinner is getting cold."

Peter turned to Josie. "Miss, I have to go. My wife and I are in the middle of dinner. I'm sorry."

With that, Peter closed the door in Josie's face. She stood motionless, staring straight ahead, not wanting to move, not wanting to believe what she had just heard. She thought about pounding on the door or barging into the house and confronting him in front of his wife, forcing him to admit he remembered her. Instead, she picked up her suitcase, turned, and walked away. She walked along Harlech, and Bridge, and the Mersey Road, past the church, and up Agnes, retracing her steps to the bus station. She felt numb, lifeless. She was in a trance, going through the motions. No thoughts, her mind blank.

The next bus for Liverpool was arriving in thirty-five minutes. She purchased a ticket and sat on a hard wooden bench to wait. She had nothing left. No hopes, no dreams, nothing. She was utterly and totally defeated. The minutes ticked by but not fast enough. She wanted to get out of there as quick as possible, as far away as she could.

All of a sudden, she felt a light tap on her shoulder from behind. She turned. It was him. She jumped to her feet. "Peter!"

Peter reached into his pocket, pulled out a small photograph, and showed it to her. It was the photograph she had given him on the sidewalk in front of Miss Bennett's the last time she saw him. "I didn't forget you, Josie," he said softly.

"But, but…your look, your face. There was no reaction. You didn't seem to recognize me."

"I couldn't let on that I knew you, with my wife there. How would I explain you to her? I saw you through the peephole before I opened the door. I recognized you right away. I had to put on an act. I had to make you believe I didn't remember you."

"So, you do remember me."

"How could I ever forget you? The woman I had fallen in love with. My first love."

"And the letters?"

"They were mine. All of them. I wrote them from my heart. I meant every word. I was devastated when you didn't write back. I felt like a fool. I had given you my heart and I thought you had just discarded it like a piece of trash."

"I never got your letters, Peter. My landlady kept them from me. I waited and waited for them, but they never came. You had promised to write. I thought you had lied to me. I was heartbroken. Completely heartbroken."

"I was heartbroken, too. I even tried to look you up when I was back in Halifax about a year or so later. I went to your boardinghouse, but the girl who answered the door had never heard of you and said there was no one living there by that name. I asked to speak to the landlady, but she wasn't in. I remembered you had a sister, but I couldn't remember her first name, so I asked if there was anyone else living there named Bourdeau. She said there wasn't. I had to get back to the ship. We were only in port a short time. I didn't know where else to look."

Josie sighed. "I moved out of there a few months after we met, "she said. "Becky got married."

Josie stared deeply into Peter's eyes. His hypnotic blue eyes. Emotions raged through her. Longing, anguish, despair. She had found her true love, and he had found her, but it was not to be. Tears filled her eyes. Peter put his arms around her, pulled her toward him, and held her tight. There they remained for what seemed like an eternity, frozen in time. Eventually, she pulled herself away from his embrace and wiped her eyes.

They looked at each other and smiled. There was so much to say but so little of it mattered now.

"I have to get back, Josie. My wife will begin to worry. I told her I was just going to the corner for a newspaper."

Josie nodded and wiped her eyes once more. "When did you get married?"

"About a year ago. My wife is expecting. She's due the end of December. We might have a Christmas baby."

Josie smiled. "I'm happy for you."

"What about you?" said Peter. "You said you were supposed to get married? Will you go back to him now?"

"No, I don't think so. As you sailors say, that ship has sailed."

Peter chuckled. Then he reached out and took Josie by the hand. "Do you remember our first dance? Our only dance?"

"On the sidewalk in front of Mrs. Bennett's. The night we met."

"You were shaking."

Josie smiled softly. "I told you I was chilly."

Peter returned the smile. "How about one more dance?"

Josie put her arm around Peter's waist and pressed herself against his body. They began to dance slowly, holding each other tenderly. Peter began humming a familiar tune, the same tune he had hummed on the sidewalk that first time. They danced and danced and danced, oblivious to the outside world, consumed with the moment. Josie felt a calm come over her. A sadness. Not one of despair, but one of resignation.

Peter reached the end of his tune; the dance was over. He gazed into her teary eyes. "I want you to know, Josephine Bourdeau, that I loved you. I loved you deeply. With all my heart. And I always will. I will never forget you. Never."

With that, he kissed her softly on the cheek, then turned and walked away. Josie watched him, never taking her eyes off him, until he disappeared into the early evening dusk. She sat back down on the bench. A peacefulness came over her. She smiled. She had been loved. Truly loved. Deeply loved. And she had loved in return. Completely. With everything in her heart. And if she never loved again, or was never loved again, that would be fine. She would be content. At least she would have this one time, this one time when she knew what real love was, more than most people ever get, and it could never be taken away from her.

The bus pulled in to the station.

Chapter 46

Josie still had some of Miss Bennett's money left, so she decided to splurge on the trip back to Canada. She booked passage on a big ocean liner sailing from Liverpool to New York City, selecting one of the nicer cabins. She'd always been fascinated by the pictures she'd seen of New York, so she'd spend a couple of days there doing some sightseeing, then take the train to Halifax. By the time she got home, the money would be all gone. It seemed appropriate.

When she'd get back to Halifax, she'd make her round of apologies. Hector, of course, Becky, even Albert. She'd go visit her father for a few days, try to explain why she had done what she had done, tell him she loved him. Maybe she'd look for a different job, give up waitressing. Maybe she'd learn to read better, get someone to teach her, someone like Captain Stewart. Then she could read the classics on her own. Maybe. Time would tell.

A brass band was playing in the lounge on the ship. On the second night of the voyage Josie decided to check them out. There was a good crowd, with several couples on the dance floor, and the band was playing her kind of music. She found a large, comfy leather chair and ordered herself a gin and tonic.

As she sat sipping her drink and watching the moves of two young lovers on the hardboards, she felt the presence of someone standing next to her. She looked up. It was a man. But not just any man. A Roman god of a man—dark eyes, jet black hair, flawless tanned skin, strong jaw, strikingly handsome.

"I'm Silvio," he said in a Latin accent.
"Josie."
"Would you like to dance?"
Josie smiled. *Would she like to dance?*
"I'd love to."

CPSIA information can be obtained
at www.ICGtesting.com
Printed in the USA
BVHW070007241121
622204BV00003B/19